ADRIFT

ADRIFT

A KARI SHARPE THRILLER

K. T. KONKOLY

THOMAS & MERCER

This is a work of fiction. Names, characters, organizations, places, events, and incidents are either products of the author's imagination or are used fictitiously. Otherwise, any resemblance to actual persons, living or dead, is purely coincidental.

Published by Thomas & Mercer, Seattle

www.apub.com

EU product safety contact:
Amazon Media EU S. à r.l.
38, avenue John F. Kennedy, L-1855 Luxembourg
amazonpublishing-gpsr@amazon.com

ISBN-13: 9781662526886 (paperback)
ISBN-13: 9781662526879 (digital)

Cover design by David Drummond
Cover image: © Felix Cesare, © Marc Guitard, © Karl Hendon,
© jose carlos cerdeno martinez / Getty

Printed in the United States of America

To my husband, Steve, for his steadfast love and encouragement

Siblings are a volume of childhood memories; a nostalgia that cannot be easily deleted.

—Vincent Okay Nwachukwu

Prologue

Lori Kady took a cautious sip of her steaming coffee, her legs dangling over the sailboat's bow. She absorbed Casco Bay's early-morning quiet and stillness, the few intruding sounds entirely at place and welcome. The gentle lapping of the water against the boat's hull. An occasional seagull flapping its wings in the distance. Seals splashing just out of sight in the heavy fog. Pure heaven.

Lori and her husband, Dan, sailed up from Newburyport, Massachusetts, every summer, spending three weeks along the Maine coast. She cherished the time more than anything. Their jobs in Boston kept them locked into the rat race.

They'd planned their trip during the cold, dark Massachusetts winter nights. Sitting by the fire, they'd review navigational charts and dream of sailing in Maine during their precious weeks off. Boothbay Harbor had been their prime destination for as long as she could remember. Along the way, they'd navigate the heavily islanded coastal waters, stopping wherever they wanted to enjoy days hiking and swimming on deserted beaches. At night Dan collected driftwood for a roaring fire on the beach. As the fire died down, they'd make their way back to the sailboat through the inky-black sea for a cozy night of rest—after a little port wine on the bow. One of the many "maritime" traditions they'd created over the years.

Shuffling feet broke her trance.

"You're up early," said Dan as he sat next to her.

"I wanted to savor every minute of our last morning in Maine. The seals joined me, along with a few seagulls," she said. "At least I think they were seagulls."

"With this fog, I'm surprised you could see any seals at all."

"No. But I could hear them splashing around," she said. "Playing."

"We could stay another night here. The kids are fine. Mason is at school. Krissy is busy working. Frankly, I'm not even sure they noticed that we left."

Lori laughed and nestled her head into Dan's shoulder, enjoying the warmth of his body next to hers. This summer's trip was the first they'd taken without one of their children on board.

"I'm sure they aren't missing us," said Lori, reassuring herself. "But we've been gone for three weeks. It's time to get back to reality. As much as I hate the thought."

"As long as you're sure. We still have a few days built into our trip, and I'm in no rush," he said. "With this fog, it might be easier to leave tomorrow."

"We've navigated through dense fog before; we'll be fine. It'll lift soon enough."

"Okay," said Dan. "I'll get us ready to cast off."

He brushed her fingers with his as she walked past.

"I'll clean and stow the galley," Lori said as she descended the boat's ladder into the salon.

"I'll take care of everything topside," he said.

During their lengthy stay at the Goslings, a popular and picturesque island stop in Casco Bay, they had pulled out nearly everything from the boat's numerous storage cubbies. Candles, decks of cards, flashlights, and plates all needed to be properly stowed and secured.

"All set down there?" said Dan through the open hatchway a few minutes later.

"Yep. Everything's ready. I'll grab the foghorn and head up," she said.

Lori pulled the handheld foghorn out of one of the cubbies and joined Dan topside. She kissed Dan as she passed him on her way to the bow.

She knelt on the bow and waited for directions.

"Cast off!" Dan said.

She untied the thick mooring-ball rope attached to the bow cleat and tossed it overboard, back to the sea, where it would wait for the next lucky boater who needed to secure their vessel for a night or two.

"We're clear!" she said.

The powerful engine pushed the heavy sailboat effortlessly through the bay. She stood at the bow, watching for other mooring balls or lobster buoys. Coming too close to either could create a problem if the sailboat's propeller or rudder became tangled with their lines.

She would remain on the bow, providing a second set of eyes until they reached open water or the fog lifted. After they cleared the cove and turned the corner toward the open waters of Casco Bay, she relaxed a little. They would sail outside of the inner bay, eventually passing the famous Portland Head Light, before turning into Portland's busy harbor, where they'd pull pierside and venture into the city, seeking a hot breakfast of thick, starchy pancakes smothered in Maine maple syrup.

First, they'd have to safely navigate the foggy sea. Even on a clear day, Casco Bay presented a tricky sail for all but the most experienced sailors. Colorful buoys marked the submerged lobster pots that dotted the bay for miles and miles.

"How we looking up there?" asked Dan.

"We're good. You can keep going for a little while, then come to port!"

Lori heard frantic yelling, immediately followed by the deep rumbling of a boat engine, and she sharpened her focus. The fog obscured everything. *What the hell is going on out there?* The lobster boats typically headed out first thing in the morning to pull their traps—gone by the time she and Dan woke up, had their coffee, and moved on. She struggled to hear which direction the noise came from, so she sounded the horn to announce their presence. Shrillness cut through the fog but yielded no reply from a nearby boater.

"Idle it! I need to hear!" she yelled.

Lori clenched her fist and held it high, shaking it back and forth. The signal for "idle the engine." In these conditions she knew Dan would understand. Rather than stop, which would prevent him from steering, they'd idle, reducing the engine noise while still allowing them to maneuver.

Loud voices continued to cut through the fog. Sound traveled so far over open water; she had no idea if they were on top of the other boat or a few nautical miles away.

Lori listened carefully, frustrated by the impenetrable, gray-toned landscape surrounding them. Waves lapped their sailboat's hull and distant birds squawked, mingling with the low hum of the idling engine.

"Anything?" yelled Dan.

She didn't respond verbally. Instead, she raised a closed fist and held it still, shaking her head. An improvised signal for what she hoped he interpreted as "shut up." She needed to listen without any interruption. Lori stood upright on the bow, a firm grip on the forestay keeping her steady. The fog left tiny droplets of water along the safety lines, which glistened in the muted light. Suddenly the voices became louder and more pronounced.

We might be headed for a collision!

She furiously signaled to go to starboard, believing the boat to be on the port side of their vessel. As Dan reengaged the engine, the tendrils of fog parted to reveal two lobster boats directly to their port.

Five or so hard-looking men turned in their direction almost in unison.

The two vessels had been tied side by side, the men having filled the fuel tank of one of the boats from a portable jug. Fuel spilled down the lobster boat's hull with every swell of the sea. Lori's eyes traced the contours of the fuel jugs, struggling to make sense of the scene. Then she locked eyes with a goateed man. The hot sting of fear shot through her. She quickly looked away. They needed to get out of here. Now! Nothing about this was right.

A male voice rang out. *"They saw us!"*

"Dan!" Lori screamed. "Turn us around!"

She wasn't sure Dan's vantage point in the cockpit allowed him to see the men on the lobster boats—until he responded. Dan spun the helm hard to starboard while pushing the engine speed to full throttle. The sailboat responded immediately. They heeled hard as ocean water sprayed over the bow, drenching her.

Lori chanced a quick glance back at the men, hoping to see them rooted in place. Wishful thinking. One of the boats sliced through the water, quickly gaining ground on them. Within seconds the lobster boat's overpowered engine assaulted her ears, sending a cloud of acrid exhaust across the sailboat's bow. She coughed as the lobster boat moved swiftly alongside their sailboat. *The men clearly intended to board them!*

Lori grabbed the foghorn and depressed the sounding button several times, back-to-back, hoping to catch the attention of another boater or ward off their pursuers. She prayed someone would recognize the distress signal, or at least be curious enough to move toward them.

"Get inside!" yelled Dan. *"Get my gun!"*

Hastily she grabbed a stanchion to steady herself as she reached for the metal post. The lobster boat banged hard on the sailboat's hull, nearly knocking her over the side. A tattooed beast of a man grabbed the deck railing stanchion and pulled hard, clanging the two boats together. Moments later another man jumped over the safety line and moved swiftly in her direction.

"Dan!" she yelled as the stranger roughly clutched her shirt and shoved her down.

A second plea for help earned her a kick to the side. She dropped flat, a firm boot to the center of her back keeping her face down against the rough fiberglass deck. He muttered something as he yanked her ponytail and pulled her head skyward, exposing her neck. A sharp burning sensation seared across her throat, her breath suddenly a struggle as she began to choke on her own blood.

The man dropped her head onto the deck, a red pool expanding in her fading vision. She lay dying, unable to move or scream. Barely able to think. She hoped that Dan had somehow managed to get away. Her eyes flitted between the sea and sky. Voiceless witnesses to the violence that met them on a lovely, quiet morning.

Just as quickly as they boarded, the men scurried back onto their boat and tore off into the fog, leaving the sailboat behind. Lori tried to lift her head but only managed to turn her gaze aft toward Dan. Bright-scarlet stains covered the plastic Bimini cockpit windows. And then everything faded to black.

Chapter 1

A sharp horn cut through the fog. One of those handheld thingies. One. Two. Three. Four. He lost count. Christ. Didn't these people know the rules? Did they plan to blow the horn all the way back to Portland? All Chet wanted to do was pull his traps and head into port. The day promised to be a long one. The old lady nagged the snot out of him about the crap she wanted done around the house. No way he would rush home to work on the "essentials," as she called them. Instead, he would hurry to Dry Dock for a much-deserved drink. If a man couldn't sit with his buddies and have a cold one at the end of the day, what sort of life was he living?

"Okay, boys, time to head in for round two!" said Chet to the lobsters in his hold.

The silence got to him sometimes. Then again, so did the rattle of the tourists' boats. Damned place would be much nicer without them. Who the hell blows their horn like that first thing in the morning? Like an emergency. Well, news flash, no one was coming, because you people got the signal wrong. "Looks like you're going to sink! Right, boys?" he said and laughed toward the hold.

The rumble of his powerful engine decreased as he throttled down in the no-wake zone of port. A few minutes later, the vessel's bumpers squealed as Chet lassoed the cleat, securing the boat pierside. The pier bustled with activity at this time of the morning—the boats returning with their daily haul.

Chet knew everyone in the lobstering community. He either apprenticed with them or mentored them as they worked through the onerous Maine lobstering requirements. Not much escaped Chet's notice or his wife Sissy's rumor mill. Besides, he had one of those minds, the type that easily got to the bottom of everything.

"Okay, let's see who walked into my traps." He opened the hold. "Dang, this is gonna take me a minute. You guys just couldn't resist my secret sauce, huh?" he said to the pile of crustaceans. Their glossy, vacant eyes stared in blank reply.

"You talking to the lobsters again, Chet?"

Chet looked up to see Fred May standing next to his boat. The man ran the harbor and seemed to have the uncanny ability to appear anywhere at any time. Nobody risked trying to pull anything over on Fred.

"Best company I've got these days. Beats talking to the tourists. Hell . . . at times it even beats talking to Sissy!"

"I'll be sure to mention that next time I see her," said Fred.

"Won't make a difference. Without me, the damned woman would have no one to boss around," said Chet.

"Sounds about right. I've got one of those myself."

"Hey, you hear about anything odd out there this morning?" asked Chet.

"Sure did," said Fred. "Several guys called in—"

"Let me guess . . . a foghorn repeatedly blaring? I couldn't tell if the guy was trying to signal a navigational shift or danger," said Chet. "Or they just didn't know what the hell they were doing? Wouldn't be the first time."

"You think you heard five short blasts?" said Fred.

"Not sure. I didn't count until it went beyond the first four. Could've went to ten for all I know. Sounded like panicking."

"All I can think of is that some inexperienced summer boater overestimated their skills, then freaked out once in the fog," said

Fred. "Either way, I've sent out the pilot boat to have a look around, just in case."

Chet stood on the sideboard of his vessel and stretched. Lobstering made him stiff as hell.

"That's what I thought too. Just no way of telling. Maybe those guys know something?" Chet nodded toward a neighboring lobster boat.

Several men crowded the ship's deck as they lifted portable fuel jugs onto the pier.

Fred glanced over his shoulder at the men. "They ain't the friendliest bunch," said Fred with a thick Maine accent.

Chet felt the thrill of one of his "theories" swirling.

"Well, if you ask me, nothing's right about their setup," he said.

"They took over Randy's operation for the summer. Seems fine to me."

"That's what I thought too. But what happened to Randy? Sissy said she ran into his sister at the IGA. She said Randy decided to take the summer off and go Down East to fish. That seem odd to you?" asked Chet.

Most of the guys considered Randy to be one of the hardest-working lobstermen on the wharf. He'd been at it for longer than most, probably the best at the job, considering the relative lack of scars on his arms.

"Sure does, given who Randy is."

Chet glanced up at the men on the FV *Ginny*. They were big and strong looking, not uncommon on the waterfront, but they didn't move with the ease of experienced lobstermen. *Out of place* was the first thing that came to mind. Chet had no idea why Randy would use them to pull on his license.

"Those guys are trouble, if you ask me. I can feel it in my bones," said Chet.

One of the men from Randy's boat glared in Chet's direction, prompting him to lock the hold of his vessel. Something neither he nor anyone else ever did on the waterfront. Each lobsterman provided security and safety to the others. Fred noticed his unusual action right away.

"Can't be too sure anymore," Fred said.

"Ayuh," said Chet, shrugging his shoulders.

Chet made his way up the long pier toward his hard-driven pickup, pulling a heavy dolly loaded with his daily haul. As he approached his truck in the parking lot just beyond the pier, one of the rough-looking guys from FV *Ginny* pushed by him and headed toward a pristine-looking F-250.

The vehicle looked like it hadn't seen a day's work on the dock. No bird crap or dents on the hood from clamshells dropped by seagulls.

Theories continued to swirl in Chet's imagination.

Chapter 2

Kari Sharpe rose slowly. She sat on the side of her bed, doomscrolling the news. She marked the day on her calendar and then willed it to disappear. Choosing to return to Maine to help her brother had been a hard decision. Today it might bite her in the ass.

She took a shower, barely noticing the hot sudsy water, the smell of her citrus soap. Then she ate her breakfast, unable to taste her bagel and coffee. She clicked off the small television and headed out to her car, dreading the rest of the day.

The glistening deep-blue Atlantic Ocean faded in her rearview mirror as she drove away from the rocky coast into the rugged interior of Maine. Small variety stores dotted the occasional intersection, providing the only commerce for miles. Several stark white wooden churches stood ready to receive the faithful, their adjoined cemeteries a testament to time. The ancient moss-covered stone markers had witnessed the passage of many souls through the land.

She flipped through the radio stations, unable to focus. A talk show about something political? Nope. Cool jazz? Not today. Nothing took the edge off as she returned to the place of so many childhood memories. She returned her gaze to the road just in time to swerve away from hitting a dead raccoon. Its body lay lifeless, feet stretched to heaven.

The final five miles to the Pine Tree Residential Rehab facility dragged. The winding drive through the lush, tree-packed landscape of western Maine filled her with trepidation and regret. She'd made it as a lawyer, finally leaving her dead-end hometown behind, only to be yanked back. Her life as a litigator in the navy, and then in New York City, had taken years to build. And it was all hers. Her success. Away from Maine, away from family.

She cursed herself for allowing her brother's alcoholism to change the course of her life. She should have stayed in New York instead of making the same tired drive yet again to Pine Tree. She knew alcoholics needed to help themselves. Years of support groups had taught her that. Yet guilt and loyalty combined to make her return to her origins.

She yelled at the empty car and punched the steering wheel. "Damn you, Jimmy!" The only words her exhausted brain could muster.

Kari lowered the front windows, welcoming warm, fragrant air. It blew through her hair as she drove. Thick walls of towering pines, maples, and oaks lined each side of the two-lane road. The dry weather sharpened the smell of heated pine needles.

The beautiful forest fragrance calmed her momentarily. She turned back to the radio and flipped through stations, finally settling on AC/DC's "Back in Black" as a distraction. She shouted the words into the air and thrummed her hand on the window frame as she drove and tried to forget reality.

Jimmy Sharpe, her only remaining family member, had once again spiraled out of control in an alcohol-fueled race to nowhere. Logically she knew alcoholics never "decided" to drink. The addiction made the choice for them. Her mind tumbled back into blame. Stupid drunk. She swiped a lone tear before it could roll down her cheek.

A horn jarred her out of her thoughts. *Shit.* She yanked the steering wheel right, barely avoiding a head-on collision with a snazzy-looking SUV.

"Shit!" she yelled, screeching to a halt on the crumbly road.

She considered turning around. Why pick him up? Kari shook her head, trying to dislodge her anger. Turn toward compassion, she'd learned in therapy. Yet in the moment, the compassion she'd felt for her brother from the safety of New York seemed like an inaccessible dream. She pounded the wheel again. Let him get an Uber home. The idiot.

After a moment she let out a sigh, placed her hands back on the steering wheel, and navigated back onto the road. She sped forward through the rolling hills as sunlight poked through the forest and intermittently blinded her. Several minutes later she turned into the hidden-away facility. The chipped, faded sign read "Pine Tree Residential Rehabilitation Center—Where the Future Begins."

Some future. She'd passed this pathetic sign more times than she could count. And it never got better. First with her mom when they went to visit her alcoholic father, then with Jimmy and their eldest brother, Doug, when they went to visit their junkie mother. As far as Kari could tell, the facility did nothing but remove the toxic person from their environment. Over time each Sharpe returned to their addiction of choice, rendering the time spent at the facility meaningless.

Am I really back here? She felt small again. The years of successes washed away and replaced by the familiar sinking feeling that she hadn't been enough to prevent the relapse. Her stomach lurched, and the sudden urge to vomit overcame her as the gravity of leaving her life in New York City sank in. Her perfectly manicured nails and hair looked painfully out of place in Maine, just as out of place as Jimmy looked in Manhattan during his infrequent visits. His rough Mainer dress and mannerisms at odds with the slick urban environment. She had been too embarrassed to introduce him to her New York friends. They romanticized about life in Maine. Why ruin it for them?

She sat up straight, tried to compose herself before facing the condescending facility staff and Jimmy. Over the years her brother had been tight-lipped about his issues. She'd appreciated that. No news was good news. Fairy-tale thinking took hold, convincing her everything was just fine. So foolish, so naive, to think he would get his life together.

Several male blue jays squawked at each other as they defended their territory. The slamming of the car door quieted them momentarily.

As she approached reception, the smell hit her. Just as she remembered. A curious mix of antiseptics mingled with false promises of *This time will be different.* The facility remained the only hope for those in need despite its less than stellar track record.

"I'm here to pick up Jimmy Sharpe, my brother," she said to the bored receptionist. The words tumbled out on their own. Words said countless times had a way of doing that.

The receptionist sat comfortably behind a window. As a child, Kari wondered what it must have felt like to view the world from behind the protection of glass.

"Have a seat. He's just finishing with the last group meeting of the day. I have some information for you about supporting the work he has done in here." The middle-aged heavyset woman leaned over to reach for a pamphlet. She looked at Kari with the same understanding and manufactured kindness as all the other receptionists she'd met over the years. Kari's jaw clenched tight. Heat worked its way across her chest. Small beads of sweat glistened on her forehead. Pine Tree had that effect on her, even before she'd had words to describe the feelings.

"Don't bother. I've already seen it," said Kari as she turned to walk away.

Kari sat in the small waiting room on one of the hard plastic seats. As a small child she'd waited on the same chair, legs dangling, too small to touch the ground. *This time everything will work out. We'll be fine.* She almost laughed out loud at the false hope her younger self had once maintained.

Now she knew the truth. Staying sober took constant work. She took a long inhale, counted the hold, and then exhaled slowly, just as she had been taught. A stress-reducing technique she'd learned in the navy. Over and over, she forced herself to do the hokey breathing routine, hoping her anger and resentment would pass, even just a little.

She looked at her watch. Ten on a Tuesday morning. If she were in New York, she'd be thinking about asking her partner and friend, Elizabeth, whether she felt like heading out for a second cup of coffee.

They'd walk across the street to Le Haricot. A very expensive, pretentious French coffee bar that boasted the best pastry chef in Manhattan. Kari would treat them to bowls of steaming lattes and pastries. Gazing upon the dingy, sad room where she now sat, the memory faded like a dream upon waking. She inhaled sharply, willing herself not to cry. The heavy weight in her chest constricted her breathing as she wrestled to gather her emotions.

A faint buzz sounded somewhere, and the only other door to the waiting room opened. Her brother stepped inside, glancing around before his gaze settled on her. A warm smile followed, his eyes moistening. He wiped them before taking another step. She feigned a smile.

"Hey, Kari," said Jimmy.

She nodded, still unsure what to say. He looked clean shaven, rested, and well. *They all do at this stage. Just a veneer covering the rot inside.*

"You good?" asked Kari.

"Yep," said Jimmy. "As good as . . . you know." He ran his fingers across his chest, looking down. He held a small tote bag of the few things he'd brought with him.

"Yeah. I do. Let's get out of here. I hate this place."

"Sorry to drag you out here," said Jimmy, closing in for a hug.

Kari allowed him to embrace her stiff body. She wouldn't return his warmth.

A cool forest breeze welcomed the siblings as they walked side by side out of the building. The sound of their footfalls on the gravel walkway filled the void created by unspoken words. They drove back to Portland, as they had done so many times—Jimmy finally breaking their heavy silence as the traffic picked up.

"You want Amato's for dinner? On me," he said. His voice gravelly, heavy.

"Yep. And since you're paying, I want the cheesy bread too. It's the least you can do," she huffed.

Kari had paid $25,000 for the in-person treatment. They both knew it. *My savings are depleted now, thanks to his crap.* She clenched the steering wheel, unable to calm herself. She was hot, perspiring. Her stomach rose and fell with her deep breaths as she searched for relief.

"I'm so sorry, Kari, for everything," Jimmy said. "More than that, I'm embarrassed that I spent four years mostly sober, just to relapse. Just like he always did."

His words barely registered through her brain fog. "You should be," she blurted.

"What?" he asked.

"You heard me. You should be sorry and embarrassed, in spades! How many times are we going to go through the same stuff? How many times?" she yelled. "All I do is worry about you. I'm distracted at work twenty-four seven, checking your location, wondering if you're okay. It sucks!" Her chest felt heavy, stress constricting her breath and mind.

Jimmy looked away from her and peered down at his tightly clasped hands.

"You didn't have to move back here. I'm fine. I can handle this," he whispered.

"Yeah, sure. They all 'can handle it.' Looks like each of you use the same sad coping technique. Or have you switched from vodka to something else? That'd be a change. Maybe it's working for you? Oh yeah, it's not! I just snagged you from Pine Tree," she screamed.

Jimmy's head snapped in her direction. His face a deep red. "Go to hell, Kari! You made your own choice to come back. I had nothing to do with it. Don't blame me if you wanted to get out of New York!"

"Nice. That's what you think this is? An escape plan? From a life I worked my butt off to build?"

"We built. If it wasn't for me, you would have never made it through law school. Don't forget that. You owe me!"

She barely paid attention as they drove the familiar roads back toward Portland. She glanced down at her speedometer and realized she'd gunned it to over eighty miles per hour, well above the posted speed of forty-five.

"I don't owe you a thing. I worked for everything, and you know it. Cut the crap."

He looked away from her and fumbled with his seat belt. His head hung low with shame. Her words had cut him deep, and she knew it. *What am I doing?*

She decelerated quickly, then opened the window for air. Their fight had no real beginning and no real end. She let out a long exhale and then spoke. "We're getting the damned cheesy bread too. I don't care how much it costs you."

He swallowed hard. "Fine."

A small victory, shallow, but she'd take it.

Jimmy clicked on the radio. A good-enough distraction. The Eagles' "Peaceful Easy Feeling" blared as they drove back to Portland, back to the life she'd fled.

Chapter 3

Detective Clark straightened his tie as he walked to the lectern of the crowded conference room. Public speaking never sat well with him. He preferred a low-key, back-of-the-room vantage point in meetings. Today had to be different. Circumstances required it.

"Okay, party's over! Take your seats!"

The gaggle of uniformed officers standing around folding chairs, most of them white men, kept talking. The large room glowed brightly under the fluorescent lights, the hum taking over for a few moments. The smell of burned java dominated the air, compliments of an ancient Bunn coffee maker in the back of the briefing room. The assembly finally started to come to order once someone in the back yelled for the group to shut up. The officers slowly took their seats and turned their attention toward Clark. He had spent years attending these morning meetings as a patrol officer, mostly waiting for them to be finished. He never envisioned himself leading a meeting, not even when he'd become a detective.

He tapped his knuckles on the wooden lectern, cleared his throat, and started, "Okay—I'm filling in today to give the morning briefing. As you might have heard, the station received a call from a jogger this morning regarding an unconscious woman found on the trail in Portland behind Commercial Avenue. Milton and Ramsey arrived on the scene, where they found the deceased. The evidence crew rolled onto the scene shortly after, along with yours truly."

The group leaned forward, listening intently to the briefing. Several of the officers scribbled notes on their field pads as he spoke. Nervous energy cracked through the space. Most murders in Maine took place inside a home or apartment, the vast majority being crimes of passion or spur-of-the-moment family-related homicides.

"The victim has been identified as Irene Simmons of Portland, Maine. We don't have anything further about the victim. Once cause of death is determined, I'll send out an update. Questions?"

"Is this related to the death of the two tourists? What's the status of that investigation?" asked one of the officers.

Clark shifted on his heels. The Kadys had been murdered far enough out on Casco Bay to involve the Coast Guard. The Portland Police played a supporting role, at best.

"We don't know yet. Hopefully the crimes aren't related. As more info comes in, I'll update everyone."

The noise level in the room increased. The buzz of several discussions erupting at once. Only a couple of weeks earlier, the Kadys' murders had shaken the small insular Portland community. Their violent deaths during the summer tourist season had scared locals and potential visitors alike.

A newspaper reporter from the *Portland Press Herald* had written an exhaustive article detailing the lost hotel revenues as bookings plummeted following the murders. The reporter also interviewed various restaurant owners who complained that the summer season had been vital to keeping their businesses afloat, considering the tight margins. This season, many worried they would have to shutter their businesses. The day the article had appeared in the paper, the mayor had unleashed a torrent of blame toward the Portland Police, despite knowing they had little to do with the US Coast Guard's investigation.

Irene Simmons's death would only exacerbate the pressure on the local police to solve the crimes.

"Simmer down," said Clark, managing to lower the side talk to a manageable level.

"What do we say to people?" said Dempfey. "Locals routinely stop me to ask if we found the murderers. People are scared."

"Sorry your coffee sipping and newspaper reading is interrupted by concerned citizens, Dempfey," said Clark.

The room erupted into laughter. The young patrolman's face turned a deep shade of crimson.

"As I learn more, you'll know more. For now, we wait for the Coasties to do their job investigating the Kady murders. Our focus is on the murder of Irene Simmons—something we can control. That's all for now."

Clark abruptly closed his file and walked away from the lectern. The meeting hadn't offered the usual cheery team building their captain spewed out every morning. Oh well, tough shit. He needed to rush to join the captain for a meeting with the mayor.

The brass had been up their asses trying to push the Kady investigation. Like the Portland PD could do anything about it. And now this. The last thing they needed was another murder. What would the *Portland Press Herald* print next? A story about how the police failed the public with their sloppiness? It was bad enough the reporter's article included numerous graphs clearly explaining the revenue lost, especially from the boating community. Anyone glancing through the paper would quickly understand the economics involved.

"I just wish the Portland Police Department would do something already. We've waited long enough for answers! It's not like Maine is that big. They need to get off their well-paid asses and make an arrest," said one desperate restaurant owner. The quote stung many department members who'd traditionally enjoyed public confidence in their work.

Clark knew something needed to break. They had to make an arrest. And make one fast. The problem with investigative police work was that speed and accuracy didn't always go hand in hand. A lesson he'd learned the hard way over the years. Ambition and bravado had caused him to rush to judgment on more than one occasion, his strong-arm tactics having made him question whether he'd arrested the right person in more than a few of his cases. He wanted to believe that the courts would ultimately figure things out. *But had they?* He ran his fingers through his hair and looked down as he walked quickly toward the conference room.

Years on the force had given Clark the seniority to attend the high-profile meeting. Years had also given him the time to reflect on his work. The faces of several of the men he'd arrested still burned in his mind. Guilt forced the images to linger. Painfully linger. He desperately wanted his remaining years on the force to be clean as a whistle. Exemplary. Go out on a high note. No regrets. Whatever that meant. He was determined to get this one right, regardless of the pressure pushing down from above.

Chapter 4

Kari set a six-pack of Allagash White on the deck behind her house and fished a key out of her pocket, holding an overstuffed bag of Thai food in her other hand. The key took some wrangling to open the door. Just one of a thousand little issues she'd get to one of these days.

The century-old saltbox overlooking Portland's Back Cove remained in rough condition, but she owned it outright. Improvements would have to wait. Location was all that mattered, and the Back Cove was coveted real estate. Leaky roof, temperamental furnace, and drafty windows be damned. She knew someone would scoop up the property if she ever decided to leave Maine again, something she thought about on a daily basis.

Still, she could never go back to her partnership at Barnes & Smith, even if she left Maine. Her clients had either scattered to other firms or been reassigned to her partners. Despite being the youngest attorney to ever make partner, returning wouldn't be possible. Her seat had been filled. Officially, she'd left to care for her brother through an illness. She'd neglected to mention the illness in question involved alcoholism and the crushing waste the disease caused to the lives impacted by it. Their eldest brother, Doug, had died in a prison fight. She and Jimmy had only each other. His relapse had sealed the deal, despite all her misgivings. He needed her and she would return to Maine.

Jimmy had, of course, strongly discouraged her return. He'd said Maine had nothing for her but bad memories and scab-picking locals. "Stay in NYC," he'd said after his latest relapse, his voice a ragged, irritating mess.

In retrospect, her decision to take the job in New York City was probably a mistake. She should have stayed in the Navy JAG Corps. But at one point in her career she'd thought . . . Well, why not go for the brass ring? Maybe earning five times the navy salary plus reservist pay would somehow finally erase the years of bullying, the stench of her father's liquor bottles, and the aches of the sofa springs from her back. Instead, it just made her return to Maine even harder, rural life striking her as dull and draining. Away from the city, her mind constantly returned to the memories of her childhood, unearthing things she preferred to keep locked away.

Coming home to a dark, empty house made her wish she had a dog or a cat, even a bird to whistle to her when she came in. Nothing but a few neglected houseplants greeted her with silent acknowledgment.

The bottle hissed as she cracked it open. Gulping down the ice-cold elixir felt good. Almost too good as she took a drink right from the bottle. She had to watch herself or she risked tumbling back into the life most expected of her. *I won't do it to myself. Not again.*

She grabbed a fork and headed to the couch with the containers to eat with her nightly companion—the local news station. As she settled in, the broadcast was interrupted by breaking news.

"Woman found murdered in Portland . . ."

Another violent crime? The news in New York always included an array of crimes. She had assumed she would leave that behind once she got here. She had only been living in Maine for less than six months. In that time three bodies had piled up.

Kari downed the spicy pad thai as she watched the news. Her phone chirped. Jimmy.

"You doing okay today?" she asked, fearing the worst.

"Yep, living the dream."

They'd agreed that he would call her nightly to check in, even though the last thing she needed was to monitor Jimmy as she tried to get settled and build a law practice. She could hear the loud creak of his La-Z-Boy chair as they spoke.

"Can you believe they found another murder victim?" she said.

"Yeah, I heard all about it. Chet thinks all three murders are related somehow."

"Chet? You mean the guy who talks to his lobsters?" she said.

"One and the same. He might be a little nutty, but even a broken clock is right twice a day."

"You need to report this to the cops, even if he has only vague ideas. Maybe it'll help them with the case," said Kari.

"No way. You know our family and local cops don't mix. I'm steering clear of this. They don't need my help. I'm keeping my head down, nose clean. Besides, what would I report? Chet's conspiracy theory? He's on a tear about this and that, and the water just seems . . . off. Gives me the creeps. Reminds me of the week Mom died."

"That bad?"

"Yep, that bad. Something's off and I have no idea what, but it's unnerving."

Kari leaned back into the thick cushions of the sofa, reflecting on the day their mother died. The week before had been particularly hard. Back then, she and Jimmy had both known something was "off." Their mom spent most of the week either wasted at home, passed out on the floor, or out trying to score more drugs. She had started using heroin, a Maine special. The difference in her behavior had been stark. Kari grew up not expecting much from her mother by way of food, cleanliness, or love, but the heroin took away the crumbs of care the woman provided.

Kari had gone through the motions of school, all the while carrying an unshakable sense of dread, a foreboding. Something was off. One day, dressed and ready, she'd silently walked to her mother's room. "Mom? I'm leaving for school," she'd muttered. Her mother's deep breathing the only reply. She hated leaving her mom passed out, or asleep—she never really knew. Lingering at the bedroom door, she'd tried one last time. "I'll see you later today!" she'd said as she softly closed the door behind her.

"What's up with her?" she'd asked Jimmy.

He'd stretched on the couch and said, "Who the hell knows."

"Something is definitely off."

Dread, guilt, and mostly relief had mingled as she'd plotted her way to meet the school bus. "Thank God I'm out of there," she'd thought. She'd wiped away a fresh tear before it had rolled down her face. The last thing she'd needed was to invite more scrutiny from her middle school classmates.

The night before Pam Sharpe had died, Kari had sat on the old wooden swing in the side yard, oblivious to the warped wood digging into her bare thighs. She and Jimmy had spent weeks getting the rickety thing to stay on a tree branch. She'd stared at the ground and lazily swayed, too locked up with emotion to do much else. The creaking of the rope against the strong branch had kept time as the afternoon passed.

Soon enough Jimmy had joined her. "You okay, kid?"

"Not really. What's happening with her? She looks like a zombie. Is she going to be okay?" she'd asked him.

Jimmy had just sat at the base of the tree, staring at the ground. He'd brought his sweaty palms to his tired face and rubbed his eyes. His usual stall tactic. No words had been needed. Her brother's hands had shaken ever so slightly. Another tell. At sixteen years old, he'd tried to be brave for her yet again. They'd both known the only direction their mother would travel. Neither had wanted to admit it.

Snapping herself from the memory, Kari said, "You're probably right about reaching out to cops. Well, just be extra careful out there. You never know what might happen."

"Yeah, it's been a little wild. The gossips on the waterfront are going nuts with all of this. I'm trying to keep my nose out of it."

Kari wanted to ask if he also kept his nose out of the booze, but she chose to remain silent.

"Okay, see ya. My food isn't going to eat itself," she said and hung up. Right now she wanted to concentrate on her pad thai, not Jimmy and his problems or the murders. She grabbed a tangled mass of perfectly cooked noodles and shoved them into her mouth. Then she washed the bite down with another swig of beer. Perfect.

Chapter 5

Kari rose early for a long run along Portland's Back Bay. The fresh air and vigorous exercise did her wonders. Mile after mile she drained the worry over Jimmy from her body, finally feeling like herself at the seventh-mile mark. After a quick shower, she picked up coffee on the way to her closet-size office in the Old Port, Portland's vibrant waterfront. She'd thought about renting space a little farther out of town to save money, but Jimmy had talked her out of it. *All the successful people work on the waterfront.*

Maybe he was right. The old adage held true everywhere, apparently. *You have to spend money to make money.* It certainly held true at Barnes & Smith. Their marketing budget alone dwarfed most Maine law firms' entire bottom line. Of course, firm politics demanded that junior partners paid the lion's share of the advertising budget from their cut of the profit. Every system required a toll payment. In Maine, she had ponied up a ridiculous deposit, draining a significant portion of the money she'd saved, and grabbed some prime real estate right in the heart of Portland. The jury, pun intended, was still out regarding the decision.

Money aside, she liked working on the waterfront. It took the sting out of leaving New York. Walking the uneven brick and cobblestone streets of the Old Port, hearing fishing boats, and inhaling the distinct heady aroma of the salty water mixing with the strong smell of a fresh catch proved to be satisfying. It also kept her in touch with her military background. The ocean was one of many reasons she loved her job in the navy. Maybe it was in her blood to be close to the water.

Someone had set up a makeshift memorial for the murdered tourists. She walked past the pictures of them, the flowers, and the candles every day. Despite the passage of over six weeks, people stopped to place fresh flowers or to throw roses into the harbor. A touching tribute to the lives taken so violently. She wondered whether the location where they found Irene Simmons's body would receive the same treatment.

"Morning, Ruth," said Kari, briefly addressing her receptionist and paralegal before dashing up the narrow steps to her office. The shabby office looked pathetic compared to her previous firm. Dinged-up furniture, threadbare carpet, and squeaky filing cabinets would have to suffice until she could afford better.

"Yeah, mooorning," said Ruth slowly, after a long pause.

Ruth was a bit of a downer during the early hours, and no amount of coffee or snacks remedied her malaise.

Kari smoothed the crease of her Italian wool trousers and settled into her chair. Ruth's footsteps slowly ascended the creaky stairs to her office.

"Here's your mail folder," Ruth said. "Looks like . . . the court granted your request." She paused, then added, "In the Riley property matter. Nice work on that one. I didn't think the court would find in our favor. You must've nailed the oral argument."

"Thanks. It was a tricky, novel approach. Glad it worked out for them," said Kari with a smile.

Before Ruth could start in with her usual rant about what a do-nothing freeloader her husband was, Kari swiveled in her chair, turning her head away, and added, "I'll be busy all day drafting a complaint for the Willis real estate issue."

"Well, you know, poor Mrs. Willis. Do you really think you'll be able to get the fence moved?"

Ruth started to say something else and then stopped, tilted her head, and said, "There's my line! I'll be right back." She shuffled down the stairs, moving as quickly as her general "Ruthness" would allow.

Minutes later, Ruth called Kari. She blurted, "Captain Pearson from the Defense Service Office in Washington, DC, is on the line. He needs to speak with you right now. Something big is happening."

Kari glanced at her clock and then said, "Okay, transfer the call."

After a few seconds, her phone buzzed.

"This is attorney Kari Sharpe. How may I help you, sir?"

"Lieutenant Commander Sharpe, this is Captain Pearson, commanding officer of the Defense Service Office North in DC."

She was familiar with Captain Pearson. Solid reputation. Earmarked for rear admiral, if all went well.

"Good morning, sir," she said, shifting her tone.

"Good morning, Ms. Sharpe. I'm calling about an unusual situation that just developed up at Bath Iron Works. I assume you're familiar with the facility?"

"Yes, sir. They've been building vessels for the navy for decades. I believe they have a few precommissioned ships up there right now, in various building stages. Arleigh Burke–class destroyers, if I'm not mistaken."

"You're not mistaken. Glad to hear that you've been keeping up," said Pearson.

"It's part of being a Mainer. Shipbuilding is baked into the DNA. My brother's a lobsterman and had occasionally taken us up the Kennebec River to see the ships up close. From the water."

"Sounds like a great outing. Unfortunately, the scene at BIW this morning is far less than ideal."

"What's happening?"

"I just received a call from the future commanding officer of the soon-to-be-christened USS *Patrick Gallagher*. Commander Lucas and most of the ship's crew have been stationed up there for over a year. Some of the crew just moved on board."

"So the ship has been officially delivered to the navy?" said Kari.

"Very good, Lieutenant Commander," said Pearson. "Commander Lucas signed the dotted line about a month ago. They've been transitioning the crew from nearby hotels and rentals in stages."

"Let me guess," said Kari. "One of the sailors saw the light at the end of the tunnel and vanished?"

"If only it were that easy," said Pearson. "Apparently, detectives from the Portland Police Department, accompanied by the Bath police chief, are on the pier demanding to question one of the crew members. A sailor by the name of Petty Officer First Class Youseff Ahmed."

Interesting. "In connection with what?" she asked.

"The cops are playing this close to the vest. All we know is that it's in connection with the death of Irene Simmons. I thought I'd reach out to you. You're a legend in these halls. People still talk about you snatching a win in the Jarvis larceny case. You made quite a name for yourself."

Kari put down her pen and looked up, a slight smile on her face. Jarvis had been one of those dead-end cases with nothing for a defense attorney to work with. Yet she had argued the hell out of facts during closing arguments. Argued hard enough to persuade the jury to find him not guilty.

"We need a JAG up there to represent him through the police encounter. The commanding officer won't let the cops on board, and things are heating up on the pier. The police are getting more and more insistent, and a few local news stations have arrived. You're thirty minutes away, right?"

"Yes, sir. I'd be happy to shoot up there."

"That's what I was hoping to hear. If you head over right now, I'll send a set of duty orders to the ship, giving you full authority to temporarily represent EW1 Youseff Ahmed."

"He's a first-class petty officer and an electronic warfare specialist?" said Kari. "Not the type you'd expect to get into deep trouble."

"That's why I'm asking you to head to Bath. He needs the best."

"Thank you, sir. I'll leave right away," she said. "I just need to run home and change into my uniform."

"I'll have your orders faxed to the ship as soon as we hang up," said Pearson. "I should've asked, Are you okay handling this? I know you're busy. If you have court appearances or other obligations, we can try and fly someone up from the Naval Justice School in Newport."

"I'm good to go, sir," she said.

"Music to my ears." He paused. "I have a bad feeling about this."

"Yeah, me too. The city is on edge, looking to place blame on someone for the murders of two tourists and now a local woman. I'm hoping the police aren't there about the murders. Mistakes happen when things are rushed."

"Exactly. Thank you, Lieutenant Commander," said Pearson. "If you run into any snags, don't hesitate to call me. Commander Lucas has my direct line."

"Understood, sir."

Kari placed the phone back into its cradle and yelled for Ruth. Her paralegal loved nothing more than hearing about "navy stuff," as she put it. Kari suspected that this one trip alone would fuel Ruth's gossip for weeks.

"Ruth, I'm heading up to BIW to handle a criminal investigation. While I'm gone, I'll need you to prep motions to continue on the matters I had to deal with today. I'm not sure what's facing me up at the shipyard, but it doesn't sound like an easy case. I might be out of the office for a few days."

"Wow. But what would you want me to do?"

"I'm sending you a draft motion from another case with the exact language I need. I'm also sending you an email with the matters in which I'll need the motions to continue. I'll circle back here tonight to execute everything to go out in tomorrow's mail." Kari's fingers moved quickly over her keyboard as she sent Ruth a list of matters.

"No problem, Kari. I'll have everything ready for you," said Ruth excitedly.

"I know. And I can't tell you how much I appreciate that."

Kari grabbed her briefcase and now-cold cup of Indy Roasters coffee and dashed back out of the office. A trip to Bath Iron Works had been the last thing she had time for this morning, even if the prospect of getting pulled into a police investigation involving one of the three murders intrigued her. She'd struggled to bring in clients as quickly as she would've liked. Between Jimmy's rehab, the cost of the office, and Ruth's paycheck, hardly any money remained for Kari. Perhaps a little free press would do her fledgling firm some good.

Chapter 6

Kari pulled up to her house and haphazardly parked on the street. This needed to be a quick turnaround. She had completed her monthly weekend reserve time just a couple of weeks ago at the Naval Justice School in Newport, Rhode Island. She unwrapped her freshly cleaned khakis from the dry cleaner's plastic, then set to the task of turning the plain shirt into a proper uniform by affixing the JAG insignia, her collar rank, ribbons, and name tag, a process she'd completed countless times.

Several minutes later, Kari jammed the final piece of the precision ensemble into place on her blouse lapels before donning the uniform. Her shoes could use a shine, but that would have to wait. She grabbed her briefcase and rushed out the door. Looking at the clock in her car, she noted the transition from civilian to military attorney had taken her around twenty minutes. Not a bad turnaround. Her car groaned as it came to life, reminding her that she needed to ask Jimmy to look at it when he had a chance.

Kari picked up speed as she merged onto the 295 North toward Bath Iron Works. The redbrick-and-cobblestone cityscape yielded to a thick mass of towering deep-green pines. Occasionally the forest opened for glimpses of the deep-blue gulf just beyond the tree line. The vast sky echoed the color of the sea on the glorious sun-filled day.

It had been a while since she'd visited BIW. In fact, she hadn't been to the shipyard since returning to the state. Even though she remained in the navy reserves, she spent most of her time in either Norfolk or San Diego. Perhaps this would change everything for her. The thought of doing her reserve time at BIW seemed too good to be true. She didn't even know whether such a thing would be allowed as a reservist.

Arriving at BIW always underwhelmed her. The shipyard that built the world's most advanced warships appeared to be little more than a disorganized jumble of run-down warehouses and crumbling office buildings. She navigated her way through the maze of structures to the waterfront, where the navy's newest ship sat pierside. The clean lines of her steel-gray hull contrasted sharply against the blue sky. A pang of familiar regret filled Kari as she witnessed the life she could've had if she'd chosen to stay in the navy. She parked a good distance away and walked to USS *Patrick Gallagher*.

Police vehicles with lights flashing surrounded the gangway. Nothing normal about that. Typically civilian police wouldn't be so close to a navy vessel. The Naval Criminal Investigative Service took the lead on any law enforcement issues arising on base. As she approached the ship, several police officers paced about. One of them, a man in a suit, probably the lead detective, chatted on the phone.

She decided not to address them until she had a chance to meet with Ahmed. She hoped to wrap things up in short order. Dodging their glances and slipping through their ranks, she strode up the gangplank, the only entrance to the ship from the pier.

The petty officer of the watch at the quarterdeck saluted her before examining her identification card.

"You Lieutenant Commander Sharpe?" asked the chief standing close by.

"Yes. I'm here to meet with EW1 Ahmed. I guess those guys are as well," said Kari, nodding toward the police cluster on the pier.

"I'm Chief Canton. Nice to meet you, ma'am. I've heard great things about you," he said. "And yes, ma'am. Those assholes have been trying to climb on board for the better part of an hour. Nothing we can't handle." Addressing the petty officer guarding the quarterdeck, he said, "No one gains entry until the captain gives the all clear. You got it?"

"Yes, Chief."

"Ready, ma'am? Ahmed's in the wardroom, waiting for you."

Kari jammed her identification card into her breast pocket and followed Canton through the sprawling new vessel. It shone like a brand-new Christmas gift that hadn't yet been broken by a child's morning exuberance. Civilian contractors with "General Dynamics" printed on their collared polo shirts hustled alongside the naval personnel throughout the passageways, everyone pushing to put the finishing touches on the ship.

Canton led her through several passageways and up a ladder, before he made a hard left turn, then heaved open a heavy steel hatch, revealing the glistening blue tile of "Officer's Country." The blue floor tile of Officer's Country stood in sharp contrast to a ship's uniform gray haze. It gave everyone an unequivocal message—only officers or those with official business requiring officers' attention were allowed in the area.

As Kari entered the wardroom, Ahmed sprang to his feet.

"Ahmed, this is Lieutenant Commander Sharpe. She was nice enough to drop everything to come down here to meet with you."

"Good morning, ma'am," Ahmed said. He folded his arms tightly around his chest as he sat back down.

"Apparently, the police want to talk with Ahmed about the death of a female BIW employee." Canton paced closer to Ahmed, glowering over him. "Some lady named Irene Simmons. The lady they found in Portland on the trail."

"Has anyone spoken with the police? Or given any information to them?" asked Kari.

"No, ma'am. We stopped them at the quarterdeck and chose not to engage any further until you arrived," said Canton.

"Thanks, Chief. I've got it from here."

Canton handed her a card and said, "Text when you're ready, and we'll escort them up." He closed the heavy hatch softly, leaving them alone. Kari moved around the well-polished table to sit across from Ahmed.

"Now that he's gone, you want to tell me why they want to talk with *you* about the murder?"

He continued to stare downward, never looking at her. "Hello? Ahmed? I'm here to help you, but I can't do it without you."

She waited for him to decide to talk. The loud echo of riveting somewhere in the ship assaulted her senses, reminding her of the ongoing construction.

Kari adjusted herself in her seat and said, "Fine. Have it your way. I have shit to do."

She closed her notebook, stood, and turned to leave.

"Wait. Please. Ma'am. I'm sorry. I just . . . just . . ."

He sucked air into his lungs hard and fast as he ran his fingers through his short hair. "Help me. Please. I don't know what to do. They want to talk to me about a murder. It's unbelievable," he said and finally met her gaze. Tears poured from his eyes.

"Okay."

She sat back down and reopened her notebook. Most of her criminal clients acted in a similar way to Ahmed at this stage. Over the years she found that trust needed to be established before the client would open enough to assist her representation. Trust and, at times, a little tough love.

"I get it. This is a stressful situation. Let's start over. Is that your service jacket?" she asked as she pointed to the folder.

"Yes, ma'am," said Ahmed as he handed her his military record, then reached across the table for a box of tissues. He turned his head away from her and noisily blew his nose.

The unassuming brown folder contained everything about a sailor's history, starting with the Armed Services Vocational Aptitude Battery, or ASVAB. All service members took the test to determine their aptitude. Most sailors scored an average of sixty on the test; Ahmed scored a ninety, indicating a high degree of intelligence. Kari knew Ahmed's high score, combined with other factors, probably accounted for his selection on the precommissioned ship.

She continued through his service jacket. He'd earned numerous awards for excellence. In addition, he'd earned the highest possible score on every one of his annual fitness reports. Interesting. This kid didn't fit the norm for her typical client. Generally, her criminal defense clients scraped the bottom of the ASVAB score and had troubled fitness reports and numerous reprimands by the time their behavior rose to the level of criminal charges. By all accounts, Ahmed looked like a model sailor, which piqued Kari's curiosity. Why would such a hard-charging, clean-cut, smart sailor be questioned by the police? And for murder, of all things?

"How long have you been attached to the *Patrick Gallagher*?" she asked. Ahmed's service record provided this information, but Kari wanted to put him at ease by asking run-of-the-mill opening questions.

"Just over one year, ma'am."

"Where are you from?"

"Right here in Maine, ma'am. My parents and baby sister live in Portland. I was born here. My parents own the Khadra Market in Portland."

"I know it very well. It's the African store near Saint John Street, on the left?" Kari had passed the store numerous times since returning to Maine but had never gone inside.

He cleared his throat again. "Yes, ma'am."

"Have you moved on board?" she asked.

"Not fully, ma'am. A few guys and I have an apartment in town. The lease runs out this month. That's when we planned to move here. We only have a couple of weeks left."

Tap, tap, tap . . .

What is that sound? she thought, then realized Ahmed's leg was bouncing uncontrollably. A loud riveting and banging added to the clamor.

"I'll bet apartment living has been sweet for you guys."

"Yes, ma'am," he said with a hint of a smile. "But I mostly like being in Maine because I can go home on the weekends." He quickly looked away from her, cheeks reddening.

"Do you do that often?"

"Yes, ma'am. I go to Portland nearly every weekend. I like to be with my family. I help in the store and eat my momma's cooking. Nothing's better." He smiled.

Ahmed visibly relaxed when he spoke about his family. Many sailors ran toward naval service to escape the dead end that a dysfunctional home offered as their future. She also knew most people in their twenties preferred the company of their peers over that of elder family members.

"Why'd you join the navy?"

"My father encouraged me to enlist. He said this beautiful country gave our community a second chance, so we needed to repay its kindness."

Ahmed rubbed his hands across his pant legs as he spoke. His eyes darted around the room, managing to avoid looking directly at Kari.

"Did your parents immigrate here?"

"Yes, ma'am, long before I was born. They're from Mogadishu, Somalia."

Before she could respond, her device chimed and lit up.

There's a detective down here bothering the watch stander on the quarterdeck, the text message read. Throwing around all sorts of nonsense like he doesn't know he's standing on a United States war vessel. Time estimate?

Just him? she replied.

Yes. Uniformed cops are on the pier.

She glanced at Ahmed and thought for a moment.

Fifteen. Tops.

OK, let me know when you're done and we'll bring up the detective.

No need. I'll go down and snag him.

You sure?

She gave the thumbs-up. Turning back to Ahmed, she said, "There's a Portland Police detective waiting for us at the quarterdeck. Any idea why they want to talk to you about this?"

"No, ma'am."

"Did you know the victim? Irene Simmons?"

"No, ma'am."

She quickly googled the date the police found Ms. Simmons's body on a trail in Portland. Then she turned to him. "Looks like this happened in July. It took the police roughly four weeks to investigate before coming to speak with you. Would you have been visiting your parents on the weekends in July, like you do now?"

"Not likely, ma'am. July involved major operations on board in my shop. That month we worked our tails off to pass inspections. Everyone either hot racked or stayed very close." He rubbed his forehead as he spoke to her.

"Including you?"

"Yes, ma'am."

"Okay. When we meet with the detective, you let me do all the talking. The only thing you do is confirm your name. Nothing else. Got it?"

"Yes, ma'am."

"And maintain eye contact. You're a respected member of the navy, chosen for a plum position because of your hard work. Sit up straight, maintain your military bearing and a thousand-yard stare, even if you feel nervous." She closed his service jacket. "Right now, they likely don't have anything concrete on you. At this stage of an investigation, the police will try to lean on someone they deem to be a person of interest. Sometimes they get lucky when the person volunteers incriminating information. That's not going to happen here. You got it?"

He nodded.

"I'll ask you one last time. Any wild guesses as to why they're interested in you?" Kari knew there had to be more to his story. His inability to look her in the eye told her everything she needed to know about the young man. He was lying, but for now she could only proceed with the facts as he presented them.

"I really don't know, ma'am," he said as he glanced away from her. A second later, his eyes shot back to hers and he said, "Sorry, ma'am."

"Okay. Let's find out. I'll be right back with the detective."

Ahmed grimaced slightly and let out a long exhale. He stood when she left the room. Most of her clients were people who had grown accustomed to police interaction. Accordingly, rather than being tense, many in similar circumstances took police interaction in stride, at times appearing to enjoy the attention. With Ahmed, something didn't add up. Maybe he lied on behalf of someone else? Or he saw something but refused to get involved? All she knew for sure was that the city had been on edge after the three murders. And now the police were focusing on a young Black man who by all accounts was a model sailor. Not the sort of person she would pin for a murderer, even if he was hiding something from her.

Glancing at him, Kari felt the pang of heartbreak. She wanted to protect him from what may be a rush to judgment from the larger population. The Sharpe family had been through enough police "investigations" over the years to make her suspicious. The ship's rumor mill probably raged hot when the cops showed up on the pier. News of police demanding to board and question a service member would be the topic of discussion for weeks. Suspicion over Ahmed's involvement in the murder would fuel baseless "theories," none of which would be favorable to him.

Even if the police chose to move on, many on the ship would assume he pulled some "legal magic" to get out of trouble. He would eventually find himself not assigned plum tasks, reducing his promotional chances. Instead, his superiors might assume that where there was smoke, there was fire.

The sad fact existed that Ahmed's command would never view him the same after today, regardless of his innocence or guilt.

Chapter 7

As the attorney walked out of the wardroom, Ahmed stood. He paced back and forth, racking his brain for answers. The cops had searched his apartment, but he felt certain they would find nothing. He'd done nothing wrong. His only crime had been going to Portland for the weekend. Stupid. Should have stayed with the guys. They planned a farewell-to-the-apartment party with others from the command. He should have stayed and ate pizza like everyone else. But no. He just couldn't resist his mom's food or the comfort of being with family. What a momma's boy. The guys mocked him for going home on the weekends. Maybe they were right.

"Come home, Youseff," his mom would say. "I want to hug my boy." "Are you eating, Youseff?" "Your sister misses you, Youseff. Come home." His mom's words worked like magic, drawing him to her, to home. He loved visiting them. Sitting on the floor, enjoying her cooking, visiting with other folks from the community who dropped by unexpectedly. It provided a needed respite from the coldness of navy life. The shouting, the filth of the ship's construction. His chief. At times he just needed a break.

During high school, his father had suggested he enlist as a way of repaying America for welcoming them. At first, Ahmed had flatly refused, but then he'd reconsidered. College had been financially out of reach, and Maine offered no real industry outside of tourist-related positions. Unless he wanted to work on a lobster boat or at a restaurant, he needed to make a choice. And he did.

Enlisting gave him flight. He trained and worked with all sorts of guys. Some women. They were nice too. The guys accepted him in a weird way. Everyone had a story. No one cared to hear it.

Damn it. If he had just stayed and gone to the party, none of this would be happening right now. Why the hell had he lied to Lieutenant Commander Sharpe? He knew she wanted to help him. Probably the only person who could. He should have told her everything. All of it. Instead, he sat there like a dope. Now he had to continue to play it cool. He had no choice.

He wore a freshly pressed set of dungarees. For what? Glancing down at his work uniform, he brushed away a thread.

At one point, she'd knocked her knuckles on the table to get his attention. He'd jerked back. Jumpy with nervous energy. She'd continued to say something to him, but he couldn't seem to connect to her words. The last time he'd felt this way had been in basic training. Standing at attention and being shouted at elicited a knotted beast of nerves. His ears would ring, buzzing with an electric live-wire energy.

Lieutenant Commander Sharpe had stood and told him to wait. That much he understood. The buzzing returned. Images of his family cluttered his mind. How would he explain what happened? *Shit.* He cracked his knuckles. The sudden urge to bolt hit him hard. His legs bounced, ready to flee.

Why did I lie to her? The only person that could help? Deny everything. Wasn't that what people did? His parents would admonish him to tell the truth. No way. How could he? No one would believe him.

Chapter 8

Kari quickly navigated to the quarterdeck. She sweated heavily from the numerous ladders she climbed on her journey. Impatient, she swiped her hand across her brow and slicked sweat away.

A bulky man dressed in an ill-fitted suit stood stiffly near the edge of the gangway. The man stared intently at his device, oblivious to his surroundings.

Oh crap.

Not him. I can't do this.

She held her breath. The sharp taste of bile stung her throat. Her carefully crafted litigator persona vanished in an instant. *How could it be him?* The man of so many nightmares. He hadn't seen her yet. She could bolt. Tell Ahmed he needed to get someone else, that she had an emergency. Anything but face him.

She felt her knees buckle and grabbed the bulkhead to steady herself.

Get your shit together, Kari! You have no choice! She steeled her body and willed herself to face him.

Kari let out a slow breath, cleared her throat, and said, "Detective?"

"Finally," he said, turning to her.

She extended her hand, straightened her back, and said, "Lieutenant Commander Sharpe." Her steady voice concealed her terror.

"Sharpe? You don't say. Little Kari Sharpe? Is that right?"

"Yes, I'm Kari Sharpe. And you are?"

Detective Clark smiled and said, "We both know you remember me. How's Dougie?"

She pretended not to hear his question. Instead, she looked away and signed the logbook, officially allowing Clark's entry on the *Gallagher*. She swallowed the rising bile in the back of her throat, squared her shoulders, and looked him straight in the eye.

"I don't remember you at all, but then again everyone ages differently."

She allowed her eyes to trail down his body to his ample potbelly, where they lingered for just a moment before returning to meet his gaze. Her barely veiled insult hit him hard.

He fidgeted, clearly uncomfortable with the current state of his middle-aged body. His rumpled cheap suit, stained shirt, and unkempt greasy hair were also on full display. She'd bested him, turning the tables on him in an instant. Kari had bested him, this demon from her past. It had to hurt seeing her, one of those Sharpe kids so successful and beautiful, and him, like this.

The last time they met had been the night of Doug's arrest. She'd stood silently, helplessly, on the weatherworn porch of their home, watching the events unfold. Officer Clark had slammed Doug to the ground, which had elicited a loud groan from her brother. The second shriek came when Clark cuffed Doug so tight that his hands turned a bluish color. He lay face down in the dirt as a stream of tears ran down her cheeks. Her brother, helpless, a feeling they shared. She desperately wanted to do something, shout or kick at the police, anything. Helplessness in the face of abject cruelty.

Kari ran toward Doug as Clark jerked him off the ground. Standing between Doug and an open police cruiser door, she flung her arms around her brother and pressed her face against his dirty body. Small stones stuck to his shirt, poking at her skin. The odor of his fear stung her nose. Clark grabbed her thin arm with so much force she shrieked in pain.

"What the hell, man. She's just a kid!" yelled Doug.

"She better watch it or her ass will join yours. There's plenty of room for all you Sharpes." Clark hissed the words at Doug, then turned to smirk at her. The jerk actually smirked. She would never forget that look.

His viciousness shot through her like a hot flame, searing the last vestiges of helplessness. A steely resolve roared to life. Never again. She had vowed to protect herself and others from men like Clark.

Meeting Officer Clark, now Detective Clark, after so many years unearthed a web of emotions. She had never considered this might happen when she'd chosen to leave New York. Never thought she'd face him like this.

"Give me one minute," she said.

She yanked her phone out. Jabbing furiously, she texted Canton. Change of plans. We meet in the hangar bay. Set up a table, a few chairs, and get Ahmed down there.

Ma'am? It's a mess in the bay. Between the exhaust, the riveting and clanging, you can barely hear yourself think.

Perfect. Let me know when it's ready.

Without waiting for a reply, she turned to Clark. "It'll be a few more minutes."

"What the hell? Why?"

"The ship's under construction. They're trying to make it safe for a civilian. Wait here."

Moving away as quickly as possible, Kari positioned herself just outside his view. Leaning against the bulkhead, she let out a slow breath. *You've got this.* She counted each breath, waiting for relief. After several rounds, she stopped clenching her jaw.

Her phone buzzed. Ready, ma'am.

Got it. I plan to take the detective on the scenic route.

If you're referring to the guy in the suit, careful. That overstuffed soft civilian is likely to have a heart attack if he climbs too many ladders.

Exactly what I had in mind, she thought.

"Detective Clark? We're ready for you."

She moved quickly up and down the ladders, over numerous hatches, and past multiple routes to the hangar bay. Kari's legs burned in protest, but she could take it. Clark's legs probably hurt far worse. Good. He huffed and puffed; red faced, he barely kept pace. Maybe he would collapse from exertion. Exactly what he deserved.

"What the hell, Kari? How much farther?"

She stopped and spun on her heel to face him. She jabbed her finger at Clark and proclaimed, "You will address me as either Lieutenant Commander Sharpe, Ms. Sharpe, or Attorney Sharpe. We are *not* on a first-name basis. Got it?"

He stared back, stunned. Sweat stained his cheap dress shirt.

"And not far. To answer your question."

Over the years, Clark had made a point of harassing Doug with near-constant police interactions. He'd pulled Doug over to check his ID or stopped by to "discuss" crimes committed in the area. Clark had seemed to focus on the Sharpes, Doug in particular. Today, payback felt great.

As a kid, Kari had looked up to her brother Doug. He had stepped into the role as sole parent for her and Jimmy after their father drank himself to death and their mother died from an overdose. Rather than accepting the arrest as something her brother brought onto himself, she'd viewed the police with hard, cold hatred, especially Officer Clark. The contours of his face permanently etched into her memory. The ease with which he'd chatted and smoked with the others while her brother had lain on the ground with his face planted in the earth . . . she felt as though they had enjoyed his humiliation, extending it for as long as possible.

That night had marked the turning point in her life. A bright line had been drawn between "before Doug's arrest" and "after." It marked the beginning of Kari's life with Jimmy as her only parent, her only family. At eighteen, Jimmy was old enough to be her legal guardian. If Jimmy had been a year younger, they would have both been placed in foster care, likely in separate homes. She also met Detective Mack Bowen that night. Detective Bowen had broken the case against Doug, which resulted in his conviction for two counts of vehicular manslaughter, possession of narcotics, and distribution of narcotics. The quantity of drugs found in Doug's car, combined with the deaths of two Portland-area pedestrians whom he'd plowed over during a high-speed police chase, had secured him a lengthy sentence. His continued bad behavior while incarcerated guaranteed he would never be let out on parole.

"Okay, that's it. You're just taking me in circles. This stupid shit can ain't that big," yelled Clark.

"We're here," she said as they entered the hangar bay.

Clark's eyes darted around the bay. His thin lips turned white as he clenched his jaw. His chest heaved rapidly.

"Seriously? This is where we're meeting?" he growled.

"Yes. The ship is a construction zone. It's unsafe for an untrained civilian. Captain's orders."

"That sure didn't stop you from taking me through every square inch of the place."

Kari ignored his comment. She made the appropriate introductions and sat down next to Ahmed, bracing herself for a tough interview. Maintaining the upper hand, not allowing her client to give in to the typical temptation to speak, would be tricky. Police interrogations proved to be unpleasant at nearly every step of an investigation. But precharging interviews always struck Kari as something a little sinister, because the police used these interactions to convince people to speak against their own interests. She once saw her father admit to crimes during a routine vehicular stop. The officer barely asked him anything, and then Larry Sharpe spewed a string of profanity-laced confessions.

Focus, Kari. Focus. She curled her toes, clenched her leg muscles, and released. Another stupid relaxation technique. Kari looked at Clark, at the roughness of his sad, lined face, and quickly looked away. Thoughts of Doug distracted her. She needed to be sharp, but instead her mind drifted to one of her fondest memories of her deceased brother.

The school bus had rumbled over the last large pothole before arriving at her stop. The breaks hissed and the door creaked open. Kari stood, slung her heavy backpack over her ten-year-old frame. Her book bag bumped against the seat backs of the narrow school bus as she made her way to the open door. She almost made it before Greg Stadt stuck his foot out, tripping her, like he'd done so many times before. She fell face down on the dirty floor to a round of laughter.

"Walk much, loser?" shouted Stacy Marc.

"Hurry up, we need to keep rolling!" yelled the bus driver, oblivious as always.

Kari scrambled to her feet, her face red with a flush of embarrassment. She tumbled down the steps, jumping onto the dirty road with a thud.

The sun poked through the canopy of trees as she ambled down the dirt road to their tiny ranch house. The early June flies bit at her bare legs and flew into her eyes and nose, but she barely noticed. Today had been the last day of school before summer. Most kids welcomed the two-months-long break, but Kari dreaded it.

"Mom? Jimmy? I'm home!" she yelled.

A strange man's voice came from the kitchen. "Who the hell is that? Some kid?"

"Don't worry about her, honey. She's just one of mine. Won't bother us one bit."

As she walked past the kitchen's swing door, she peeked through the crack to see her mom sitting on the man's lap. A thick haze of cigarette smoke seeped into the hall.

"Kari! You're finally home! Doug and I have been waiting for you," said Jimmy excitedly as he ran into the house. The screen door slammed behind him with a loud racket.

"Why?" No one ever waited to see her. No one seemed to care.

"Come on!"

Jimmy grabbed her hand. His palm felt clammy and dirty, like he'd been working outside.

"Where are we going?" she asked.

"You'll see."

They headed around the small home to the woods in the backyard. A robin squawked as a car engine rumbled to life in the distance.

"Cover her eyes!" yelled Doug from a distance.

"Right. Close your eyes, Kari. We have a surprise for you."

Jimmy held her shoulder, guiding her forward. She could barely contain her excitement. He pushed her into the cool woods.

"Okay! Open them!" yelled Doug.

She blinked open her eyes to take in her surroundings. The boys had made a small shelter out of branches they found in the forest. Long branches and sticks leaned up against a large tree in a triangle shape, with one side of the structure remaining open.

"What do you think? It's our place now. Away from *them*," said Doug excitedly.

"We've been working on it for days. Wanted to surprise you," said Jimmy.

"It's amazing! Can I go inside?" Kari said as she ran toward the shelter.

The inside was surprisingly large. The three of them sat on the ground, looking over the brothers' handiwork. The shelter was crude but nice.

"We plan to bring chairs out here, maybe even a TV," said Doug.

"The most important thing is that they don't know about it. This is our secret," said Jimmy proudly.

An oasis from the drinking, drugs, smoking, fighting, and random men coming and going before their dad returned in the evening was pure heaven to Kari.

"Can I sleep out here?" she asked.

"Not yet, but once we finish it, who knows?" said Doug. His face beamed with possibility.

She got up and hugged both Doug and Jimmy tightly. The three amigos, supporting each other. They gave each other strength even during the worst of times. Without them, she'd have been lost.

Butch Clark had taken Doug away from her. Or at least that was how she'd always remember what happened. Her hero gone forever because of a cruel cop.

She swallowed hard, trying to push the torrent of memories from her mind. Something she'd done countless times growing up, yet something she rarely had to do when she lived away from Maine. She exhaled all her air, imagining the memory of Doug leaving her body with the exhale. Glancing around the hangar bay, she took a quick sensory inventory of her surroundings. The gray metal bulkheads, overheads, and hatches. The loud riveting. The sharp banging. Acrid chemical smells. One by one she noticed and categorized everything around her. She needed to do her job, not relive her past. Finally, the relaxation tool started to work. She felt grounded.

As they settled in, the pause in the loud riveting came to an end. The sound of an air compressor mingled with the banging and loud drilling. Noxious fumes of diesel fuel and chemicals, combined with the dust created by the drilling, made it difficult to breathe. Beads of sweat poured down Clark's beet red face as he struggled for breath.

"As you know, I'm here to talk with you about the death of Irene Simmons," he yelled over the noise.

"Is Mr. Ahmed being charged with anything?" Kari asked.

"No. We just want to talk with him. That's all. Maybe he can offer us some help. You aren't in any trouble."

Kari knew this song and dance well. The let's-be-friends tactic persisted in police interviews because it remained remarkably effective. At their core, most people wanted to be viewed as helpful and kind. Even hardened criminals repeatedly fell for the trap, offering information against their own interests.

"Ahmed has no information that could assist you," she said.

"Is that right? Where were you the morning of July sixteenth?" asked Clark.

"What?" Kari yelled. Loud riveting picked up the pace, preventing her from hearing his words. Clark looked annoyed but shouted the question out again. Spittle flew from his mouth as he struggled to be heard.

"Detective Clark, direct your questions to me. Mr. Ahmed has nothing to say to you."

"Fine. Then you tell me Ahmed's location on the morning of July sixteenth."

"Mr. Ahmed, along with the rest of the ship's company, have been working night and day to meet their deadlines. The morning of July sixteenth would have been no different."

Clark adjusted his ample body on the small metal chair, clearly uncomfortable. Sweat continued to run down his face.

"Has Mr. Ahmed retained your services? A lawyer like you must be expensive."

"The financial relationship between myself and my client is none of your business." Kari knew the comment about her fees was meant to belittle her. "We're finished here. As I said, Mr. Ahmed has nothing to offer your investigation."

Instead of getting up with her, Clark eased back into his chair, a look of satisfaction overtaking his face.

"Oh, I very much think he *does* have something to offer. An eyewitness can place him on the trail behind the deceased's usual place of abode on the morning of the attack. Your boy here knows much more than he's telling you." Clark rolled the word "boy" around his mouth, elongating the "oy" sound.

"What witness?" she hissed. Maybe Clark was bluffing?

"Betsy Roth. Ring any bells, Ahmed?"

Ahmed's head jerked up. His eyes darted between Kari and Clark. He ran his fingers through his hair. His leg started bouncing again. Poor kid looked like he was about to flee or pass out.

Kari needed to end the conversation. Quickly.

"Unless you're charging him, we have nothing further to say to you," she said as she stood again. She turned to Ahmed and said, "You can go back to your appointed place of duty. The master-at-arms and I will show the detective to the quarterdeck."

"This won't be the last you've heard from me, Mr. Ahmed. Once the boys in blue get done searching your place, I'm sure I'll be in touch."

Kari's stomach tightened into a painful knot.

Clark continued: "In fact, I think I'll call down to the officers who are at your little shit domain right now. See if they've discovered anything. You don't mind waiting a minute, do you, Kari?" Before she could correct him, Clark added, "My mistake, Ms. Sharpe."

The detective smirked. They had no choice but to sit and wait for him to call the team who were searching Ahmed's apartment. He strode away, a spring in his step.

"You lied to me? You said you spent most of July on board," she snarled at Ahmed once she was confident that the detective could no longer hear them.

"No, ma'am. I just forgot. It was a busy month. I barely made it back to Portland at all that month." He wrung his fists as he spoke.

"Fine. Did you know the cops searched your apartment?"

"Yes, ma'am. They showed up this morning after I left. One of my roommates texted me. The cops waved around a piece of paper and demanded they be allowed in to search my room and the rest of the place. He didn't know what to do, so he let them in."

"Nice. That'd have been good to know about an hour ago."

She held her facial features together to present a blank, unemotional facade, unwilling to allow Clark to read anything into the conversation between her and Ahmed when the detective returned.

"Do you know the victim, Irene Simmons?"

"No, ma'am. They said she worked as a civilian at BIW, but I never met her. We only meet certain people connected with BIW."

"You better be telling me the truth. If I find out you withheld information again, I'm leaving, and you can deal with this yourself. Got it?"

"Yes, ma'am. Sorry," he said. A reddish hue passed his cheeks.

A distant memory of Doug using the same sort of tough love tactic with their obviously drunk father interrupted her train of thought. "Are you drunk again?" shouted Doug at their inebriated father. "What's it to you?" yelled Larry Sharpe. It always started the same and ended the same, with Doug on the receiving end of Larry's angry blows. Kari wrestled the unpleasant memory back into the cage where it resided. Reliving one of the countless nights Doug had taken a beating while she hid in her room needed to stay out of her professional life.

She glanced at Ahmed. He repeatedly rubbed his hands on his thighs, stopping only to pick at his cuticle. In her experience, nervous energy could be a sign of either innocence or guilt. She reminded herself that without knowing more, nervousness alone proved nothing, even from a client who had withheld vital information.

Her phone chimed and lit up.

How's it going down there? You need anything from me? asked Canton.

Not sure yet. Apparently the cops had a search warrant for Ahmed's apartment and are still there now. I'll let you know if anything comes of it.

A search warrant? That can't be good news.

Nope, usually not.

She put her phone down and turned to Ahmed. "I told your chief that we'd update him if anything changed down here."

Ahmed nodded his head and said, "Thank you, ma'am. I'm sorry I didn't tell you about the cops at my place."

She could give a damn whether he did it. She had one goal—to make Clark's job as difficult as possible. Slow him down. Make him prove everything. Make him work. Shielding Ahmed from criminal processes while disrupting Clark felt cathartic. The detective would never cause another family the pain he had caused hers. Not if she could help it.

Officer Clark paced around the hangar bay, occasionally glancing over his shoulder at Ahmed. He jammed a finger into his free ear in a futile attempt to dampen the noise as he used his phone. Kari suspected that either Clark purposely kept them in suspense, or he, too, was waiting on something from the police officers who were searching Ahmed's apartment. The dirty, hot, noisy hangar bay made Kari rethink her decision to hold the interview down here rather than in the wardroom.

Clark strode back to them, his gait victorious.

This can't be good.

"We found a sneaker in your apartment with what appears to be a bloodstain," he said to Ahmed. "We also found the same substance on a pair of gray sweatpants, which had burs on them. The burs are the same one the victim had tangled into her hair. Anything you care to tell me?"

"How do you know it's blood?" Kari demanded. "There's no way Augusta turned anything around that quickly."

The State of Maine's forensic labs located in Augusta, the capital of Maine, suffered from a notoriously long backlog of cases. She had heard the backlog extended into months for routine items. Clearly someone had pulled strings to expedite their investigation.

"They ran a field kit to test the substance. It's biological. They bagged and tagged the items, then drove them up to Augusta. While I waited for you to bring me into this hellhole, I pulled a few favors from the mayor's office. Both the mayor and the governor are anxious to get the violent killer off our peaceful streets. As you can imagine, murders aren't good for the tourism industry." He refocused on Ahmed. "I'll ask again: Anything you want to tell me?"

Ahmed looked at Kari. She shook her head.

"No, sir," answered Ahmed. He sat up straighter and maintained eye contact as he spoke.

"Fine. I'm bringing you down to the station. You'll be held until we get either an all clear from Augusta or they confirm it's blood."

"He is absolutely not leaving this vessel without the express permission of the commanding officer," said Kari.

"Bullshit. I don't need permission. This is a state criminal investigation into the murder of a civilian in Portland. Your captain has no authority to impede our investigation. Ahmed leaves with me."

"You'll have to wait."

Kari furiously tapped a message to Canton.

Chief, is the brig ready for use?

Brig, ma'am? Our vessel is too small for such luxuries. We have a room we can use as a cage if that works? It's sort of like a brig.

She turned back to Clark. "The ship has a perfectly functioning brig. If you'd like, we can hold my client here pending the results of the forensics evaluation on what you claim to be his personal property."

Clark appeared to think about her offer as he intently stared at her.

"Not good enough. He comes to Portland, where he can sit until we hear from forensics and the attorney general's office."

Clark stood, abruptly placing his large hands on the table. He leaned forward.

"Get up. This charade is over." He jammed his finger in the air at Ahmed.

Before Kari could say anything, Ahmed started to get up.

Then Canton strode in.

"Lieutenant Commander Sharpe, I thought I'd check in. We're in the middle of precommission qualifications and could really use Ahmed back to work. He's one of our best sailors. What's the delay?" asked Canton.

"Officer Clark here thinks he can pull Ahmed off the ship based on suspicion that they found blood on his clothing. We're trying to work out a solution that would serve the needs of the navy as well as the Portland Police Department. He isn't satisfied that the brig would be secure. Or at least I assume that's your objection," she said, turning to Clark.

"I can give you a tour of it. I assure you, we can secure anyone," offered Canton.

The detective glared at Canton with pure rage. "Nice try, but I don't need a damned tour of this tin can, because Ahmed comes with me. Talk to the damn president if you need to. I don't care. This ends now. You've got twenty minutes. In the meantime, I'm going to lean on the boys in Augusta. See if they can work their magic as quickly as possible." Clark turned to Ahmed. "You might be charged with murder before the end of the day, my friend."

Ahmed sat stock still, listening.

"Hmm . . . twenty minutes might be difficult, Officer Clark. Our skipper just went into a meeting with Washington brass. Those blowhards love to hear themselves talk. You never know how long it'll take," said Canton.

"How about you wait by the pier? Assuming he's cleared to leave the ship, I'll escort him to your location," offered Kari.

Clark rolled his eyes. "Fine. I need to get out of this hellhole."

Kari turned to Ahmed and said, "Let's go."

At first he didn't move. Kari assumed the noise prevented him from hearing her. She leaned in closer and yelled "Let's go" as she gently touched his sleeve.

Ahmed continued to stare straight ahead. The sharp aroma of nervous sweat wafted from his drenched uniform blouse. She recognized the signs of shock. The far-off stare, disassociation from one's surroundings. Even professional criminals looked like this at certain points during their interaction with the legal system. Normally she expected her guys to get the "shock stares" at sentencing, not during a prearrest interview. Typically the hardened criminals sat like peacocks during initial police interactions, smug in their ability to hide their crimes. Not Ahmed.

She needed to protect her client from Clark. Right the many wrongs this idiot detective had inflicted on her family. The kid faced a rough road. The search warrant. Strings pulled in Augusta. They wanted him for this. Bad. She'd slowed them down for now. If the toxicology report confirmed the existence of blood, they'd arrest Ahmed, which was the direction she feared they were headed in. She wondered about all the decisions he'd made to bring him to this juncture. Where had he gone wrong?

Chapter 9

Ahmed and Kari made it to Officer's Country in record time. Kari breathed a sigh of relief, needing a minute from the noise and filth of the hangar bay. She grabbed the pitcher of water set out by the mess staff and poured herself a drink. Then a second one, not realizing how dehydrated she was.

"Would you like some water?" she asked Ahmed.

"Yes, ma'am. Thank you."

She handed him the tumbler of cold water and sat down across from him. Before she could say anything, Canton entered the room with a noisy bang of the door.

"What the hell is going on? They searched your apartment?" he barked at Ahmed.

Navy chiefs, as senior enlisted personnel, spoke to the sailors working under them in harsher terms than most officers might do in the same situation. In many ways the chief's tough directives kept the entire enterprise running smoothly. Kari had learned to stay out of their way and allow them to deal with their sailors in a distinctly "chief-like" manner, even if these interactions seemed overly caustic at times.

"The last thing this goddamned ship needs right now is dancing around the bullshit you created for yourself. I should've just let the detective take you out of here. I can replace you in an instant and would probably do the navy an injustice if I don't. None of us have time for this crap. Lieutenant Commander Sharpe, what happens next?"

Kari leaned in to speak, but Canton cut her off.

"I thought you were a squared-away sailor. You were handpicked by your last command and recommended for this position. You have any idea how lucky you are to be here? Only the best of the best are selected for a precommission tour."

Ahmed continued to silently stare at the ground, taking in his chief's words. What else could he do?

The wardroom's intraship phone line buzzed. Canton answered on the second ring.

"Canton," he said. "I see. Okay. We'll be right down, with Ahmed."

Canton hung up the phone. "Detective Clark has some sort of update for us. He said Ahmed needs to come down. Time's up."

Ahmed's pallor changed from gray to green within seconds.

"I'll bet Clark heard from Augusta. Normally these things take a considerable amount of time. However, this case's notoriety fueled a political charge to get somebody in lockup. Hopefully they'll have the right somebody. I'll need to speak with Ahmed before we go down."

"Fine. I've got a division to run with sailors who are here, ready to work," said Canton. He gave Ahmed one last glance and strode out.

After Canton left the wardroom, Kari turned to Ahmed. "Let's assume they have enough to charge you. If that's the case, you should call anyone you need to call right now. You will also want to memorize any phone numbers you might need."

"Why memorize phone numbers?" he asked.

"They'll take away your device and then give you the right to a local phone call. If you haven't memorized any numbers, you're out of luck."

"Thank you, ma'am. I wouldn't have thought of that."

"Yeah, no one does. If they do take you into custody, do not say anything to anyone. Not even to anyone in your cell. They might seem nice, like a friend, but those guys will sell information to the police in exchange for a shorter sentence. Do not tattle on yourself. I repeat, do not say a word, even though it'll be very tempting. Anything you say will be used against you. You should assume the police are listening to everything you say, always, except in a private room with your attorney. Do you understand?"

"Yes, ma'am. Will you be with me?" Ahmed asked. A glimmer of hope shone in his eyes.

"Negative." Kari paused, ignoring the pang of sadness in her heart over what the future may hold for her client. She had to be clear, straightforward. "Assuming you're arrested, this is where I leave you. You should contact family to arrange for legal counsel. If you're deemed to be indigent, the clerk of the court will assign you counsel. But we are getting ahead of ourselves. Let's go down there to hear what Detective Clark has to say."

"Ma'am, I'd like to call my mom before we go. She should probably know what's happening. I planned to go home for dinner. It's my little sister's birthday this weekend. I don't want them to worry if I don't show up."

Kari hated birthdays. Her eleventh birthday, the last one she had with both brothers and her father, ended unceremoniously. Larry sat at their cramped wooden kitchen table drunk out of his mind. He never tried to conceal his inebriation like some boozers did. Instead, he sang "Happy Birthday" with so much gusto he toppled over.

"What a jerk. We should've gone to Subway," Doug had said as he'd rolled his eyes at their dad crumpled on the floor.

Jimmy had tried his best to create a celebration for their birthdays, but they'd never had extra money for presents or an expensive cake. On most birthdays, they each had a cupcake. Jimmy would reuse a few different candles for the occasion. Usually, a pink one for her and a blue one for him. "Another year gone." His favorite refrain as he blew out the candles.

Shaking off the memory, Kari gulped down the rest of her water and stood. "Okay. I'll wait right outside."

She started to walk out of the room and then stopped to hand him her business card.

"Here, you can give her my number if she has questions. As I said, if you're charged, I won't represent you unless I'm retained or hired by you as a civilian attorney. Otherwise you'll be provided no-cost or low-cost representation."

"Yes, ma'am, just like the movies."

"Yeah, except movies are fun to watch. This is anything but."

Ahmed nodded, then cracked his knuckles.

Kari shut the door and leaned against the bulkhead, waiting for Ahmed to call his family. She feared the worst for him. The criminal justice system had a way of injuring the already broken. For the unbroken, the weight of the justice system could be crushing. Ahmed's interaction with the police had probably already hurt him in ways she could never imagine.

Chapter 10

Ahmed stared at his phone. What could he say to his mother? How could he possibly explain what happened? Sweat poured down the back of his uniform shirt despite the chilly air.

He hated to admit it, but he desperately wanted the safety of his family right now. The loving words his mother would say to him, hushing his fears, soothing his frayed nerves as she'd always done. "Hush, Ahmed, Allah will protect you," she'd say.

Her phone only rang once before she picked up. *"As-salamu alaykum, huuno!"* his mother said cheerfully. The rhythmic sound of her knife hitting the cutting board in their kitchen, a familiar cadence.

"Wa-alaikum-salaam, Hooyo," he said.

"How's your day? I'm busy getting things ready for your sister's feast. What time should we expect you?"

Ahmed froze, unsure of how to begin. His heartbeat pounded in his ears. "Something has happened," he finally said. "I don't know if I'll be there tonight."

"What? It's Bilan's birthday feast. What could be more important?"

Embarrassment burned on his cheeks. "Something big is happening at work, and I can't get out of here. Please tell Bilan I'm sorry. I know how much this day means to her . . . to everyone. I'm sorry."

He choked up, fighting back tears as he chose to lie again. He'd never lied to his mother, not even as a child.

"Are you okay? You're scaring me, *huuno*," she said.

He fell silent. Tears flowed in an even stream, dotting his shirt. His ears buzzed as he paced the wardroom. Jittery legs burned with pent-up energy, ready for flight. He wanted to protect her. *Damn it.* He shook his hand, snapping his fingers, searching for purchase as his mind reeled in every direction.

She put his father on the phone.

Ahmed rolled his eyes and rubbed his forehead. Construction grime and sweat mingled, forming a gross sheen on his skin. "Youseff? What is happening?" His father's voice was jagged. Breathless. Fear of his father yanked the words from him. They tumbled out with a violent force before he could grab ahold of himself as he revealed everything. Although his father started to reply, Ahmed couldn't connect to the words. A loud buzzing filled his ears. The sharp blade of fear deafened him.

Betsy Roth turned me in to the police. Why? What the hell?

He had helped the old lady countless times. Why would she do this?

He disconnected the call abruptly. Rudely. He'd never been disrespectful to either of his parents. What was happening to him?

The door swung open, startling him. He stopped pacing and straightened his hunched back.

"You about ready?" asked the lawyer.

"Yes, ma'am."

Using the back of his hand, he hastily wiped away tears. His parents and their shared faith had taught him to face adversity with strength and confidence. He needed every ounce of both to navigate what lay ahead.

Ahmed followed Lieutenant Commander Sharpe through the ship. Several shipmates glanced at him and quickly looked away. He felt so stupid. He should have told her the truth.

Chapter 11

A few minutes later Kari and a crestfallen Ahmed returned to the quarterdeck, where Detective Clark and two uniformed police officers waited for him. Ahmed glanced at Kari, unsure what to do.

"It'll be okay. The officers are probably here to take you to the Portland Police Department," she whispered to Ahmed as reassuringly as possible. Then she spoke up. "Detective Clark, you have an update for us?"

Clark spun toward them and said, "Augusta confirmed the biomatter is blood. That along with the burs gives me enough to arrest Ahmed in connection with the death of Irene Simmons."

The detective took a step toward Ahmed. Kari took a sidestep, blocking Clark.

"The blood could be his. I'm sure Augusta didn't have time to run a full DNA analysis of the sample. As for the burs, everyone picks up the occasional bur on their clothes. We live in Maine, surrounded by forests. The blood and burs by themselves are hardly conclusive. It seems like a stretch to pull him off the ship. Like I said, the captain is willing to allow the Portland Police to use the brig until the matter gets sorted."

"I have a duty to the people of this state who are scared that a murderer is on the loose." Glancing at Ahmed, Clark said, "This is hardly the sort of thing that happens with real Mainers. And let's not forget that I also have an eyewitness who saw a Black man creeping around the trail on the day of the murder."

"What do you mean by that? Real Mainers? Ahmed was born here, just like you and me," Kari shot back. She made a mental note to complain about Clark's behavior to the department. Not that it would change anything.

The uniformed officers quickly flanked Ahmed. The petty officer on watch stood wide eyed.

Clark took a moment to look Ahmed up and down and replied, "Could've fooled me. Officers, we're ready here. I have nothing else to tell you, Ms. Sharpe. It's up to the attorney general's office at this point."

"Youseff Ahmed, you are under arrest for the murder of Irene Simmons," the patrol officer said as he handcuffed the sailor. Ahmed appeared to nearly black out as the officer turned him around for the cuffs. The officer Mirandized Ahmed as they walked down the gangway toward the waiting patrol car.

"Are the cuffs necessary? He's hardly a threat to your officers," Kari said to Clark.

"Can never be too certain," the detective said with a wink as he followed the other officers off the ship.

Kari sucked in a ragged breath, momentarily stunned.

She texted Canton. They've arrested Ahmed. Unless you need me for anything further, I'm heading back to Portland. He'll need civilian counsel from this point.

Seconds later he responded. Can he hire you to handle this?

Of course, but I'd have to charge him my usual rate, minus a slight navy discount. I'm not sure it's in his cards to pay for counsel. He is entitled to no-cost or low-cost representation.

Got it, ma'am. Thanks for your help on such short notice. I'll let everyone know what happened. He's a good kid, sharp as a whip, never in trouble. I'm not sure how to feel about any of this.

That makes two of us.

Kari waited until the police left the area before heading out. Her head pounded as she drove back to Portland. She massaged her temples, trying to collect her tired thoughts. She had no energy to face the office. Instead, she called Jimmy.

He answered on the second ring. "Hey, Kari."

"I hope you don't have plans for dinner. I'm getting pizza. I should be there around six."

"Everything okay?"

"Not really."

She hung up the call and reconsidered her words. She didn't want to worry Jimmy unnecessarily, especially considering he'd recently left rehab.

She thought about calling him back to cancel but reconsidered. After seeing Clark, she desperately needed Jimmy's support. Dumping what happened on him would be selfish, but she didn't care, because in that moment she needed the only person in the world who could truly understand.

Chapter 12

Ron Baker walked through the full parking lot to his waiting truck. The baking blacktop stank in the afternoon's sun. Normally he chose to stay at work until the "Seventeen Hundred" warriors left. The guys who chose to leave immediately at quitting time irritated the brass, making sailors look like slackers despite working a full day. His long navy career had taught him to never quit at quitting time. Always stay after the dust settled, preferably after his boss left. Today, however, was an exception.

His hot truck smelled of the stale coffee he'd left in the cup holder. *Crap . . . that's gonna be a pain to clean.*

The powerful engine rumbled to life, drowning out the near-constant buzz of BIW's busy waterfront. He'd spent his entire career close to the water, enlisting at eighteen. After twenty years, he'd continued to work with the navy as a civilian so he could be close to Irene, whether she wanted him to be or not.

He sped toward home, feeling light from the day's events, almost giddy. The police spent the morning at BIW interviewing some poor sap on the *Gallagher*. His coworkers said they heard the cops had arrested the kid for Irene Simmons's murder. Now they could all go back to normal. Relax just a little. Put it behind them, end the entire chapter.

Ron fumbled with the dials on his radio until he found something he liked, thrumming his way to the music of Eric Clapton's "Lay Down Sally."

Despite the celebratory mood, his mind lingered on one of the dead tourists. The man's body had been recovered from the sea. The news reported that the corpse contained heavy amounts of diesel fuel. The Coast Guard had asked the community for help in understanding the murders and the recent diesel fuel dumps just off Casco Bay. Another problem for him to solve, thanks to his idiot cousins.

A loud honk caught him off guard, startling him. Mainers usually never honked at a person sitting on a red light. Instead, custom dictated they wait patiently until the bozo in front of them finally noticed the green light. *Rude jerk.*

Normally he'd flip a honker the bird. Maybe get close enough to their bumper to make them sweat a little. Not today. No, today not even a rude jerk had the power to dampen his mood. Today he felt like celebrating. A quick stop at Dry Dock would do the trick.

Chapter 13

Kari balanced the pizza pie on her hip as she opened the side door to Jimmy's house. The loud bang of the screen door announced her presence.

"Hello? Pizza here!" yelled Kari.

"In here," Jimmy shouted back.

"You have paper plates? I don't see any out."

"Just got some. Hold on." He rummaged through his overflow cabinet, where he stowed an odd assortment of items. Kari suspiciously eyed the interior of the cabinet, looking for booze.

Peering into the pizza box, she said, "Looks like good old Chuck finally got our order right."

"The man is one for five at this point."

Kari and Jimmy loved pineapple and onions on their pizza. As kids they'd begged Doug mercilessly until he'd finally given in and ordered the combination on their pizza. The idea came to them after watching an episode of *Fantasy Island*. They thought pineapple on pizza seemed like something Mr. Roarke, the host on the island, would eat. She imagined Mr. Roarke in his signature white three-piece suit, impeccably groomed, licking pizza grease off his fingers like everyone else. Eating pineapple on pizza made her feel as though she lived on a tropical island, away from snowy Maine. Away from complicated problems. A silly childish notion that had stayed with them mostly through sheer stubbornness.

"You brought a huge bottle of Mountain Dew?" He placed the two-liter of soda on the island and looked at her inquisitively.

Kari craved Mountain Dew but never allowed herself to drink the sugary concoction. She found once she started, she couldn't stop. Besides, her friends in New York joked it was white-trash Perrier. Tonight she didn't give a shit. She needed something to take the edge off. Jimmy's fledgling sobriety meant she couldn't bring over the bottle of Bourdon she would have liked.

"Look, I had a shit day. Not everything's about you."

"Fine, fine." He held up his hands in mock surrender.

They took their slices to the adjoining family room in silence.

Holding up a glistening glass of Mountain Dew and ice, Kari said, "Here's to us!"

"Living the dream," he said, holding up his soda. He glanced at the pizza. "You really went all out tonight with the good stuff."

"I needed something special to balance the day I had."

Taking another sip of his soda, Jimmy said, "Yep."

Jimmy waited patiently for his sister to spill the beans. Kari took another large bite of the pizza. The warm grease oozed off the top of the curled slice and slid down the side of her hand.

Finally, soda and pizza worked their magic. The sugar from the highly caffeinated drink gave her head a zing. Bull's-eye.

"This morning I was asked to drop everything and run up to BIW. They needed a JAG to cover a police interrogation of a sailor on the precommission ship."

"You're talking about the *Gardner*, or *Gallen*. I don't know. Something Irish, right?"

She laughed. "Yes, the *Patrick Gallagher*."

"Yep, knew it was something Irish. Did you go?"

"Course I did. I can't let the navy down. Besides, I thought it might be a good way to get more business from BIW, either through a navy gig or civilians. You know I'm not even close to profitable yet. I'm still paying Ruth from my savings."

"Paying for my rehab couldn't have helped." He rubbed his eyes, embarrassed, and then he muttered, "What a bozo."

She let the comment and thoughts of her dwindling bank account pass with another slug of Mountain Dew. Then she leaned back into the well-worn plaid couch and took in her surroundings.

"What are you looking at?" Jimmy asked.

"Did you clean up or something? Looks like you threw out all the old newspapers and magazines. And did you wipe down the table? What's going on around here?"

Jimmy's house had never been clean. They'd grown up in squalor. Neither of them knew what living in a tidy house felt like. Their only clean "home" had been the shelter they had spent a few months in while she'd attended law school. "Daily chores ensured a healthy environment and mind," the director was fond of saying. Kari found that she agreed, having kept her New York apartment practically spotless.

"Can't a guy improve his surrounds without raising suspicions?"

"Nope. Not when that guy is you."

"Very funny." After a minute, he said, "So you went up there?"

"Yes, and I sat through what I'm sure the police had hoped would be a fruitful interrogation of the young sailor. The kid is from Maine. A Black kid."

"So what went wrong?"

"Butch Clark was the detective doing the interviewing."

Jimmy let out a loud whistle and looked at her. The deep scowl lines on his face became exaggerated.

"Now I get it," he said, glancing at the Mountain Dew. "I probably would've hit something way stronger. And don't start with your soda-is-a-gateway-to-obesity nonsense. It isn't the worst thing you could drink, considering the options." He took another bite of pizza and spoke with a stuffed mouth. "Did he recognize you? A lot has changed since that night."

"Oh yeah, he recognized me, or at least recalled the Sharpe name once I introduced myself. He made a point of asking about Doug."

Jimmy's eyes flared wide. He punched the armrest and whispered, "Bastard."

Kari suddenly felt small for imposing her problems on him. His recovery and continued sobriety depended on a calm, stable, supportive environment. *I shouldn't have come,* she thought, even as she found herself continuing with her story. She had to share what happened with the only person who fully understood how awful Clark was.

"Yep, and then he reminded me about the use of handcuffs and forcing an arrestee onto the ground to subdue them. A real charmer, like he enjoyed rubbing it in my face."

Kari quickly downed her soda, wiped her mouth with the back of her hand, and reclined into the worn couch. The springs jabbed her stiff back.

"I hope you didn't give him anything. A guy like that will only become even more cruel if he sees his victim suffering."

"No, I didn't react. But I did make sure to take him on an entirely unnecessary arduous walk-through of the ship before meeting Ahmed in the filthy and loud hangar bay. The noise, heat, and fumes nearly killed me, but it was worth it."

Jimmy almost spit out his soda. He swallowed hard to stifle the laugh.

Kari joined him in laughing so hard she wept.

Jimmy raised a slice and said, "To shitty days and Doug. The best older brother two lost kids could hope for!"

"I'll eat to that! To Doug," Kari said as she waved her slice in the air, besieged by yet another memory of her previous life. Toasting had been something they'd learned from their parents. Larry and Pam Sharpe had always had a drink in hand, with a fresh toast to kick off their inevitable slide into inebriation. As kids, Jimmy and Kari had copied their parents by toasting with anything they had on hand—candy, pizza, a potato chip. As time passed, they toasted with whiskey and pot.

A few minutes later Jimmy asked, "So what happened to the kid he questioned?"

"They arrested him for the murder of Irene Simmons. Poor guy looked sick. Frankly I thought he'd hit the deck before they could shove him into the patrol car. He seemed seconds away from passing out." Kari wiped her greasy hands and said, "She's the woman they found on a trail here in Portland. It was all over the news. Still is."

"Right," he said, shaking his head. "Her murder really freaked everyone out, especially after the death of the tourists. Geez, people are still scattering flowers into the sea and maintaining the shrine to the dead sailors. I see all of it every day on the waterfront. You think he killed the Simmons woman?"

"How should I know? He maintained his innocence. Then again, most of my clients at Leavenworth would say the same thing."

"We both know you don't have many clients in Leavenworth. In fact, you might have a few former clients who should be there but aren't because of your legal magic work." He gulped more soda and said, "Well, I hope for everyone's sake the cops have it right. I'd hate to think the real murderer could be still out there."

"And I'd hate to think the Portland PD focused on Ahmed because of his race."

"Me, too, but you know how people are around here. Race? Family history? They'll use anything to keep a person out of their little clubs."

Kari remembered Clark and his comments about "real Mainers." "Tell me about it," she said to her brother and finished off the rest of the pie.

Chapter 14

Kari arrived at work early. Her morning run had done wonders for her mental state, helping her to mostly shake off the heaviness of the previous day. Ruth wouldn't be in for at least another hour. She found the pre-Ruth quiet time to be the most productive minutes of her day. Surveying her electronic calendar, she noticed how many hearings and meetings she'd attended over the past month. Her next couple of months appeared to be similarly full. Her bank account seemed to be the only thing that wasn't filling up.

Kari scrolled through the district court docket to see if Ahmed's name appeared for arraignment. Finally, she found it listed on the afternoon docket. She decided to call her law school friend who still worked at the Maine Commission on Indigent Legal Services. An attorney from the organization would be assigned to represent Ahmed if the judge determined it necessary. Kari wanted to be sure they knew something about him ahead of time.

Kari searched the internet until she found the number for the Maine Commission on Indigent Legal Services. She picked up her phone and dialed, hoping to speak with her former classmate. A cheery-sounding woman answered on the second ring. "Attorney Meade, please," Kari said. "This is Attorney Sharpe calling from the Sharpe Law Offices."

"Just a moment."

Kari listened to numerous clicks as her call made it through their offices. Finally, her friend answered, "Kari, nice to hear from you. I heard you're back in Maine. I also heard you made partner at Barnes & Smith. Kudos."

"Thanks. I appreciate that. I wanted to give you guys the heads-up that you might be asked to represent Youseff Ahmed. He's a Maine resident and navy sailor. Yesterday the Portland PD arrested him and charged him with the murder of Irene Simmons."

"Right . . . yeah, I heard about the case. I think he's up for arraignment today."

Rachel audibly shuffled through papers. Kari imagined Rachel's ancient state-government-supplied desk. Somehow the state offices boasted less luxurious accommodations than even the navy, a very low bar.

Kari didn't miss sitting on worn-out, mismatched furniture. Her firm in New York City had engaged a specialist to measure her for an appropriate chair. Not only had a custom chair been provided for her, but she'd picked all-new furnishings from a catalog of very luxurious office furniture. She had never been treated so well. She'd bought the custom chair from the firm and shipped it back to Maine with her other belongings. Now the chair looked painfully out of place in her shabby surroundings.

"Yes, it is. If your office is appointed to represent Ahmed, I'd like to send you a copy of his personnel record. I think he's a good kid. There's a lot to work with, even if it only comes in during sentencing."

"Okay, no problem. I'll shoot you a quick email after the arraignment."

After hanging up, Kari braced herself for a meeting with Jan Farry and Mack Bowen. Ms. Farry had hired Kari to investigate whether her husband had cheated on her. She didn't want to file for divorce unless she caught him in a lie. Kari gave the woman credit for slowing down before taking the irretrievable step of proceeding with a divorce filing. She had hired Mack to investigate Walt Farry on Ms. Farry's behalf. Today they would both hear Mack's conclusions.

The front door chimed. Seconds later she heard Ruth's voice.

"Mack! I saw you were on the schedule for today," cooed Ruth.

"Well, hello, Ruth. How's the prettiest paralegal in Portland?"

"Oh, Mack, you're making me blush."

"I'm sure your lucky husband tells you how pretty you are all the time."

"That'd be the day! I'm not sure he knows I'm alive. Let me call Kari for you."

"No need. I know where Grumpy's office is."

Seconds later, Mack appeared in her doorway. He wore his usual uniform—an old dirty dress shirt and wrinkled khaki pants. From the looks of him, he'd decided to give himself a break today by not bothering to tuck in his shirt. The fabric hung over his rotund middle, exposing its frayed edges. The stink of cigars and cigarettes preceded him.

Glancing over him, Kari said, "Glad you dressed up to meet with a client."

"No problem. Looking professional is easy for me," he said with a smile.

Kari couldn't help but laugh. Ever since her adolescence, Mack had had a way of making her smile, despite herself. Mack had inserted himself into their lives after Doug had been arrested. Kari never knew if he did so out of pity, genuine concern, or professional obligations. As the years passed, Mack seemed to have an uncanny ability to show up at their place when she and Jimmy needed him the most. Over time, he simply let himself inside. Mack brought food and basic household supplies to their sparse home. He always went out of his way to explain that the items came from overstock, either at home or at the station. Occasionally Jimmy, too proud to accept charity, would refuse. Yet Mack always managed to convince them that they did him a favor by getting the items off his hands. Somehow Mack's kindness broke through Jimmy's stubborn ego to give them the things they desperately needed. Kari also struggled to accept his gifts, the jagged edge of suspicion a constant companion. But over time, as he had repeatedly shown up for them, her trust had grown.

Kari turned to her long-standing friend and asked, "She's going to be here in a few minutes. Did you find anything?"

"Oh yeah. Just not what she's expecting."

The door chimed on the heels of his comment.

"Showtime."

Kari punched Mack's soft, thick arm as she moved past him. He quickly reciprocated and winked at her.

She wondered what page of the L.L.Bean catalog Ms. Farry would wear today. L.L.Bean, a Maine company, had been the woman's clear retailer of choice, and she'd sported a seemingly new outfit for every meeting. As a kid, Kari had pored over the L.L.Bean catalog. She and Jimmy could never afford the preppy, well-made outfits. However, she loved to see the smiling models in beautiful clothes. Kari invented stories around the pictures, pretending she lived in the perfectly appointed homes or that she attended one of their parties as a favorite guest. The L.L.Bean Christmas catalog kept her busy for weeks as she created stories about a life she'd never know. The snowy scenes of homes decorated with pine boughs, candles, tinsel, and love made her ache with longing. Despite the pain, she couldn't look away.

She imagined playing in their yard with the L.L.Bean golden retriever by her side, wearing cozy boots and one of their parkas, a hip-length rust-colored number that matched her imaginary canine. Perfection in a Maine winter.

Jimmy hated that she spent so much time with the catalog. He would say, "Why the hell are you looking at that thing, Kari? You know we can't afford it. You just make yourself miserable."

One year, when she was around sixteen, her Christmas edition of the catalog went missing. She searched everywhere for the dog-eared, marked-up fantasy life she pored over.

"Where's my catalog?" she shouted at Jimmy.

"How the hell should I know? You know how I feel about you looking at it."

"It's my escape!"

A week later Mack showed up, like he'd done so many times.

"I brought good tidings for Christmas and all of that," he said.

He brought gifts and a pie from Hannaford. A luxury.

Jimmy looked embarrassed. They had nothing for Mack or one another.

"Come on, Jimmy. It's just a pie. Probably not even good," said Mack. "The gifts shouldn't be opened until Christmas."

For the next few days, Kari stared at the wrapped gifts. "What the heck is in there?" Even when the five Sharpes lived as a family, the little affection in their home never translated to Christmas or birthday gifts. Unless a bottle of booze passed for affection.

Finally, Christmas morning arrived. Jimmy had gotten up to make a fire, taking the chill out of the cold, snowy Maine morning.

"It feels nice in here. Thanks for getting the fire going," she said.

"Hey, it's Christmas. Why the hell not? Chestnuts roasting and all that crap."

"I can't take it any longer. I'm opening my gift!"

"Let's open the joint gift first. Who knows what the old meddler got us!"

Jimmy handed the large package, which had been carefully marked with both their names, to Kari. Her nails grabbed at the shiny red ribbon as she clawed at it excitedly. Once she ripped the ribbon off, she tore away the emerald green paper dotted with little yellow Labs decked in perfect Christmas sweaters.

"Yum!" yelled Jimmy.

Mack gave them the L.L.Bean Christmas morning of her dreams. The package contained all the fixings for their signature blueberry pancakes, complete with Maine-made maple syrup.

"Oh my God!" had been all Kari could say.

"I'm opening my gift. I want to eat," said Jimmy excitedly.

She watched him tear into the next parcel, unwrapping a pair of black L.L.Bean gloves. Jimmy desperately needed gloves. Trying them on, he whistled approval.

Next, she opened her box. Mack gave her the L.L.Bean Fair Isle sweater in her size. At that moment she put it together. Mack must have taken the missing catalog. She couldn't believe she possessed such an expensive article of clothing. *New* clothing. Typically Jimmy took her to Goodwill for their shopping. Her lower lip trembled with emotion. She felt seen by Mack. Oddly seen. He'd taken the time to figure out what she really wanted. No one had ever done that for her. Jimmy tried but barely managed the essentials.

"Enjoy it for today only. Then it goes back to Mack. He can't keep giving us shit like we're a charity case."

"Not a chance. This sweater is all mine." The wall of Sharpe false bravado cracked ever so slightly. Although difficult to admit, she never trusted Mack's love or kindness. However, the simple gift, the generosity and warmth it offered, melted her resistance to his affections ever so slightly.

She wore it to shreds for years, ultimately using the ripped garment as a home-only sweater. Mack had gotten them through a lot during those years. Now he was helping her professionally. They walked down the narrow staircase toward the conference room and Ms. Farry.

Ms. Farry sat on one side of the massive wood table, waiting. The petite brunette was dressed in a Bean T-shirt and khaki pants. Kari wondered whether she realized her great fortune. The entire L.L.Bean catalog effortlessly worn. Carefree. Probably not. The lucky people never knew they were lucky.

"Thanks for coming in today. This is Mack Bowen. He's the private detective I hired on your behalf," said Kari.

"Nice to meet you. I hope you have something. He went out again yesterday," she said.

She sat on the edge of her seat, leaning onto the table. The number eleven etched between her brows. Ms. Farry wrung her hands over and over as she waited for Mack's report.

"I hired Mack because he is considered the best in Portland," Kari continued. "He worked for the Portland Police Department for over twenty-five years, starting his career as a patrol officer and moving through the ranks until he retired as a detective. The youngest patrol officer to make the rank of detective, I might add. If anyone can get to the bottom of things, it's Mack."

The investigator looked down and blushed.

Kari knew clients needed the warm-up to build trust in the process. Otherwise, the client would second-guess Mack's work.

"I've spent the past two weeks following your husband. This is a folder containing all the places he's been and a list of the people I suspect he met with," said Mack.

He handed her a thick file that had a chocolate smudge. *Typical Mack,* Kari thought.

"The file is yours to keep, Ms. Farry. My conclusion is that your husband isn't cheating on you. Probably never was."

"Then where the hell has he been going?" the woman said, incredulous. She slammed the folder on the table and looked at him.

"He's been spending all his time at either Maine Medical, various clinics in Portland, or in Boston at Dana-Farber. Details are in the file. It appears that he needs medical attention. What I don't know is what he's being seen for. HIPAA laws make that impossible for me to get."

"Medical appointments? Like something's wrong and he isn't sharing it with me?"

"Yes, that appears to be the case. I'm sorry, ma'am. I know this is difficult to hear."

"What do I do?"

She absently twirled a strand of hair, lost in thought. Ms. Farry looked out the window and then turned back to them. "What about the nighttime outings? He can't be going to appointments after five in the afternoon."

"Yes, I thought he might have been going out to see someone at those times. However, I tailed him every time he left your home in the evening. He drove to the waterfront and just sat there, looking out at the sea."

She covered her mouth with her hand. Her eyes welled with tears. "That's not good. It's what he does when he's stressed out. The jerk. Why wouldn't he tell me?"

"My only guess is that he loves you very much and didn't want you to have to carry the burden with him. He's likely shielding you the only way he can."

Mack said the words in the most tender way possible. The warmth and compassion in his voice clear, the same voice Kari heard so many times growing up.

"So that's it? What do I do now?" Ms. Farry asked, on the verge of tears.

"You need to talk with him. Leave out our involvement and just ask how he's doing. Eventually he will confide in you," said Mack.

Ms. Farry's loud, heavy sobs continued for several moments as Kari brought her a tissue box. Kari winced at her client's pain. She knew the heaviness of grief and desperately wished she could say something, anything, to relieve Ms. Farry's sorrow.

"I think I would have preferred that he cheated on me. How bad is that?" She hiccuped.

"I would probably feel the same way. Somehow anger is easier to handle. It's more familiar than a potentially devastating diagnosis," said Kari.

Ms. Farry wiped her eyes, took a deep breath, and continued.

"I guess I don't need your services anymore."

"No, you don't, but we're here in case you do need anything else," said Kari.

Kari started to continue, then clamped her mouth shut. She'd just stopped short of offering to draft their wills. She would have never done that in New York.

As they finished with Ms. Farry, Kari heard the soft sound of the door chime in the reception area. Emotionally worn out from the meeting, she hoped the door had chimed for the mail delivery. She really didn't think she had the bandwidth for anything else.

Chapter 15

Hani pushed back the edges of her draped *guntiino*. Even though she and her husband, Omar, had lived in the United States for decades, she still chose to wear traditional garments, like the white *guntiino*, both at home and in public. Their daughter, Bilan, chose to do the same. She looked on with pride as the young woman left home in a colorful hijab. Many Somali women wore a hijab even through the coldest of Maine winters.

Living in the United States for the past several decades didn't change the roles she and Omar had fallen into once Allah had graced them with Youseff. They'd chosen to send both Youseff and Bilan to Quran classes, as they would have done if they still resided in Mogadishu. Unlike in Somalia, the children's Quran classes were an addition to American-style compulsory education, something she'd been happy for them to attend.

She pressed her hand flat against the fermented, spongy injera bread she molded into neat circles in preparation for dinner. Other dishes for tonight's feast simmered on the stove of their cramped kitchen. The scents wafted through the air, filling the space with the heady aroma of cinnamon and cardamon reminiscent of life in Mogadishu. Cooking traditional Somali food immediately brought her mind back to her parents' home, to a simpler time in her life. She and her mom had sat together, making the sour bread. Once it was made, they'd passed the time chatting and laughing as they rolled the bread into long bundles, ready to be enjoyed. Female family members had come and gone throughout the day, adding to the relaxed environment.

After war broke out again in their corner of the world, Hani's brothers chose to fight. She and her sisters stayed home or tried to work as best they could. One by one, word came to the family that each of her brothers had been killed while fighting. Hani's family sought the safety of a foreign land, as her father became convinced the war would take each of them if they chose to stay.

Hani, her sisters, and her parents settled in Georgia, as so many Somalis had done before them. As the years passed, her parents died, and her sisters married and moved in with their in-laws, leaving Hani alone. With neither her father nor brothers alive, she relied on her eldest sister's husband, Abdi, to find her a suitable marriage.

"I might have a suitable match for you, Hani," said her brother-in-law.

"Remember, Hani, sparks are not necessary for marriage, only decency. Love will come later," counseled her sister Faduma.

Meeting Omar, she felt no physical attraction. Yet his unmistakable goodness shone through his eyes, making her trust him. Every day she felt grateful for her marriage to Omar. He proved to be tender and loving even as he provided financially for the family. Love grew between them as they navigated life together, shoulder to shoulder.

She and Omar wed, and they moved to Maine after hearing about the peaceful lifestyle the state offered its inhabitants. It even boasted a small but growing Somali community. After using up the spices she brought with them from Georgia, it became difficult to acquire the ingredients she needed to make the traditional dishes she and Omar craved. A two-and-a-half-hour drive to Boston was their only option. The necessity for a steady supply of recipe ingredients and clothing brought Omar and Hani to the decision to open a Somali import store in Portland. They named their place Khadra, meaning "lucky."

Smiling, Omar often said, "Hani, we are *khadra*. We owe this beautiful country and its generous people everything." Today, however, she didn't feel lucky—or happy, the meaning of her name.

Yesterday, their beautiful boy had called to inform her that he wouldn't make it to his sister's birthday party because of something on the ship. He later called to tell them he'd been arrested.

At first, the words made no sense to her. *How could this have happened? Surely a mistake has been made,* she'd thought as he repeated himself. Youseff spoke softly in Arabic during their call. She noticed he chose to use the formal version of the language, a way to stamp a solemn note on the conversation as he gently explained the situation to his mother.

Youseff had used formal language with her only once before. Friends had come over to visit after school. The group of four fifth graders watched television, played catch in the yard, and ate more food than she thought possible. Somehow, while they played, one of the boys broke a dish on display in the living room. The dish had been the only gift Hani had from her long-departed mother. Although not an expensive item, it carried deep emotional weight. Youseff came to her that evening in tears. He apologized for his friend and took full responsibility for the boy's actions. He asked if he could somehow fix the dish or repay his mother in another way. He'd always been like that, a responsible, honest young man.

This must be a mistake.

Omar had happened to be home when Youseff's call came. He asked to speak with Youseff midway through the conversation, relieving Hani of the burden. After hanging up the phone, he held her tightly, softly reassuring her. As Youseff's mother, she bore the sole responsibility for making him a respectable Clan member. That afternoon she knew she'd failed the most basic tasks given to her.

Where did I go wrong? Hani thought she had taught her children proper values. "Always do the right thing, no matter the circumstances. Allah will know. Let others do as they will. Your light will shine through," she would say to them. Youseff had been her smart, predictable, hardworking boy, helping the family, never getting into trouble. *And now this?*

Her shame felt like a heavy weight had been placed around her neck, weighing her down as the time passed at an excruciatingly slow pace. Omar, to his credit, never said a word to her of the failure, and she loved him for it.

"Why did Betsy do this to our boy?" Hani had said after the call, her words buried in the fabric of his shirt.

"She didn't do anything to him, Hani. It must be a mistake. Our boy is a decent young man. *Mashallah.*"

"No *Mashallah*! God can't bless this. It is the *nazar*!"

"Come now, let's not talk of *nazar*. We are Americans now. Our children are American. The evil eye cannot touch us here."

She wanted to trust her husband's words, but like so many Somalis, she deeply believed that someone else's jealousy could yield tragedy for a family because of an evil eye hex.

It had been her turn to open Khadra the next morning, but she couldn't face the store. More precisely, she couldn't face the familiar faces of the other women as they shopped and chatted. Logically she knew they had no way of knowing the family's shame, but still, she couldn't face their community. The other women would sense a change and insist on knowing the details. "Hani, are you ill? What can we do to help?" they would say to her.

Generally, the entire small Somali community knew everything about each other's business. They shouldered pain together, often cooking for each other or crowdsourcing funding for catastrophic medical bills. Hani didn't know if the community would rally around their family in this situation. She feared they would become outcasts.

"Salaam!" said Bilan.

Their daughter worked in an office near their store. During the summer months the young woman walked to work, head held high.

Her beautiful high cheekbones and forehead jutted from her hijab. She often wore bright colors to contrast with the deep tones of her skin.

"In the kitchen, Bilan!" Hani yelled.

"It smells amazing in here. You must have been cooking all day. Let me help you," Bilan said as she pulled on an apron.

"Not a chance. It's your birthday, child. I want to serve you today, my Bilan."

Hani often referred to their daughter as "my Bilan," to mean "my first daughter." She and Omar thought Bilan and Youseff would be just the beginning of a large family. However, the financial reality of raising children in the United States dashed their romantic ideas of creating a large family to add to the Clan. They had no realistic ability to afford all the expensive things children needed to thrive. Besides, they had one perfect boy and one perfect girl. Allah had provided.

"No, please. You've done so much," Bilan continued.

Lost in her thoughts, Hani barely heard her daughter. "Please, let me do this," said Bilan. The young woman gently touched Hani's shoulder.

Suddenly Hani burst into tears. *Not again,* she thought. Not in front of Bilan.

Bilan put down the large wooden spoon she'd used to stir the fragrant food and hugged her mother.

"You don't need to comfort a silly old woman, child."

Hani tried to force a smile for Bilan's sake but knew she failed at that too.

"You don't have to be strong for me. I'm scared for Youseff as well."

Bilan had walked in shortly after Youseff called. Omar and Hani would have preferred to shield her from the devastating news. Bilan's arrival at their apartment at just the wrong moment ensured they had no choice but to share the news with her, even though they hadn't had a chance to make sense of it themselves.

"I just want to see him. Where have they taken him? Why can't we contact him?" Bilan pleaded. Frustration laced her words as they tumbled from her mouth.

"We've been through this already, *beta*. Youseff said they would take his phone. He gave us the number for the lawyer who met with him on the ship. He said we needed to talk to her."

"Do you think he is okay?"

Suddenly the brave young woman looked frail, childlike. She leaned on Hani for support as the two of them held each other and cried. The fate of the most cherished member of their family unclear.

"I don't know, *beta*. Only Allah can help him at this point." Hani openly sobbed with her daughter for a moment. It felt good. The strain of putting on a brave face had become almost too much to bear.

The people of Maine hadn't always been friendly to the Somali population. Police harassment of the male members of their community had been commonplace when they first arrived. Things had improved over the years as the local population grew accustomed to their presence. However, police interaction remained the same. Law enforcement either hounded them or completely ignored their requests for assistance. No medium ground existed for the Somalis in Maine. Hani feared for her son as she thought about the gentle, kindhearted boy being held and mistreated by the police.

That evening, parents and daughter sat on the floor of their small living room, eating the feast Hani had prepared. Normally the men ate separately from the women. However, tonight, Omar said they needed each other more than formalities. None of them ate with the gusto such a feast should engender. A dark cloud of shame and dread chased them.

Under different circumstances, a birthday would be cause for a large, joyful, weekend-long celebration with music, dancing, and storytelling. The Ahmeds had invited several families to crowd into their small home to celebrate. After the news came, Omar made the decision, as the head of the household, to cancel the party in favor of the three of them marking the day alone. Hani knew it had been the correct decision.

After they'd finished eating, Hani presented Bilan with a gift. She carefully pried open the rough paper bag her mom had used as wrapping.

"Wow!" Bilan exclaimed as she removed the sparkly, colorful *dirac*, a formal dress Somali women wore for major events. The beautiful royal-blue silk accentuated the bluish undertones of Bilan's skin, as Hani hoped it would.

"I love it! Did you order this from Somalia?" asked Bilan.

"Of course I did! You are a proper woman now. You need something other than homemade clothes," said Hani.

Hani had bought the elaborate garment in the hopes that someday Bilan would wear it for her brother's engagement party. Omar had been approached by the father of a young woman who lived in New Jersey. The families had wanted to arrange a meeting of the potential couple within the next few months. She had hoped to be helping with wedding arrangements within a year. The realization that all their plans for Youseff would be put on hold reignited her pain.

Hani swallowed hard and said, "I'm glad you like it."

She shared a knowing look with Omar. The sadness in his eyes revealed his thoughts to her. They both mourned the potential loss of the future for their children they'd hoped for. Homes filled with love, children, and family might never happen for them if Youseff had committed the horrible act. He would endure a life of incarceration while his sister would remain in a different sort of jail. Families of eligible Somali suitors would never accept her if they believed *nazar* followed. Bilan, as an American-born woman, had dated several Mainers. It never worked out. Omar said it was because Mainers never cared to learn about their culture. Hani, for her part, had welcomed the suitors, placing Bilan's happiness and providence over stuffy cultural notions.

Hani pulled her scarf close to her body and once again whispered a traditional prayer for protection, begging Allah to come to their rescue.

Chapter 16

Kari had spent hours in a small room in the superior court in Portland. She and her opposing counsel had engaged the assistance of a semiretired superior court justice to hold a judicial settlement conference for a real property case both lawyers knew should settle. Justice Bowley listened intently to the parties and then separated them into smaller conference rooms. Over the course of the morning, he communicated hard-acquired, reasonable settlement offers, only to have those offers shot down by the clients, who each thought they deserved more.

Kari needed a break. Sitting for so long with a client had a way of wearing down most attorneys. Finally, Bowley suggested they break for lunch and a "think," as he put it. She advised her client to grab a sandwich and reflect on the latest offer to settle, which would probably be the best they could do, even at trial. Once her client left the building, Kari ventured out into the main hallway of the courthouse.

"Kari! Kari!"

Can't I just get a minute to myself? She let out a heavy sigh and rolled her eyes.

She turned around to her friend. "Rachel, are you in trial today? I usually don't see you this late in the day."

"No, just finished with a return day. Not sure how we did. You win some, you lose some. You know how it is."

"Totally," said Kari.

Despite Kari's response, she couldn't fully appreciate the public defender's sentiment, because private practice attorneys were paid to win. Reputations hinged on success. Too many losses could mean a professional death sentence for most lawyers.

"I planned on calling you this afternoon anyway. Ahmed was arraigned earlier than scheduled. A few matters were moved on the docket to clear the justice's afternoon schedule for something else."

"Thanks. I hadn't heard."

"He pled not guilty, as we advised. The bad news is that the assistant attorney general assigned to the case successfully argued that he should be held pretrial without bail."

"Oh crap. I had hoped he would be released today, or at least that bail would be set."

"No such luck. He's stuck in there until trial. If he's convicted, he'll get credit for time served."

"A thin consolation prize for losing his liberty before being convicted. The kid is hardly a threat to the community or a flight risk," said Kari.

"The fact that Maine doesn't have many nonfamilial murders didn't help his situation. Plus, it's summer tourist season. We did everything we could to get him released on his own recog," said Rachel.

At times the government of Maine seemed entirely too focused on tourist revenue. Tourist money brought life to their hotels, restaurants, gift shops, and guides. News of a seemingly random murder of a middle-aged white woman in the heart of Portland probably had a chilling effect on some vacationers, especially after the two sailors had been killed in Casco Bay. The news media fueled paranoia. Dozens of murders occurred around the country each year, yet somehow the three murders in Maine had become national news.

"He said you'd be representing him from this point forward."

"No, his command only engaged me for the initial interview."

"That's what I thought you'd say," said Rachel.

"Who did they send down from the attorney general's office?" Kari asked.

"Bob Parker."

Kari rolled her eyes. "The worst."

"I know. I've had cases with him too. If the Maine bar allowed people to fail only twice, we wouldn't have to deal with the likes of Parker," said Rachel.

Kari spotted her client riding the elevator back upstairs for the next session of the conference. She needed a couple of minutes to regroup before dealing with the second half of what she hoped would be a successful mediation. Kari bade Rachel goodbye and dashed into the nearby counsel room for a break. She hated her client, the courthouse, and the case. She stood, stretching her aching back, arching side to side for relief. The woman needed to settle. She grabbed her phone.

Ruth called and left a couple of voice messages, which seemed odd even for Ruth.

"Kari, Ahmed's parents are here in the conference room waiting for you. They said they don't care how long it takes."

Then the next message came an hour later. *"Kari, they're still in the conference room. I don't know what to do."*

Ruth seemed unusually frazzled in her voice messages. She also seemed to be whispering.

Kari rubbed her forehead, took a slow breath, and quickly typed out an email reply to Ruth, trying to shelve her annoyance.

> I hope to be back a little before five if everything goes as planned. They can either continue to wait or I can call them when I get back. It's the best I can do until I'm out of here.

Maybe Justice Bowley would bang some sense into her stupid client's head. She could only hope. It had not looked good when they'd broken for lunch. However, fresh air, a sandwich, and some personal time had a way of making people soften to reason.

After the judicial settlement conference ended, Kari walked as quickly as she dared to her office. She watched her steps as she carefully traversed the uneven cobblestones of the Old Port section of Portland. The fancy heels she bought in a swank store in Manhattan were borderline useless here, and yet she still wore them, holding hard on to the past. Eventually she'd have to purchase a pair of warm, rugged boots for the Maine winter.

Despite growing quickly over the past few years, the city had retained its old-world charm. The redbrick buildings, narrow cobbled streets, and locally owned businesses added to the cozy feel that tourists and locals loved. Still, she didn't give a damn about quaint architecture and cobblestones. She preferred Manhattan and walking in the heels she loved.

Turning down the narrow street near her office, she hoped to see only two cars in the parking lot. Instead, three vehicles sat waiting for her. Ahmed's parents were still in the conference room. She did not feel up to meeting potential new clients, especially considering the case they wanted to discuss. However, at this point Ahmed's parents had waited close to four hours for her return. Most people would simply have called or emailed to make an appointment.

She let out a long, slow exhale and entered the building, hoping the meeting would be quick.

"Hello, Ruth," she said, sounding more chipper than she felt.

"Kari, you're back."

Ruth flicked her head toward the closed conference room door and said in a low, conspiratorial tone, "I tried to get them to make an appointment, but they wouldn't hear of it. I also offered them beverages, but they refused. So I just left them in there." She shrugged her hunched shoulders.

"That's okay. They're dealing with a stressful situation. I'll be right back down."

She dashed up the stairs to her corner office, where she dumped her hunter green Dooney & Bourke satchel in a corner of the room. Then she grabbed a quick drink, a fresh legal pad, and a few business cards before returning downstairs to meet with them.

"Ruth, it's getting late. Please feel free to leave at five."

"I wouldn't dream of it. We leave together."

Ruth would never leave her alone with a client, and she appreciated the gesture.

Opening the door to the conference room, she said, "Hello! I'm very sorry to have kept you waiting. I'm Kari Sharpe."

"Hello. Thank you for seeing us. I am Omar Ahmed, and this is my wife, Hani Dihoud. We are Youseff Ahmed's parents."

"It is very nice to meet you both. Sorry it's under less-than-ideal circumstances."

"Yes, sadly," said Mr. Ahmed.

Mr. Ahmed wore a neatly pressed dress shirt tucked into his slacks. Ms. Dihoud wore a gold-colored jeweled hijab which covered her head and shoulders. The couple stood stiffly when she walked into the room but quickly sat once Kari took her seat. They looked remarkably fresh for people who'd waited hours in a conference room without refreshments.

"You have a very nice son. I met with him yesterday on the *Gallagher* at Bath Iron Works. We then met with a detective from the Portland Police Department. Detective Butch Clark."

She winced ever so slightly when she said his name.

Ms. Dihoud stared at Kari, a vacant look on her face. She occasionally produced a small cloth from her hijab to wipe her wet eyes. "But they took him. Why?" Ms. Dihoud interjected.

Mr. Ahmed flashed Ms. Dihoud a stern look and touched her hand.

"Yes, they searched his apartment during the interview and found a few personal items containing blood smears. They also have an eyewitness who can place Youseff at the scene during the time of Irene Simmons's murder."

Mr. Ahmed grimaced and looked at the floor. Shame flashed across his face as he tried to cope with the news.

"So that's it. Will we ever see him again?" he asked after a long pause.

The question took Kari aback. They came to her thinking their son would be gone forever. No wonder they chose to sit waiting for hours to see her.

"Of course you will. In fact, they are holding him here in Portland. You can go and visit him. I will write down the times when visitors are allowed. Unfortunately, the judge decided to hold him pending the trial. Otherwise, they would have released him already," she said. Kari attempted to convey a reassuring tone, unsure whether it struck the right chord.

"Can you help to free him? I don't want him to be held there like an animal," Ms. Dihoud blurted out. Omar frowned and looked away. He opened his mouth to say something and then stopped.

Kari's father had been treated like an animal by his arresting officer after driving around like a drunken madman, his daughter in the back seat. She pushed the painful memory aside. Since coming back, she'd felt herself being routinely pulled into the past by random words or smells or condescending looks. She refused to go on like this. There was too much work to do.

She cleared her throat. "Your son will be treated fairly while he's incarcerated." Or so she hoped. "Please know that nothing will happen to him in police custody." What a lie. Cruel things could happen. Doug had been killed while he was imprisoned. Nonetheless, she hoped her words sounded sincere.

"Thank you. Thank you," whispered Ms. Dihoud.

Looking at the strained faces of Ahmed's parents, Kari had not anticipated that handling a criminal case in Maine would unearth so many things she had long forgotten. The knot in her stomach confirmed that she deeply understood their pain.

She sat up straighter, pushed aside her emotions, and said, "I can represent him. However, I am in private practice and would require him to pay me for my services. The navy paid me for my assistance on the ship. The court then appointed him an attorney for his arraignment, when he entered his plea of not guilty. If he qualifies, he could continue to receive free or low-cost legal representation. I'm not sure paying a private attorney is something he can do on his salary."

Mr. Ahmed stiffened at the suggestion of a free or low-cost attorney. The proud man had probably never taken a handout of any sort in his entire life. She hoped her suggestion didn't offend the couple.

"Our son will only be represented by the best. He told us you fought hard for him yesterday and he trusted you. That is all we need to hear. You are the only attorney for our son. We will do everything necessary for him, including paying your fees," said Mr. Ahmed.

"Okay. I would require a ten-thousand-dollar retainer and will charge two hundred and seventy-five dollars per hour. This is a substantial discount of my usual fees. I'm willing to do that for him as a navy discount." She quoted a pathetically low rate. Nowhere close to what she fetched in New York.

Mr. Ahmed's lips turned white as he pressed them together in a tight line.

"No, we do not need your charity. We will pay your usual rate," he said.

"I assure you it is not charity. I would extend the same rate to any other active or former member of the armed services. It's my way of showing appreciation for the work they do. Youseff is no different."

"Fine. We will have your money. *Mashallah,*" he said with resolve.

"*Mashallah,*" Ms. Dihoud repeated softly as she sobbed.

Ms. Dihoud never spoke during the meeting after the initial exchange. Instead, her continual sobs filled gaps in the conversation, eliciting an emotional response from Kari. At one point Kari's emotions became nearly overwhelming as she struggled to repress memories of Doug's last arrest, or of when she learned that he'd died. She needed to get it together. Almost crying in front of a client? What had she become?

After they left, Kari said good night to Ruth and went back upstairs to her office. She needed to clear some email traffic before tomorrow. From her desk she could see Ahmed's parents getting into their old car. Mr. Ahmed opened the door for his wife and then helped her arrange her hijab, careful not to allow the silky fabric to get caught in the car door. Kari worried for them. The case wouldn't be easy, nor cheap. *Maybe I should have given him a better discount,* she thought. Then she remembered something a professor in law school had said: "No client wants to hire a cheap lawyer." Clients didn't want to pay a high fee, yet they also wanted someone who could win. A high fee signified a winner in the eyes of most potential clients. The inherent tension between the two interests caused lawyers to struggle over fee setting, always seeking a Goldilocks approach and possibly never reaching it. She hoped they'd be able to raise the funds. She needed the work.

Chapter 17

Later that evening Hani and Omar sat on the thick rug in their living room. They sipped tea and shared a small plate of the nuts Bilan had set out for them. The couple hadn't spoken a word since meeting Attorney Sharpe. Hani knew Omar wanted to pay for the fancy private attorney. She just didn't know how they would afford to do so.

She worked side by side with him at Khadra. The store did best during the holidays, Ramadan being the most profitable. Women drifted in and out of their shop all day, purchasing ingredients for the feasts they planned to serve at sundown for the entire month. Other times of the year could be very slow, even resulting in little to no sales for substantial stretches of time. A reality that had been a source of stress for the couple.

To make steady money, Hani accepted sewing work from other women in the community. In the evenings she sat on the floor, legs crossed, embroidering beads or tiny mirrors onto the raw silks that would be worn as hijabs. Women preferred to personalize their silks with their own chosen embellishments, creating unique looks others couldn't easily imitate.

Over time, word spread of Hani's excellent embroidery skills, causing her to become extremely busy, even receiving orders from women in the Boston area. Many projects came from outside the Somali diaspora, including from Indian, Persian, and Afghani women. The exacting, delicate work had been exhausting at times, but she loved it. The feeling of making her own money, outside of her husband's work in the store, exhilarated her.

Omar didn't object to Hani adding to their family's resources. She never knew if his silence had been an acknowledgment of the need for more money or a sign of his remarkable indifference to "women's work." Most of the time he seemed to barely notice her toils. Hani's mother told her not to feel ignored or underappreciated. Instead, she advised Hani to enjoy the freedom. Over time she understood her mother's advice, especially after she'd managed to save a tidy sum from her embroidery work.

Omar crunched on a tea biscuit. Strain lined his face. She desperately wanted to offer him a lifeline, but even her successful sewing business and secret savings would not yield the money they needed. A knock on the door interrupted her worried mind.

"*As-salamu alaykum.* Bilan, are your parents home?"

"*Wa-alaikum-salaam.* My parents are having chai. Please come," said Bilan.

Hani quickly covered her head and stood with Omar to greet their visitor. Guests arriving without warning had been a common and welcome occurrence to Hani until tonight. They needed some time to consider everything that had transpired over the last day.

"*Adeer* has come to visit," said Bilan. She walked the elderly man into the room.

"We are so pleased to see you," said Omar and held the elderly gentleman's hand with both of his.

Hani and Bilan quickly excused themselves to the kitchen, where they prepared fresh chai and snacks for the men. As the eldest man in the community, *Adeer* took on the role as "village leader." Even in their new home in Maine, the tight-knit group of immigrants relied on his sage advice. A visit by him, without his family in tow, meant official business. Normally the entire extended family would visit. On such evenings, it would not be uncommon for Hani to provide food for over twenty people.

She carried a heavy silver tray loaded with nuts, fruits, chai, and biscuits down the long, narrow hallway to the living room. As she turned the corner, she saw the men standing at the front door.

"*Adeer*, don't leave so soon. You haven't had chai. Please stay," she said.

"Next time, Hani, I will enjoy your hospitality. I must go now."

Omar gently closed the door and turned to her. Tears filled his deep-brown eyes.

"Omar? What is it? Has something happened?"

"They know. Everyone knows that Youseff was arrested. Our shame is on full display."

Hani put the tray down and began to weep, as she had done so many times since the arrest. Visions of being ostracized from their only source of support and comfort in this strange country seemed almost too much for her to shoulder. Her mind returned to the woman she'd begun to despise.

"She did this to us, Omar! Betsy Roth! How could she?" Hani's lips trembled as she spoke. Leaning against the wall, she dabbed her swollen, tearful eyes.

Omar touched her cheek. Wiping her tears. A small gesture of kindness. Then said, "*Adeer* made sure to stop the gossips and support our family. He raised nineteen thousand dollars for Youseff's legal fund."

Omar said the words with great deliberation, as though he needed to hear them again to believe the news.

"*Mashallah.* Allah has provided for us. All will be well now, Hani. It will be okay."

Omar pulled his wife close and held her gently for a moment. She leaned into his warm body and allowed herself the luxury of believing his words.

Chapter 18

Kari couldn't unwind from the day. Between the stress of worrying about Jimmy and her cases, she'd been a bundle of nerves. Her legs bounced with an electric nervousness as she tried to eat dinner, barely tasting her sandwich. Instead of trying to settle in for the night, she laced up her running shoes and headed out. Running through the Old Port in the evening had become one of her favorite things to do. The warm golden glow of dim lights poured through the leaded glass of the historic old-brick buildings. At night the city looked no different from how it must have looked over one hundred years prior. The simplicity and character of the buildings calling back a simpler time.

Jimmy's boat bobbed gently pierside. Foghorns and the deep tone of chimes from maritime buoys kept her pace as she pressed past the wharf. Jimmy and his counterparts would have been finished with their labors hours ago. Their work involved early mornings, not late nights. As she continued along the quiet waterfront, she looked out to the harbor. Two lobster boats headed out to sea. *Why would they be going out now? They aren't lobstering.* She stopped for a minute to look more carefully at the shape of the vessels. Jimmy had taught her how to identify a lobster boat from other civilian vessels. The navy had taught her how to recognize warships.

Kari had no doubt in her mind that she had witnessed two lobster boats leaving the harbor. She made a mental note to ask Jimmy why a lobster boat would need to head out late in the evening.

Chapter 19

Kari sat in the counsel room, waiting for Youseff Ahmed for their first meeting as attorney and client. The Cumberland County Jail housed inmates who received short sentences or those who awaited trial, such as Ahmed. Chipped paint, scuffed linoleum, and fluorescent lights made the facility feel tired. Its stale air smelled like a mix of school cafeteria and vomit. She hated the place. Too many bad memories.

The small attorney room contained nothing but a banged-up table bolted to the floor with heavy-duty steel plates and a couple of affixed chairs. The thick metal shackle rings provided the only other indication of the nondescript room's location inside a jail. Kari found the use of shackles, especially for a client, barbaric. She had needed to exercise the option of restraining a client only once in her career. Her New York firm had been hired by a wealthy estate couple to represent their son in a criminal proceeding. The partners had not wanted to turn away the business for fear that the clients would develop a new relationship with a different firm, risking the loss of the lucrative estate matters. Although a young attorney, she'd had extensive criminal defense experience from her years in the navy, logging more courtroom time than many of her more experienced civilian counterparts. They'd told her they had handpicked her for the assignment because of her vast experience. Later she'd wised up and realized she'd been picked because no one else had wanted to touch the work.

The young man had had a host of mental issues resulting in violent, cruel tendencies. When he'd walked into the counsel room at Rikers Island, Kari had assumed she could allow the guards to release his shackles. Instead, the guard had insisted that "you're going to need them." He had also assured her that he would be directly outside the door in case she needed anything. She'd assumed the guard's protective stance had been rooted in some sort of sexist nonsense about protecting a woman. Within moments, the inmate had lunged at her, stressing the wrist and ankle shackles to their max. Metal had soon dug hard into his wrists, drawing blood. After that interaction, if a guard suggested restraining an inmate during her meeting, she'd listened. Her work on the case had cemented her winning reputation in the firm because she'd managed to wrangle a lighter sentence than anyone had thought possible. His parents had ended up requesting her for other work. Then they'd referred their rich friends to her.

Earlier in the day, Mr. Ahmed had come to the office to engage her services. He'd paid the retainer she'd requested and then lingered to talk about the case. His wife hadn't been present. Kari had made it clear to him that although he'd paid for her services, Youseff would be her client. Accordingly, she wouldn't be allowed to discuss the case with him unless Youseff gave her explicit instructions to do so. Visibly disappointed, the gentle man had silently nodded and thanked her for taking his son's case.

The door opened with a loud bang. A very tall, broad-shouldered deputy sheriff stood in its threshold. "Attorney Sharpe?" he said in a deep, booming voice.

"The one and only," she replied.

He turned away from her and led Ahmed into the small room.

"You want me to keep the cuffs on, or chain him to the table?" he asked.

"It won't be necessary. Please uncuff him."

After the sheriff left them alone, Kari sat for a moment to collect her thoughts. Ahmed's crisp navy uniform had been replaced by an orange jumpsuit. The uniform of crime. The intelligent young man shrunk in her eyes.

"I'm here because your parents retained my services on your behalf. They believe in your innocence and are doing everything they can to support you. However, I will not discuss any aspects of your case with them unless you allow it. Do you understand?"

The vacant look in his eyes flitted to hope as she told him she would represent him.

"Yes, ma'am," he said. She noticed Ahmed addressed her as he would if they sat on board the *Gallagher*.

"I will be honest with you. I thought about passing on your case."

His head jerked up. Eyes finally meeting hers. A deep crease formed between his brows.

She continued: "You lied to me about your whereabouts the weekend of the murder. I simply can't work with you if you continue to lie. Do you understand?"

"Yes, ma'am."

Ahmed dropped his head at the mention of the lie, a slight blush reddening his complexion. Then he looked up and said, "I'm sorry, ma'am. I should never have lied to you. I know you're trying to help me."

"Fine. That said, I also do not want you to tell me that you committed this murder unless you intend to change your plea. Do you understand?"

"Yes, ma'am, but why?"

"There are many ethical implications for lawyers handling criminal matters, and I do not want to get caught up in those. If you did it, and want to change your plea to guilty, then I will do everything I can to ensure you receive a fair sentence. If that isn't the case, then we have our work cut out for us. I plan to make the prosecutor work hard for a conviction. Prove everything. As they should. Got it?"

He sat up straighter and nodded. "Yes, ma'am. Thank you."

She pulled a thick file from her satchel. "I received the evidence file from the attorney general's office, and they have several things working against you."

Her words felt forced, mechanical. Sitting in a counsel room of the Portland lockup messed with her. In New York or the navy, this meeting would have been easy. Her mind kept turning back to her family. *Doug probably sat here with his attorney.* She struggled with repeated thoughts of her eldest brother.

"Ma'am? Why is the attorney general's office involved? From the movies I thought it was a district attorney who does this, right?"

She let out a breath, pulling herself back to the room. She needed to focus. Ahmed needed her to focus. *Did I really take this case, forcing me to sit here?* Her stomach knotted at the passing thought, anxiety cutting into her body.

She smoothed her hair back, picked up a pen, and continued: "Normally it is. However, in Maine the statute requires that the attorney general's office handle all murder cases. And before you ask, Maine doesn't have a death penalty."

His shoulders dropped almost imperceptibly. He turned to look out the window. Ahmed jingled his hand and snapped his fingers. Other inmates probably told him all sorts of tall tales, filling the gap in his knowledge. Probably scaring the crap out of him.

"The lab results for the blood they found on your clothing and sneaker matched the DNA of the victim, Irene Simmons. There were burs on your pant legs consistent with the ones at the scene. In addition, as you know, they have an eyewitness who can place you at the location where the crime occurred. Why was the victim's blood on you? What were you doing when the witness saw you?"

"I don't know, ma'am. I don't even know where they found that poor lady. I just remember hearing about it from my parents. They didn't want my sister to go out at night or anywhere alone. They wanted her to walk everywhere she went with a friend or one of them." With a slight smile he added, "I don't think she liked the idea, but she had no choice but to follow their wishes. Our parents are very strict."

"Okay. Let's look at a map." Kari reached into her satchel and pulled out a map of Portland. She'd highlighted the location of the body in yellow and the location of the eyewitness in green.

She used her pen to point out the highlighted sections. "They found her here." Then turning to the green highlighted section, she said, "This is where the eyewitness lives. She would have probably seen you here, I guess."

Ahmed leaned closer to examine the map. His face remained expressionless.

Yelling outside the door caused them to glance at it almost in unison. Several guards rushed past, their feet pounding loudly in the hallway.

Returning to the map, she said, "Okay. Now that you have a better idea of where Ms. Simmons was found, why would the witness, Ms. Roth, place you there?"

A look of astonished realization quickly transformed his face, and he said, "I know exactly why, ma'am. I take that trail every time I visit my family. I park my car on the side street over here; then I walk this way to my parents' house here. She's old. Maybe she remembered me from another time?"

He pointed out his route to Kari as she looked on intently. The route he outlined placed him at the murder scene, just as an eyewitness had sworn.

"Fair enough. Why do you have to park so far away? The walk must be tough in the winter."

"Yes, ma'am, it sure is. No one shovels the trail, so I walk on the sidewalk over here." He pointed to the map again. "It takes twice as long, or at least seems to in the cold. My place has street parking, and the area around there is always congested, I think because everyone is looking for parking."

"Yes, that area has a lot of apartments and, from what I can tell, no parking garages. Not unusual for Portland."

She handed him a pencil and said, "Circle your usual parking spot and your parents' home."

He did as she instructed, carefully marking each location on the map. His hand shook slightly as he drew neat circles.

"Thank you. Did you know Ms. Simmons?" She'd already asked him the question when they first met but thought she'd try it again.

"No, ma'am."

"Did you ever see her before? She worked at Bath Iron Works, just like you do. Ever run into her? Even in a parking lot?"

"No, ma'am," he said. His voice cracked.

Ahmed fought back tears, the strain of his circumstances weighing heavily. *Doug went through all of this.* Kari had to look away momentarily before continuing.

Finally, she said, "I'm going to work hard on your case. We'll get the best outcome possible. The state must prove beyond a reasonable doubt that you killed Ms. Simmons. The burden of proof in this case is the highest the law provides. That means the jurors must have absolutely no doubt whatsoever that you are guilty. If they even have the slightest question about your guilt, they must acquit. We are going to do our very best to make sure you get a full acquittal. Do you understand?"

"Yes, ma'am. That would mean I get to go home? I'd get out of this shithole? Sorry, ma'am."

"Yes, you would be free and the State of Maine would never be allowed to bring charges against you again for the murder of Irene Simmons. Got it?"

"Yes, ma'am. That would be amazing."

He considered his next words. "I really appreciate you, ma'am."

"I know you do."

She paused for a moment to give him a break and a chance to digest the information. Jailhouse meetings had a way of being fraught with desperation and fear. The combination often rendered her clients unable to participate in their own defense. For both of their sakes, she needed to take a soothing, patient approach.

"Why would the victim's blood be on your clothing and shoe?" she asked.

His jaw quivered from clenching as he searched the floor for answers. Finally, he said with a whisper, "I don't know." He shook his head, snapped his fingers, and said, "I'm sorry, ma'am. I really don't know." He bit into his lower lip as he looked at her.

He persisted in withholding information. Obviously. Maybe a few more days in custody would convince him to work with her to develop his defense. She'd seen it before. Her guys tended to change their stories while incarcerated.

"Fine. I would like you to really think about my questions. If your case goes to a jury, we will need to explain how the victim's blood ended up on your clothing and why an eyewitness places you there. A jury needs an alternate explanation of the facts to believe in you. Do you understand?"

"Yes, ma'am." After a pause, he asked, "Ma'am, are my parents okay?"

In all her years representing criminal defendants, not one had asked about their family. Even when that same family paid the legal bills.

"They're very worried about you. I gave them visitor information, so you might be seeing them."

He gasped. "No! Please . . . I can't face them. I'm so ashamed. I can't allow them to see me here. Please tell them not to come." Ahmed's self-control broke. The strain of his circumstances rushed out of him with every deep sob. "Please, ma'am. Tell them not to come. My poor mom, I don't think she could take it. And my father, he'll be so angry. Please."

"Ahmed, I cannot stop them from trying to visit you. Nor can I stop people from your command from doing the same. However, when the sheriff tells you there's a visitor, you can refuse to see them. I don't recommend this. I know facing them seems daunting, but over time those meetings will be a great source of comfort for you." Kari thought once again of Doug, how she'd never visited him in prison before he died. Visiting her father while he was incarcerated had been terrible enough.

"It will be a long haul to get you to trial," she continued. "The road will be filled with ups and downs. You'll need all the support family can offer."

"I know, ma'am. I really miss them. I just don't want this to be harder on them than it is."

"Seeing you will comfort them. Believe me," she said. "I'll plan to visit every week or so as I dig into the evidence and prepare your case. For now, please remember not to talk to anyone while you're here. Like I said, inmates may try to get close to you to extract information to sell to the prosecution in exchange for reducing their own sentence. Don't fall for it. None of these people are your friends."

As she spoke, she noticed for the first time that the side of his right jaw appeared to be slightly misshapen and bluish. How could she have missed it? Had she been so far into her thoughts that she'd failed to truly see her client? What did that say about her?

"Is your jaw swollen? Did something happen in here, or was it like that when we met and I didn't notice?" she asked.

"It wasn't like that, ma'am, but it's not a big deal. I'm fine. Boot camp was way worse for me, ma'am."

"You shouldn't be mistreated while you're in here. Did a guard hit you or another detainee?" she demanded as she remembered Ahmed's parents, and her lying words to them that their son would be safe.

"No, ma'am. I fell. That's all."

His eyes darted nervously toward the closed door. *Is he worried about a guard or another inmate?*

This was all more than Kari could bear.

"All right. I'm going to let this go for now. If you 'fall' again, I'm doing something about it."

Chapter 20

Jimmy's lobster boat, the *Magpie*, sliced through the calm sea as he left the harbor to haul his lobster traps. He dreaded the morning. Rehab made him lazy, unaccustomed to the rhythm of his life. However, today calm seas and a colorful sunrise accompanied him during his chores, easing him back to reality. Rehab had a way of making a man forget life. Somehow everything about the real world seemed manageable from the sterile vantage point of the facility. The names ascribed to feelings helped. "Triggers" and "compulsion" were the labels the doctors stamped on behaviors he knew simply as crashing out.

Like clockwork, alcohol found its way to him. Always did. Sometimes the need to drink came as a gentle breeze. Other times the desire to drink roared to life with a vehemence that demanded his attention. He wanted to keep his latest relapse from Kari. It had worked before. However, months of drunken calls to her in the middle of the night had changed their lives.

"Damn it, Kari! I'm just like him!" he'd slurred.

"Jimmy? What the hell? Are you drunk?" Those had been the only words he remembered from the call. Apparently it had gone on for some time. Then in the spring Kari had announced her decision to move back to good old Maine. In a call shortly after she'd made her decision, he had tried to convince her not to. "It was just one night, Kari." "No big deal. People get drunk sometimes." "I'm fine, no need to panic." Then she'd told him about the nightly calls he'd made over the course of a few months. Slurred stupid drunk shit. Night after night. He'd had no recollection of the calls, but a quick look at his phone log had confirmed it. Some nights he'd called her number repeatedly. Like a stalker. Damned drunk. No wonder she moved back. *I scared the crap out of her.*

His latest stint at Pine Tree had followed shortly after her return.

Numerous lobstermen also headed out to Casco Bay. The loud rumble of their diesel engines added to the chaotic clamor of his own. At times he thought he would go deaf from the noise. Kari had suggested hearing-protection earplugs or over-the-ear headsets. But none of the other men wore ear protection, so neither would he. End of story.

Kari's run-in with Butch Clark seeped under his skin. Clark epitomized everything that could go wrong with a police force. The detective's cruelty had no place working under a motto of "Protect and Serve" or, more accurately, "Sworn to Protect. Dedicated to Serve," the department's motto. After hearing about Kari's experience, he knew that Clark had never mellowed with age or station. Instead, his horrible behavior had probably hardened into an unbreakable mix of habit and entitlement. Jimmy didn't know if Kari's representation of the service member would require further interactions with Clark, but he hoped not. For all their sakes.

His fledgling sobriety depended, in part, on manageable circumstances. Resurrecting their childhood boogeyman had the potential to derail him. Who knew what it could do to Kari.

The roar of a powerful engine approaching Jimmy's boat caught his attention. Chet, his friend, pulled starboard to chat. Usually the men stayed to themselves on the water, merely honking or waving to acknowledge other lobstermen. Most preferred to concentrate on their work and leave the chatting for shore. Many things could go wrong when hauling traps. An added distraction could result in a severed limb, as many had unfortunately experienced. Chet's chatty nature prevented him from yielding to the dangers of the sea. Instead, he seemed to disregard the danger in favor of gossip sessions. Jimmy hoped this one would be quick.

"Hey, man—how's it going?" said Chet as he threw Jimmy a line.

Jimmy grabbed the line and pulled Chet's boat close to his starboard side, tying it to a cleat on his deck. Tying together prevented the boats from drifting apart as they talked. They idled their engines to reduce the noise. The thick diesel exhaust from their boats clung in the air despite the crisp ocean breeze.

"I can't complain," Jimmy responded.

"How are your traps looking this morning?" asked Chet. He jetted his chin toward the hold in Jimmy's boat.

"It's been a light day today. You?"

Normally lobstermen would either complain that the catch had dried up or brag about how much their traps had pulled. Every lobsterman thought he had the secret sauce for success. Jimmy knew some of the industry depended on luck. Sheer luck, indeed, that a line of crustaceans would choose his traps over the numerous other options in the bay as they marched across the seafloor.

"So far, I haven't pulled enough to justify coming out here. It'll be hard to face the missus if this continues. I can barely afford to fuel up anymore with the way diesel's going these days."

Jimmy's bottom line had been squeezed as well. He'd noticed two factors weighing down profits—rising diesel costs and empty traps. Surprisingly empty traps. If it continued, the combination might drive out many struggling lobstermen. Jimmy didn't want to be one of them.

"I get it. Things have been unusually tight," said Jimmy.

"The only ones who don't seem to be hurting are those assholes."

Chet flung his head to the side to discreetly point to the men who piloted Randy's boat. The men looked very relaxed as they casually moved from buoy to buoy, emptying their pots. Most lobstermen hustled between locations to chip away at fuel costs.

"I noticed one of them sported a brand-new F-250. I'd like one of those too," said Jimmy.

After he made the comment, he immediately regretted it. Chet could be hard to defuse. Once he settled on a conspiracy theory, Chet had a habit of not letting go. Jimmy knew he needed to avoid fanning the flames or he faced an extended conversation while burning expensive fuel.

"Yep, but it's not in the cards for either one of us. Those guys are up to something. I just can't figure out what. First Randy leaves town, then they're driving his catch. Now I see them flashing success while the rest of us suffer. I don't know, but the whole thing's fishy to me."

"Not sure what they could be doing differently. Maybe one of them came into money somehow. The new truck might have nothing to do with their hauls. Who knows?"

"You think? How would anyone come into so much money they could buy a truck like that and be lazy about work?" asked Chet.

"How should I know? If I did, I'd do it myself," Jimmy said.

"Heck yeah! Me too! All right, man, I've gotta go. Lobsters don't wait for anyone."

"Don't you mean Sissy doesn't wait for you?"

Chet pulled away with a laugh and wave. Chet often complained that his wife kept him on a short leash. Despite all Chet's protests, he seemed like the happiest married man Jimmy had ever met.

A return to solitude allowed Jimmy's thoughts to wander as he worked. In his mind, he created the scaffolding to build a happy future with a woman, maybe a few kids. Images of warm, cozy meals and snuggling by the fire as a Maine winter storm raged kept him company as he worked his way through Casco Bay. *Who're you kidding? No one will want a drunk.* He sure as shit wouldn't marry one.

A chill crept over his body. The thought of spending his life alone scared the crap out of him. *No one will want you once they know your past.* His mind's usual refrain. *Just one drink. That's all.* He lifted the cover off the storage bay to check his stash. Several bottles of Jack sat waiting to assuage all fears. The bottles sung to him. Just one small sip.

He exhaled a long, tortured breath and closed the hold. Give it time. He needed to stay sober. Beat his dad's sobriety record.

He yanked his final trap, noticing right away that it contained only a couple of lobsters. Given his absence while at rehab, the traps should have been full with ten to twelve lobsters. Normally most of the traps contained at least eight to ten, especially in the fall, when the catch increased. Not two to three—or none, as had been the case not only this morning but over the past couple of months before he left for rehab. Something had changed for everyone except the guys running Randy's ship, the FV *Ginny*.

As soon as the thought formed, he shook his head. A few minutes with Chet and he was creating conspiracy theories with the best of them. Theories couldn't fill his traps. If this continued, he might consider hauling in the winter.

Chapter 21

Chet scrubbed his palms one last time. The damned stench of lobsters and bait bags never quite left his calloused hands. "Damned things reek!" he yelled to the empty bathroom in Dry Dock.

He pulled up the stool next to a fellow lobsterman named Pete Bradford.

"Hey, Pete, how's it going?" asked Chet.

"Hey, Chet."

"Ronny, snag me a Blue Ribbon."

The bartender nodded once and then cracked open a cold bottle of beer.

"You look like shit, man. Someone take away your birthday?" asked Chet.

"Nah, not that bad, but close. I've been pulling empty traps for weeks now. I'm going broke. With the price of diesel . . . I don't know how much longer I can hold on."

Same story with everyone. "You see those guys running Randy's boat?"

"Can't miss them. Why?"

"They're the only ones hitting it out there. The rest of us are dry," said Chet.

"You don't say?"

Chet knew he could count on Pete to listen. He always did.

"Yeah, I think they've been stealing lobsters from the rest of us."

Pete leaned back on his stool, then shook out a smoke. It was a luxury to smoke inside in Maine. The management at Dry Dock decided they didn't give a hoot about the new ordinances given by the fancy shits in Augusta.

"Something's been happening to our hauls. All of us empty at this time of year? Makes no sense," said Pete.

"Sissy told me that a friend told her that those guys bragged to a few chicks they tried to score with about getting free diesel from BIW. Can you imagine? Free diesel and three to four times the traps to haul?"

"Wait a minute . . . You saying they're stealing diesel from somewhere?"

"It's a theory I'm working on, yeah," said Chet.

"Crazy, but yeah, could be true. Those guys are fat and happy while we suffer."

One last swig of beer and then Chet said, "That's it for me, man. I've got a ton of crap to do for Sissy."

Chet walked out of Dry Dock onto the cobbled streets to distant sounds of the Casco Bay Line blowing its horn to announce its departure from the harbor. He knew in his bones that those men had to be up to something. They just had to be. He was determined to watch them a little more carefully.

Chapter 22

Kari circled the block one more time, frustrated that she couldn't find a spot near the location Ahmed indicated on the map as the place he frequently parked. She decided to drive around a few more minutes; otherwise she'd head to a parking garage and walk back to the trail. Finally, she managed to squeeze her vehicle into a tight spot, which slightly straddled a no-parking zone. Hopefully today wouldn't be the day the Portland Parking Police team decided to be extra vigilant, she thought as she pulled out her map.

She knew every inch of Portland. As a teen she'd spent many weekends and more than her fair share of weeknights in the Old Port, drinking like only a Sharpe can. None of her friends could match her alcohol tolerance, especially for shots of tequila.

Reviewing the map, she decided to start at the south end of the trail and walk in the direction Ahmed would have walked the morning of the murder. If the case went to trial, she needed to understand every nuance of the facts to be effective. She walked down a quiet residential street, where she quickly found the trailhead Ahmed indicated on the map. The trailhead poked out of the woods between two of the small homes on the street. The unmarked trail would have been easily missed by anyone who didn't know it existed. Kari wondered whether the city had created the trail as part of its greenway or if the locals had developed the trail over time as a convenient shortcut.

The hot August sun felt great on her skin, warming her. The warmth quickly passed when she entered the deep shade of the forest trail. After a few minutes she arrived at the crime scene, where six weeks earlier Irene Simmons lay dead. Someone had marked it with a simple wooden cross and a picture of Irene Simmons smiling for the camera. A small glass jar of wilted wildflowers her only company.

Who would place flowers here? Her family? A stranger? Would anyone care enough to do the same for me?

Kari retrieved the picture of the crime scene she had received from the attorney general's office. Irene's body lay at an odd angle, her head off the trail in the forest underbrush and her legs on the trail. Anyone walking the path the morning of the murder would have seen part of her body. The underbrush prevented a passerby from seeing the victim's torso and head. It also would have prevented a pedestrian from knowing the extent of Ms. Simmons's physical condition.

She quickly pulled out her pad of paper and took copious notes as she thought about the case. Then she snapped a few pictures using her phone. The coroner's report indicated Ms. Simmons had died of blunt-force trauma to the back of her head. The force had been so powerful that her skull had shattered, causing fragments to push into her brain. Kari leaned over and pulled back some of the branches of the thick brush lining the path, where Ms. Simmons's head had landed. Numerous rocks in various sizes and shapes lined the forest floor. *Could she have simply fallen and died an accidental death?*

She stood and assessed the entire scene again. Moving the thick layer of underbrush caused her pants to be covered in burs. She tried to brush them off, but the burs clung to her clothing. The same burs the police had found on Ahmed's clothing.

The coroner's report also identified several contusions on Ms. Simmons's face consistent with numerous open-hand hard hits across her cheeks. The police had crafted their case around those contusions. They assumed the killer had beaten up the victim and then forced her to the ground, where the murderer bashed her head onto a stone. Kari needed to develop an alternate theory to explain Ms. Simmons's death.

"What happened was so sad and scary. Are you family?" said a voice behind her.

Kari turned to see a young, fit, petite woman jogging in place as she spoke.

"No. Just passing by and saw all of this," said Kari.

She held her legal pad behind her to hide her previous note-taking. She wanted to informally interview the woman. If she knew Kari represented the defendant, the woman would likely keep running.

"I just can't believe it. This sort of thing never happens in Maine. It really freaked me out!"

"Do you usually run on this path?" asked Kari.

"Sometimes, but I stopped when they found her."

"What made you come back?"

"They caught the guy! It was one of those Sumerians or Ethiopians. I don't know. Something like that. He's one of the Black people who came here in droves years ago. It figures. They really don't belong in Maine and should go back to whatever crap country they came from." The woman stopped slow jogging, pulled out a water bottle from her waist pack, and took a long gulp. Water ran down her chin onto her T-shirt.

Her misidentification of everything about Ahmed except his skin color told Kari all she needed to know about the woman. And a potential jury pool.

"Do you usually jog at this time of day?"

"I always do. Gives me a nice break from the office."

Kari wanted to get back to work without racist gossip interrupting her thoughts. She looked at the woman and said, "Enjoy the rest of your run," then turned away.

"See ya!" said the runner as she jogged off.

Normally she might try to develop a witness in a situation like this. However, the jogger's timing did not match the time of the murder. A dead-end conversation for developing the case.

The prosecutor's witness list included the name and address of the state's eyewitness, Betsy Roth. Kari intended to interview the woman today, if possible. As Kari walked down the shaded trail, she questioned her plan. Ms. Roth lived in one of the houses lining the trail, but Kari had no way of knowing when to exit the trail to find the house. According to the maps app on her device, the home should be close. She hoped if she kept walking, she would eventually find the house. A long shot at best. Worst-case scenario, she would drive to the witness's house.

Finally, Kari saw a second offshoot from the main trail, which headed into a residential street. She took the side trail and searched the small road for a street sign. Maine notoriously lacked street signs. Instead, locals used big trees, rocks, or buildings as markers. People from "away," as anyone not born in Maine were referred to, found the lack of signage particularly frustrating.

With tremendous relief, she confirmed the street and found the eyewitness's house. She walked up the narrow, cracked driveway toward the small Cape Cod–style home. The little house looked as though no one had cared for it in years. Its white walls and black shutter paint were visibly peeling away, leaving sad bare spots where the paint should have glistened. The overgrown landscape exceeded the skill of most amateur gardeners' ability to adequately remove.

She rang the small round, gold-circled doorbell and waited. An audible soft chime sounded in the home. The front porch suffered from the same lack of care as the rest of the home. Several soggy newspaper bundles had disintegrated from neglect and rain on the filthy, unswept porch. She waited a few more seconds and rang the bell again. The white sheer curtain lining the window moved slightly, and soon the lock disengaged. A middle-aged woman opened the door wide and smiled at Kari.

"Sorry to keep you waiting," she said.

"No problem at all. Are you Betsy Roth?" asked Kari. The report indicated the witness's age as eighty-seven. Based on the age provided and Ahmed's comment, Kari knew the woman in front of her could not possibly be Ms. Roth, but she wanted to appear as having no prior knowledge of the facts.

"No, I'm Debbie, her caregiver. Can I help you?"

"I'm Kari Sharpe, an attorney here in Portland. I need to speak with her regarding her statements to the police in connection with the murder of Irene Simmons. Is she home?"

"Yes, she is. Betsy is homebound at this point, so she's always here. Come on in."

The door squealed a loud protest as Debbie opened it and allowed Kari to enter. The home had a strong odor, suggesting the windows hadn't been opened in a very long time. Aromas of food mingled unpleasantly with the scents of mold, urine, and antiseptic cleansers. Kari nearly gagged. She hoped the interview would be a quick one.

"She just finished lunch and is resting in the family room."

The family room sat in the back of the house, just off a small eat-in kitchen. The room boasted a large bank of windows looking onto the forest where Kari had emerged. Small breaks in the thick trees revealed the interior of the forest. The elderly woman sat quietly on her recliner, facing both the forest and a television situated in the corner of the room. An afternoon game show kept the elderly woman's attention. Kari wondered whether she watched out of habit or interest.

"Hello, Ms. Roth, I'm Kari Sharpe. I represent Youseff Ahmed, the man accused of killing Irene Simmons."

Before she could continue, Debbie interrupted her. "I didn't know you represented that animal! I would have never let you in. How can you do such a thing? You need to leave."

Debbie's words had an immediate impact on the older woman. Betsy looked shocked and agitated. She pulled a crumpled tissue from the side pocket of her cardigan sweater and dabbed her nose.

"Mr. Ahmed is currently innocent of the crime he is charged with. As part of his defense, it is essential that I understand Ms. Roth's testimony. She's the only eyewitness in this case. I'm sorry to upset you and do not mean to in any way. I just would like to speak with you for a few moments."

Kari's words calmed the old woman and placated Debbie just enough to settle her down. She pressed on.

"You told the police you saw Mr. Ahmed walking on the trail the morning of the murder. Is that correct?"

Betsy turned to Debbie for an answer, unsure of how to respond. "Remember the day you saw the Black kid running on the trail? The day that nice lady was killed?"

Betsy nodded her head slowly. "Yes, I saw him," she said.

"Where were you when you saw him?" Kari asked.

Again, Betsy turned to Debbie. "I need to hear from Ms. Roth," Kari said, force in her words. "Only. In her words, not yours. She'll have to testify in court under oath, without your assistance. You never gave a statement to the police. Inexplicably." Debbie stiffened at the rebuke.

"Are the police here, Debbie?" asked Betsy.

"No, dear, everything is fine. She's just a lawyer. I can ask her to leave, if you want me to."

"That won't be necessary," Kari said. "What is necessary is my interviewing the only eyewitness that places my client at the scene of the crime. She can either do it here, or in my office, subject to a subpoena. Her choice."

Wasting Ahmed's family money on a deposition was something she'd intended to avoid. However, allowing the likes of Debbie to feed the witness information couldn't be tolerated.

Visibly angry, Debbie had started to say something when Betsy spoke.

"Am I in trouble? Who is this lady?" asked Betsy as though she had just spotted Kari for the first time.

"She's the lawyer representing the Black kid. Remember?" shouted Debbie.

Eyewitnesses were notoriously unreliable. Building a case around a statement from one could be difficult at best. The use of Betsy Roth as the prosecution's only eyewitness made no sense, given her age and mental infirmities. Kari decided to take a different approach. She needed to move on before she got booted.

"Do you always sit in that chair when you're in this room, Ms. Roth?"

"Yes, I always do. I like to watch the birds in the trees. They can be more entertaining than what's on that thing," she said as she pointed to the television.

Kari nodded. "Is that a picture of your daughter?"

Kari pointed to the single oak-framed picture on the mantel of the ancient, dusty fireplace. The picture's frame had a fuzzy white coating of dust on its edges. Clearly Debbie let things slide when it came to cleaning.

Instead of quickly responding, she said, "Which picture is that? I can barely see it."

"It's Martha's picture," Debbie said. "She lives in Massachusetts now, with your grandkids. Remember?"

The picture sat roughly five feet from Ms. Roth. The forest path at least seventy-five feet.

"Debbie, were you here the morning of the murder?" Kari said.

"Yes, I stay over most nights or arrive very early so I can help Betsy out of bed."

"Yet you never gave a statement?"

"Well . . . I . . ."

"Didn't see anything. I get it." Glancing to the threadbare carpet, which clearly had not been vacuumed in a long time, Kari added, "It's hard to see everything."

Debbie dropped her eyes to the floor.

Kari needed to continue. "Ms. Roth, did you see someone on the path the morning of July sixteenth?"

Debbie started to say something, but Kari held up her hand and added, "Ms. Roth?"

"Oh, honey, I can't be sure of the days anymore. They all seem to blur together nowadays."

"You identified my client, Youseff Ahmed, as a person who was on the trail the morning of the murder. Is that correct?"

Betsy appeared uncertain and looked at Debbie, who nodded.

"Yes," she said, her response sounding more like a question than an answer. "I see the Black kid a lot of the time. He's always running back there."

"How do you know the boy you saw was Youseff Ahmed? The trail is quite a distance from your chair."

"I know them. When I could walk, I used to go to their little store, just down the street. They make the best food. Black-people food. It's different than ours, but good."

The old woman had suddenly had a bout of clarity. Kari needed to ride the wave as long as possible.

"You enjoy Somali food?" she asked.

"Oh yes. When they first moved here and set up the store, I didn't know what to make of it. Just like everyone who lives around here, I suppose. The group seemed out of place. Then I decided to go to the store and see for myself. Maybe I could get a few things? You never know."

"What do they sell in the store?" asked Kari. She hoped to keep the woman's lucid streak going long enough to obtain more impeachable statements for use at trial.

"They have all sorts of things. Spices, pots, colorful cloths for their dresses. It was stuff I'd never seen before and had no idea how to use. Real exotic. But, you know, I didn't want to be rude, so I really looked around for anything small I could buy."

Betsy's face went blank and she looked away. Kari prompted her: "Did you find anything?"

"Where?"

"At the little Somali market?"

"Oh, that place. They are the nicest people. You know, the first day I went in there, the mom worked with her two kids. She probably could tell I had no idea what to buy. She came over and offered me some of their bread for free. She said she felt honored I came to her store. I still remember it, the way she said 'honored.' The boy helped me to my car. Such a nice kid. I didn't need the help, of course, but the mom insisted."

"I have a picture of Youseff Ahmed," Kari said. "Can you look at it, please?"

She handed the photo of Ahmed in his uniform to Ms. Roth and asked, "Is this the boy?"

"Sure is. Such a handsome boy. The family loved talking about how he enlisted in the navy. Their proudest day. What a nice family."

"You went to the market frequently?"

"Oh, sure. I got hooked on the spongy bread. I like to spread jam on it. I told Hani, the mom, how I ate it, and she just laughed. The next day she showed up at my home with a large bowl of some beans or something and more fresh bread. She said to sop it up. Like I said, they are the nicest family I've met in years."

"How did she know where you live?"

"The boy, Youseff, must've told her."

"How would he know?" asked Kari.

"She made him walk me home whenever I came to the store on foot. The place isn't too far from here. She said she wanted to be sure I made it home okay, so she sent her boy or girl with me. I didn't need the help, until I did. Then I was grateful for her kindness. It's hard to ask for help sometimes, especially when you get old. You'll see. No one wants to admit it. Humans are a stubborn lot."

Betsy paused to wipe her nose again. Her eyes softly floated closed. Kari looked to Debbie, who shrugged.

"She needs her rest. This is her usual nap time. It's like clockwork," whispered Debbie.

Debbie accompanied Kari to the front door. Kari produced her business card.

"Thanks very much. I appreciate your time. Please feel free to call if she thinks of anything else."

"I doubt that'll happen. He did it and everyone knows it," snarled Debbie. "And that won't be necessary." She glanced at the offered card.

Kari chose not to engage the woman. Instead, she waved another quick goodbye over her shoulder and walked away.

Chapter 23

A dark-haired woman moved swiftly from the redbrick house across the street to her car. She stuffed a large vacuum cleaner and bucket into her truck and slammed the door, catching Kari's attention.

Kari needed to speak with the woman, who may have information about the day of the murder. Her shoes noisily clamored on the pavement as she picked up her pace.

"Hello!" yelled Kari as she crossed the street.

"Hey there!" replied the woman.

"My name is Kari Sharpe. I'm talking to people on the street about the murder of Irene Simmons. Are you familiar with the case?"

"Of course, who isn't? Between her and those dead tourists, everyone's talking. It's the biggest thing to happen in Maine since that rash of car thefts a few years ago."

Mainers considered two vehicles driven by teenagers looking for fun to be a "rash" of thefts. Kari loved the innocence people of Maine had with respect to crime. The state's low crime rate ensured an overreaction from its population whenever something happened. Charming, but dangerous to those accused of a crime.

"Are you usually here this time of day? In the afternoon?" Kari asked.

"Yes, I clean ten houses in this part of Portland. This street is the second-to-last stop on the days I'm here. I'm Jillian, by the way."

Kari shook her hand and offered her a card. Jillian examined the card, turning it in her hands. Then she looked back to Kari.

"Did you manage to talk to the old lady over there? I saw you came from her house."

"Yes, and her caregiver, Debbie. Do you know them? Or clean that house?"

"No, I've never met the older woman, but I know Debbie. I see her kissing her cop boyfriend all the time when he comes over. Probably for lunch."

"He shows up in his patrol car?" asked Kari.

"Oh no, he's not that kind of cop. He's a suit. Name's Clark."

Now Kari's interest had been piqued even while she stamped down a wave of disgust.

"How do you know Detective Clark?" she asked.

"Unfortunately, my oldest got himself into a bunch of trouble a few years back when he was in high school. Nothing too bad, just teen stuff. Clark investigated the incident and arrested my son, along with a couple of his friends, for a break-in. He claimed the boys stole things from people's garages and sheds."

"You don't think it was your son and his friends?"

"No way. Mostly because Clark's the one who accused the boys. That guy's a real jerk. The way he handled a bunch of kids was terrible. He scared the crap out of them. I complained, but of course nothing happened. I still see him kissing that hag Debbie goodbye. He should spend more time studying police stuff and less time eating lunch. Would do him some good!"

"The victim lived one street over. Did you know her?"

"No, I never met the woman or her sister," said Jillian.

"Thanks, I appreciate your time. If you think of anything, feel free to call me anytime."

Disappointment dogged Kari as she crossed the hot blacktop street toward the forest. She had hoped the woman might shed some light on the case. Instead, Jillian only hardened Kari's view of Clark. She wondered if Ahmed would suffer the same fate because Clark had targeted him. He had managed to move mountains to quickly obtain DNA confirmation. What else had he done?

She crossed a yard toward the forest. Her mind swirled, and anger filled her chest as she imagined Clark pressuring Ms. Roth to make a positive ID of Ahmed.

Chapter 24

Kari had made it halfway to the woods when a large golden retriever jumped on the back of her legs, nearly toppling her. The drooling dog wagged his tail with excitement as she scratched behind his floppy ears.

"Good boy, you are sweet, aren't you?" she cooed.

Golden fur blew everywhere as she scratched and patted him.

"Baxter! There you are," said a woman.

A bottle redhead with a short pixie cut effortlessly jogged over to Kari and Baxter, quickly closing the gap.

"I'm so sorry! I had him outside with me to clean up the yard. I went in for just a minute, and he dashed. I hope he didn't startle you. He's a jumper."

Kari laughed and said, "I don't mind at all. I love dogs."

"We're trying to work on the jumping, but so far it's been a spectacular failure," the woman said.

Right on cue, Baxter jumped up on Kari, placing his front paws on her chest. He leaned in for a slobbery face lick.

"Baxter!"

Kari smiled at the dog's exuberance. The distraction felt great.

"You live here?" Kari said. She pointed to the dark-gray colonial home adjacent to the forest path.

"Yes, for the past fifteen years. It's the only good thing to come out of my marriage." She winked at Kari.

"It must be nice to live near the trail with Baxter. Do you walk him here often?"

"Sometimes. But after the body was found, I stayed away. I've been locking my doors since. At least they caught the guy. I feel much better now."

"Yes, the murders really rocked our community. I feel it too. First the tourists and now this. It's been hard, to say the least."

"I guess I've always taken for granted that I would be safe living in Maine. Maybe I was wrong." She turned toward the forest, her eyes silently searching the deep shade of the trail.

"Sadly, many people feel that way, including me. I'm here investigating the murder of Irene Simmons. Would you mind answering a few questions?"

The woman stepped back slightly, then said, "You don't look like a cop."

"I'm not. I'm attorney Kari Sharpe. I represent the accused. I only have a few questions."

She stiffened and then, after a moment, said, "Okay. I'm Meg Shore. We can chat, but I'm not sure I'll be of much help."

"Were you home the morning of the murder?"

"Yes. I'm a nurse at Maine Medical. I'd just gotten off a forty-day cycle of four tens and took a few days off before transitioning from a night schedule to a day schedule."

"A night schedule seems overwhelming to me. I was in the navy and had to 'stand watch' over nothing as part of my training. I could barely stay awake without standing upright the entire time. As soon as I sat down, I'd start to drift off."

"You get used to it. It's not as hard as it seems."

"I'm not sure I ever would, but I'm very happy others can do it. So you were here on the day they found the body?"

"Yes, Baxter and I were home together."

Meg pulled the large slobbery toy out of Baxter's mouth and threw it. The dog tore off with an admirable singular focus on fetching the ball. The loud squawk of a blue jay cheered his efforts.

"Did you see anything unusual that day?"

"Sort of. I don't know if it's unusual in a bad way or just different. The day of the murder, I heard the rumbling of a large truck coming down the street. I was asleep and started to dream about snow trucks plowing the street. Weird, I know," she said, waving her hand. "Then, slowly, I woke, and once I did, of course, Baxter needed to go out."

The woman leaned over to scratch the large dog, who sat close to her leg. He pushed the retrieved toy into her leg for another throw.

"Did you see a vehicle on the street?"

"Sure did. I saw a silver Tundra parked just over there."

She pointed to a section of the street between the houses directly in front of the path to the forest.

"Was there anyone in it?"

"No. Not when I happened to look out."

"Did you ever see the driver? Or grab the license plate number?"

She shook her head. "No. I didn't see the driver and couldn't make out the plate that far away. It was a Maine plate. That's all I know. Then about twenty minutes later I heard the rumble of the truck, and it sounded like the person accelerated fast."

"Why do you say that?"

"Well, it went sort of like . . . *roooom!* Really loud."

Kari smiled and said, "That sounds about right. I assume you told the police everything you just told me?"

Kari knew Meg hadn't been interviewed by the police. The police logs never mentioned speaking with a neighbor. Either they hadn't spoken with her or Detective Clark had chosen not to put the witness account in the report.

"No, no one ever came over. I saw Debbie with her detective boyfriend and assumed they saw the same thing over there. Betsy has a better view of the forest than I do anyway. I thought they probably got enough information from Debbie and Betsy."

"Sometimes the police will leave a card in a doorjamb, asking for the person to call. Did they do that?"

"Nope, I never received a card or a visit."

"Are you close with Betsy?"

"Oh yes. I've known Betsy since Mark and I moved in here. She was such a love to me when things got bad between us. A real godsend."

She relaxed when speaking of her friend. Baxter lay in the warm grass of the yard near her feet, content to chew on his toy.

"And Debbie?"

"I don't really know her. Only through Betsy."

"How did you know her boyfriend is a detective?"

"I went to have tea with Betsy one day when he stopped by. He wore plain clothes and a gun. The gun sort of freaked me out. He must've realized and told me he wore it for his work."

"Is there anything else you can tell me about that day?"

"Not that I can think of."

"Thanks, Meg. Do you mind if I grab your contact information in case anything further comes up?"

"Not at all."

Kari obtained the woman's contact information and said her goodbyes. Before she made it back onto the path, Meg yelled from behind her, "Hey, wait. There was one more thing about the Tundra I remember."

"What was that?"

"It had one of those large NAVY bumper stickers on the rear bumper. I just managed to see it before it turned out of the street."

"Thanks so very much! You've been extraordinarily helpful," Kari said with a wave.

As she walked through the cool, damp forest path back to her car, she thought about everything she'd learned. The police had interviewed only Betsy Roth. They'd failed to canvass the neighborhood to garner additional corroborating information. Instead, they'd chosen to simply rely on one easily impeachable witness.

Damned Clark.

Chapter 25

Debbie allowed the dusty old curtain to fall back into its original place and stepped away from the window. She'd witnessed the entire conversation between the lady lawyer and the cleaning lady from across the street. Lord only knew what that gossipy bitch told the lawyer. As though that hadn't been bad enough, then the nosy idiot stood around talking to Meg. She glanced at the sleeping Betsy and then the clock on the mantel. She picked up her device and hit the first number on her favorites list.

Butch Clark answered on the second ring. "Yeah?"

Debbie hated it when he answered her calls like that. Over the years she'd commented that his tone made her feel like she was bothering him. He didn't seem to care.

"A lady lawyer for Ahmed just left here. I thought you should know."

"So what? I expected her to talk to Betsy. She has to. It's part of her job."

"Then she talked to a couple of other people on the street, including Meg from next door."

"Interesting."

"That's it? Interesting?"

"Yeah, interesting. What the hell else do you want me to say? We got the right guy. End of story."

"I hope so, for your sake," she spat. Then she hung up the line. The man never seemed to care about anything that concerned her. At times she thought habit had been the only thing keeping them together. Habit and few other options. He'd been confident about other arrests in the past, only to be wrong. She feared a mistake in such a high-profile case had the potential to be the thing that finally caused the police to fire him. Well, she'd tried to help him. If he wanted to go it alone and continue to make mistakes, so be it.

Betsy rustled slightly in her La-Z-Boy chair. The crochet afghan slid off the old woman's frail legs. Debbie sighed and glanced at the clock. Nap time was over, and she hadn't even gotten a proper break.

Chapter 26

Kari's phone buzzed and lit up on her bedside table.

What the hell? she thought as her groggy mind focused on grabbing the device before it slid onto the floor. The screen said "Blocked Number."

She considered putting it down and going back to sleep. Then she remembered Ahmed. Something might have happened.

Two forty-three a.m. "This better be good," she muttered.

The springs of her bed creaked as she sat on the side of it, dangling her feet toward the carpeted floor.

"Hello?" she said groggily, her voice heavy with slumber.

A recorded voice asked her to accept the charges.

"Kari! It's me. I need you!" said Jimmy.

Jimmy? She glanced at the alarm clock to confirm the time.

"Where the hell are you?" she asked, rubbing her eyes.

The clicking and chatting behind him indicated somewhere public.

"Are you okay?" The words tumbled out of her as her mind reeled with possibilities. A car accident? Medical emergency?

"I'm in Portland PD's lockup. Can you bail me out?" he slurred without a lick of humility.

Her mind grappled to understand him. She shook her head and stood in the small room. Stretching, she said, "You're drunk. Again." The accusation landed loud. Caustic.

"Are you coming? Or leaving me to sit here all night?" he demanded.

She glanced at the clock yet again. "No way. I have shit to do in the morning. You can just sit there for all I care!" She moved the device away from her ear to hang up.

"Kari! You can't just leave me here all night!" he pleaded. His loud, slurred voice filled the room despite not being on speaker.

"I sure as shit can leave you there! It'll do you some good to sober up with the rest of the drunks!"

"Just get over here! You owe me!"

His words felt like a slap in the face. He was manipulating her, and she knew it. She paused, unwilling to answer.

"*Paleeeze?* Kari?"

"This is the last time I get your ass out of the drunk tank." Her voice was low, deep. Defeated.

She forcefully pressed the red disconnect symbol on her device and flung it across the room before he could say anything else.

Kari shrugged on a hoodie, pulled on some jeans, and headed to the jailhouse she knew so well. She'd been the only Sharpe from her immediate family *not* to be detained in Portland. Or anywhere, for that matter. Despite years of partying in high school, somehow she had managed to stay clear of police interaction.

The harsh fluorescent lighting of the police station glared down at her as she filled out the paperwork, bailing her brother out of jail. She barely needed to read the familiar documents. Thirty minutes later, a door opened, disgorging Jimmy.

"Let's get out of here. You hungry?" he said as he walked past her. His flippant words only added to her anger.

"No! I'm not hungry! I'm tired, Jimmy. It's the middle of the night, and I just bailed your ass out of jail. This is absolutely the last time! You hear me? The last time! And for the record, I don't owe you shit!"

He quickly turned to face her.

"If it wasn't for me, you'd be no one! I put you through law school, you uppity little bitch! I did that!"

He moved closer and yelled in her face. Jabbing his finger at her chest for emphasis. Alcohol-laced spittle peppered her.

She shoved him hard. "And there it is! Somehow you manage to take credit for my success, you self-centered asshole! You did so much for me, like making me live in a homeless shelter while you drank. You're just like them, every inch of you nothing but a stupid Sharpe!"

She turned and walked away.

"You're one of us, too, Kari Sharpe. You think you're better than us, but you never will be!" he shouted.

"I am better than you! Better than all of you! I actually got out of this shithole and made something of myself."

"Really? Some fancy attorney? So fancy that you just quit everything and ran home? You're no hotshot, you're just another Sharpe loser. You didn't come back for me! Something happened in New York and you know it."

He screamed at her loud enough to wake the dead. Taunting her to fight. Continue the cycle.

She needed to get away from him. Far away. She had reached her limit. Why the hell had she moved back here? She picked up her pace.

He quickly caught up. They walked side by side. The strong odor of alcohol wafted from him. He looked so pathetic . . . bruised face, bloodied knuckles, glassy red eyes. A glimmer of compassion stirred, taking the edge off her anger. Her regret.

"What the hell happened?" she demanded.

"Some no load shot his mouth off at me and I let him have it. Pop! Right in the kisser. The jerk deserved it."

He shook his blood-crusted fist in the air as he loudly recanted the night's events. Punctuating his story with loud, lip-smacking pops and grunts. Like only a drunk could.

"Lower your voice," she said.

A woman walking nearby glanced over and made a wide arc around them.

"Where the hell were you? And, by the way, glad to see you decided to get drunk after I paid for rehab! You idiot. You just shit away my money all down the drain for nothing!"

"Well, I wouldn't say 'drunk,' just comfortably numb."

They walked a little farther in silence until he said, "So . . . you gonna give me a lift?"

"Asshole. Get in. And next time don't bother calling me. I won't answer."

What else could she do? Leave the idiot on the streets to get into another fight? It would just cost her more money.

◆ ◆ ◆

The sun began to rise on her return home. She let go of the pipe dream of sleep, opting instead for a hot shower and strong coffee. The local newscasters predicted yet another glorious Maine day; then the "breaking news" started.

"Local attorney Kari Sharpe bailed out her brother Jimmy Sharpe after an alcohol-fueled fight in the Old Port. The incident is nothing new to the Sharpe family. Larry Sharpe . . ."

Kari watched in horror as the reporter recounted the various ways her parents and Doug had ruined their lives. The drugs and alcohol. The vehicular manslaughter conviction. Doug's death in a prison brawl. All of it neatly summarized for the entire community to enjoy as they sipped their lattes.

She slammed her mug down on the speckled Formica countertop. *Damn him.* She should have never returned to Maine. Nothing had changed in the isolated world.

A few hours later, she fidgeted in her office chair as she filtered through emails from various clients. "We will not need your services anymore . . ." "We decided to go in a different direction . . ." Several more clients chose to fire her. Word traveled fast in Maine. Too fast.

In one drunken night, Jimmy had reminded everyone in town just how messed up their family had always been. All their secrets, laid out for public consumption. No more hiding.

"Good morning, Kari. Here's your mail folder," said Ruth.

The paralegal placed the thin folder on the corner of Kari's messy desk and walked out quickly without eye contact.

Kari's cheeks burned hot. A familiar feeling of embarrassment clouded her thinking. She wondered whether Ruth planned to resign. Kari's past had never come up between them before. She shivered and absentmindedly tugged her tailored suit jacket closed.

The morning passed slowly as she attempted to do damage control. She could barely afford to lose the clients she had. Maybe she could reassure those who'd fired her that Jimmy's problems wouldn't affect her work. Maybe she could reassure herself. The memories, Jimmy . . . all of it had taken a toll on her since returning to Maine. She barely made deadlines, seeking continuances for the first time in her professional life. What was happening to her?

The navy had given her a gift. Her first day as a JAG officer, she'd met with her skipper. He'd told her that the navy gave everyone a clean slate. "Present your best self. It's the only one people will know," he'd advised. She'd taken his words and run with it. She'd presented her shipmates a sanitized version of herself. The one she wanted to believe. Unencumbered, she'd suppressed every painful detail about her childhood. Her standard MO until she moved back.

Jimmy and the *Portland Press Herald* had taken away her anonymity. Exposing her.

Kari jammed her fingers onto the keypad and listened to the rings of yet another unanswered call to a client. She threw the headset onto its cradle and walked out of the office, furious.

Chapter 27

The silvery light of the moon shone on the water, illuminating the calm sea. Greg idled the engine of the lobster boat, waiting for his cousin to meet him in the designated area. He double-checked the waypoint on his GPS against the current location of his boat to be certain he was stationed in the correct spot.

Everything about lobstering repulsed him. The stench alone made him reconsider the plan. Then the money started rolling in. He made more in one week doing this job than he managed to eke out in a month of working at the Getty on Route 1. As a bonus, this gig didn't involve interaction with tourists. Giving the same directions for the starry-eyed lost "Massholes" grew old. The only tourists they ran into out here had been the unlucky chumps on the sailboat.

A soft rumble of a diesel engine traveled over the water. He turned in its direction, unable to see anything in the darkness. The shadowy outline of a boat formed as though from thin air, prompting him to turn off his running lights. No one needed to see their labors.

"Hey, man!" said his cousin Ron.

The driver of the small boat yelled over to him. So much for stealth.

"Hey, cuz!" he replied.

The other man pulled his vessel to the side of Greg's lobster boat. The man yelled "Here, grab it" as he tossed a rope into Greg's waiting hands.

"You have the empties?" said Ron.

"Sure do."

Large plastic fuel containers made clunking sounds as he struggled to hand the man several jugs.

"Careful! Last thing we need is to have one of these babies go into the drink!" yelled Ron.

"No shit. I'm doing the best I can. These things are a pain to hold."

He handed his cousin the final container. After double-checking the boat, he said, "That's the last one."

Ron stacked the empty containers on the deck of his boat and then turned to the upright jugs, which lined the boat's perimeter. The shadowy figure grunted from the exertion as he lifted the heavy jugs and handed them to Greg.

"What the hell? That's all you have for me? It's hardly anything," said Greg.

"That's it for now. Take what you can get. I'm the one risking everything, you shithead."

Leave it to his cousin to place himself at the center of everything. As though no one else risked anything to run their little business.

"Fine. I'll let you know if anything changes on our end, but I'm sure selling the liquid gold won't be a problem," said Greg.

"About that, I need to take a week off, just to be safe. The cops have been swarming BIW because of the Simmons murder. I need to cool it and let things go back to normal," said Ron.

"Seriously? That'll cut into the bottom line. Jeff won't like it."

"I don't give a shit what Jeff thinks. We take a week off. Final word."

Ron tugged hard on his rope until it pulled free from Greg's boat. Greg moved back to the control console and slowly put his vessel into gear. He wanted to race away from the location and the annoying conversation. Prudence told him to move toward the open ocean slowly and quietly so as not to attract unnecessary attention. The few fuel containers had to suffice for now. At least until things cooled off.

Chapter 28

The next afternoon Chet made his rounds, checking a portion of his traps. Like most lobstermen, he rotated which traps he checked daily, ensuring he never left one unattended. Only one area remained for the day's cycle. He pushed the engine to move toward the next area. His boat struggled and whined in reply, moving slow.

"Oh shit! I'm stuck!"

His rudder had snagged a lobster pot line. If he continued to run the throttle, the line would completely stop his movement and likely burn out his engine.

"Shit, some poor sucker is gonna miss that one! Right, boys!" yelled Chet.

Instead of risking damage to his boat, he cut the line. Cutting another person's lobster pot caused countless feuds among those who relied on the pots for their living. None of the true professionals wanted to cut a line if it could be avoided.

Chet reached down and sliced the thick rope of the pot, allowing the pot to sink to the ocean's floor, never to be retrieved from the deep water. Once freed, he leaned over and grabbed the buoy from the water and gave it a good yank. He pulled the buoy onto his deck. He made sure to set a waypoint as a marker for the location so he could share it with the owner of the pot.

The color of the buoy indicated it belonged to the guys who'd taken over Randy's boat for the summer. *Not those guys.*

Ever since they came onto the scene, things had changed. The waterfront felt far less friendly than it had in previous years. Something everyone noticed and felt.

The sun warmed Chet's weathered skin as he pulled the boat into the harbor. The first half of his day, finally coming to an end.

After he finished banding the day's measly catch, he grabbed the buoy and walked over to one of the guys on Randy's old boat.

"Hey, man, sorry, but I snagged your pot and had to cut it!" he yelled.

The man looked up at him inquisitively.

"Just toss it over there," said the man roughly.

"I'll pay for the pot and a few lobsters to make up for it. I have the waypoint for you, so you can reset the trap in your location."

Chet pulled out his phone, ready to provide the man with the coordinates. This would allow the man to reset the trap exactly where the previous one had been cut without infringing on another lobsterman's maritime territory.

"No need," the man said.

"No need to pay or no need to give you the coordinates?" asked Chet.

The man stopped his work, straightened up, and said, "I'll take your money, but I don't want the damn points. I couldn't give a shit about those."

The full lobster crates on the deck beside the man's boat had more lobsters than Chet snagged in an entire week.

"Your call. I'll bring by a hundred in cash tomorrow," he said.

"That's it? A hundred bucks doesn't cut it. You can pay me two hundred and fifty dollars for my loss, or you'll see who loses out."

The man tossed the banded lobster, straightened to his full height, and stared at Chet, who stepped back under his glare. He considered his options.

One hundred dollars usually sufficed under the circumstances. Over the years, the lobstermen had developed a going rate to compensate the loss while also not punishing a person for accidentally getting snagged on a line. Most professional lobstermen knew the current local rate. The man's response demonstrated that he either had no idea of the custom or intended to shake Chet down for every penny possible.

Chet cleared his throat and said, "I'll give you two hundred. Not a penny more."

"Fine. Have it tomorrow. In cash."

Chet nodded, then quickly retreated. The full crates meant the guy made more than he had on the same day. *Asshole.*

He wished Randy had been the one on his boat instead of that guy. Randy knew the customs and was a decent guy who would give a fellow lobsterman a break. *What the hell happened to him?*

Chet considered his theories about the men running Randy's boat. The unusually large haul confirmed everything he suspected. The men were clearly thieves. Now he had to prove it.

Chapter 29

Mack Bowen drove his late-model Buick LeSabre faster than he probably should have. The wide, comfortable car provided a smooth ride at any speed. It effortlessly cruised at eighty along the I-95 as he headed north to Portland, Maine. Even though his beige Buick didn't scream "eligible bachelor," he preferred the car over flashier models. He took a noisy sip from his orange Big Gulp and tossed the empty onto the floor of the passenger seat. The freedom to toss his trash anywhere had been an unexpected gift of divorce.

One day Jinny had decided she just couldn't deal with him anymore. Whatever that meant. They'd been together for nearly twenty-five years when she pulled the plug on their life. "You're too much work," she'd declared. He wiped his sweaty hand on his stained dress shirt and grabbed a cigarette, a habit he knew he should quit. A person needed things in life that gave them pleasure. Other indulgences included whiskey and cigars. He wanted to add women to the list but hadn't been lucky with the ladies for as long as he remembered. But Ruth, Kari's assistant, was the type of woman he wanted to date. Fun loving, smart, snarky, and a little rough around the edges, just his style. Maybe she would walk out on her husband, just as Jinny had done, giving him an opportunity.

Kari had hired Mack to serve papers to a real loser scumbag who bounced around southern Maine, occasionally crossing into New Hampshire. As if New Hampshire wanted him. She intended to file a divorce action against the man on behalf of his wife, who was seeking child support. Commencing the court action required serving him the complaint. Mack started by paying a visit to the man's normal residence.

The second-floor apartment in Standish, Maine, appeared abandoned. Mail overflowed from the small dinged-up plastic mailbox, and paper advertisements littered the front stoop. As he looked around the building, the landlord approached him. The landlord said, "That pile of crap never paid rent for months. Then just disappeared." Not surprising. The man refused to pay for his children's food and clothing, so why would he pay rent?

After several dead ends, Mack finally managed to track him down. He had been bouncing around, crashing on friend's couches probably to avoid service of process. Several late nights watching the residences of friends resulted in gold. He saw the man pull up to the house and into the garage, quickly closing the garage door behind him, concealing his vehicle. Mack had been trying to locate the man for the better part of a month. Finally, he had gotten the scumbag. Now for the fun part.

Mack grabbed the documents and rang the bell. Movement in the house stopped. Mack suspected the occupants were weighing their options. Finally, a young, wasted woman opened the door a crack. She kept the chain across the threshold. Her red, glassy eyes were barely able to focus.

"Hey, I'm a friend of Bob's. I need to see him right now," he said.

She hesitated, then said, "He's not here."

"Cut the crap. I just saw him drive into the garage. You either get him or I come in," he demanded.

Technically he had no right to enter the woman's dwelling, but she didn't know that.

"You a cop or something?" she asked.

"Yeah—or something . . . get him or I come in," Mack demanded.

A skinny guy forcefully shoved the woman aside and yelled, "You have no right!"

Before he could say anything else, Mack jammed the documents at him and said, "Add a divorce to your losses, chump. You've been served."

After several months of searching for the guy, Mack finally nailed him. Kari had to explain to her client why the case had not begun. Mack's work helped her immensely. If he had been unable to find good old Bob, Kari would have had to file a motion for alternate service and then pay for an ad in the newspaper, giving the man "notice" of the proceedings. Everyone knew only lawyers read those notices, but the fiction allowed things to progress. Mack leaned into the comfort of the cushy seat in his Buick, satisfied with his efforts.

He had known the Sharpe family for as long as he could recall. Jimmy and Kari had received the raw end of life at most turns. They'd been dealt crappy parents who never cared about them. Drug use and alcohol abuse had been standard fare at the Sharpe home. Finally, when the eldest brother had been arrested, Mack had known he needed to help Kari and Jimmy. He'd wanted to prevent them from falling into the same life choices.

Over the years, Mack had made a point of checking on them. He'd brought small gifts when he could, of food, clothing, and household basics like cleaning supplies. During Kari's rough years in high school, he'd leaned on his fellow officers to give her a break. She'd raged during those years—screaming at teachers, getting into fights, doing more drugs and alcohol than humanly possible. At one point, things had gotten so intense he wondered whether she'd survive.

Despite wanting to walk away from them, Mack had stayed close, helping when possible. He never told Kari or Jimmy how many times he had intervened on their behalf. Eventually, the heavy makeup, stark black hair, and countless piercings had faded away, as did Kari's self-destructive behavior. She'd emerged strong and determined, plowing her way through university and then law school.

Much like Jimmy's, Mack's heart had broken when Kari left Maine to start her military career. He never had children of his own but knew his pride in her must have been what parents experienced as they celebrated their children's successes. The tough, scrappy, skinny kid had managed to break out of the Sharpe family rut and make something of herself. Jimmy's life seemed to meander in different directions. Mack wanted to believe the dude would somehow straighten out, but the latest bout of drunken nonsense hadn't been particularly reassuring.

Mack slowed his car down to negotiate the highway exit ramp to Portland. He needed to meet with Kari about several cases. Then he hoped to snag dinner before heading back to Old Orchard Beach. He'd moved down to the coastal community after his divorce, joining the other divorced men whose wives had had enough of them.

Mack yanked the door to Kari's office open and entered the cool space.

"Mack! Hi, I didn't know you were coming in today," said Ruth.

"Hello, beautiful," he said as he leaned into the reception desk. He paused to smile at her, then added, "Yeah, I didn't know I was coming in today, either, but you know how the boss lady is, always needing something."

"Tell me about it," Ruth said with a sweet laugh.

"How's life treating you? I hope that husband of yours knows how lucky he is," he said with a raise of his brows and a wink.

"Oh, Mack!"

As he started to walk away, Mack glanced at her over his shoulder. Ruth smiled and blushed like a schoolgirl. Just as he hoped.

The office smelled of fresh, spicy food. Mack couldn't be certain of the type, but he hoped Ahmed's mom had dropped off another banquet for them.

"Geez, is that Somali food I smell?" he asked as he stopped at the steps.

"Sure is. Hani dropped off enough to feed all the lawyers on the waterfront. Have some. I left it in the break room. There are containers up there if you want to take more for later. Kari won't, and my husband flips out if I try to put anything in front of him but meat and potatoes," Ruth said.

"You cook too! Your husband sure is a lucky guy, Ruth."

Mack loaded a paper plate with the freshly cooked homemade food. The weight of the meal caused the thin paper to sag, necessitating a second plate to prevent a total collapse.

"Enjoying yourself?" asked Kari.

Mack jerked in his seat. "Crap, you almost gave me a heart attack. Why are you creeping around like that?"

"Creeping? I just walked in."

"You need to wear a bell. Damn. I nearly dropped my bread!"

Kari sat with him until he licked his last finger clean of the savory food. The large stains covering his stomach marked the meal as a success.

"So you finally found our shifty little friend Bob McIntry?" asked Kari.

"Yes, I nailed him hiding at a friend's house. The guy bounced around so much, I started to lose faith that I could serve him for you."

"Thanks for all your work on it. I really appreciate it and have an affidavit ready for your signature." She glanced at his still-greasy fingers and added, "After you've washed your hands."

"I thought divorce officially ended my time getting harassed by a woman."

"Funny guy. If you're done, let's go downstairs. I have Ahmed's file in the conference room and need your opinion on a few things."

"Lead the way."

They settled into the conference room to review the file. Mack had often lent Kari his expertise as a former police officer turned private detective. He helped her strategize a defense for numerous cases. As a former officer and detective, he'd never envisioned himself working on a criminal defense team, but he wanted to help Kari.

"Yesterday I walked the trail to view the location of the murder."

Kari stretched her well-worn map onto the table in front of them.

"I interviewed Betsy Roth, the state's one and only eyewitness. She lives here." Kari jabbed her finger on the pencil-circled location.

"Is she credible?" he asked.

"Not really. She's in her late eighties and can't see worth a damn. She does, however, personally know Ahmed and the entire family from their store. Apparently, Hani occasionally brought her food."

"And she's acting as a witness against Hani's son? Nice show of gratitude."

"Seriously. I also talked with another neighbor. She saw a truck on their street the morning of the murder. She claims that the vehicle pulled off in a hurry."

"Did she see the driver? Or get the license plate number?"

"No. Neither. She said the silver Tundra had Maine plates and a NAVY bumper sticker on it. That's it."

"So you have the workings of an alternate theory. The stranger in the truck killed Ms. Simmons and then tore off to parts unknown."

"That's what I'm looking at. I hope it's enough."

"To raise reasonable doubt? Maybe."

"I know it's a stretch, but can you search for a Maine-plated silver Tundra? Maybe narrow the search to veterans?"

"I can, but we will get way more from such a search than might be helpful. And some veterans don't register as veterans with Motor Vehicles."

"True, maybe cull the search to those within a one-hundred-mile vicinity?"

"I'll give it a shot. You never know," said Mack.

He flipped through the file and said, "I don't see an entry on the police log for the interview with the neighbor, Meg Shore. It's only in your notes. Am I missing something?"

"No—they never interviewed her. Nor did they leave a card. Don't you find that odd?"

"A little. You said Clark is the lead investigator?"

"Yes. And his girlfriend is the caregiver for Betsy Roth, the only witness."

"Interesting. It seems a little too easy, even for Clark. The guy is lazy, but knocking on doors is standard. He would have given the task to a uniformed officer. I'll poke around to see if anyone at the station has heard of anything. I know Clark was in trouble for sloppy work a few years ago. I assumed he improved his performance, because he made detective. Who knows. The PD is under a tremendous amount of pressure from the bigwigs to button up the case. They could have skipped a few steps."

"Yes. As much as I would like to think Clark has some nefarious plan, I know you're most likely right. They rushed the investigation."

Mack closed the witness file and turned to the medical examiner's reports and photos. He had become accustomed to the gruesome photos in death cases. Anytime a person died at home, their body had to be examined by the medical examiner's office. Families found the state law very intrusive during a difficult time. The stack of photos of Irene Simmons looked like so many he'd viewed over the years. The once-vibrant woman looked pale and alone on the cold stainless-steel table, a terrible place for a body to spend its last days on earth.

"This is interesting. Look at this," said Mack.

He handed Kari the close-up photo of Ms. Simmons's face. Numerous bruises of various shades of purple and green soiled her skin. Mack used a closed ballpoint pen to trace a small area on her face.

"This imprint could have been from a ring. Something substantial. The perp would have worn it on his right hand, judging by the location of the bruising."

Kari leaned into the photo for a closer look. "Yes, I saw that as well. The report failed to mention it."

"They pin the cause of death as blunt-force trauma to the back of the head, right?" he asked.

"Yes, from the condition of the back of her skull, I'd say they got that right."

Mack turned to the photo of the victim's head. The skull had been shattered. Then he looked at the police photos taken at the scene. Brain matter, blood, and a gooey whitish substance dripped down the side of the rock under her head. It hadn't taken a genius to determine the victim's cause of death.

"Have you talked to the family of the deceased or anyone in her workplace?" asked Mack.

"Not yet. I'm going to BIW this week and plan to poke around her office. Then I'll go out to see her family. A sister, I believe."

"You might also consider hiring an expert to opine on what could have caused that faint circle line on her cheek," said Mack.

"Yes, I'll do that after I meet with the medical examiner. Perhaps I can have their office look at this again and add an addendum to the report. If possible, I'd like to keep costs down for Ahmed's family. Apparently the Somali community chipped in to pay my retainer fee."

"Wow. Lucky kid. Most young Black men are swept up into the system so fast, they don't even know what hit them."

"He has a lot of people behind him. I'm trying to do everything I can for him."

"You always do."

Mack stood and stretched. He needed to shoot up north for an off-the-books meeting with an abusive spouse, and his watch told him to leave soon. The father of the man's young wife decided he had enough of seeing bruises on his daughter's face from "falling." He'd hired Mack to pay the man a visit. A stern "conversation" had the potential to scare the man enough to set him straight, at least for a while.

"Okay, Kari, if we're done here, I need to head out."

"Thanks, Mack. You've been helpful. I needed a second set of eyes."

"I didn't do anything. You have a good handle on it. Remember, just throw enough spaghetti at the wall to create some doubt. A little is all you need to meet a reasonable doubt standard. And I saw the news about Jimmy. Sorry. The last thing you need right now is him going sideways. And nice of the news to identify you by name. That was cruel."

"Thanks. I wasn't sure if you knew. I feel so embarrassed, exposed. Like the whole community knows who we are. Who I am."

He ran his fingers through his thinning hair and said, "You didn't do anything wrong. This is on Jimmy. He effed up. Plain and simple."

"I wish everyone could see it that way. I've been fielding calls all morning about it, mostly from clients. Some asking to have their matter transferred. I'm in damage control mode at this point."

"What a shit show," he said.

Kari's eyes welled with tears as she mentioned her clients leaving. In that moment she looked just like the frail, skinny kid from all those years ago.

"You'll get through this. If I know one thing about you, Attorney Sharpe, it's that you're a survivor. People forget. This will blow over, eventually."

"Thanks, Mack. I appreciate your support. Somehow this feels different. Being here, in this place. In Maine. Handling a criminal case and Jimmy's shit. I don't know. It's just all too real for me. It's bringing up all sorts of stuff I'd rather forget." She paused to look at him, then added, "But I'll get through it. What choice do I have?"

Mack shifted uncomfortably on his heels, unsure of what to say. How to make her feel better. Finally, he said, "You'll be okay. Give it time and remember that you're one hell of an attorney."

Mack carried a bag stuffed with Somali food to his car. Ruth had prepared it for him while he'd met with Kari. The aromas filled his vehicle as he drove north. He hoped his next stop scaring the abusive husband didn't take too long. He could hardly wait to get home to dig into the homemade food, a real luxury for a bachelor. Most nights he ate takeout in front of the TV, just like the other men living alone in Old Orchard Beach. Served him right. He'd never fully appreciated Jinny's freshly cooked meals. Until now. He navigated south on the I-95, strumming his fingers on the doorframe to a familiar tune.

Chapter 30

Kari stood in line at the small coffee shop near her office. The Port Roasters roasted the beans for their delicious coffee on site. It made their java taste far superior to the coffee sold at other locations. Jimmy always said, "Caffeine is caffeine. Get it hot. That's all that counts." However, her time in New York City had schooled her in the subtle nuances of the delicious beverage. Most of her colleagues at Barnes & Smith had specific, extremely detailed coffee orders for the staff. Over time she'd included herself as one of those people with an overly complicated drink order, a double caramel macchiato with light foam, half-decaf coffee and soy milk being her go-to. Before moving to New York, she'd thought Dunkin' Donuts had been an exemplar of good coffee.

The smell of roasting beans combined with the aromas of vanilla, nutmeg, and sugar. She peeked behind the counter into the back kitchen, where an older woman wearing a stained apron placed a tray of muffins on a cooling rack. The blueberry muffins released their steam into the already fragrant air. Kari imagined slathering the warm muffin with a thick coat of butter. She felt her resolve crumbling as temptation took hold of her. Normally she limited herself to a once-weekly indulgence, typically for Sunday brunch. Today would be an exception.

As she drove to the Office of the Chief Medical Examiner in Augusta, Maine, she nibbled on her fresh, still-warm blueberry muffin and sipped hot coffee. She tucked a napkin into the top of her white blouse and laid a second one across her lap. She preferred not to arrive at their offices looking like Mack, with food and drink stains creating a mosaic across his gut.

The state created the Office of the Chief Medical Examiner in 1968 for the purpose of examining sudden or unexplained deaths. Maine typically had over three thousand deaths that needed the medical examiner's office. But only around two thousand of those deaths per year required an autopsy.

Kari placed a few business cards in her navy blue suit jacket before getting out of the car. Today had promised to be hot, and it didn't disappoint. The short walk from her car to the entrance of the office resulted in a bead of sweat slowly trickling down her back. She wished she had worn something other than a navy pantsuit. A skirt suit would have been slightly cooler.

Her mind drifted to Jimmy. Her anger had subsided ever so slightly. In its place, anxiety. She gnawed on her lower lip as she thought about the life he could have had if he remained sober. She also considered the alternative. The image of her father in his casket flashed in her head momentarily. Her stomach lurched in response. "Nope. Not today," she said to herself as she shook off the image. She couldn't go on like this, phantoms assailing her at every moment.

Walking into the reception area, she said, "Hi, I'm Attorney Sharpe. I have an appointment to meet with Dr. Jesper."

The receptionist looked distracted and unconcerned about Kari's offer of her business card.

"Sharpe? Kari Sharpe? I recognize the name," said the woman. She scrutinized Kari's face, then said, "Oh . . ."

Kari's face reddened as her jaw clenched. *Not again.*

The woman quickly looked away from her and said, "Have a seat over there. He's in an exam room. It could be a while."

Kari reviewed Ahmed's file as she waited. She needed a few distinct things from the medical examiner.

The scuffed door in the waiting area opened with a bang. A tall, slim balding man stepped out and said, "Attorney Sharpe? I'm Dr. Jesper."

"Yes, nice to meet you, Doctor."

"Please call me Mike. In my business, we don't have to stand on titles. I've figured out over the years that the dead don't really care," he said.

Dr. Jesper's amiable greeting relaxed Kari immediately. For the first time in ages, her smile felt real.

They walked through a narrow hallway to Dr. Jesper's large office. Pictures of a smiling family on trips in the mountains and on a sailboat covered the walls. The photos felt staged, as if they wanted to prove their happiness to the world. "Aren't we perfect!" shouted the pictures.

Kari's smile vanished.

"Sorry I kept you waiting. We had a rush of tangled skin to sort through."

"Yikes. That doesn't sound good."

"No, it wasn't. The three-car accident on the 95 really pushed our limits. It would be nice if people could slow down so I could have a relaxing summer!"

She cocked her head to the side, unsure how to respond.

"Sorry, gallows humor." He shrugged his shoulders and added, "It's not for everyone but gets us through the day. Uh, what can I help you with?"

Kari pulled out her file for the Ahmed case and spread the crime scene photos on the table. Then she laid out the pictures from the medical examiner.

"As you know, I represent Youseff Ahmed. He's been accused of Irene Simmons's murder. I need to get a handle on the investigation and ask you a few questions about her injuries."

"Sounds easy. Ask away."

She pointed at the picture of Ms. Simmons's body at the crime scene and asked, "Was someone from your office at the scene of the crime to assist in taking these photos?"

"Yes, we were called that morning. I usually like to view the scene when homicide is suspected. However, in this case, I had to send one of our other examiners. I spent the morning in court, testifying in another matter. Our examiner took a few pictures in addition to the ones provided to you by the police."

"Why the extra step of visiting the scene when the police and their evidence unit are already there?"

"We like to view it to help us develop an understanding of the nature of the death. We might notice something in the vicinity of the deceased that others may not. You never know. It's our practice and has been helpful for our work."

"Do you think visiting the scene could lead a medical examiner to simply follow the theory of the death as presented by the police?"

"What do you mean?"

"Well, if the detectives and the evidence team are at the location audibly discussing their theories, I'm wondering if their chatter concerning the cause of death might influence the findings of the medical examiner who performs the autopsy. Sort of creating a scenario where the physical autopsy merely confirms the initial findings set forth by the detectives."

Kari chose her words carefully. She wanted to avoid insulting the man's lifework, but she also needed to be able to question him on the stand and understand whether bias existed.

"Oh, sure, that can absolutely happen," he replied. "I've walked away from a crime scene with an idea of what I would find on the body. But bodies have a way of telling their own story. Once we start to slice and dice, we get to what happened. Sometimes our findings confirm the working theories set forth by the detectives and evidence team. Other times, the body sings to us in a way that creates a totally different picture of the cause of death."

"In this case, Irene Simmons's cause of death was blunt-force trauma to her head, cracking her skull, correct?"

The doctor picked up a few photos and pointed as he spoke.

"You can see here where the skull has been broken. It seemed clear to us what happened."

"Is it possible that she merely slipped and fell? It happens all the time."

"Sure, it's possible. Her cranium hit a jagged edge of a rock at just the right angle. Given her weight and the velocity of a fall, the force exerted on her cranial bones would have been enough to open her up. No bone saw needed!" He chuckled at his own joke. "Sorry. Just trying to keep it light."

Kari relaxed into her seat. "If a fall is an alternative cause of death, why was it ruled a homicide?"

He picked up the picture of Ms. Simmons's face and said, "Because of the fresh contusions on her face. These bruises occurred contemporaneous to the fall. Someone had been with her when she died, perhaps causing the death."

"Is it possible the person punched her and then she fell and accidentally died?"

"Yes, that's possible. Like I said, the velocity of a fall with her height and weight and the jagged edge of the rock cracked her open. The question as to why she fell remains open to different interpretations."

Kari pointed at Ms. Simmons's face. She circled the bruised jaw area with the eraser side of her pencil and asked, "What do you make of this?"

Dr. Jesper picked up the photo and looked a little closer. "Hold on. Let me grab my file."

He crossed the room toward a large gray metal filing cabinet. The drawer creaked loudly as he pulled with a hard yank.

"Government crap. You know how it is. The mantra of 'do more with less' is great until your filing cabinets don't even open," he said.

He thumbed through the files and then pulled one out. Dr. Jesper reviewed the documents carefully before turning to Kari.

"My notes indicated the existence of a rounded abrasion embedded in the contusion on her left cheek. However, since the cause of death had been the cranial fracture, our team chose not to run down the cause of the imprint. It seemed clear to us that she'd been attacked and fell."

"I would think everything about a death would be noted, especially in a homicide case. Why didn't this make it into the report?"

"Not everything does. We focus on the cause of death to assist the police and give families closure. That's all."

Kari sensed the man was holding something back from her. She carefully moved forward. "This is a high-profile case. I noticed irregularities in the police procedure throughout the investigation. Did your office receive any pressure to work quicker than usual?"

"Yes, our staff fielded calls from all the bigwigs . . . mayor's office, governor's office. You name it, they called. People seriously freaked out, especially since we have two dead tourists as well. That case is still unresolved." Dr. Jesper inhaled sharply and released an audible exhale.

"I know—and having three murders in a relatively short period of time, during tourist season, probably caused a bit of a panic. I'm sure the tourist board pressured everyone too."

Dr. Jesper looked away. He cracked his knuckles loudly and turned back to Kari.

"Probably. We were asked to make this matter a top priority. Generally, we turn around a body in twenty-four to forty-eight hours. The family can then bury or burn the corpse as they see fit. The examination is done relatively quickly, but our report could take a few weeks to complete."

"Is that roughly the timetable of this investigation?" Kari held her breath, waiting for his reply. She needed him to admit they rushed the case.

The doctor rubbed the back of his head. "No. Uh, for Irene Simmons we did our magic in less than twenty-four hours and then turned in our report to the Portland Police Department in just a few days. We had to lean into the lab to rush the toxicology reports to get everything together."

She let out a slow exhale as she moved back into her chair. Relieved.

"If there hadn't been so much pressure to get this done, would you have included the indentation on the side of the victim's cheek?" she asked. Her question hung in the air between them momentarily.

"Most likely. My report had been lean and mean, right down to the immediate cause of death," he admitted.

"Do you think it's possible that a large ring could have cause the faint mark?"

"Yes, but the outline is so faint that it would be hard to connect to an actual ring. Or another object hitting her face, like a buckle. Its existence doesn't change the cause of death, but could help you, if your client doesn't wear rings," he said with a smile.

She laughed out loud despite herself. Her tension eased.

"Yes, that's *exactly* what I was hoping. If this goes to trial, I'd like to get into this issue when you're on the stand. Are you comfortable repeating everything we talked about while under oath?"

"Of course. You must do your job. If your client didn't do this, it's in everyone's best interest to find who did."

Finally, someone got it. She stifled a sigh of relief. Dr. Jesper would be a key witness in Ahmed's defense. She almost felt giddy as she realized what his testimony could mean for the case. Something legitimate to grab the jury's attention. Something she could spin into reasonable doubt.

"I just have one more question," she said. "Am I correct to assume that the victim was identified at the crime scene?"

"Yes, they found her identification in her purse. Most people are identified where they died by something either on them or in the location. The dramatic scene of a family member identifying the body isn't something we do. We leave that to Hollywood. In fact, we don't allow families to come over here. It's not where anyone would want to see the body of their loved one. After we're finished, the funeral home will pick up the remains and prepare them for viewing. Things are better that way."

Irene Simmons's purse lay next to her body as though she'd merely placed it there. The poor woman had been on her way somewhere when she'd been killed. The suddenness and simplicity of Ms. Simmons's death shook Kari unexpectedly. She dropped her watery eyes to her satchel and pretended to look for something.

After taking a beat, she looked back up at Dr. Jesper.

Clearing her throat, she said, "That should do it for me. I know you're busy. You've been very helpful. I'll get out of your hair."

"Not a problem at all. Feel free to stop by or call if you think of something else."

She collected her files and stood to leave, then hesitated, not wanting to go. The peaceful, open man felt like a balm to her frayed mind.

"Any thoughts on the two murdered people on the sailboat? I haven't heard anything about them in a while," she said.

"Those cases are odd. They were killed with what appears to be large hunting knives. Not the sort of knives a person might bring with them for a day of boating. They pulled the man out of the bay. His body was covered in diesel fuel, like he floated in a spill of some sort. Personally, I think they were killed by someone who isn't too familiar with boating. The office is full of theories. My assistant Genie thinks the guy who killed Ms. Simmons also killed the sailors. Your client doesn't own a hunting knife, does he?"

"I doubt it. I also doubt he would have had any way to get out onto the water. He's just a young navy kid, not a boater. I think Genie needs to reconsider her theory."

"Yeah, she isn't winning the office pool with it, but I don't have the heart to tell her. The wager is lunch at the Red Barn, a staff favorite. Hope of winning the pool keeps everyone working."

Kari smiled and extended her hand. "It was a pleasure meeting with you. Thanks again," she said.

"Pleasure's all mine. It's a nice break to chat with a person who has a pulse. The dead aren't great conversationalists."

"I'm not sure if that's a compliment."

Kari nestled into her vehicle. For the first time in a while, she felt her shoulders relax. Her grip on the steering wheel light. It felt great to focus on work instead of Jimmy's crap.

She looked at the clock on the dash. Their meeting had gone way over her allotted time. Her hearing on a money-judgment matter started in just under one hour in Portland. She would make it in the nick of time if she could snag a parking spot without too much trouble.

Chapter 31

Ruth Morgan flipped off her shoes as she walked into the small ranch house she shared with her husband, David. They'd lived in the tiny brown home for as long as she could recall. Over the years they'd made numerous changes to accommodate their growing family. One year they'd invested in finishing the basement, even including a bathroom. The kids loved the additional room for sleepovers. Ruth loved not having a messy mass of youth in sleeping bags on their family room floor.

She walked through the kitchen past the family room. Her husband, long retired from his position with the rail yard, sat in his recliner, gently dozing. Whenever she thought about retiring, she thought about sitting in the room with him. Watching David picking at his toes and talking over their shows hadn't been the retirement she'd dreamed for herself. Even on the worst days at work, thoughts of not leaving the house on a daily basis kept her going into the office.

"You home?" he yelled.

"Yes, just changing. Any ideas for dinner?"

She didn't know why she bothered to ask. He never offered solutions, just a body to feed. Their terrier followed her to the back bedroom and anxiously awaited his reunion love. She knelt over to pat him. "Good boy, Reggi. Did you have fun today? Did you see the babies?"

David kept goats in the backyard. She never really understood his interest in goats, but it kept him busy. The babies born in the spring had grown over the course of the summer. Unlike as had been the case with previous kids, she thought her husband favored this crop of brood. She often saw him in the little wooden pen, holding the babies and talking to them. Maybe he would find homes for the goats that didn't involve a dinner plate.

Kari had been out of the office in Augusta and then at a hearing, enabling Ruth to finally take a breath. Keeping up with an attorney with exacting standards had been difficult. Kari often returned the documents Ruth prepared with red ink covering the entire page. The process of revising her work until Kari deemed it perfect enough to file wore Ruth out, even on the best day. In the morning, she faced a stack of revisions from the work Kari had done the evening before. Ruth had no idea how the woman kept up the pace. After the revisions, she then had to prepare the documents Kari gave her during the day. The cycle repeated itself every day of the week. Week after week.

Working with a solo practitioner had not been the most glamorous employment Ruth could have found. Her friend at Morgan & Price often crowed about the importance and prestige of "her attorneys." But Ruth had something her friend didn't, a former navy JAG and a former partner from one of those fancy New York firms. In Ruth's estimation, the JAG thing trumped all of it, fancy firm included. She held her head high and bragged about Kari at every turn possible. The case against Ahmed fueled her bragging. Kari had landed the hottest client in Portland. Everyone talked about it, and Ruth was on the inside. The hell with the women who stuck up their noses at her taking a job with a solo attorney.

After a day out of the office, Ruth knew Kari would have to work extra hard on things that had piled up in her absence. That meant only one thing for Ruth—a very long day when she returned from her day off. At least today, without Kari in the office, she'd had the opportunity to watch her daytime shows at the correct time. Though, of course, she would have traded watching her shows for a little time with Mack. Every time a car pulled up, she glanced outside, hoping it would be him. The two of them alone. Without Kari in the office? Who knew what could happen? Maybe he'd finally embrace her, give her a kiss, or maybe . . .

"Ruth!" her husband shouted from the other room.

Just like him, to wreck her dreams yet again.

Chapter 32

Fred May settled into his well-worn desk chair and yawned. He moved various sheets of paper, dusty paperweights, and dirty cups to the side, searching for a pen in the cramped harbormaster's office. Various jobs had kept him close to the sea his entire life. He wore a constellation of sunspots on his face and arms as a badge of honor. All "men of the sea" looked weathered. "Move over and let someone younger take over, ya ole faht," said his wife. Nothing like a Down-Easter to call a spade a spade.

Today started extra early to oversee the arrival of yet another cruise ship to the Portland Pier. Fred and his counterpart, the second harbormaster, Jared, shared the responsibility of overseeing the entire Portland Pier. South Portland also had two harbormasters, and Fred knew those guys worked their tails off too. The men monitored the flow of traffic in and out of their busy locations. In addition, they maintained the waiting list, sometimes years long, for the mooring balls in their respective harbors.

Fielding calls from angry, rich out-of-town people who expected they could just make a phone call to arrange a mooring-ball rental for the summer, while real Mainers waited their turn for the precious commodity, really annoyed him.

He rummaged around for a bite to eat. Usually he stashed nuts and granola in his desk. Not today. His grumbling stomach would have to wait.

The Casco Bay mailboat blew its loud horn in concert with a nail gun being deployed somewhere close. The clatter of that thing nearly made him lose it.

He glanced at the dusty clock. Detective Clark had said he would be at the pier close to two o'clock. Fred had about fifteen minutes to sip his cold coffee, freshly prepared hours ago. Clark had said he needed more information from him. After the murders of the two tourists on their sailboat, the police had coordinated efforts with the Coast Guard to find whoever had committed the crimes. As part of their investigation, Detective Clark had asked Fred for a list of all slips and mooring-ball rentals he'd acquired for the summer. Turning over the names of fellow boaters seemed like a betrayal of their community. But despite his reservations, he'd complied, just like the harbormasters from South Portland.

"Boss, you there?"

The voice on his handheld radio interrupted his thoughts.

"Yeah, I'm here. What's up?"

"Your appointment for two o'clock is here. You want me to walk him back, or are you coming out?"

Their summer hire had a way of grating on him. Fred had gone to high school with the kid's dad. As a favor, he'd hired the tenth grader to do something he typically reserved for someone who had a little experience on the waterfront. Fred hadn't been sure the kid even realized he worked on a waterfront, not to mention a busy one. A few more weeks and the kid would quit to go back to school. Then things would be nice and relatively quiet for the fall and winter months.

"I'm coming out. Thanks."

Before the appointment with Clark, he'd instructed the kid to call him when the detective arrived. The tiny "office" had no room for a proper conversation. It was littered with charts, maps, lists, and various mechanical pieces in case one of their watercrafts required a quick cheap fix. Not exactly a suitable place for a meeting with a member of the law enforcement community. As with many of his instructions, this one had gone in one ear and out the other.

"Detective Clark, nice to see you," he said.

Clark extended his hand for a quick greeting. For a while there, the fancy-pants people had chosen to do the elbow bump instead of a real handshake. That little ritual never took off on the waterfront, thankfully.

"What brings you back to our neck of the woods, Detective?" asked Fred.

The glistening blue sea sparkled in the distance. Various leisure and working boats moved lazily across the water. The Portland Head Light stood in the distance. The large stone structure of Fort Gorges sat prominently in the bay, drawing Fred's eye.

"Thanks for seeing me today. I know you're busy. I just have a few follow-up questions," said Clark.

"Go for it."

"You provided us with a list of the mooring-ball and slip rentals for the summer. Some of those folks have rented their piece of the waterfront for years, we noticed."

"Yes, many people hang on tightly to the few we have. Causes a big problem for the newcomers."

"I'll bet. Do you also keep track of whether people use their ball or slip on any given summer?"

"No, not really. Over the years there's been talk up in Augusta to limit a person's time on a rental or delete the accounts of those who don't actively use their rental. If they ever legislated to do one of those things, we'd have to keep track. As it is right now, we don't."

A summer renter circled their assigned mooring ball for the second time, prompting Fred to wonder whether they'd be able to hook the line. Inexperienced boaters often needed several passes to accomplish the tricky task.

"But do you have a good idea of who's coming and going?"

"Oh, sure. Informally we do. Of course. The two of us and our staff are here day in and out. We know everyone who's coming and going. Do you guys think the murderer came from down here and not up the coast?" Fred's Maine accent was thick with dropped *R*s.

Clark looked at the water and then the sky before speaking. "Yes. The Coasties have been investigating a series of fuel dumps just outside of the Portland Harbor. They seem to think the fuel dumps and murders are related."

"Interesting. Have you seen the price of fuel? Wicked expensive. Who in their right mind would dump the stuff? It's like liquid gold," said Fred.

"Seriously. The prices have gone through the roof. Considering the price of fuel, I'm thinking it must have been spilled by accident," said Clark.

A nail gun resumed its loud punching, causing Fred to step slightly closer to hear the detective. "I don't know about that. Most watercraft have refueling ports that need to be opened with a key when refilling. Opening the tank to refill is not something one would do by accident. No, the spillages out there aren't accidental. There's something else going on," he said.

"That was my thought too. But then again, what do I know about the sea? I'm a landlubber. All that rocking tends to make me sick."

"I felt the same way about forty years ago. Turns out, you do get used to it."

"Good to know in case I decide to get on one of those." Clark pointed at one of the large cruise ships berthed on the Portland waterfront. *The whole damned place would be better off without those cans pulling in,* thought Fred.

"Can you think of anything that struck you as odd this past summer? Anything different than in previous years?" asked Clark.

Fred rocked back and forth from his heels to toes. A little tick he picked up years ago. The rocking always grounded him when he pondered something.

"Now that I think about it, there is something. Randy's boat comes to mind."

"Randy owns which vessel?" asked Clark as he thumbed through the small notebook in his hand, reviewing his notes.

"He's a longtime lobsterman. Hell, he's been around for as long as I've been. Maybe longer. He owns the FV *Ginny*. But this summer he isn't here at all. He turned his boat over to a few new guys without saying a word about it."

"Would you have normally expected him to mention that he planned to rent out his boat or take the summer off?"

"Oh, sure. During the winter almost everyone has their boats up on chocks. It's the time to do repairs you can't get to in the summer. Only the desperate are out there in the winter for a measly offseason catch. He would have mentioned taking the summer off, something he's never done. Randy is the guy who is here first and leaves last. Always has been, for as long as I remember."

"Maybe he had a family emergency that took him away unexpectedly?" offered Clark.

"I don't think so. His mom got real ill a few years ago. When that happened, everyone knew about it and supported him and his family. The guys took turns pulling his traps, and the wives took turns cooking for Randy's entire extended family. Taking care of our own is something we do, without question."

"The new guys? On the . . ." Clark flipped pages and said, "FV *Ginny*?"

"They keep to themselves, come in late, leave early, unlike everyone else out here."

"Maybe they're just getting the hang of things? Or content to not make much money this summer?"

"That's the other odd thing," Fred said. "From the looks of it, they're the only ones making money."

"Why do you say that?"

Fred glanced toward the parking lot. The glistening truck sat there as usual. He jutted his chin toward the vehicle. "The flashy new truck, the new pots . . . you name it. They bought everything new. And then Chet, one of the guys down here, told me about an incident he had with one of the new guys. Chet told me that while he did his rounds, he accidentally clipped one of their pots. It happens. He offered to pay for the lobsters and the pot. One of the guys demanded more money than is customary and told Chet not to bother giving him the buoy or coordinates."

"Coordinates?"

"Yeah, so he could reset the trap. Lobstermen have a delicate balance out there. Placing a cut pot in the exact same spot guarantees peace."

"I see. And the man didn't care about the buoy or the location?"

"Exactly, like he didn't plan to reset the pot. It's odd because this time of year is make-it-or-break-it time out there. Winter's lean if those pots aren't full during the summer. I can't imagine why anyone would be okay with just trashing one of their pots."

"Do you think the new guys are maybe doing this as a hobby? Not a real business?"

"No. The cost of running the boat, not to mention renting it from Randy? No way. I mean, who would do that?" He thought about it for a second and added, "Maybe some rich asshole, but not these guys. They look like they're making money, not just enjoying it, if you get me."

"So you think they're making money some other way and don't care so much about the lobster pots?"

"Bingo," said Fred.

A cloud passed overhead, dimming the bright sunlight. Fred collected his thoughts and added, "There's also been a string of break-ins this summer, something that's never happened before."

"I haven't seen anything about break-ins down here, and I made an internal request to be notified of every call related to the waterfront. Did I miss something?"

"No, most lobstermen won't call the police. We tend to stick together and police our own. Most guys don't take kindly to getting cops involved in waterfront business."

"I see. Maybe they should start reporting things. It could make our investigation easier."

"Maybe, but I doubt anyone will."

"What do you mean by a string of break-ins?"

"Several lobstermen have reported that items have gone missing from their hold. Little things that cost a fortune to replace, like radios, knives. General gear. I've also heard that their traps are unusually empty for this time of year." A high pile of empty lobster crates sat near the water's edge, punctuating his point.

"Do they often see peaks and valleys in the supply of lobsters? In other words, could this just be an off summer for everyone?" asked Clark.

"Could be, but I don't think so. A few guys have said one trap would be empty, while one close by is full of lobsters. Usually when the population is low, every trap is low or empty. We've weathered that scenario before. Some guys took second jobs just to keep food on their tables. This is different."

"Are you thinking the same guys responsible for the break-ins could also be stealing from traps?"

"Ayuh, just no way of provin' it is all. One guy thinks it's all related. The dead lady in Portland, the dead tourists, the break-ins—all of it," said Fred.

"We got the guy who killed the lady in Portland. It can't be related."

"So you think. People down here ain't too sure. Everything is off," said Fred.

"'Off' isn't really something I can work with, but reporting crimes as they occur? That'd be a real help," said Clark.

"I get it, but ain't no one down here willing to talk to the cops. That's for sure." Fred looked out to see the summer hire tripping over his own feet on the pier. The kid was a mess.

"Can you think of anything else?"

"No, but if I do, I'll call you. I have your number inside the shed."

"Do you know the names of the guys renting the boat from Randy? I only have the names of the vessel owners per your list."

"No, I don't. They've been all tucked into themselves. I don't need the information for official business, so I haven't pushed the issue."

"Would be helpful if you did."

Fred nodded, knowing he had no intention of tangling with those guys.

"Hope you get whoever killed those tourists. It's really freaking out the waterfront community. If that ain't bad enough, then the lady turns up dead. Place is goin' to shit, if you ask me. A gosh-darn crime spree that's hurting everyone's wallet."

Fred stood for a moment, waiting for the detective to leave; then he grabbed his pack of reds and shook one out. Although it felt childish to hide his habit from anyone other than his waterfront family, he chose to do so anyway. In this town, one never knew who knew who. The last thing he needed would be for his wife to get wind of the fact that he'd never quit smoking, like he'd promised. He took a long drag and exhaled an extended plume of whitish-gray smoke. Quitting could wait until tomorrow.

Chapter 33

Kari swiped through her emails on her device as she waited for Ahmed to be brought into the counsel room. The stale air in the room felt heavy and oppressive. Finally, the door opened and a sheriff appeared. "You ready for him?"

"Yep, sure am. Thanks."

The sheriff led Ahmed into the room and then paused to look at Kari. She said, "The cuffs aren't needed. Thanks."

Ahmed sat down. "Hi, ma'am. Thanks for seeing me," he said.

"I'm happy to come down anytime you have questions or think of something that could assist with your defense. I had planned to visit with you to update you on a few developments, so this works out nicely. What's up?"

"There's no need to update me, ma'am. I'm pleading guilty."

Shocked, Kari put her pen down and asked, "What happened? Every time we've spoken, you reiterated your innocence. Why the sudden change?"

Ahmed teared up, then slowly wiped his glistening eyes with the back of his hand.

"I can't continue to put my family through this. I'm going to be convicted anyway. I just need to get this over with. It's been terrible for them."

She wondered whether Ahmed had heard about Jimmy's crap. Maybe he no longer trusted her lawyering abilities.

"I know it's been extremely difficult on them. They're really worried about you, but they also support you one hundred percent. I've had the chance to speak with your mom on numerous occasions. She's a lovely woman. And her food is amazing."

Ahmed smiled softly and said, "Yeah, that's my mom. She feeds the people she loves. If she's taken to feeding you, that means she really cares about you."

He sniffled back mucus in a loud snort, then took a deep inhale of the stale air as he rubbed his hands vigorously against his pant legs.

"What makes you so sure you'll be convicted? I have a few things we need to discuss that can create a decent defense," she said.

"My mom said she talked to some guy who told her I shouldn't be bothered with any of this. Just have him plead guilty, he told her. It would save everyone the money and time."

Great. The legend of Jimmy Sharpe strikes again.

"Well, the decision to change your plea is entirely yours. I'll support you no matter what. However, I'm uncomfortable with the idea that someone talked to your mom about your case. Do you know the person? Was it maybe someone from the Somali community, or from the navy?"

"No, she said it was some lawyer. He claimed he worked with the state and knew all about the case. He really scared my mom and probably everyone else."

"Did she mention his name?"

Kari leaned toward Ahmed, eager to hear his answer. Another attorney speaking with the family of her client? Unacceptable. Her stomach tightened at the thought of someone infringing on her work. A territorial instinct rooted in fairness and the bar rules of professional responsibility.

"Yes, but I can't remember. It was something sort of easy too. It's like right on the tip of my tongue."

Kari thought about it for a moment. Who would want him to plead guilty? Who could possibly benefit from a speedy resolution to a potential trial?

"Did she speak with an attorney named Bob Parker?"

"That's it! He's the guy trying to keep me locked up. That's what he told her. He said he knew everything about the case, and I would be found guilty anyway, so why bother? It's just a waste of money," said Ahmed excitedly.

Kari's fists balled, open and closed. Open and closed. Trying to calm herself. She let out a long exhale. The inexperienced assistant attorney general had been assigned to prosecute the murder case. She thought carefully about what to say next.

"Attorney Parker had no business speaking with your mom. It is highly unethical for him to have done so. There's no way you should listen to a desperate, inexperienced prosecutor trying to make his life easier by making this case and you go away. Do you understand me?"

"Thank you, ma'am. I felt like no one believed in me anymore. None of us wanted to listen to the guy, but my family is scared about using our community's money. Saying all of this is a waste of time and money really hit." His voice cracked with emotion. He ran a shaky hand over his head.

"I understand how that would strike a chord. Defending yourself is not a waste of money. I believe in you, and so does your family. We're all behind you and will work as hard as possible to get you out of here."

Ahmed looked down, and a sliver of sunlight poked through the small, grimy reinforced window, touching his cheek. He softly sobbed.

Through his sobs he whimpered, "I just wanted to help her. I didn't do anything."

"What? What do you mean you tried to help? Who? Irene Simmons? The victim?"

Ahmed had maintained that he never saw Ms. Simmons on the morning of the murder. He claimed that he'd walked through the trail as always, but saw nothing, not a body or another soul.

Kari slammed her open palm on the table. "Ahmed! Get it together and tell me what you mean! I'm trying to keep your ass out of jail. You just thought of telling me this? Whatever this is?" she said.

Her body temperature rose as she lost control. Ahmed shrank away.

"Yes, the dead lady. I saw her that morning. I didn't want to tell you. I was worried you would think I did it."

"What the hell? You lied to me? Lovely."

He stared down at the table, tracing his finger in one of the numerous dimples on its surface. His cheeks reddened with embarrassment.

She needed to re-collect herself. Anger had a way of blinding her, making it hard to do her job. *Breathe, Kari,* she told herself. *Breathe and let it pass.*

After a moment, she said, "I need you to be one hundred percent honest with me. Otherwise, there's no way for me to help you. Do you understand?"

He nodded his head slightly. The razor-sharp military-style haircut had grown since they first met, removing the last indication of his profession. At least the bruises had healed.

She ran her hand through her hair, flipped the page of her legal pad, and said, "Okay. Let's start over. Tell me *everything* about that morning. And this time, do not leave anything out." Her words came out snarkier than expected, but at this point she didn't care.

"Yes, ma'am. I will."

He grabbed a few more tissues and blew his nose loudly before continuing.

"I left my mom's house and walked through the back trail to my car. That's when I saw her legs."

"By 'her legs,' you mean Irene Simmons's legs?"

"Yes, but I didn't know her. I just saw the old-looking legs sticking out from the brush and figured an old person toppled over. It used to happen to my auntie all the time before she died. She would just sit there, unable to get up."

He maintained eye contact as he spoke. A first for him.

"So you see her legs, and then what did you do?"

"I thought she needed help. I had no idea she was dead! I called out to her and then leaned over to see if I should call for an ambulance. You aren't supposed to move old people when they fall. We learned that the hard way with my auntie. My dad fractured her arm pulling her off the ground. They break very easily."

"Ms. Simmons wasn't exactly old and frail." Kari jotted down notes as he spoke.

"I guess, but her legs looked old. Anyway, I knelt and nudged her shoulder, but she didn't budge. I even tried to shake her to wake her up. Then I moved her head around and saw the blood. It was so gross! The blood and creamy stuff . . . I can't get the image out of my head. Not to mention the smell. Worst damned thing I ever smelled."

"Then what did you do?"

"I freaked out. I'd never seen so much blood. As I looked at her closer, I noticed the bruising on her face and realized that something bad had happened. Like maybe someone attacked her and cracked her head open. So . . . so I ran!"

"You ran? Why?" What sort of person would just run? His story made no sense. She wondered whether he'd just lied to her again.

"Ma'am, I'm a Black kid living in a small, very white community. The last thing I wanted to do would be to get myself involved with a white lady getting hurt. I worried they'd suspect me, so I bolted. Lots of good that did me." He shook his head and lowered his gaze, absentmindedly snapping his fingers.

Kari considered his story. It was plausible, just like the last version he told her. "Was she dead when you saw her?" she asked.

"I don't know for sure, ma'am, but she wasn't answering and looked like no one was home."

Kari jotted down a quick note as he spoke. "I'll ask you again: How did the smears of blood get on your shoes and pants? This time you need to be honest with me."

"I've wondered the same thing. All I can guess is that when I touched her, I must have gotten gook on me and didn't know it. Other than that, I have no idea."

"Okay, show me what you did when you touched her."

He stood and moved around the table, where he found a little more space to maneuver in the cramped room. Then he squatted down all the way to the ground. His backside must have grazed the back of his calves as he took the position. Kari's astonishment that he'd been able to bend like that must have registered on her face.

"Yes, I'm flexible. We sit on the floor at home. Most Westerners sit on chairs. We don't. I think it keeps me limber. My family too." He moved forward. "I leaned over to touch her shoulder, like this. Once I got a good look at her face, I freaked out and stood up. I bolted out of there as fast as possible."

"Did you see anyone else?"

"No, ma'am, but that wasn't too unusual. The trail is usually quiet in the morning. What was unusual were the legs."

Kari considered everything and said, "Did you hear anything out of place?"

The sailor rubbed the side of his face and looked to the ground. Then he added, "I did hear something different that day. I didn't think anything of it until you just asked. There was some sort of loud rumble, like a big truck engine. It sounded like it was taking off real fast."

"You heard that when you were still near Ms. Simmons?"

"Yes, ma'am."

"Interesting."

"Why, ma'am? It could have come from anywhere."

"True, but Betsy Roth's neighbor Meg Shore said she heard what she described as a loud truck taking off. She only managed to see a large silver pickup with a NAVY bumper sticker as it sped out of the neighborhood. No license plate or physical description of the driver."

"Crap. If the lady was killed, that could have been the guy!"

For the first time since she met him, a flash of hope crossed Ahmed's smooth face. Although she wanted to avoid giving him false hope, she knew the existence of a second person at the scene would go a long way to explain what had happened to the victim. Or at least cast enough doubt in the minds of jurors to free him.

"I don't know the neighbor, but I do know Betsy Roth," he continued. "My mom made me walk her home from our store for years. She's a nice lady. Ancient too."

Remarkably, he harbored no resentment for the woman who had provided the only eyewitness identification of him. The sole reason for his arrest. Did he understand?

"Yes, she is. She's also the only eyewitness in the case. Her testimony, combined with the blood, put you in here."

"I can't see how she could place me at the scene. She can't see the nose on her face. But she does know me, and I do walk behind her house all the time."

Kari spent the remainder of their time together discussing what she'd learned from Dr. Jesper. Once they finished, Kari reached for the button to call the guards to escort Ahmed back to his cell. Before she could press the button, he said, "Ma'am, um, would you please talk to my mom for me? Tell her the other attorney doesn't know what he's talking about? It would mean a lot to me."

He focused on his feet. Deep lines carved an eleven between his soft chocolate eyes.

"Of course I will."

Kari walked away from their meeting with renewed vigor to defend Ahmed. His explanation of the events made sense. She needed to run down the other vehicle, find someone else to fill his cell. But first she needed to speak with Hani. Damage control, once again. Then she planned to have it out with Bob Parker.

Chapter 34

Hani flipped through the worn pages of their family photo album. Ahmed's baby pictures were scrambled, with this first tooth loss alongside his first day of school. She vowed, not for the first time, to better organize the jumble of photos that captured their lives together.

The soft gurgling of boiling water caught her attention. She made chai every day for customers of Khadra. The small back room became kitchen, community room, and, on the days she worked without Omar, a space for women to relax together.

Pots of lentils simmered with cardamon, onions, and garlic. She rotated her wooden spoon in each of the fragrant dishes, ensuring they cooked perfectly.

Glancing toward the store, she wondered whether anyone would come today. Maybe she was making food and chai only for their family. After Ahmed's arrest, the community had showered the family with support. However, little by little, their generosity had waned, and so had their willingness to visit.

Returning to the small wooden table, a picture of Ahmed caught her gaze. She caressed the photo, turning it in her hand to see the day, although she knew it well. His second-grade picture. Missing teeth, a bright smile. The world in front of him.

How could this have happened? Anxiety tightened in the pit of her stomach. She stiffened in the chair, feeling alone.

The male attorney had called her about the case, claiming Ahmed's defense would be nothing but a waste of money and time. Disbelief followed by searing anger mingled with her already confused emotions. She wondered why Kari took their money for nothing. Then the news of her family had broken. She and Omar had sat in their cramped kitchen, watching the small television as they'd shared a simple breakfast. "What sort of a person is she?" had been all he'd said.

The front door chimed, bringing her back to the present.

"Hello . . ."

Hani knew the voice.

"Kari, what brings you to us today?" she said. Her tone formal, cool.

She navigated from the back room to stand behind the counter. This was the first time she chose not to embrace Kari. She closed her scarf tightly around her shoulders, as she would do if a man or stranger entered the store.

"I just finished meeting with Ahmed, and I need to discuss a few things with you. Do you and Omar have a minute?"

Hani's eyes darted to the closed front door. Omar thought they needed to stay away from Kari because of her family's alcohol abuse. Alcohol was considered haram, forbidden. Associating with those who used it excessively would bring even more shame to the family. Scared, she didn't want to defy Omar but desperately wanted answers.

"Yes. Please come back, Kari. Omar isn't here today, but we can talk," said Hani as she motioned for Kari to follow her into the back room.

Without asking, Hani poured two steaming cups of chai and set a plate of nuts for them to share on the small wooden table.

Hani took a sip of her chai and spoke softly. "We have decided it is best for him to tell the truth." Her gaze remained fixed on the small table, never looking directly at Kari. Kari had betrayed them. She'd stolen the money the community had raised for Ahmed's defense. Hani tugged at her scarf. She eyed the entrance to the store, praying to Allah that no one would see them talking.

"Yes. He told me he wanted to change his plea. I discouraged him from doing so. He did nothing wrong and deserves to defend himself. There's new evidence to suggest . . ."

Hani's eyes darted to Kari. Was she just doing this to take their money? The sharp tendrils of anger gripped her spine. She sat ramrod straight in the little wooden chair.

"No. This ends now."

"I see. You probably heard the news of my brother's arrest. Maybe that's what's happening here? Yes, my family has problems. We've always had problems. However, that doesn't mean I'm not an excellent, experienced lawyer who can help your son. I believe in him. He's innocent and doesn't deserve to be locked up. Please allow me to help him."

The small timer chimed, prompting Hani to turn off one of the burners. Returning to the table, she said, "But the attorney said he is guilty and this is a waste of money. Why would he say that but to help us? He tried to warn us about you. About the case."

Hani gripped the silk of her red-and-gold blouse, waiting for an answer. Her trembling hand tightened around her cup of chai.

"Do you know his name? The attorney, I mean? Ahmed said it was Attorney Parker—is that correct?"

"I wrote it down. Let me get the paper."

The wooden bureau squeaked as she yanked open the drawer. She shuffled scraps of paper before finding the one she sought.

Hani handed Kari the scrap and said, "Attorney Parker." Hani's accented English made Parker sound like "Paaarker" as she elongated the first vowel in the name.

"I'm sorry he contacted you, Hani. He had no right to do so. Ahmed is innocent. I'm sure of it. He never hurt Ms. Simmons, and we'll prove it when the case gets to trial." She took a deep breath. "As for my family, I can't change my past. None of us can."

Hani peered into Kari's face, searching for truth. The attorney's eyes showed her desperation, her pain. To Hani she looked like a lost child.

Hani softened slightly and nodded. She desperately wanted to believe in Ahmed's innocence.

They spent the rest of the visit discussing the case. "You really believe in him?" Hani asked, hopeful in a way she hadn't been before.

"Absolutely. After all my years with different clients, I've learned to trust my gut. It's a simple case of being in the wrong place at the wrong time. The truth will come out at trial."

"Inshallah."

Hani relaxed slightly as they sat together. She believed in her son and in Kari. Despite Kari's horrible family. Maybe her family had been victims of the evil eye, the *nazar*? She shouldn't think such things but couldn't help herself. Only time would tell whether her trust had been misplaced.

As Kari prepared to leave, Hani said, "Let me pack some *sambusa* for you. I know how much you like them."

"Thank you. Those are quickly becoming my favorite late-night snack."

She closed the container, wrapped it tightly in a sack, and turned to Kari. "I trust you, *my Kari*. Help Ahmed. He needs you, and so do I."

Hani's voice quivered as she spoke. Kari stood and embraced her. Hani noticed that for the first time, Kari initiated a hug. She opened her arms to the embrace. The thick material of Kari's suit foreign to her touch, so accustomed to silk. Kari held Hani tightly, something she had never done. In the past, Kari's hugs had always felt distant and awkward. Today, something had changed.

"I will. You have my word."

They hugged for another second before parting. Hani watched her as she walked down the street, holding her *sambusa* and Ahmed's future in her hands.

Hani glanced around the tidy store as she returned to the back room. She needed a second cup of chai to fortify herself for the conversation she would have with Omar.

Chapter 35

Kari thumbed through Ahmed's file, looking for Attorney Parker's cell phone number. She'd bypass the office rigmarole to talk with him quickly. He'd given Kari his cell phone number and joked that the number might come in handy if her client decided to come clean. The prick. He'd intended to influence Ahmed the entire time. She wondered whether this had been a consistent practice of his. Did he railroad every opposing party?

"Ms. Sharpe . . . why am I not surprised to hear from you. Let me guess, your client finally realized the jig is up?" said Parker.

Kari's cheeks flamed red with anger. Stay professional. Even with this jackass. She mindlessly turned his card between her fingers.

"No, and nice try, you unprofessional piece of crap."

Parker softly chuckled in the background. The man lived life knowing his deep, old family connections ensured he could do the most unethical things without repercussions. Kari carried the weight of the Sharpe family reputation, which provided the opposite experience in the world. *And* she was a woman. Kari earned every break, building her reputation one step at a time.

"I have no idea what you're talking about."

Soft jazz played in the background of his office. A metallic tapping mingled with the music as though the smug jerk played in tune with the beat. He didn't seem to have a care in the world.

"You called my client's mother to influence Ahmed to plead guilty. You should know better. That was easily the most unethical thing I've ever seen an attorney do."

"Who? I really don't know what you're talking about," he said.

"Cut the shit, Parker. Hani Dihoud. You know very well she's the mother of Youseff Ahmed. You called her to have an ex parte communication with my client."

"Ms. Dihoud? Hmm . . . You mean the lady that runs the little ethnic store?"

"You know damn well that's who I'm talking about, and you know what you did."

"Oh, sure. I called over there to see if I could try some of their cuisine. Dee-lish. Anyway, she and I just had a friendly little chat about the case. I can't help it if she went to her son and told him she wouldn't pay for a no-win defense? Besides, Kari, we both know the bar rules only prevent me from speaking with your client, not his family. Not my problem that Mommy talks to the kid."

She imagined Parker with the smug smile of a wealthy, entitled person.

"They've been alerted to your despicable behavior and are now wise to your tactics. They also know that you barely deserve your bar card, given how many ethical violations you've racked up. Not to mention failing the bar several times." She paused for a moment, then added, "If I get wind of any other ex parte communications, I'll not only report you to the overseers, but also to the attorney general. And I'll file a motion for Rule 11 sanctions. As part of my motion, I'll request that you be removed from the case and that a Chinese wall be put in place around you at the attorney general's office to insulate the case from your grubby hands. Do we understand each other?"

"You wouldn't dare!" He sounded more scared than casual. Bingo. Finally, a shift Kari had waited for.

"Try me. I will not have my client or his family intimidated by you or anyone else."

"If that's the case, then you can kiss your little career goodbye. I'll make sure you and your drunk brother never work in this town again. Who knows? Maybe all of you Sharpes are drunks."

She stood abruptly at the veiled threat to spread lies about her sobriety. "Here's the difference between us, asshole. I started at the bottom and worked my way up. I'm more than capable of doing it again. If your little escapades ruin your career, good luck rebuilding. Even your country club connections won't want to touch someone with this serious of an ethical violation, and we both know it. So don't bother threatening me. I'm not afraid of you. *You* should be afraid of *me*."

Parker's only reply came in the form of a soft click when he disconnected the call.

Chapter 36

Kari pulled up to the home Irene Simmons had shared with her sister, Samantha. She had delayed the uncomfortable meeting for as long as possible. Samantha, the victim's only remaining family, had no reason to speak with her and might flatly refuse.

The tidy Cape Cod–style shingled home sat on the end of a dead-end street. Each of the homes on the eight-house street boasted a large one- or two-acre lot. Many such neighborhoods existed in Maine. The large idyllic yards drew people from New York and Boston to the state, seeking the quiet space Maine offered.

An older woman answered the door shortly after she rang. "Hello?"

Kari knew her face from somewhere but couldn't place it. Then the woman said, "Kari? Kari Sharpe?"

"Yes, but I'm so sorry. You look familiar, but I can't place you."

The woman laughed heartily and said, "No worries. I'm what they call a 'super recognizer.' They tested me and everything. Turns out I can recall faces better than most. It's a gift. Well, not much of a gift, truth be told, but I'll take it. Came in handy when I taught middle school."

"Oh my gosh, Ms. Simmons! I was in your seventh-grade math class. Of course! Now I recognize you."

"Please come in, Kari. Keeping the door open is letting out all my flies."

Kari walked into the neat home. The hardwood floors gleamed with a fresh coat of polish. The sparse decor had a pleasant, uncluttered, clean feel. Even the air seemed fresher than outside in the spotless home.

"Thank you," said Kari. She flipped off her shoes and padded across the floor, following Ms. Simmons.

"How are your brothers? I taught them too. I think I taught half of Maine!" Ms. Simmons asked the question without a hint of malice, as though genuinely curious.

"You probably have. Jimmy is fine. He's been lobstering for years now. He has his own boat and a small seasonal crew to help."

Is it possible she hadn't seen the news?

"That's a terrific accomplishment. Jimmy was always a nice boy."

Kari paused, unsure of how to tell her that Doug had been killed in a prison fight. She hadn't planned on divulging any details about her life to Ms. Simmons or anyone else. Her eyes darted from the floor to the wall and back. She shifted in her seat, uncomfortable.

Ms. Simmons must have seen Kari's strain and interjected, "Can I offer you anything?"

"Sure. I'd love a drink. Water is fine, thank you, Ms. Simmons."

Turning the conversation away from Doug eased her slightly. The last thing she needed would be to explain Doug's sad ending and Jimmy's latest round of self-destruction.

"Oh, please, call me Samantha. We aren't in school anymore."

Samantha led them to the kitchen table and turned to bring over drinks. Kari slid one of the wooden chairs out from the table and took her seat.

"What brings you to visit me? It can't be a social call after all these years."

"First, I'd like to say how sorry I am for Irene's passing. The way she died, so suddenly and violently, no one deserves that. It must have been a real shock," Kari said gently.

"Yes, my sister and I were very close. She lived in the little flat above the garage. We liked to be together but also needed time apart. This gave us the best of both worlds." Samantha looked down toward the table and lifted her head to glance out the kitchen window. She mindlessly produced a tissue and dabbed her soft eyes. The pain was so evident and raw in the way she turned the frayed tissue, dabbing and grasping.

"Do you work with the police?" she asked softly.

"No, er . . . Samantha. I'm an attorney and represent Mr. Ahmed. He's the man currently charged with Irene's murder."

Samantha's eyes quickly cut into Kari.

"I know exactly who he is. I don't mean to be rude, Kari, but you can leave right now. I have nothing to say to you or anyone else trying to get that vicious animal off the hook." Samantha sounded forceful, certain, and mad as hell as she stood. She pushed her chair under the table, banging with a loud clatter. The table shook, nearly toppling Kari's water glass.

"I fully understand why you'd feel that way, Samantha, really. But I'm not trying to get him off the hook. Instead, I want to find the man who killed Irene. Please hear me out. Then if you want me to leave, I certainly will."

Samantha broke eye contact and gazed out the large bay window. She lifted a wobbly hand to sip from her water glass. Strain contorted her features as she considered her options. Kari remained seated, hoping to not be kicked out. Finally, the woman turned back to Kari.

"Okay, Kari. Fine. I'll give you just a few minutes for old times' sake because you were a good kid from a hard situation. You've done very well for yourself, I might add." Samantha folded her arms tightly across her chest. She stared at Kari and waited.

"Thank you. After law school I joined the navy as an attorney. That's my connection to Ahmed. He's also an active duty member of the navy. He's based out of Bath Iron Works."

"I see."

Samantha sat stiffly, listening to Kari with a chilly reserve. Neither the laser focus of her stare nor her tight posture shifted as Kari spoke. Kari turned her pen over in her fingers. A nervous habit.

"The morning of Irene's death, Ahmed walked the trail behind your home, to his parked car. He's very close to his family and comes to Portland on the weekends to be with them instead of staying in Bath with his shipmates. His entire family and the whole Somali community are behind him in this matter. They believe in his innocence, and so do I." Kari paused to let her words sink in. "He's a smart guy, a good sailor, and comes from a decent, hardworking family who encouraged him to join the navy in service to our country. In fact, he was hand selected for the BIW job on a precommission ship. This is something the navy reserves only for the best of the best."

Kari's chair creaked as she shifted. The weight of Samantha's gaze had started to unnerve her.

"So why did he kill my sister?" she demanded forcefully.

"I don't believe he did. However, as I mentioned, he was there that morning and saw your sister on the ground. Ahmed stopped to render aid. He said that when he saw her legs, he thought an elderly woman needed help to get up. He kindly knelt by her and checked on her."

"Oh . . ."

"He quickly realized that she was deceased and panicked. Instead of calling for an ambulance, as he thought he might have to do, he ran to his car and drove north to Bath."

"Why would he panic like that? Maybe she could have been saved if he'd just called 911!" Samantha stood and crossed the room to the refrigerator. She yanked a picture of Irene off the front of it and threw it at Kari, saying, "So we don't forget who she was!"

"Thank you. I haven't forgotten, and yes, I agree. He should've called for help. But we'll never know if Irene could have been saved, or if he was right, that she'd already passed. The coroner placed the time of death before his arrival. He ran because he knows that as a young Black man, people would assume he did it."

Samantha turned away from her. Disgust carved the contours of her face. The soft chime of a clock and music from the kitchen radio filled the silence.

"He's right. Everyone around here thinks he's guilty. I never understood racism. All of God's children are the same to me. That's why I loved teaching so much. They all deserve the same treatment.

Since this started, people have been saying the unkindest things about the Blacks in Portland . . . the Africans."

"His parents came here from Somalia, but he was born here. He's as American as the two of us."

Samantha's arms uncrossed as her shoulders dropped slightly. She looked up at Kari with gentle eyes, nodded, and said, "Poor Irene. Just lying there like that. And the Somali boy skewered by everyone. Including me. The whole thing is awful. Who could have done such a thing?"

Samantha softly sobbed, wiping the tears from her deeply lined gray eyes.

"We don't know. However, a witness places another person near the scene around the same time. Said witness saw a silver Tundra with Maine plates and a NAVY bumper sticker leaving the area near the trail."

"That could be the guy who did it," Samantha said with a glimmer of hope.

"Do you know anyone who drives a truck like that?"

"No one comes to mind," she said.

"Whoever drove the truck could be the person who killed Irene. Do you know of anyone who Irene feared or who gave her trouble?"

"No, like I told the police, Irene never ruffled any feathers. People liked her. She had a small circle of friends and mostly kept to herself."

Kari had read the statement Samantha had provided to the police, which answered most of the questions she'd just asked. However, she wanted to keep the woman talking to open her up.

"Did she like her job at Bath Iron Works?" asked Kari.

"She loved her job at BIW. She was a veteran too. Served in the navy. She eventually got out because she missed Maine. BIW was the closest thing to the navy she could find up here. Hold on, I'll show you something."

Samantha rose from the table and went into the adjoining family room. She picked up one of the few items on the clean fireplace mantel and returned to Kari.

She handed over the photo. "Here she is with a couple of navy pals. She hated this picture, but just look at her. She's so beautiful in that uniform. Despite her protests, I kept it up there."

Kari took the picture. A young, vibrant, uniformed Irene smiled at the camera. She'd been flanked by two uniformed men, who'd linked arms with her.

"I agree. She looks great. Who're the men?"

"That's why she hates looking at the photo. She dated the guy on the left. Didn't end well. I guess she just didn't want the reminder. I don't know what her problem with him was. He seemed like such a nice man."

"I can appreciate not wanting to see a former boyfriend."

Irene's ex-boyfriend had unique facial features. His wide nose and small, squinty eyes gave his face a birdlike quality. Not an unattractive man but not good looking either.

"Did she have anything unusual going on at work? Anything that stressed her or bothered her?"

"She *had* seemed stressed at work. She was working on something big, she said. I have no idea what she was talking about. You navy people speak using more letters than words at times. It all went over my head."

"There are times we don't know what we're talking about either. The acronyms can get a little out of control."

"Would you like to see her place? The police already went through it, but you can have a look too."

"I would really appreciate it. Thanks for the offer." Kari grabbed her empty water glass, then deposited it in the spotless kitchen sink as they passed.

Samantha yanked open the door to the garage. The walls of the room contained shelving of various heights that housed garden tools. Another area had an assortment of small wooden hanging drawers.

Samantha, noticing Kari's attention had been drawn to the unusual drawers, said, "I saw a TikTok video about garage organization. The woman uses the little drawers to store various nails and screws."

"Ingenious. I love it." Kari's eyes moved quickly over the area.

"Me, too, but especially because it kept my Rick busy all winter making the drawers!"

They walked through the garage to an outside staircase at the back of the house. The staircase led to the flat's entrance. A burst of fresh air greeted them as they went outside.

"I always told Irene we needed a fireman's pole for her. Keeping the stairs clear in the winter was always a real challenge." They walked the creaky wooden stairs to the second-story entrance.

Samantha unlocked the small knob. Neither the lock nor the door had the potential to stop anyone who might want to enter the flat. In New York City, Kari had had several dead bolts securing her heavy door, and she'd never felt safe.

"Take your time. Just lock up when you're finished. And sorry for the staleness of the place. I haven't been up here to clean in a couple of weeks. After Irene died, I had been cleaning once a week, but it has been hard on me to be in here. Eventually, I'll need to pack everything. Irene would have wanted her things to go to a charity."

"Thank you, Samantha, for everything. I can't imagine how difficult this must be for you. I appreciate you hearing me out and allowing me into Irene's space," said Kari.

"Everyone deserves the benefit of the doubt," she said with a wink. Kari watched as the spry woman walked quickly down the faded wooden staircase. *She knew about Jimmy. Of course she knew.*

The stale flat contained a simple kitchen, small living room, and a single bedroom with an en suite bathroom. The furniture and appliances stood in desperate need of replacement. Irene's ancient bathroom tile and fixtures must not have been updated since the seventies, judging by their sky blue color.

Kari didn't need to spend too long in the flat. She mostly searched for anything that might give her a clue as to who would have wanted to hurt Irene. The police had already visited the residence. Their report included a search, but no list of items seized. Kari wanted to become more familiar with the victim as part of her defense preparation.

She walked past the couch, running her fingers across the handmade crochet throw blanket. Then she went to Irene's bedroom. She picked up one of the displayed perfume bottles for a whiff. Although lived in, the apartment seemed barely used. Everything placed in just the right location. Perhaps Samantha had cleaned her sister's apartment but didn't want to admit it?

After a few minutes of quietly looking over the deceased woman's lifetime belongings, Kari left the small flat, locking the door behind her.

"Hey, Kari!" yelled Samantha. Kari had reached her vehicle and almost didn't hear Samantha's call.

"I'm all set up there. I locked up. Thanks again!" she yelled to Samantha.

"I'm going to open the garage door. I want you to have something," she shouted across the street.

That was odd. The garage door opened slowly, creaking its protest. Samantha navigated around her sedan with a navy seabag. All navy personnel kept a seabag packed with an extra uniform and toiletry essentials. The bag served as a quick pack in the event a crisis required a speedy deployment. Kari maintained hers to this day.

"Maybe you can bring this back to the navy. I have no use for old uniforms, and I'm sure Goodwill doesn't either."

She handed Kari the heavy, overstuffed bag.

"Sorry about the combination lock. I don't know the code."

"No worries. I can get someone to snap off the lock. Do you mind if I look at the contents before I bring it to the ship?"

"I don't care at all. You can keep anything in there if you want."

"Thanks, Samantha. I'll see it gets a good home."

Kari lugged the heavy seabag back to her car. Maybe the contents of the bag would shed more light on Irene. Her apartment certainly gave no clues to the identity of her killer. She slammed the car door, tugged on her seat belt, and drove away.

Chapter 37

Ron Baker took a luxuriously long drag on his cigarette, then sipped his black coffee. He drank from the same stained plastic coffee mug he'd used in the navy. The mug, like many other things from the navy, would never leave him. It served as a reminder of his twenty-year military career. He felt like a god when he put on the chief's uniform. It had given him satisfaction to see his underlings scramble for scraps of the approval he had no intention of giving. He'd wielded his senior enlisted rank like a sword against those in his command, continuing the practice even as a civilian defense contractor.

Like so many before him, he knew a position with a defense contractor enabled him to leverage his naval experience in a lucrative second career. Bath Iron Works had scooped him up faster than he had expected. Lucky, too, because he would have chased Irene Simmons to Maine anyway. A job just made things easier.

Although his position at Bath Iron Works allowed him to utilize the skills and knowledge he had gained over his career, working among so many civilians grated on him. The lack of discipline shown by his coworkers annoyed him to no end. The fact that he no longer had the power to punish them galled him. At times he thought several people in the office would benefit from a good swift kick in the head.

He enjoyed the last few exhales of his second cigarette during the break. As a civilian, the smoking area never failed to bring him a moment of rest. However, smoking on board various ships he'd been assigned had been a different experience. Half the crew smoked. The smoking area presented the opportunity for the sailors to pester him. The problem never repeated itself in his current position, because few of his colleagues at BIW smoked. Something about it being bad for one's health. He had never cared, preferring today's enjoyment over the risk of future illness.

Returning to the break room, he removed the lid from his plastic mug and refilled it. The steaming contents would keep him awake through the next string of useless meetings. Civilians loved nothing more than holding meetings for the sole purpose of crowing about their performance. During these times he chose to remain silent unless someone directly spoke to him. His wall of silence had been the only thing preventing him from unleashing a steady stream of choice words about whatever idiotic topic they flapped on about.

He knew keeping quiet also prevented him from being tasked with yet another to-do item. The navy taught him to "Never Again Volunteer Yourself," a maxim he adhered to at all costs. A clipboard, scowl, and harried walk worked wonders to prevent coworkers from approaching him in the corridors with questions or assignments.

He settled back into the measly cubical BIW had assigned to him. Most of the BIW workforce suffered the indignity of cubical "offices," something he'd grown to like. The vantage point from his desk allowed him to look over the sea of his shitbag colleagues. He'd even been able to watch Irene Simmons most of the day, while she tried not to notice.

The inbox on the corner of his desk teemed with new arrivals. Someone had been busy while he stood outside in his "second office." Probably Rainey. She never left him alone, always tasking him with nonsense that never amounted to anything. At times he found himself fantasizing about beating the shit out of her. He relished the thought of knocking her flat on her back and stomping on her slack-jawed face until he erased the stupid look off it.

Another few years and he could retire from this place and enjoy two retirement incomes, one from the navy and the second from BIW.

Time couldn't pass quickly enough. No need to engage in violence, he told himself.

His device buzzed in his pocket. He yanked it out and glanced at the caller ID. Another jerk to contend with.

"What is it? I'm busy," he barked.

"Are we on for tonight?" The gruff-sounding man was unfazed by Ron's tone.

Ron looked around to be sure no one was nearby. "Maybe. It's the best I can do for now."

"What the hell? We have—"

Ron pressed the red hang-up button on his device. They could argue later. Right now he had something he needed to take care of.

Chapter 38

Mack circled the streets of Portland, looking for a parking spot. Kari had asked him to stop by when he had a chance, to crack a lock on some sort of bag she'd obtained from the victim's sister. Finally, he found a free spot. A little tight for his Buick, but he would make it work. Desperation had a way of improving his driving skills. He had a busy day in front of him and hoped Kari's issue wouldn't take long.

"Hello? Anyone home?" he yelled as he walked in.

The office was empty. He waited a few more seconds, then looked at the multiline phone on Ruth's desk. A blinking light on Kari's line indicated her use of an extension. Mack hoped Ruth had taken the day off as a mental health day. Kari tended to be a handful at the office as she cranked out documents. Ruth complained about it all the time. The poor woman probably needed a break.

He walked into the still conference room. A large, overstuffed green duffel bag sat on top of the table where Kari had left it for him. The rectangular bag opened only on the short end. The opening had several metal grommets that threaded through a ring, enabling the owner to secure the bag's contents with a Master padlock. Easy to break.

He rotated the rough bag for better access to the lock. The name Simmons was stenciled on the side.

"Hey, Mack, thanks for coming. I see you found the bag," said Kari.

He dropped the lock and turned toward Kari. She was dressed in jeans, a short-sleeve sweater, and a pair of slippers.

"I assume you aren't in court today or meeting a client?"

"No, and Ruth is out today, so I can really relax and enjoy the office. Hopefully she isn't out looking for another job. Thanks to Jimmy's little stunt, I'm now a pariah."

He let go of the bag to look at her. Poor kid looked worried. Again.

"Don't stress it. It'll blow over," he said, despite knowing better. Jimmy followed a predictable Sharpe family trajectory. Maybe in time Kari would get it. She couldn't help him, but she could help herself. "What do you expect to find in here?" Mack said, pointing at the seabag.

Her moist eyes moved from him to the bag and back. "Not sure. Probably a bunch of uniforms. Irene chose to store the bag in her sister's garage, not in her apartment, as most people might have. Weird."

"Maybe she lacked the space? This thing is a beast." He patted the bag with a loud thunk, thunk.

"Could be, but I don't know." She shrugged. "Everyone I know keeps their seabag in the back of a closet. Seeing the bag at the bottom of a closet tends to make people open it occasionally to refresh the items. Something about her leaving it in her sister's garage, even as a retired navy member, just doesn't feel right."

They both stood for a moment, staring at the dust-covered green bag. It looked filthy. "Looks like it was neglected, judging from the grime," said Mack.

"I thought so, too, but check out the top, where the lock is located. The rings are all clean, like . . ."

"Like someone had used it enough to keep garage dust from settling on them," Mack said.

"Yep, exactly what I thought."

Mack dug into his satchel for his bolt cutter. Kari held the lock in place for him to snap it off. The metal loop broke apart with a loud snap. Mack threaded the broken pieces out of the ring and opened the bag.

"And just like that, here we are. Let me know what you find. I need to hustle out of here. I'm following a potential thief for a very wealthy family. It could be a long, boring stakeout tonight, but I can't screw this up."

"Another wealthy family? That's great. Just don't get too busy to remember us little people!" said Kari.

"How could I forget you?" He smiled and winked.

Mack left Kari's office and hustled back to his car. Lugging the heavy tool bag into the hot midday sun made him sweat like a pig. Fortunately, part of his stakeout kit included deodorant, a toothbrush, and eye drops. All essentials. He might need to crack out the deodorant soon; otherwise he faced a long night of breathing in his own stench.

Chapter 39

Kari would finally get her hands on the contents of the seabag. She cracked her knuckles with anticipation. Maybe she'd find something useful for Ahmed's case?

She pried open the narrow opening and peered inside the musty interior. After jamming her hand into the bag, she pulled out several neatly pressed and folded uniforms. Irene had clearly been an overpacker. She'd been prepared for any shipboard occasion with the neatly pressed assortment of uniforms. Kari made a detailed inventory for Samantha.

After making note of the initial pile of uniforms, she stretched her slim arm into the long, dark bag. "Damn it. Why did they make the seabags like this? No one can get to the bottom. It's a ridiculous design," she muttered. Her hand blindly moved around the dark contours of the bag. Not feeling anything, she lit up the interior with her device's flashlight and peeked inside.

She spotted something yellow tucked between the folds of one of the pairs of sweatpants just beyond her reach. She held her breath from the stale stench of the bag and reached into its depths to grab the object. A yellow file folder.

Kari tore open the folder. Irene had hidden a thick stack of log documents with the BIW logo on each of them inside her seabag.

The various logs marked the date and time when an individual acquired the key for BIW's skiff. Various people had checked out the skiff over the four-month period preceding Irene's murder. Someone, presumably Irene, had circled one name in particular: Jesse Helm. Then she'd placed a letter *C* in the margin of each circled entry. Kari ran up to her office and ripped the puppy calendar off her wall, then ran back to the conference room. She circled each date on her own calendar, seeking a pattern. The circled entries happened twice a month, like clockwork, on the first and third Wednesday. Interesting. *What had Irene been looking at? Why the secrecy?*

One of Irene's responsibilities at BIW had been procurement. As part of her job, Irene had anticipated the needs of the office, ordering things one step ahead of a particular supply item running out. The Excel spreadsheet of her orders included everything from break room items to paper supplies. It also included a diesel fuel marine reorder log. She marked up the spreadsheet with various highlights and calculations. Her highlighted sections showed an increase in the quantity of fuel ordered for BIW. Kari compared the dates of the starred entries on the Excel document against the circled dates on the skiff sign-out log. Each order for fuel occurred approximately one week after the skiff had been signed out by Jesse Helm.

On a separate document, Irene had meticulously compared the increase in fuel usage to a baseline norm. She'd estimated that BIW ordered approximately 20 percent more fuel each week following Jesse Helm's use of the skiff. In addition, several weeks over the course of the summer exceeded the extra 20 percent usage, tipping the scales at an extra 40 percent of fuel needing to be replaced by the navy. Irene had been working on some sort of investigation involving the theft of fuel by Jesse Helm.

Kari wondered whether Irene's concerns had been taken seriously by her boss at BIW. Or had she even brought her notes to the attention of her supervisors? Perhaps Irene had been investigating the losses when she was murdered? Kari sat lost in her thoughts as she considered the implications of finding the logs. She needed to go to BIW for clarification.

"Hey ho! You home?" yelled Jimmy from the reception area.

Jimmy's familiar voice broke her concentration. She glanced toward the conference room door.

She'd been so engrossed in the documents she'd forgotten their lunch date. The first since Jimmy's very public relapse. From what she could tell, he had maintained his sobriety, for now. Even though she burned to ask him if he was drinking, she refrained. Countless Al-Anon meetings had schooled her to not ask an alcoholic whether they'd been drinking. They would never admit it.

"In here!" she yelled.

"Hey, sis," he said.

Jimmy kissed the top of her head softly as a greeting. She looked at him carefully. Searching his face for signs of drinking. His tired eyes, sagging jowls, and mottled face were nothing new. Par for the course as alcohol ravaged his body.

"What's all of this?" he asked.

"Irene's sister gave me her seabag to bring back to someone in the navy. I had Mack crack the padlock for me," she said, lifting her eyes to meet his momentarily.

"From the smell of this room, seems to me that Irene never opened that bag. I'm not sure how you can stand going through this stuff. Just shove all that dusty old crap back in and let's go have lunch. I'm starving." Jimmy bounced from one foot to the other as he spoke. Impatient.

"That's just the thing. She did go into the bag. She even hid a BIW file in there. I think it might hold the key to her murder."

"What do you mean?"

He sat next to her at the conference table, facing a window overlooking one of the working decks on the Portland waterfront.

"Look, she had all of this tucked into her sweatpants. Everything is dated as the four months preceding her death. Plus, she kept the seabag outside of her flat, in her sister's garage. As though she knew someone would search her apartment and wanted to make sure they never found the bag."

Jimmy rubbed his cheek, creating a scratchy sound on his stubble. Realization hit him. "So you're thinking whatever this is got her killed?" he asked.

"It could have. Yes, that's what I'm trying to figure out. Irene concealed the file. Why? The only reason I would hide something outside of my home is because I'm afraid someone might search my belongings. I'd want the item close, but not with me."

"Yep, especially if you needed to get into it frequently. Or maybe she tipped her hand, alerting the killer, then needed to make sure the evidence wouldn't be found and destroyed."

"Exactly. That someone could be our real murderer." Kari twirled a yellow highlighter between her fingers as she remained fixed on the logs. Then she picked up one of the logs and brought it close to review.

"I don't like any of this, sis. You need to just turn the evidence over to Clark and let the cops deal with it."

"No way I'd ever give this to Clark. He'd just ignore it. As far as he's concerned, they caught the kid. Just another Black kid who committed a horrible crime. End of story. They even have blood and an eyewitness, an ancient eyewitness, but still. No. He won't do a thing. I need to figure this out myself before I go to them."

"At least have Mack help you. If this is what got Irene Simmons murdered, you need to steer clear of it."

On some level Kari knew Jimmy's instinct to leave the mess to the professionals made a great deal of sense. She wanted to vigorously defend Ahmed, not get herself killed.

"Okay, you're right." She rolled her eyes and added, "For a change. But first I need you to help me make sense of this. I think she discovered someone had been stealing fuel from the shipyard. I just need you to look at this stuff and tell me if you agree."

She handed him the fuel order logs and the sign-out sheets. Jimmy carefully reviewed the documents and then brought his eyes back to hers.

"So what am I looking at?" he asked.

"Irene worked in procurement. She would have placed orders for everything, or at least most things, at BIW. The Excel sheets are orders for fuel."

"Oh, okay, I see it now. So she must have noticed something funky going on with her orders?" His eyes moved down the columns, searching for answers.

"Maybe. I really don't know. None of these numbers make sense to me beyond the labels. I'm trying to make the same connection that Irene had made."

She rubbed her temples. The dust from the old clothes had given her a terrible headache. The eyestrain she'd developed while reviewing the logs did not help her already pounding head.

Jimmy concentrated on the pages for a few moments and then said, "Oh shit! Look at this! She did figure something out. You're right!" He slapped the table with excitement before pushing the documents to her.

"Show me." Kari straightened her back again and flipped to a fresh page of her yellow legal pad.

"Okay, here are the fuel orders from four months ago. If you look down the line, you see roughly the same numbers. It's sort of like me. I always buy roughly the same amount of fuel for my lobster boat, because I take the same route each time I check traps."

Jimmy traced his finger down the column.

"Sure, just like a commuter who goes back and forth to work. They could probably estimate the costs of their commute based on the fuel usage."

"Exactly. But here you see a spike," he said.

He turned the Excel sheet around for Kari to see and then jabbed at one of the underlined entries with a pencil.

Kari leaned in. Her eyes focused narrowly on the line item. She let out a long exhale and sat back in her seat.

"So Irene started to notice a bump in how much fuel she had to order. Just as I suspected."

"Exactly. This seems like the first time the amount changed."

Kari carefully considered the figures and then said, "It almost looks like whoever did this started off slow and then gained speed. Look how the number starts to increase."

Jimmy took the Excel sheet from her outstretched hand and reviewed the entries again.

"Wow, almost like he wanted to see if anyone would notice," said Jimmy. "This is a ton of fuel, Kari. I don't even go through that much. What the hell was he doing? Selling it? Using it? For what? Daily trips to Nova Scotia?"

"I don't know, but I think Irene knew."

Jimmy shook his head, ran his fingers through his hair, and said, "All right. You're freaking me out. You have enough here. No need for you to do anything else. Turn it over to Clark. He might be an asshole, but even he can't refute math."

Her eyes moved from Jimmy to the logs and back.

"Maybe. But I'd like to put a little more meat on the bones of this thing before I turn it over. For some reason, Irene hadn't done it yet."

They both stared at the log, pages strewn across the table.

"Or maybe she confronted the person, and that's why she got killed?" Jimmy finally said.

"Yeah, I don't know. Either way, I need to understand this more. Otherwise I risk losing the opportunity to use this as part of Ahmed's defense."

"You remember those dead tourists? The ones killed on a sailboat here in the bay?" asked Jimmy.

"Sure. Why?"

"A few of the guys were talking and mentioned that when they found the husband's body, it was covered in diesel fuel. Almost like he fell into a slick or had been drenched before going into the water."

"I forgot about those two. You never know, maybe the stolen fuel somehow made it from Bath to Casco Bay, and the tourists saw something that got them in trouble," she said.

"This shit's getting too real, Kari. You need to give it to the cops. End of story." Jimmy shook his head, pushed away the papers, and leaned back.

Kari didn't want to deal with her brother's discomfort. "Let's get out of here," she said. "I'm going cross-eyed looking at this stuff."

She put Irene's file back into its file jacket, grabbed her notepad, and said, "Give me a minute. I'm going to store this in my safe upstairs."

She dashed up the short flight of stairs to her office. The tall burn-proof, locked file cabinet she used as a safe stood in her office. The rest of her fledgling firm lacked the space to accommodate the bulky cabinet. Clicking the lock closed, she felt satisfied the documents were secure.

"Ready?" she said to Jimmy.

He waited for her in the shabby, dated reception area of the firm. "You know, Kari, I just thought of something," said Jimmy.

"What's that?"

"The additional fuel would have taken a long time to pump out. If whoever did this had done so during the day, everyone would have seen it. Plus, they'd need to pump it into something or there'd be a parade of boats going to the refueling area."

"Crap, you're right. Maybe a bunch of people were involved?"

"Could be. I'm not sure how else to explain it."

Her stomach noisily growled at her as they stepped outside the office. The warm sunlight felt amazing on her skin. She knew Jimmy had a point. She needed to turn everything over to Clark. Get the cops involved. But first she'd poke around BIW.

Chapter 40

Turning into BIW, Kari decided to drive around the quasi-base before parking to meet with Irene's former supervisor. She had a few extra minutes before the meeting and thought an overview of the entire operation might make it easier for her to piece everything together.

She turned toward the water and searched the rows of parked cars until finally settling on an opening. Gazing across the lot to the water, she tried to find the marine refueling station. Many marinas had floating fuel pumps at the pier. Others used a raft near the marina. Boaters could then dock at the raft and dispense the amount they needed right into their fuel holds.

"Hello! Can I help you?"

She turned to see a young, tanned man approaching. He waved and jogged toward her.

"This is a secured area, ma'am. I'll have to ask you to please park in the visitors' lot."

She realized that her civilian clothing and lack of a work badge made her appear very out of place. Which she was.

"Hi, I'm Lieutenant Commander Sharpe. Sorry for the civilian clothes today. I had meetings in Portland requiring civies."

"Sorry, ma'am. You can park anywhere. Do you need help finding something?" asked the young man.

"I'm just curious, where's the refueling dock? I don't see it here."

"No, you can't see it because we use a floating dock. If you look to your left, just a smidge, you can see it out in the river, just there."

He pointed to something that looked like a bump across the horizon from their distance. The orange flag marking the dock fluttered in the breeze.

"How do BIW personnel pull fuel from it?" she asked.

"That's simple. Certain people have been given the tank's combo. They just pull up and pump what they need. Then we ask that they reengage the lock. We had some kids stealing fuel a few years ago. Before that, we never really locked the pump."

A stiff gust of cool marine air tossed her loose hair around, lashing her face.

"How many BIW boats refuel over there?" Kari asked. She jutted her chin toward the dock.

"All of them. It's our only tank. So I'd say probably thirty or so, give or take."

She whistled. "That many? I didn't realize BIW had so many watercraft."

"Oh, sure, we have skiffs, tugboats, a dredger . . . you name it, we have it here," he said.

The young man suddenly hacked into his elbow, the deep cough of a chain-smoker.

"Are you aware of any recent fuel losses?"

"Well, I don't get into the numbers on the gauge with too much detail, but I have noticed more refueling happening at the landside refueling port. We fill the dock the same way gas stations fuel their pumps, with underground storage tanks."

"And you think the refueling trucks have been here more frequently?"

He leaned back on his heels and jammed his hands into his pockets. He looked at her, held his hands out, and shrugged. "Maybe? Probably? That truck has shown up tons for a while now. Must have been something to do with the ship." His eyes turned toward the ship as he pointed in its direction. "Anyway, I need to get back to it. Nice talking with you, ma'am."

The young man jogged back to a small work shed just off the pier. He confirmed Irene's findings. More fuel had been needed for several months. But did Irene get killed because of it? For the first time, Kari felt exposed. Naked. How quickly would the killer figure out Kari was onto him? Despite the warm day, a shiver ran up her spine.

◆ ◆ ◆

Kari yanked the door open to her vehicle and got in. She quickly engaged the engine so she could put down the windows. The stifling car caused her to start sweating almost immediately. The last thing she needed would be to present as a "sweaty lawyer."

She quickly drove through the campus to the visitors' lot. She had an appointment with Sheila Rainey, Irene's former supervisor. Meeting the kid near the waterfront had been an unexpected bonus.

Kari struggled with how much to tell Ms. Rainey regarding the fuel logs she had found in Irene's seabag. Irene hadn't yet disclosed the information to her supervisor. Or had she? And the logs obtained by Kari had been a copy. Without knowing Irene's actions, Kari knew she risked tipping her hand and ruining the opportunity to defend Ahmed with the logs. If she turned over the information prematurely, she risked it languishing on a bureaucrat's desk without further investigation. She also risked alerting the real killer, something she desperately wanted to avoid.

"Hi, I'm attorney Kari Sharpe, here for Ms. Rainey," she said.

The young man at the front desk barely made eye contact before picking up the phone to call Ms. Rainey.

"The lawyer's here. Okay, I'll let her know."

Turning to Kari, he said, "Have a seat and someone will be right out."

Her shoes clicked on the gleaming floor as she walked toward the waiting area.

"Wait a minute, I need to grab a picture of your ID and have you sign in on our guest logbook."

A look of satisfaction crossed his face at the job well done. Kari surmised that the young man had been counseled, numerous times, about failing to obtain proper identification of visitors. Most defense contractors employed a certain level of security. A common, minimal effort had been to ask for a picture of an ID card and a log of who had been in the facility, as the man had done. More sensitive facilities required a passport, name badges, and the use of restricted buffered areas to protect sensitive US technology research. Kari had been surprised BIW hadn't required more from her.

The door to the office area opened slowly.

"Ms. Sharpe? I'm Sheila Rainey. Please come in."

Kari followed the middle-aged, worn-looking woman through a maze of grayscale cubicles to an enclosed office. The walls of the cubicles sat lower than most cubicles Kari had seen. The design allowed individuals to look over the top of the partition at their fellow employees. Cubicle work had a way of sucking the life out of people. She wondered whether lowering the partitions helped or hurt the deplorable work environment. Fortunately, she had no plans to test out the workspaces.

"Thanks for seeing me, Ms. Rainey. As you know, I represent Youseff Ahmed in his defense in connection with the death of Irene Simmons," said Kari.

"Yes, I'm well aware of who you are."

The woman's eyes flashed annoyance, then looked away from Kari. The steely response had been something Kari had anticipated. She had to tread lightly to learn anything from this woman.

"I'm so sorry for your loss. I never had the pleasure of meeting Ms. Simmons, but I did know her sister. She came from a very nice family and by all accounts loved working at BIW."

Finally, Ms. Rainey smiled and looked directly at Kari. The closed arms remained tightly clasped across her chest.

"Irene was a special person. We all loved her around here. She had a way of making everyone feel at ease," she said with a hitch in her voice.

The smell of microwaved food wafted in the air, mixing with the usual stale stench of an office.

"How long did you work with Irene?" asked Kari.

Ms. Rainey sat back into her seat and looked out the window, thinking. She finally said, "We worked together for over ten years. She was like family to all of us."

Her eyes glistened as she wistfully spoke of Irene. Kari knew the interview had the potential to end abruptly if she failed to choose her words carefully. She looked past Ms. Rainey toward the parking lot.

"Yes, I can well imagine. Seeing someone five days a week, every week, working toward a common purpose has a way of cementing coworkers as family. Again, I'm so sorry for your loss."

"Thank you. I appreciate it very much. How can I help you?"

Kari pulled out the legal pad on which she'd written several questions in preparation for the meeting.

"It is my understanding that Irene worked in procurement. Is that correct?"

Ms. Rainey placed her elbows on her desk and steepled her hands. She looked directly at Kari.

"Yes, she had the monumental task of making sure this place ran smoothly. She had a background from the navy, where she worked in disbursing, so she could handle spreadsheets with the best of them."

"What type of items would she order?"

"Everything from break room supplies to machine parts."

"I can appreciate getting low on break room supplies, like Goldfish or even soaps and toilet paper. Those are easy to see and order. But how would Irene know she needed to order parts? Or other items less noticeable around the office?"

Kari hadn't wanted to dive in and directly ask about the fuel orders. She needed to allow Ms. Rainey to become comfortable answering questions before she moved to the main point of her visit.

"We have a standard supplies-requisition form all personnel are required to fill out. They had to give the form to Irene on Tuesday to get certain items by the end of the week. Otherwise, most items were delivered the following week."

"With all the shipbuilding at BIW, I'd imagine she had her hands full ordering various parts as vessels are constructed," said Kari.

"Not as much as you'd think. The parts for a particular ship arrived in stages as the ship had been built, not all at once. Our waterfront facility could never house everything at the same time. The engineers placed orders according to the specifications of the ship design; then Irene took it from there."

"I see. So she only had to anticipate a need for general office supplies. Much like we do at home. When things get low, we reorder."

"Exactly. Everything else she ordered based on requests from our cohort partners—the men and women out there—doing the work we support." Ms. Rainey leaned back into her chair and gestured toward the window.

"I assume she needed permission to order certain items?"

"Yes, but only for dangerous things. Irene had been given a longer leash than someone in her position would have normally had. Over the years she'd been in so many roles around here and participated in several successful builds that everyone really trusted her corporate knowledge. She really didn't need much supervision. In fact, she often acted as my acting supervisor when I needed coverage for an out-of-state meeting."

"She'll be a difficult person to replace on many levels."

"Yes, you're right about that."

Ms. Rainey looked down at several metal baskets on her desk. Each piled high with paperwork needing her attention. Somehow, as she reviewed the messy desk, she aged. A tired look of resignation firmly planted on her delicate face.

"I'm a little embarrassed to admit it, but I managed to get turned around when I first drove onto the facility," said Kari.

"It's not hard to do." Ms. Rainey snorted.

She glanced down at Kari's expensive tailored civilian suit, allowing her eyes to trail toward Kari's lap. In that moment Kari regretted not wearing her uniform.

"I finally turned around near the skiff shed and noticed a floating dock out in the river. Is that a refueling station?"

"Yes, you have a good eye for detail. Most people never notice the dock."

"I grew up on the water. My brother is a lobsterman down in Portland. I've slugged cleats on the side of more than a few gas docks over the years. I was surprised to see it. I would have thought BIW would use a land-based refueling port."

"Yes, I think years ago, way before my time, that's what they did. But as the facility grew, we needed more of the waterfront for building, so the fuel had to be moved off the land. The refilling ports are still on land."

Kari jotted a note on her pad, then returned to Ms. Rainey. Several people walked past the small office, laughing and clacking plates of reheated food.

"That makes sense. Is fuel something Irene ordered as well?"

"I don't understand what this is about. Why are you asking so many questions about Irene's work?" demanded Ms. Rainey.

Shit. Kari had hoped to keep the woman talking. "As you know, I'm preparing a defense for EW1 Ahmed. He's a local kid who enlisted in the navy and was hand selected for his position on the precomm. Due diligence requires me to find out everything I can about Ms. Simmons. I apologize if my questions seem unrelated or overly intrusive."

Ms. Rainey considered Kari's words, glanced at the clock, and continued: "The tanker comes once a week and fills the tanks to the maximum capacity. Then Irene would pay the invoice as part of her duties." Her tone was once again cold, distant.

Kari put her pen down. "That makes sense. Otherwise, she would have to look at a gauge. Something I'm sure she didn't have time for."

"No, not likely. And marine fuel is a critical need. We can't afford to allow the facility to run dry. The system we have prevents it."

"Is the amount ordered roughly the same over time? I wouldn't think there could be much variability."

"No, fuel ordering is tricky. At times it seems like we don't use much, and then suddenly there's a spike in demand. It happens."

"Did Irene ever flag a spike as excessive?"

Ms. Rainey started to laugh and said, "Irene thought every order was excessive. Part of what made her great at her job was her cheapness. If someone wanted an extra set of pencils, she wanted to know why."

"Wow. I'm sure she saved a ton of money and annoyed people in the process."

Ms. Rainey clapped her hands and shook her head. "Yes to both. But everyone loved Irene, so they didn't mind. Or at least no one ever said anything to me about it. Probably knew better."

"Did Irene ever flag marine fuel orders as excessive?" Kari held her breath after asking the million-dollar question. She moved to the edge of her seat.

"Yes, she did so several times over the years, even right before her death. I asked her to investigate and let me know if she found anything."

"Did she bring anything to your attention?"

She shook her head. "No, usually her suspicions died of natural causes once she followed up with the partners needing the item. That's why I tended not to get too involved at first. I learned not to waste my time until she confirmed her suspicions."

"But was she ever correct? Did she catch anyone stealing?"

She pressed, hoping to get more from Ms. Rainey. Kari glanced out the window toward the river behind Ms. Rainey.

"Oh, sure, over the years she caught people placing extra orders for food or drinks, stealing from vending machines. That sort of thing. Nothing too substantial, but it's always better to weed these things out."

"I couldn't agree more."

Kari paused and then added, "You said everyone loved her. But this is a big place with lots of employees. Were you aware of anyone who didn't like her? Maybe someone who she rubbed the wrong way?"

Without skipping a beat, Ms. Rainey said, "No, not that I can think of."

A buzzer sounded and a shrill voice interrupted them. "Your afternoon meeting is starting in five, ma'am."

Ms. Rainey's eyes returned to meet Kari's. "Unless you have anything else, duty calls."

"No, you've been very helpful. I appreciate your time." Kari shoved her pad back into her satchel and stood.

"Are you heading back to Portland?"

"Yes."

"Would you mind bringing a box of Irene's personal belongings back to her sister?"

"Not at all. I'd be happy to."

"Thanks. Everything is still on her desk. If you don't mind, I'll have you wait a moment in the break room. It'll just take a minute to assemble."

"It's no problem at all. I'm happy to wait a few minutes," said Kari.

She soon sat in the break room waiting for Irene's belongings. The drab beige room contained one round table, a full-size refrigerator, and a microwave. A dangerously slim woman entered the break room and rummaged through the refrigerator. She hadn't seen Kari yet. She roughly clanged things to the side, looking for something. "Damned idiots. Where is it?" the woman muttered.

"Hey there!" said Kari.

The woman jumped. "Geez, I didn't even see you!"

"Sorry to startle you."

Lunchtime had come and gone, yet the slim woman heated food.

"Afternoon snack?" asked Kari.

"Yes, I sort of just eat whenever I feel like it. Sometimes I don't eat at all, then realize days passed. Oh well. It happens." The woman looked Kari up and down, then said, "Are you visiting today?"

"Yes, I had a meeting with Sheila Rainey. I'm just waiting to take a box of Irene Simmons's belongings back to Portland to give to her sister."

"I still can't get over that." She shook her head, allowing her long hair to graze the top of her leftovers. Kari sensed the woman wanted to talk about the murder. Before Kari could probe a little further, a voice interrupted her.

"Hello, ladies!"

A loud, deep male voice boomed behind them.

"Hey, Ron," the woman said without looking at him.

She quickly collected her things and scurried from the break room for her cubical, without even a parting glance at Kari. Something about the man had clearly driven her away.

"Hi, I'm Ron Baker."

The man's deep voice had the jagged edges of either malice or plain old insincerity. Kari couldn't be sure which. "I'm Kari Sharpe," she said without extending her hand to shake.

"What brings you to our humble home away from home today?"

The man's eyes trailed down the length of Kari and then settled on her satchel. A yellow legal pad peeked out from the top of its opening.

"I represent Youseff Ahmed, the man charged with the murder of—"

He waved his hand and said, "I know who he is. We all do. You have your work cut out for you if you think you'll get him off. Is that what you do for a living? Represent criminals?" His eyes bored into Kari with intensity.

"Some of the time. But, yes, usually my representation of navy personnel tends to lean into the criminal realm."

"Never heard of a civilian doing navy work," he said.

"I'm a former active duty navy JAG, now a reservist."

She needed to turn the conversation away from herself and toward something of value. Then she recognized him. The wide nose and birdlike eyes of the man in the picture with Irene. Samantha failed to tell her that the man had continued to work with Irene. She wanted to test his honesty.

"Were you close with Irene Simmons?"

He looked away from her, then hesitated a moment as though he ran several responses through his mind before finally settling on, "Not really. She worked here, and I probably saw her in passing, but that's about it."

Something about his intensity made Kari immediately uncomfortable. Disheveled. Like he was playing her. And it was interesting he chose to lie about his past relationship with Irene. What did he have to gain by the cover-up? More importantly, what had he calculated as his loss if he'd been truthful?

"Sorry to keep you waiting!" a woman's voice interrupted.

Sheila's assistant walked into the room with a large box containing Irene's desk belongings. Someone had gone through a tremendous amount of care to arrange her pictures for safe travel.

"I hope it's okay, but I put all the granola bars, candy, and other food things in the break room earlier in the week. I thought Irene would rather share than throw anything away."

"I agree. No need to waste. Is this everything?"

"Yep, that's all of it. She kept a clean workstation. Unlike mine, I have about a year's worth of crumbs jammed in my keyboard!"

"Tell me about it," Kari said, rolling her eyes.

Ron Baker disappeared without saying a word of goodbye. She needed to ask one more question of someone at BIW before she left.

"Do you work with Jesse Helm?" she asked.

Sheila's assistant rolled her eyes and then answered, "I know him from parties. He's the guy who drinks a little too much and then hits on every woman in the room. Of course, no one takes him up on his offers because he's so gross. He works in facilities management."

"What does that division do?" asked Kari.

"I think they mostly work outside, keeping things running. I'm not entirely sure. Sorry I can't be more helpful. Do you need a hand bringing all of this to your car?" asked the woman as she handed the box to Kari.

"I've got it from here, thanks."

Kari grabbed the box and headed back to her car for Portland. The day had been eventful and long. The brief meeting with Ron Baker clung to her uncomfortably. Something about him made her skin crawl. She most certainly needed to dig into his relationship with Irene.

Chapter 41

The next afternoon, Fred May stood near the harbormaster's shed and watched various men returning from their day of fishing and lobstering. The lobstermen arrived one by one, depending on their departure time. Some days he walked around chatting with them as they cleared traps and banded their catch. Today he had a mission. He intended to learn more about the men who took over Randy's boat. Detective Clark never requested his service. Instead, Clark wanted him to stay out of it. However, Fred felt investigating the matter properly depended on him. Civic pride, ego, and a desire to properly manage the waterfront enabled him to press ahead, even though his instincts told him to leave the men alone. Instincts and his wife.

She worried about everything. At times he chose not to tell her about things for fear it would spool up her fearful mind. Everything would lead to devastation, according to her. If he smoked, he had cancer in his future. If he failed to drink a gallon of water a day, kidney disease. Somehow she could turn anything into a potential disaster. Over the years he'd learned to manage her and his own fears. Today he pushed aside those fears and pressed ahead, intent to learn more.

He looked toward the deep-blue harbor. The two men hadn't yet arrived on the waterfront. Some days he noticed they left very early and then returned before others had even left for the morning. Other days they seemed to push off the pier after lunch and then return shortly, usually empty handed. Odd behavior for lobstermen. Most men had set schedules. Their days consisted of tasks done in a certain order. Pull trap, weigh and band the lobsters, and drive the haul to market. Every day the same set of tasks in the same order.

The men using Randy's boat followed no set pattern or rhythm. Their actions appeared, from an outsider, as chaotic and disjointed. Yet the outward flash of their new toys suggested their efforts brought in a significant amount of money, even as other lobstermen suffered financially.

Jimmy Sharpe's boat moved swiftly toward the pier. He had known Jimmy for as long as he could remember. Over the years Fred had watched Jimmy cycle through brief periods of sobriety. Very brief. Some days Jimmy returned from the bay glassy eyed and full of slurred-speech proclamations. Telltale signs of inebriation. Fred had spoken to Jimmy about his drinking on numerous occasions. Little good it did. The guy still drank, daring Fred to get the Coasties involved. As Jimmy approached, Fred walked toward the end of the pier to help him catch a cleat.

"Thanks, Fred!" yelled Jimmy.

Jimmy tossed a line to Fred's outstretched hand, allowing him to secure the boat to the pier.

"Hey, man, how's your day?"

Jimmy clicked off the idling engine and turned to Fred.

"Not great. Another day of nearly empty traps. Same as the past few months. At this rate, I'm not sure I can keep my distributor. They'll have to seek lobsters from others if I can't keep up with their demand. I'd hate to lose their business; it has been a lifeline of steady income. Steady if the lobsters cooperate."

"Yeah, I've been hearing the same thing from everyone. It's been an odd, slow summer. We've seen it before."

The briny smell of the salt air combined with a strong fish odor. Fred stood back and glanced over Jimmy's boat.

"True. I was thinking about that. There have been years when things dried up. But after they changed the rules on sizes, the population seemed to grow again. This is different," said Jimmy, straightening himself to look at Fred.

"How so?"

"Well, some days my traps are full. Like normal. Then other days, nothing. At first I thought I had bad traps. Like they walked back out," said Jimmy. He pointed at the hold in the back of his vessel and the pots on its deck as he spoke.

Fred's eyes carefully searched the pier to see who could hear them. So far, not many men had returned. He didn't want anyone to see him asking around. At least not yet.

"Did they?" asked Fred.

"Not that I can tell. I pulled each one out and inspected for holes. You never know. But everything was fine with the traps. Then I talked to Chet. He said he's experiencing the same thing."

Everyone knew Chet to be the gossipiest guy on the waterfront. Fred had no intention of speaking with him about anything. However, he wanted to learn Chet's thoughts on the matter. He might be gossipy, but he also might have insights to share. Chet knew things.

"I think nearly everyone is."

"*Nearly* is right," said Jimmy.

"What do you mean by that?" Fred took off his ball cap and slicked his hair back before repositioning the hat on his head.

"Everyone is lean except the guys who took over Randy's boat," said Jimmy with a nod to the gleaming truck in the lot.

"I've heard that before too. Any thoughts as to why?" asked Fred.

"I don't, but Chet has plenty of ideas."

"Chet can work a conspiracy almost as well as my wife can," said Fred. After a pause he asked, "So what does he think?"

"He thinks those guys are stealing lobsters out of everyone's traps. He also thinks they are getting fuel somehow."

"Why would he think that?" asked Fred.

Fred peered toward the sea and rubbed his chin. Detective Clark had told Fred that the Coast Guard had been investigating fuel dumps offshore, possibly connected to the murders of the tourists. The location of the dumps sat far outside of the range most lobstermen ventured.

"Chet said he saw the men coming back from the no-dumping zone. He said he has seen them doing that a lot of the time. So I ask myself, Why the hell would any lobsterman need to go out that far? You know us. We all stay in the harbor; it's the best spot for lobstering."

The no-dumping zone lay just beyond the harbor, as the water's depth exceeded sixty feet. Federal law prohibited the dumping of sewage, fuel, human remains, and other items in the no-dumping zone. If a person needed to dump sewage or anything else, they had to go far outside of the zone.

Turning back to Jimmy, he said, "That is interesting. Maybe Chet is onto something. Geez, did I just say that?"

"I know. I'm beginning to think he's right too. I just can't prove it. Instead, I'm going broke by the day while those guys are getting rich somehow," said Jimmy.

He jerked his head to the left, toward the parking lot where the shiny new truck sat.

"Have you met them?" asked Fred.

"Nope. They seem to keep to themselves. All the better, if you ask me. I'm not even sure what happened to Randy. Haven't heard a thing from him. He doesn't respond to my texts or calls," said Jimmy.

"Seriously. I've tried too."

Suddenly Fred's device buzzed loudly, reminding him to return to the shed for a meeting. The bureaucrats always wanted to hold meetings during the day.

"See ya, Jimmy. Duty calls. And thanks for the intel."

The gravel drive crunched as Fred walked back to the shed. He placed the call on speaker and gazed out the small grimy window.

Returning his eyes to the room, he flipped through the newspaper as he half listened to the faceless voices drone on about nothing. Today the talking heads seemed concerned about something related to beautification of the fuel tanks in South Portland. Fred chuckled to himself, knowing how painful the focus on South Portland must be for the two harbormasters on that side of the waterfront.

Again, he peered out the window almost wistfully. The day had been perfect. Clear, sunny, and with a nice crisp breeze to cool everyone. Maine summers were the envy of the country for a reason.

He spotted the FV *Ginny* approaching the harbor. "Damn it. I need to get off this stupid call," he said, knowing that he'd muted the receiver. He desperately wanted to corner the men before they left for the day.

He unmuted the phone, then cleared his throat and said, "Sorry to interrupt, but I have a critical issue on the pier. I need to go . . ." And then he hung up.

Scrambling out of the shed, he slow jogged to the pier.

The men secured their boat to the pier. Instead of opening their hull to band lobsters, they jumped onto the pier and started walking toward their truck. A few more seconds and he would have missed them.

"Hey, guys! You've been here a while, and we haven't met yet. I'm Fred May, one of the harbormasters."

Fred tried to be as casual as possible so as not to alarm them. The men barely grunted a reply. He pressed ahead, stepping between them and their truck.

"I see you're working Randy's boat. What's he doing this summer?"

"Don't know. And don't care," said one of the men. Their eyes bore into Fred with an intensity that made him shuffle backward.

They quickly moved around him toward their truck. He followed them despite his inner voice telling him to leave it alone.

"Oh, I see. Well, I need your names for the Coast Guard. Should've gotten them sooner, but I've let it slip. Paperwork isn't exactly my thing. Do you mind?"

He shook the clipboard in his hand for effect. The men looked at each other and then back at him.

"I'll also need your driver's license numbers. The Coast Guard requires harbormasters to provide the names and license numbers of all commercial fishermen. Like I said, I've been remiss. Now they're breathing down my neck, threatening to pull harbor rights for anyone who doesn't submit their information."

The men shared a stunned glance. Bingo. He pressed on. "They can be real sticklers at times. Typical bureaucrats. I'd rather they don't show up down here, poking around. Lord knows they'll find more crap I'm not doing right," said Fred. He forced a slight chuckle for effect despite his tension.

"Jeff Baker and that's Greg . . . Baker. I lost my driver's license, and he forgot his," said the big guy with a tight edge.

Fred jotted the names down on his clipboard, then said, "No worries. I can stall a little longer until you get it sorted. This your first time lobstering?" Averting his eyes from them gave him a moment away from their intensity.

Fred's eyes trailed from his clipboard to their hands. The pale skin, clean, smooth hands, and lack of scars stood out right away. Lobstermen always looked the same—deeply tanned, full of scars, and heavily calloused hands. These were not lobstermen. Not by a long shot.

"We done here?" growled the other man.

The man's murderous glare told Fred he had gone too far and needed to back off fast.

"Yep, all good! I won't hold you guys up. Just get me your licenses when you have a minute."

He held the clipboard up in the air and shook it. "Thanks again!" he shouted as he jogged over the gravel yard to the shed.

Their truck doors slamming sounded like gunshots, ringing over the low din of noise from various boats, the nearby lighthouse, and loud conversations. He shut the door to the shed and exhaled loudly. Maybe his wife had been right. He should have sat this one out.

Chapter 42

Detective Clark sat at his desk, trying to look busy. He had spent the morning at a conference on evidence-collection techniques given by a science type. The guy had droned on about clean catches and proper tagging. Like the seasoned detectives in the room had no clue about crime scene preservation. The guy's "sciencie" egghead haughty attitude irked Clark. What did he know? *Leave evidence collection to the real cops,* thought Clark.

His eyes desperately searched for a file or phone message on his desk that could help him get out of the next session. The desk offered no answers. Then the phone rang.

"Detective Clark."

"Hi, Detective. It's Fred May from the waterfront."

"Yeah, I know who you are," said Clark, sounding more irritated than he'd intended.

"I found out a couple of things I thought you should know."

Clark moved papers around on his cluttered desk until he located a pen and notepad. He flipped the well-worn pages to a fresh one and said, "Shoot."

"Well, remember I told you about the new guys on the waterfront, the ones who took over Randy's boat?"

"Yeah, what about them?"

"I finally got their names: Greg and Jeff Baker," said Fred.

"Got it, thanks. Is that everything?"

"I can also give you a plate number for their vehicle. Not sure I shared this before."

May provided the plate number and then added, "A couple of the longtime lobstermen think those guys are stealing from their traps."

"Why would they think that?"

Clark put his pen down and spun in his chair to peer outside. He looked through the heavily smudged narrow window by his desk toward the parking lot.

"The traps are randomly empty some days and full on other days, with no rhyme or reason. In a slow season everyone pulls nearly empty traps. But for the past few months, their traps are either totally empty or completely full. It doesn't make any sense," said Fred.

"That is odd," said Clark. "Maybe the lobsters are wiggling back out somehow? Maybe there's a hole in the netting?" Clark only knew the basics about lobstering he'd learned on an elementary school field trip to the Maine State Museum.

"I don't think so. One guy, Jimmy Sharpe, said he'd checked all his traps and found nothing wrong with them. Just missing lobsters. Then Jimmy told me that another lobsterman named Chet saw the FV *Ginny* returning from the no-dumping zone. Lobstermen don't go that far out. There's no reason for it."

Clark's seat creaked loudly as he leaned into it, considering the new wrinkle. Fred interrupted his thoughts. "I thought since the Coast Guard was investigating fuel dumping, you might want to look at those guys more closely."

He jotted down "fuel dumping," then tapped his pen on the desk.

"Anything else?" asked Clark.

"No, that's about it. I just thought you should—"

"Thanks, Fred. I've got it from here."

He dropped the receiver onto its base with a clatter loud enough to startle a colleague.

Normally Clark hated calls from the public. Old ladies staring out their windows and reporting on the normal behaviors of their neighbors grew tiresome. In this case, Fred might have helped move the tourist-murders case as well as the Coast Guard's other investigation into the fuel dumps.

Although Fred never mentioned anything about the two murdered sailors, Clark knew the criminal mind. If a nefarious person found himself a good thing involving making lots of money with little risk, they'd do anything to protect it, even murder. His hunch made sense. Finally, something he could sink his teeth into.

He cracked his knuckles and turned on the ancient computer that passed for a workstation. After several minutes, the screen displayed its usual tabs. He clicked on the Background tab and entered the last name—Baker. A long list of Bakers appeared in front of him. He narrowed the field to Baker, Maine residence. The list shortened considerably. He found Greg Baker and opened the window into Greg's past experiences with law enforcement.

A long list of crimes appeared. Greg Baker had been involved in numerous theft schemes, violent altercations with other males, domestic violence, and child abuse. A real winner. Usual occupation stated: None. If Greg Baker had been working lobster boats most of his life, the report would have listed it as an occupation.

The noise in the crowded detective pit killed him. "Keep it down! Some of us are working!" he shouted into the air. No one cared.

His hand moved quickly, navigating the mouse to another screen. Jeff Baker shared an address with his brother, Greg. From the look of the list of offenses, Clark assumed they committed their crimes together. Jeff's report also failed to indicate lobstering or any sort of maritime occupation.

Greg and Jeff had various relatives in the area, all losers. Each one of the cousins had been involved in petty theft or fraud schemes. Nothing too serious, but these had not been law-abiding citizens from all accounts. The question remained: Why had they chosen to rent a lobster boat for the season, and did their involvement on the waterfront result in the death of the tourists?

The names provided more questions than answers. The Coast Guard investigators thought the murders had something to do with the fuel dumps. Clark hadn't been too sure. However, knowing that two inexperienced petty criminals had managed to secure a lobster boat from one of the waterfront's oldest lobstermen indicated to Clark that the Coasties might have made the right connection.

"We're starting in five, Butch," said a man.

His pencil-necked, spectacled weasel of a coworker was reminding him to go back to the training. Clark considered the murdered boaters and concluded training could wait. He needed to investigate the Bakers.

Chapter 43

Ron Baker stood in a windowed conference room overlooking the visitors' parking lot. Yesterday, he had watched Kari Sharpe, the attorney, walk to her car and place Irene's box in her trunk and drive away. Their exchange had been short and uneventful, but still her presence at BIW bothered him. He needed to know more about the case against Youseff Ahmed.

It had been some time since anyone mentioned Irene or the case against the sailor. Maybe it had been about time he got some answers, from the source. He grabbed his device and called the Portland Police Department. The weak cell phone reception in the conference room annoyed him, but it would have to suffice. BIW monitored all calls for "security" reasons. Security, his ass. They just wanted to eavesdrop on their employees and had a handy reason to violate their privacy.

He bounced around the Portland Police Department's nonemergency line in an endless stream of transfers. Finally, an official-sounding man answered the phone.

"Detective Clark," he said. The gruff, no-nonsense greeting assured Ron he had a person in charge.

"Hello, Detective, sorry to bother you. I know you're busy. My name is Ron Baker. I'm a friend of the late Irene Simmons."

Ron cloaked his anxiety with a sickly-sweet respect he reserved for certain occasions, such as interaction with law enforcement.

"I'm sorry for your loss. How can I help you?"

He noted the man's stark change in demeanor. He glanced away from the window toward his feet.

"It's been a while since I heard anything about the case and was wondering what's happening. I hope you don't mind the intrusion into your day."

Noisy chatter from somewhere in the detective's office distracted Ron as he listened.

"Not at all. At this point we are done with the case. We arrested Youseff Ahmed, as I'm sure you might have seen on the news. He's currently locked up pending trial."

"You think he did it?"

"We wouldn't have arrested him if we didn't. It's a strong case that didn't necessitate further digging on our side."

A small, slick smile passed over Ron's thin lips.

"Yes, I heard about the arrest but nothing else."

He strained not to inject desperation into his voice. He wanted more information. He wanted a conviction because that would nail the case down as final.

"Ah, you know lawyers. Always a song and dance with these things. They drag everything out. As far as the PD is concerned, the guy did it. But innocent until proven guilty and all that . . ."

Ron created a sound he had hoped would pass as a laugh and then said, "Thanks, you've been very helpful."

"Not a problem. What was your name again?" asked Clark.

"Ron Baker. I'm a friend and former colleague of Irene's."

Ron hung up the phone, satisfied that the cops had passed over him as a suspect. They had their guy, end of story. A rush of relief filled him, buoying his spirits. The strain of forced politeness had nearly killed him, but the relief had been worth every moment of the conversation. He glanced at his watch. Nearly quitting time.

Chapter 44

Butch Clark opened his investigative file on the death of Irene Simmons and jotted down the name Ron Baker. Then he turned to his computer. Another Baker seemed too much of a coincidence to him.

Name aside, years of detective work had told him something seemed off about Ron Baker. Generally, family called the prosecuting attorney's office during this phase of a case. Not the police department after the investigative phase completed. Coworkers rarely, if ever, called. Workplaces moved on rather quickly, in his experience. He needed to know more about Ron Baker's motivations.

Within a few minutes he found Ron Baker in the police database. He had been convicted of several petty theft–related offenses as a juvenile, just like the other Bakers. Once Ron Baker entered naval service, he disappeared from law enforcement interaction. Nothing remarkable existed in his record, yet something still gnawed at Clark.

His hands moved quickly to search for Ron Baker's known relations. He expected to come up with no concrete information, because Baker was a common name, and as he knew from his previous search, a lot of Bakers resided in the New England area.

He let out a long exhale and read the screen. Nothing worthwhile had been listed under the Known Relations tab of Ron Baker's profile. However, a few clicks later he realized Greg and Jeff Baker lived on the same street as Ron Baker. Near enough to suggest a family relationship existed between the men. Maybe cousins? Another scumbag family, just like the Sharpes. Just what Maine needed.

Clark spun his desk chair to look out the window and thought about the murder of the tourists. Greg and Jeff Baker might have been connected with those murders. And now he gets a call from another Baker regarding Irene Simmons's murder. Odd.

He scratched his greasy head, then absently picked his right ear. Could the three murders be connected to the Baker family?

If a connection existed, had he arrested the wrong man for the murder of Irene Simmons? *Shit.* Not again. He cracked his knuckles, the dozen or so snaps sounding like small-caliber gunfire. Glancing at his colleagues, he felt exposed. Over the years he had arrested a crap ton of men. Not all of them deserved it. He knew it. Even if he never would admit fault, the guilt chased him. Had it finally caught up to him?

Locking someone up for a crime they never committed had to be the shittiest thing a cop could do. Doing it for a promotion? Next-level shitty. He had never framed anyone, but there had been some questionable arrests. And juries more than happy to put away a scumbag. He always blamed any mistakes on the court system. The prosecutors, the juries, the lawyers, and the judges. Never himself. His job was to investigate the crime and put a suspect in the hands of the prosecutor. Dandruff flakes drifted to his shoulders as he shook his head. He let out a long exhale, considering his options.

He leaned back in his chair. The sides of his stomach pressed uncomfortably against the armrests. Glancing out the window, he considered the case, starting with the first interrogation of Ahmed. He gnawed at his lower lip as he remembered seeing Kari Sharpe for the first time after her return to Maine. She had stood on the ship in command of the world. A real winner. He was just a sloppy loser compared to her. He had acted like a shit. Had he really asked about Doug? What a crap thing to do. Letting out a puff of held air, he tried to forget the embarrassment.

He needed to alert his supervisor right away. They might have the wrong guy. Hell no. Not gonna happen. One bad arrest could mean more. The pencil pushers would rip through years of his work. Then they'd know everything he had done. Every shitty arrest. Every brutal jump to "justice." The hell with that. He'd figure this out. Investigate the snot out of the Baker boys and get to the bottom of this mess. Maybe then he'd be able to live with himself. Go into retirement in peace.

Chapter 45

Kari blocked out a chunk of time to drop off Irene's work items to Samantha. She just wished she had been more rested. Another long yawn escaped her lips.

Hani had insisted that she attend an evening with the family. Kari assumed Hani meant a quiet evening sipping chai and talking about the case. Instead, moments after Kari arrived, Hani and Bilan strung a sheet across the living room, dividing it into two smaller rooms. Hani said she was always ready on a Friday night, because friends often stopped over for a visit.

She had been right. At one point Kari counted twelve women in the cramped, shrouded section of the living room. She had to assume the men's side contained at least as many men. Hani and Bilan served tray after tray of chai and savory snacks. Guests brought an equal number of delicious sweets to their home. Despite any previous reservations about her as a member of the Sharpe family, they treated Kari as one of their own. Kari had never experienced anything like it. The only time the Sharpes entertained had been during her dad's poker nights. The group of men had drunk and smoked all night long in the cramped kitchen. Many had simply passed out where they sat. Kari had learned to avoid the kitchen on those nights. One of the men had always grabbed her and hoisted her onto his filthy lap. Her drunken father had merely laughed it off.

She tapped on Samantha's door, hoping she would be home on a Saturday.

"Kari. What brings you here?" said Samantha.

Kari shifted the box of Irene's belongings to her other hip and said, "Irene's supervisor gave me things from her desk to bring down to you."

Kari's eyes trailed across Samantha's outfit. She wore an old-fashioned cleaning apron over her jeans and T-shirt.

Realizing how she looked, Samantha said, "Oh geez, I know it's ancient, but this apron really gets me in the mood to tackle even the grossest cleaning projects."

"Your house is the cleanest home I think I have ever been in. I'm sure there's nothing gross lurking around here. I hope you don't mind me stopping over like this."

She handed the measly box of Irene's belongings to Samantha.

"Not at all. Come in and sit for a minute, if you'd like."

They walked through the small house to the living room in the back. Kari noticed the picture of a young Irene with Ron Baker and another man. She needed to figure out why Baker decided to hide the fact that he had been a longtime friend of Irene's.

"I met Ron Baker when I was up at BIW," said Kari.

"Who?" Samantha seemed perplexed.

"The guy from the picture—the one you have on your mantel." Kari pointed to the photo.

"You mean Chief!" Samantha laughed.

"Chief?" asked Kari, confused.

"Yes, she always called him Chief. I have not heard the name Ron in a very long time. Sorry about that. I've only known him as Chief. Once he made chief, he insisted on everyone calling him by his rank instead of Ron."

Kari laughed and said, "Rank can at times go to people's heads. I've seen it before."

"Yes, he loved being called Chief. Even long after he left the navy. The nickname stuck with him."

"How was her relationship with the chief?"

"Oh, I don't know. Good, I guess?" said Samantha. Her eyes darted away from Kari.

Kari needed more information on Irene's relationship with Ron Baker. Samantha either had been left out of all the details or intended to conceal something from her. Perhaps she needed to speak with someone whom Irene would have taken into her confidence.

"Did Irene have a best friend? A girlfriend she had been close to?"

"She sure did, Lorraine Bozeli. Those two have been friends since seventh grade. They were thick as thieves."

"Would you mind sharing her contact information? I'd like to ask her a few questions."

"I'm sure she'd be fine with it. But I can do one better for you. She's helping me clean out Irene's apartment. I thought I heard her go up there earlier. If you want, you can bring these office things up to the place. You just might catch her."

Kari dashed up the back exterior stairs, carrying a small box to the apartment. Music played through the open windows.

"Knock, knock! Anyone here?" she yelled.

Kari nudged the door fully open and looked around the apartment. The living room contained several large moving boxes. They had been stuffed with the remains of Irene's life. The possessions she had surrounded herself with, those that had given her comfort, had been unceremoniously boxed with the finality of death.

"Back here!" yelled a woman.

Kari moved to the back of the apartment to meet the woman as she walked out of the bedroom.

"Hi, I'm Kari Sharpe. I represent Youseff—"

"Hi, Kari. Nice to finally meet you. Samantha has told me all about you."

Kari felt relief at the warm welcome. She had been far too tired from the previous night's activities to handle a hostile interaction with the best friend of the victim. Or, worse, to deal with the glares that only another Sharpe family incident could produce.

"Do you mind if I ask you a few questions? I'm grappling with a few loose ends and really need more insight into Irene's relationships at work."

"No problem at all. I'll help if I can. Irene would have wanted it that way."

Lorraine moved a pile of clothes off the couch to make room for them to comfortably sit. She dropped the folded clothes onto the floor and steadied the pile so it would not topple.

Kari sat on the worn couch and said, "Yesterday I went to BIW to speak with Irene's supervisor. While I was up there, I ran into Ron Baker."

Lorraine stiffened at the mention of Baker's name. She looked beyond Kari and then quickly back. She rolled her eyes. "That guy again? Poor Irene will never be rid of him."

"Can you tell me about their relationship?"

"Sure. It's long and sordid. Complicated. They met at boot camp and quickly became a couple. Irene loved him, but not their relationship." Lorraine glanced over the contents of Irene's life, neatly boxed. Deep grief etched her face as she wiped away her tears.

Kari leaned in toward her. "I'm so sorry for your loss. I can't even imagine losing your best friend."

Lorraine hiccuped, blew her nose, and said, "I'm sorry. Being here, packing her things. It makes everything so final. I can't believe it came to this."

Kari waited a moment. Frozen. What could she say? She stood and looked out the window, giving Lorraine privacy. Then she turned back and said, "Samantha has a picture of them on her mantel. They look like kids."

"Yes. Samantha loved that picture even though Irene never wanted to look at Chief ever again."

The clatter of children's passing voices outside distracted Kari for a moment. "Why not?"

"He became obsessed with her after she broke up with him. Wouldn't leave her alone. She tried, but never managed, to fully get away. He even followed her to various duty stations. Move after move, she thought she'd be free but never managed."

Lorraine shook her head and then swiped a tear as it streamed down her cheek.

"He lied to me and said he barely knew Irene. Why?"

Lorraine's eyes darted back to Kari. A look of pure fury in them.

"What a joke. Irene was all that jerk *did* know. He followed her home from work, at times parking outside of here. He called her all the time, texted, you name it. Then when she dated someone, he'd harass that person until the guy decided the effort wasn't worth it."

"He stalked her."

"If you want to call it that. In our day, that was 'normalish' jilted-man behavior. Nowadays you girls have a term for everything."

"Did she fear him?"

"Of course she did. He'd say things like 'If I can't have you, no one can.' A couple of times he even became physical, grabbing her by the wrist, bruising her arm."

"Did she ever report him to the authorities?"

Lorraine cried softly at the mention of the police, then huffed and said, "I tried to make her do it. I told her they could help. Maybe talk to him. I don't know. Anything!" Her voice quivered with emotion as she replayed the memories. "I should have done more to protect her. She didn't deserve this, to die alone like that. I know it was him. It had to be him. It just had to be."

Lorraine cried so hard she started to heave breaths uncontrollably. She kept wiping the tears and blowing her nose with tissues she reused over and over, yet still the tears flowed. Kari picked up the nearby tissue box and handed it to her.

"Why do you think she never wanted police interaction?" asked Kari.

Lorraine blew her nose loudly, sat up a little straighter, and said, "Irene was one of those rare optimistic people. She had a kind word for everyone and nearly every situation. Despite how he acted, she made excuses for his behavior. I think she truly believed he would stop. Just magically stop on his own." She waved her hand in front of her face and continued: "I know, it sounds unrealistic, but women from our generation . . . we aren't used to turning men in like you 'MeToo' girls. We just made the most of our lot in life, and that's what Irene did. She made the most of her lot. She took the good with the bad, always being optimistic as she waited for the good."

"You think Ron Baker murdered Irene," said Kari, more of a statement than a question.

"Of course I do. It's the direction I always thought he would go in. We argued over him so many times. She refused to do anything about it. And that stupid clueless sister of hers kept inviting Ron over here, like he's some old family friend. What a moron. He killed Irene. I can feel it in my bones. Then they lock up some Black kid. That figures." Lorraine bolted to her feet. She pounded the floor with heavy footfalls as she walked angrily to the kitchen.

She guzzled a glass of water. Blew her nose, dampening multiple tissues, then dabbed her face with a wet washcloth. Returning to Kari, she said, "Sorry. This has been shitty."

"I know. Talking about him must make it even worse. I'm sorry to be bringing all of this up."

Lorraine simply nodded her head. Her eyes puffy and red rimmed.

Kari waited another minute and said, "Did you ever report your suspicions?" She wondered whether Detective Clark knew about the turbulent relationship between Irene and Chief but had failed to investigate further. The police investigatory file did not indicate any law enforcement interaction with Ron Baker. Either Clark had been lazy, or he had no idea a connection existed.

"No, of course I planned to, but then the cops arrested the Black kid. I saw on the news that he had been identified as at the place where she . . ." Lorraine stopped short, sucked in a long breath, and continued: "I had my doubts that the Black kid did it, but what could I do? He was there. Maybe my bones don't know a damned thing anymore."

Kari turned back to her notepad for a moment to collect her thoughts and jot down her impressions. She turned over Lorraine's words in her mind. Then she looked up and asked, "Did Irene ever mention anything about trying to link Baker or anyone else at her work to fuel shortages at BIW?"

"Irene always thought someone was stealing from her workplace. She could lean into conspiracy theories at times," said Lorraine with a slight laugh.

"I'm concerned that she was working on something related to Ron Baker, Chief, before her death. Did she mention this to you?" said Kari, confiding in Lorraine.

"Not that I'm aware of."

"What about the name Jesse Helm? Does that ring a bell?"

A look of realization dawned on Lorraine's face. Finally, Kari had asked the right question.

"She did mention Jesse several times. She didn't seem to respect him very much."

"Why's that?"

"She thought he was, how did she put it, 'too nice of a guy to realize someone put him on their hamster wheel.' That was Irene for you. She always had a colorful description of people."

"I've never heard that expression. What do you think she meant by it?"

"She thought Jesse didn't know someone was making him do their bidding. Like he was being used and had no clue."

Kari considered her words for a moment and then asked, "Did she ever mention Jesse in connection with theft of fuel at BIW?"

"Like I said, I can't be sure. Irene had a conspiracy theory about everyone and everything. At times I had a hard time keeping up with her. Not to mention everything she said was half in English and half in navy jargon. I just listened. I always listened to my dear friend." Lorraine pulled the box of tissues to herself. She puffed out a fresh handful and wiped her damp cheeks. Then she stood and stretched her back. She picked up several things off the floor and placed them in nearby boxes.

"Okay, fair enough. Is there anything else you can tell me about Irene's work relationships, or about Chief?"

"I can't think of anything," said Lorraine after a brief pause.

After they said their goodbyes, Kari walked back to her car, worn out from the conversation. The weight of Lorraine's grief caused a heaviness in her chest. She needed to go for a run to clear her head. Anything to shake the heavy feeling.

Thinking back to the morning she spent at BIW, she recalled how the female office worker had scurried out of the kitchen when Chief Ron Baker walked in. Kari knew something was off about the guy. Very off. Now she needed to connect the dots.

Chapter 46

After speaking with Lorraine, Kari felt as though she finally had a slight break in the case. A person she could pin it on. Excited, she decided to call Jimmy to discuss her working theory that Ron Baker, a.k.a. Chief, had committed the murder either as an abusive past lover or to cover up the commission of the theft of fuel.

After she recounted the previous day's events, Jimmy whistled. "Wow. So you think he's the guy who killed her? Or maybe knows something?"

"I'm not sure. I need to figure out if there's a link between the fuel logs and Ron Baker. Once I figure that out, then maybe I'll have something."

"Baker? Did you say the ex-boyfriend's last name is Baker?"

"Yes, why?"

"The guys who are using Randy's lobster boat are also Bakers. Maybe there's a connection."

"Interesting. It's a common name; maybe they're related. Maybe not?"

"I think you need to bring Mack into this. He might be able to help sort it out," said Jimmy.

"I can't. Mack's too busy making real money in Boston investigating things for paranoid rich people. Ahmed's family can't pay him what he deserves to be paid."

"Then what's your plan?"

"I need to be up at BIW to get eyes on the fuel dock to scope things out before I watch the theft next week, which is when another fuel grab may occur, according to the pattern Irene identified."

"No way. You're not going up there. It's way too dangerous. If you're right, then Irene was killed because she figured it out. You need to stay far clear of whatever this is. If you won't use Mack, then you need to turn it over to the police."

"No, Clark oversaw the investigation. There's no way I'm going to give anything to him until I have worked out a few more details."

"You have enough now for the police to investigate. Besides, he's working with the harbormaster and the Coast Guard, investigating fuel dumps. If you're correct, the theft and fuel dumps could be connected. They all need to be brought in."

"Yes, I know, I know. I forgot about the Coasties investigating the fuel dumps. Maybe all of it is connected? Even the murdered tourists?"

"Now you sound like Chet. You just need to think about Ahmed and make sure you don't get killed in the process."

Kari thought about it for a moment. She knew Jimmy's instinct had been correct. Conducting her own nocturnal field investigation posed serious risks to her safety. On the other hand, Ahmed's defense hinged on her ability to provide the jury with a plausible alternate murderer.

"Okay. You're right. I'll call Clark and let him know what's happening. Hopefully, I can get him to agree to investigate further."

"Good idea. Let me know what he says. Maybe the douchebag will come through."

"Maybe, but I doubt it," she said before ending the call, guilt consuming her.

Kari had no intention of turning the matter over to Clark. If he chose to investigate and somehow messed up, his actions had the potential of alerting Baker. If Baker had in fact committed multiple crimes and sensed a net closing in on him, he would simply flee. No, she needed to connect the dots without involving the detective who'd ruined Doug's life.

Chapter 47

Butch Clark sat at his desk, begrudgingly moving through the tasks of the morning. Monday had arrived far too quickly for him. He'd had a blast over the weekend and didn't want it to end. A new video game, *Warlord: Britannia*, had been released on Friday at midnight. He'd joined thousands of other men as Roman generals in a quest to conquer the island of Britannia. Hour after hour he'd worked the game controls until his eyes and fingers had gone numb.

"Clark, you done with the reports? I need your write-ups by the end of the day."

Clark glanced up at his annoying bug-eyed supervisor. He'd never known becoming a detective meant mountains of paperwork and very little field time. His former position, in uniform, had given him far more latitude. During the day he'd traveled where he pleased, even stopping to visit Debbie from time to time. Those days had become few and far between once he'd joined the detective rolls.

"Almost. I just need to update my call logs," said Clark.

The fear of missing something during the Irene Simmons murder investigation kept him up at night. Then came the call from Ron Baker, a colleague of Ms. Simmons's from BIW. Discovering a connection between Ron Baker and the Baker brothers on the waterfront gave him pause. Something didn't add up. He felt it in his bones. He'd missed a key point during the investigation, but what? He combed through his field notes, looking for the obvious misstep. Nothing jumped out at him. From everything he could tell, the investigation had been solid, the arrest of Ahmed warranted. Case closed.

Yet Ron Baker, a BIW employee who worked with Irene Simmons, was related to the two Bakers on the waterfront. The longtime lobstermen thought the Baker brothers had something to do with stealing their lobsters and maybe stealing fuel. He needed to figure out the connection between the three men, the murder of the tourists, and the murder of Irene Simmons.

At this point in his career, he had more years behind him than in front of him. As he aged, a stupid sentimentality arose in him. Something he'd never experienced. Now he wanted to get things right. Not merely look right. Be less shitty to everyone. Do the right thing. Seeing Kari Sharpe on the navy ship in her uniform had thrown him for a loop. He had never expected a Sharpe to make anything of themselves. Yet she had. Despite all odds. Her success made him feel even shittier about being such a jackass on the night of Doug's arrest. Of course, feeling shitty didn't stop him from acting like an ass. Never did.

He considered talking to another detective about the case, or even his supervisor. Then he thought better of it. He needed to figure this shit out on his own.

He returned to the blank call logs. *Damn it. Why did I put it off for so long?* he thought as he backtracked his work, logging every call he made or received. The onerous task had been another stupid requirement set out by the idiots in Augusta. They had no idea how time-consuming their "initiatives" had been for those doing real police work. Resentment at the desk jockeys who controlled the purse strings had become a formidable barrier to completing the task. He needed to push through his feelings and get it done. Then he would turn back to the murder of Irene Simmons.

Chapter 48

Kari knew she needed to get her own eyes on the waterfront at BIW. Jimmy had strongly recommended that she put the matter off until Mack returned. She wanted to wait to follow the timing Irene had identified in her logs but felt like she just couldn't delay her efforts. She wanted to take her chance this Wednesday to watch the fuel dock, on the off chance something would happen. How could she look at Hani, Bilan, and Omar the same if she knew she had the opportunity to clear their son and brother, but chose to wait until someone else had time to handle the matter?

Kari spent the day on the USS *Gallagher* interviewing Ahmed's shipmates, roommates, and friends. After several hours of meeting with various people in his life, a consistent theme emerged. Ahmed wasn't the sort of person anyone would suspect of committing a violent crime. Many said he was "considerate, kind, generous, and honest." She heard numerous examples of how the young sailor readily agreed to swap duty sections with his shipmates or how he would volunteer for difficult collateral duties. She made a point of jotting down the contact information for several of the men. If convicted, Ahmed needed as many character witnesses as possible.

After leaving the ship, she set out to find the facilities management building. She needed to speak with Jesse Helm, the person who signed out the skiff on the days identified by Irene. She wound through the maze of nondescript buildings until she found the facilities management building and parked.

"Hi, I'm here to see Jesse Helm. Is he around?" she shouted to the first person who passed by.

The noise in the building reverberated off the metal structures, echoing to a deafening pitch.

Kari chose to keep her uniform on rather than changing into civilian clothing. The uniform gave her an automatic pass at BIW, leaving her free to roam without scrutiny.

"Sure, I'll get him for you."

The young man darted off into the bowels of the loud facilities building. The building looked like an old metal hangar bay that had been transformed. Several two-story garage doors sat open to allow fresh air into the industrial building. Even with the open bays, the air had been barely passable to breathe.

"Ma'am? Are you looking for me?"

Kari spun around toward the male voice. A tall, rail-thin young man stood in front of her. He wore a grease-stained work shirt that had been embroidered with his last name: "HELM."

"Hi. I'm Kari Sharpe. I represent Youseff Ahmed in the case involving the murder of Irene Simmons."

The man shook his head and said, "Oh, okay." He looked at her with skepticism and added, "I'm not a suspect, am I?" He brushed his filthy hands down the front of his stained uniform several times.

"Not at all. I just need to clarify a few things and think you can help. That's all."

She had to tread lightly. She wanted to avoid alerting him about Irene's investigation.

"Would you mind if we step outside for a moment?" she shouted over the racket. The noise and the fumes quickly gave Kari a searing headache. She desperately needed to get out of the building into the fresh air.

"Yes, I could use the break too. It gets bad in here sometimes. We try to vent it out, but even opening all the bays doesn't always clear it."

They stepped into the late-afternoon sunlight. She inhaled the fresh, briny salt air. Relief came instantly as she took a second long, deep inhale. The moist, cool air worked its magic.

"How long have you worked at BIW?"

"I've been here almost five years. I started after I left the navy."

She surveyed him up and down and said, "Have you always worked in facilities?"

"No, ma'am. I started off in acquisitions, but the paperwork wore me down to nothing. I asked to be put in a position where I could use my hands. This is what they found for me."

Interesting. He'd worked in acquisitions along with Irene Simmons and Ron Baker.

"Who's your supervisor now?" asked Kari.

"I report directly to Derrek Searts."

"Who did you report to when you worked in acquisitions?"

"Chief Baker," said Helm.

She stopped momentarily. She knew Ron Baker had been a chief in the navy but thought he had started at BIW after leaving active duty. If Jesse Helm was referring to the same Ron Baker, then he should be addressing Ron Baker as a civilian, not as Chief Baker.

"I didn't realize BIW employed active military members for the acquisitions team."

She glanced over his shoulder toward the facilities shed. Various men and women came and went. None seemed to notice the two of them talking. She wanted to keep it that way.

"You're right. They don't, but he'd rather be called Chief than Mr. Baker. Everyone called him Chief."

"Are you referring to Ron Baker?" she asked.

"Yes, I mean Ron Baker. He still works over there," said Jesse. He ran his hand through his sweaty, matted hair, looking at her inquisitively.

"Do you still do any work for Chief?"

"No, ma'am. The departments are separate business units."

"As part of your work, do you often take out the skiff?" she pressed further. She held her breath, dancing around the edges of the theft, hoping Jesse Helm wouldn't notice.

"Yes, ma'am. All of us use it. We fabricate parts for use on the marine side of the vessel. The skiff is the only way to get out there. I'll also use it to get to places quickly. I think some of the guys just check out the keys to get out of here for a little while," he said with a sly, shy laugh. Kari assumed he meant that he'd taken out the skiff at times for a break. Who could blame him? Buzzing around on the water beat the facilities-building hellhole.

"You don't have to justify why you need the skiff?" she pressed.

"No, ma'am. Paperwork isn't a big part of this side of the operations. That's what I love about it."

"Do you ever drive the skiff to the fuel dock?"

She needed to find out why, on the days Jesse took the skiff, the amount of fuel increased tremendously.

"No, never. We aren't supposed to fill it up. The tanks can only be unlocked by someone in acquisitions."

"But you can take the skiff's keys and use it for as long as needed for your official duties?"

"Yes, ma'am. Then I return the keys to the shed," said Jesse.

"Do you ever forget to return the keys?" she asked.

He laughed and said, "Yes, ma'am. All the time. I've been so busy during the day that I've taken the keys home with me."

"Have you been reprimanded for this?"

"Yes, ma'am. I'm not supposed to leave BIW with any company property, especially keys. None of us are supposed to, but it happens." He spread his hands open as he spoke. His grimy face innocent of malice.

"If you're running late, what happens if the shed near the skiff dock is already buttoned up for the night? What are you supposed to do in that scenario?"

"There's a drop box near the shed where we can deposit the keys at the end of the day. Sometimes we need to use it because we'll do welding jobs from the water, if needed. Those are time consuming and can require us to work late on the skiff."

A loud marine horn blared, distracting Kari's attention. She glanced toward the water.

"Do you ever ask anyone else to put the keys back for you? Maybe when you're running late?" she asked.

"Well . . . things happen sometimes. It's not a big deal; we all do it," he said. He had a sheepish grin and admitted, "I don't think we're technically supposed to, but how would they know?" Jesse rolled back on his heels as he spoke, staring at the ground directly in front of him, hands jammed into his uniform.

Yes, how would anyone know if Jesse gave the keys to Ron Baker. She considered him for a long second. Trying to best decide how to proceed when a voice interrupted her thoughts.

"Helm!" a man yelled from just inside one of the open bays.

Jesse peered over his shoulder, shrugged, and said, "Break time's over, I guess. Unless you need something else?"

"Nope, not at all. Thanks very much. You've been very helpful."

Jesse walked slowly back to his appointed place of duty. He dragged a little as he moved toward the shed, probably to delay his reentry into the noxious fumes for as long as possible.

"Actually, I do have one more question," Kari called out. "Have you checked out the skiff today?"

"No, ma'am. Been in here all day," he shouted over his shoulder as he returned to work.

Kari sat in her car, wondering what she should do next. Tonight could be the next possible time when fuel would be stolen. Yet Jesse hadn't checked out the key for the skiff. She anticipated he might have obtained the keys before three in the afternoon. Maybe everyone had been right about Irene? They said she saw a conspiracy around every turn. Perhaps Irene's "investigation" had been nothing more than the work of a paranoid person who took her job too seriously?

Ron Baker served as an easy alternate assailant because of the abuse and stalking, if she could prove his actions. Irene had never filed a police report. Instead, she'd weathered his abuse without the intervention of law enforcement. To throw Ron Baker at the jury as an alternate assailant, Kari needed more than Lorraine's testimony. Irene's sister, Samantha, could easily impeach Lorraine's testimony. Kari suspected that Samantha would never display Baker's picture on her mantel if she knew the truth. The facts were still crappy. Kari would have a hard time convincing a jury Irene was abused but never told her sister. A very hard time.

She needed a stronger connection between Ron Baker and Irene's death if she intended to use it in court to provide the jury with enough doubt to acquit Ahmed. She needed to prove Ron Baker had the motive and opportunity to kill Irene Simmons.

Chapter 49

Kari quickly eased her vehicle into a different parking spot on the BIW grounds. The long-term parking section of the campus served the ship's company. Anyone stationed on board the USS *Gallagher* could leave a vehicle in the lot for as long as needed. She hoped her vehicle would go unnoticed.

The sinking feeling of being watched gnawed at her. Irene Simmons had been murdered by someone hiding in plain sight right here at BIW. She shook her head vigorously to vanquish the scary images of a confrontation with the killer. *What the hell am I doing?* Not the first time she'd questioned her decision to engage in an amateur stakeout.

Paranoia or good sense demanded that she relocate her car, just in case someone had been watching her. She almost laughed out loud at herself over how scared she felt. Yet she couldn't seem to shake the feeling. The tightness in her chest, the gnarling, painful stomach.

Her hands trembled as she twisted the lid on her tumbler. Draining the last few drops of water, she waited for nightfall.

There was no way the thief and Irene's potential murderer would steal fuel during the day. No, she had to wait until night, danger be damned. Ahmed needed her. Everything fell to her to solve the case and free him. She would never forgive herself if she let an innocent man go to prison.

She let out a deep breath, trying to gather control over her shallow, ragged breathing. Breathe, they say . . . as if it works. Anyone suffering the rough edges of a panic attack knew the bullshit of that promise. *Relax, Kari . . . you're hidden. No one knows you're here.*

She tried to soothe herself, yet somehow ratcheted up her fears instead. *Crap. No one knows I am here. How could I be so stupid?* She took her hair out of her ponytail, then rearranged it again in a messy pile.

After nightfall she twisted in her seat, tugging on the black sweats and hoodie.

"Crap," she moaned after bashing her knee hard against the steering wheel shaft. She hoped her dark clothing would help conceal her as she moved on foot to the skiff dock. Kari jogged through the shadows, finally settling in a concealed location. The vantage point afforded her the best chance to view the dock while remaining concealed. A cold breeze washed over her, eliciting a strong shiver and a tug on her hoodie, closing the garment snuggly over her ears.

A low rumbling of a marine engine startled her. She glanced toward the dock and quickly realized that she had failed to notice the missing skiff. Her eyes desperately clawed the pitch-dark waterfront, seeking purchase on the contours of whatever caused the noise. Nothing. *Where the hell is the rumbling coming from?*

Seconds later, the bow of a small boat materialized from the darkness as it moved closer to the dock. The clatter from the boat's engine increased as the sole occupant navigated to the open slot on the pier. Kari watched as a man lassoed the line on a cleat, then pulled the boat close to the dock. The man struggled as he heaved large fuel containers onto the platform. He turned to kill the engine, looked around the skiff's open hull, then heaved himself out of the small boat.

She held her breath when she realized that the killer was working right in front of her. Why had she been so stupid? She shouldn't be here. She tugged her device out of her pocket, her trembling hands nearly dropping it as she unlocked the screen, careful to turn off the flash before snapping pictures.

The shadowy hooded male figure maintained a downward gaze, concealing his face. Unless he looked up, the pictures would reveal nothing useful. *Shit.* The night would be a waste if she had no proof. A stupid, senseless waste.

Suddenly her phone buzzed and lit up to announce a phone call. *Damn it.* She silenced it but forgot about the backlight. She chanced a quick peek at the stranger. He continued moving the jugs of fuel onto a cart, seemingly unaware of her presence. If he had been looking in her direction, he would have seen her. Instead, he continued to load the heavy fuel jugs onto a small drivable work cart. Just as quickly as he'd arrived, the man sped off with the stolen fuel. Damn it. *He'll get away before I even get to my car.*

She held her device with a wobbly hand and swiped through the photos. The damned low lighting, his hood, and posture hid the man's face. Was it Ron Baker? She had no idea. She needed Mack's help after all. He had the fancy cameras and high-powered lenses essential to capture the man's image, unless she could find his vehicle. Maybe she would be able to snap a picture of him loading the containers to take away.

She ran hard back to her car and cringed as she turned the key in the ignition. He could be anywhere. Turning off her headlights, she drove slowly through the maze of low buildings. Kari squeezed the wheel tightly as she crept along. No signs of him. *Where the hell did he go?*

She circled the property one more time before admitting she'd lost him. *You're not good enough to do anything . . .* Her mother's toxic words pierced through her anxiety. *Not good enough. You failed again . . .*

Frustration, anger, and disappointment clouded her mind as she gunned her engine, exiting BIW. She blew her nose hard and punched the steering wheel hard as she drove.

The investigation would have to wait another week, the next scheduled theft.

Chapter 50

The worn plaid recliner creaked loudly as Jimmy sat back into it. A cold beer sweated in his hand. One beer a week. That was all. Or one beer a day. Either way he had to hold his shit together and not have a repeat of the other night. Having your kid sister bail you out after a drunken brawl in the Old Port didn't exactly shout rehab success. Yet . . . a beer tasted too good to deny himself.

As he tried to settle into the evening, his mind darted around nervously. Kari had hatched the ill-advised plan to go to BIW to "find a murderer," as she'd put it. She was the smartest person he knew and the most foolish, all at the same time. She also had a good dose of Sharpe family stubbornness. If Irene had been killed because of the excessive fuel orders, Kari needed to turn over everything she knew to the authorities, even if Detective Clark would receive the information.

He jabbed his finger at the call button for the hundredth time in the day. She usually answered right away or called shortly after. Today she did neither. He hoped she'd been entangled in some court thing but knew his sister well enough to know she'd gone to BIW, despite assuring him she wouldn't.

He took a long pull of the glistening elixir and then slammed the bottle onto the side table. The call went straight to voicemail. Her location disabled.

"Shit, Kari. You're going to get yourself killed!" he said to the empty room.

He needed to drive to BIW, check for himself. If anything happened, he wanted to be close to her. To protect her. After he grabbed the keys, the porch door slammed behind him as he jogged to his vehicle.

Somehow he always protected his kid sister. Despite his drinking. She had a way of shooting her mouth off at the wrong times. Over the years he'd smoothed over many ruffled feathers, especially during her high school years. That period had been turbulent for both. Borderline poverty, his drinking, and her drinking had exacerbated their situation exponentially. He'd never permitted himself to truly believe she would graduate from high school in one piece, yet somehow she had. Not only graduated but become a hotshot attorney. He didn't even understand all her awards, just knew she was the best of the best in her profession.

He held the steering wheel in one hand and picked up his device. "Hey, Siri! Call Kari." As her device rang, he hoped beyond hope that she would finally answer.

"Jimmy?"

"Holy crap, Kari! Finally! I've been worried sick about you! Why haven't you answered my calls?" he said angrily.

"Sorry," she said sheepishly.

He decelerated his truck, intent to turn around now that he had proof of life. An illegal U-turn or two never hurt anyone.

"I've been trying to get you all day and half the night. I'm worried sick about you, and don't even try telling me you aren't at BIW!"

"Sorry, I know, but I had to see for myself. Ahmed is sitting in lockup. I can't just leave him there, knowing what I know!" she yelled back. His sister sounded unhinged.

"I knew it! Kari, how could you be so . . ." He pounded on the dashboard as he yelled into the device.

"Sorry! I'm leaving BIW now, and everything is fine. I'm on the 295, heading home."

"Did you see anything? Or did you put yourself in danger for no reason?"

Although he didn't want to legitimize her behavior, he really wanted to know if she'd seen anything. Curiosity had gotten the better of him.

"Yes, I did. A man loaded nine full fuel jugs off the skiff and onto a work cart. You know the kind of jugs we used to tie on the Jeep when we'd go off-roading?"

"Seriously?"

"Yep. Or at least I assume it was fuel in the jugs."

"I'll bet that's a safe assumption. Did you see the guy who was doing it?"

His eyes darted across the median on the 295, looking for a decent spot to blow a U-turn. The sooner he turned around, the quicker he could enjoy his beer.

"No, that's the frustrating thing . . ."

Suddenly a loud crash echoed through the speaker of his device. Then another, and another. Muffled, chaotic whining and road noise blared.

"What the hell!" she screamed. "No! Oh my God! He's slamming my car!"

Bang. Bang. Then a deafening crunching sound.

"Kari? Kari?" Jimmy yelled.

The headlights of two vehicles crested a rise on the southbound side of the 295. He watched the vehicles speed past him as he headed north. They drove so close together it had been difficult to see where one ended and the other began. He yanked his steering wheel to the left and careened across the thick grass. His truck violently bounded over the uneven ground, rattling all its contents. Once across the grass, he gunned the accelerator to catch up with the cars. The powerful truck lurched forward.

Sound distortion followed where Kari's reply should have been. Had she dropped her device? A loud thump, then another. His sister's voice shrilled in a bloodcurdling shout. There was the roar of her accelerating engine, the sickening sound of metal crunching, and then silence. Nothingness.

"Kari! You there? Kari! What's happening!" he shouted. His eyes scanned the side of the road, desperate for the sight of her.

As his panic increased, so did the speed of his truck, to one hundred miles per hour. In the distance, he noticed a set of taillights on the side shoulder. One set of lights.

A large truck sat on the side of the road, alone. *Where has she gone?* Something must have happened when he reversed directions. But what? Then he saw the headlights shining on the forest next to the highway. A car sat at the bottom of the ravine. Its lights still engaged in a futile attempt to illuminate the way for its driver. *Shit!*

He slammed on his brakes, lurching himself forward as he rapidly decelerated and pulled up behind the silver Tundra.

The driver's door opened, disgorging a man. Jimmy jumped out of his truck, oblivious to the danger. He had no idea whether the man had been the one to run Kari off the road, or even if she sat at the bottom of the ravine. The only thing he knew for certain had been what he heard when speaking with Kari. The man remained silent, staring toward him as he took several ominous steps in Jimmy's direction.

"I already called the police. They said a patrol car is a minute out!" yelled Jimmy. His voice was loud but strained with fear. Not exactly the robust tough guy he wanted to portray.

The man stopped in front of his back bumper, hesitating. The shadowy figure glanced between the side of the road and Jimmy.

"I'm a trained paramedic. Stay up here and wait for the police. I'll triage whoever is down there," yelled Jimmy as he rounded the front bumper of his truck.

The man simply stood, staring. He repeatedly balled his hands into fists and then moved his hand to his waistband as though reaching for a gun. Then he hesitated.

Jimmy held his breath. He tried his best not to freak out. The two remained still, locked in a staring contest, like two rams before locking horns.

Jimmy broke the intensity of the moment by pivoting toward the ravine, away from the man. Turning his back on the dangerous man may not have been wise, but he needed to find Kari.

Rough, thorny brush tugged at his pant legs as he slid and stepped down the ravine. In the distance, a car door slammed with an angry violence, followed by the acceleration of a powerful truck engine. He exhaled his held breath and shouted, "Kari! Can you hear me?"

Chapter 51

Kari sat in her car, stunned. The airbag had deployed, smashing her face as her car careened down the embankment. Someone had forced her off the road. She knew that for sure. Everything else remained foggy. She needed to get her device and call for help. Fast.

She jabbed her fingers at the seat belt button. Its locking mechanism must've jammed. The lock refused to yield. The car's safety features included tightening the seat belts in the case of a crash. Now the darn thing wouldn't allow her to escape. The heavy sound of something moving in the brush stopped her efforts. Someone approached. A scream escaped her lips as her eyes darted toward the danger. Pinned down by the belt, she sat, helplessly waiting for her fate.

"Kari! Kari!" Jimmy yelled.

"Jimmy! I'm here!" she shrieked. Tears streamed down her face at the sound of his voice. Darkness and thick brush prevented her from seeing her brother approach.

"I can't get out!" she yelled back.

Her voice was weak, shaky.

"Are you bleeding? Can you move?"

Jimmy yanked at the car door, then kicked it. "I can't get it open. It's dented. You'll have to get out from the other side," he yelled.

Dented? How had that happened? Kari wondered, her mind coming in and out of lucidity, darkness shrouding her thoughts, her eyes closed.

The next time she opened her eyes, she was somewhere else. Slowly her mind rose from the depths of her subconscious back to the surface as it clawed the edges of clarity. Her eyelids fluttered open to see Jimmy sitting next to her. An intravenous needle felt heavy in her vein, immediately bringing her attention to her location. The brightly lit hospital room came into focus. Somehow she had been pulled out of her vehicle and brought to a hospital. She vaguely remembered the night at BIW, then driving home, but not much else.

"Oh, my head," she said.

The hard, painful thud in her skull beat rhythmically, causing her to wince.

"You have a very serious concussion from the accident. Don't try to do anything. They said you need fluids and rest."

"Where am I?"

"Maine Medical. I called an ambulance and the police to use the Jaws of Life to get your ass out of the car. You tumbled down the embankment. You're lucky to be alive. The car is destroyed."

She rubbed her temples and reached for the water cup on the small tray in front of her.

"Oh shit. It's all coming back to me. Someone forced me off the road. That was no accident. I had just left BIW. Everything was fine until a truck smashed into the rear of my vehicle. I tried to speed up; then I tried to slow down, thinking he'd simply move on. He just kept coming, slamming the back of my car and blinding me with the glare from his high beams." She cleared her throat and added, "We were on the phone when it happened."

Kari's anxiety rose as she relived the accident. Or attack? Had she been attacked? She looked at her brother's tired, sad face. The face of the man who'd embarrassed the crap out of her, being a careless drunk. The man who'd saved her from more than one bad situation.

Jimmy took her hand gently and said, "I heard everything. It was the worst thing I think I've ever experienced. I saw some of what happened. The man who did this was there when I arrived."

"What? Are you okay? He's dangerous," Kari yelled, which took considerable effort.

She watched his lips move in reply. Although she listened to his words, she struggled to understand them. The brain fog returned. Her eyes closed, returning her to cozy darkness.

Chapter 52

Jimmy sat by Kari's side in the mauve-and-mint-green hospital room. She'd finally been allowed to sleep. The hospital staff had taken turns keeping her awake, allowing her brain to repair itself. The doctors had worried that if she slept, then she could have easily drifted into a coma. But at a certain point they'd stopped trying to keep her awake and allowed her to rest. He had been told not to expect much when she first awoke. Kari's condition would take time to heal. Patience and love were what she needed from him right now.

Wednesday, the night of the accident, Jimmy had cried harder than he thought possible. Catastrophic images of fabricated injuries swirled in his head. He convinced himself that she would die of internal bleeding or smashed organs or any number of other maladies he'd seen on television. The reality of possibly losing his little sister crushed him. Not being able to protect her racked him with guilt. He'd been an idiot. A stupid, drunk idiot. If it wasn't for his issues, she would've been safe in New York.

Kari had slept through Mack's and Ruth's visits. The doctors wanted her to stay in the hospital for another day of rest and observation. He determined to stay with her until they could leave together.

"Jimmy?" she croaked.

Her voice sounded delicate and hoarse.

"Here, kid, take a sip of water," he said.

He held the Styrofoam cup to her parched lips. The nurse had applied ointment to prevent her lips from cracking, but it barely helped. She sipped tentatively, then said, "I'm exhausted. I feel like I've been run over by a bus."

"And look worse, believe me."

A thin smile formed on her chapped lips. The heavy, dark circles under her eyes etched sharp lines against her impossibly pale skin. His baby sister looked like a frail child.

He pressed the call button to alert the medical personnel she'd awoken. Finally.

A heavyset middle-aged nurse strode into the room. Jimmy had seen her numerous times over the day but never learned her name. The stress of waiting and hoping for Kari to open her eyes clouded everything.

"Ms. Sharpe? I'm Nurse Spender. How are you feeling?"

"Tired."

"I bet. You've been through a lot. Any pain?"

"Just a headache and sore throat," said Kari.

"That's good news. You were in an accident. I'm going to alert the attending physician that you're awake. Someone will be in to check on you shortly."

The woman strode out of the room as quickly as she'd arrived, leaving them alone.

"Someone forced me off the road," she said.

She'd repeated herself. The doctor had said she may or may not remember their previous conversation. The soft chime of her medical equipment assured Jimmy that her heart pumped life through her veins.

"I know, kid. You're lucky to be alive. You rolled off the highway into a ravine with so much force you bent your steering wheel as you hung on."

Kari smiled slightly and said, "Ten and two?"

"Yep, just like I taught you," he said with a wink.

"Thank you for helping me," she said.

He held her hand and said, "What kind of a big brother would I be if I didn't?"

Emotion held him back from expressing all the things he wanted to say to her. The relief, the worry, the anger he felt for her recklessness, and his stupidity jumbled together. But mostly he felt relief.

"Did you see the guy? The guy who did this?"

"No, but I did see his vehicle. It was a silver Tundra with a NAVY bumper sticker on its fender. I couldn't see his face because it was so dark."

"Mack. I have to ask him to . . . ," she said.

She started to sit straighter in the bed, anxiously clawing around for her phone. He placed a hand on her shoulder, nudging her back into the pillows. "Relax. He's already searching all the databases, looking for anything that'll help."

"It's the same truck, Jimmy. The same truck," she said quietly.

"We know, Kari. It's okay. We are . . . ," Jimmy started to say.

Kari's head rolled to the side as her eyes slowly closed. She had been in an out of consciousness. The doctors had told him to be patient as she healed. The danger had passed even if she continued to look like hell.

Jimmy had provided Mack with a description of the truck and driver who had forced Kari off the road. The back of the truck had a Maine license plate and a NAVY bumper sticker. The stress of the situation had prevented him from having the clarity of mind to memorize the license plate number, leaving them to guess at the identity of the assailant. Mack assured Jimmy he would do everything possible to determine the identity of the man who had attacked his kid sister. Jimmy knew Mack loved Kari nearly as much as he did. He completely trusted the longtime friend to do everything possible to bring the man to justice.

Chapter 53

Fred May jolted awake, momentarily disoriented. The hard edges of the cot instantly reminded him he was sitting in the harbormaster shack. Rubbing his eyes, he yawned loudly and cracked open the Red Bull he kept on the desk next to him. He hesitated before taking a swig, wondering whether he needed the hit of caffeine. This was supposed to be a quiet night in Portland Harbor. No large freight arrivals were expected.

Nights like these felt like an eternity to Fred. He preferred a busy shift full of harbor traffic. Most would relish a full night's sleep, even on a cot, but Fred hadn't slept more than a few hours straight since he'd gotten back from Vietnam—so he didn't care. In fact, he preferred the night shift.

The caffeine and sugar hit his ancient system like a jolt of adrenaline, snapping him awake but not doing a thing for his aches and pains. He shuffled outside of the shack into the cool evening air to light the first of many smokes the evening would bring.

The night shift had a way of exaggerating bad habits. Binge eating junk food, alternating between coffee and Red Bulls. And smoking far too many cigarettes. And if the three-pack-a-day habit since he was a young teenager hadn't killed him by now, nothing would. Every joint felt like it could use a can of oil, his back was stiffer than a telephone pole, and he couldn't turn his head more than a few inches in either direction, but life could be worse. He could be dead.

Before he lit his cigarette, muted voices drew his attention to the parking lot. The Baker brothers chatted by their truck, unaware of his presence. Darkness shrouded Fred, concealing him from observation. Those guys were up to something. He knew it. Just had no idea what that something might be. He strained to hear their voices. A distant foghorn mingled with the gentle city noises, obscuring their conversation.

Although he desperately wanted to get closer to them, he instinctively knew staying concealed was safer. Thank God he hadn't lit up a smoke. The two men heaved heavy fuel jugs from the back of their truck onto the grass earth. Then they rolled the large red fourteen-gallon jugs on their built-in wheels to their lobster boat. One by one they moved the jugs, loading them on the waiting vessel. The task required multiple trips back and forth between the truck and boat.

"Damn it. The stupid hose keeps falling. I hate these idiotic jugs. We should've purchased the better ones," said one of the men.

"These are just fine. They get the job done. We couldn't lift the other ones into our truck, remember, dipshit?"

"Go to hell."

The two bickered and hauled the jugs back and forth. One of them slammed the rear gate of the truck shut, then jogged to the boat, where the other idled the engine. The lobster boat pulled away from the pier before vanishing into the inky-black darkness beyond the city and harbor lights.

Why would they need so much fuel? Where had they planned to go at this hour? He needed more information to provide to Detective Clark. Clark had been assisting the Coast Guard with a fuel-dumping investigation and the murder of the two tourists. Based on tonight's observations, Fred considered Greg and Jeff Baker prime suspects for both crimes.

Fred yanked the handheld marine radio from the holster attached to his belt.

"Harbor pilot. This is harbormaster. You copy?" he said.

"Hey, Fred. It's Steve. Over."

"Steve, switch over to secondary frequency," said Fred. He didn't want anyone listening in on their conversation. Couldn't be too careful.

"Switching," said Steve.

Fred shifted frequencies and transmitted. "Steve, do you guys have anyone out in the harbor tonight?"

"Not sure, let me check. Do you need a pilot? Over?"

"No, just curious about something. Over."

The Portland Pilots provided large vessels with guidance as they moved through the busy harbor. As a cruise ship or tanker arrived in the harbor, a pilot ship met them and guided the vessel to its destination. Tonight, no large vessels had been expected to berth in the harbor. Although Fred had no need for a pilot to guide an incoming ship, he could use a second set of eyes in the harbor. He wanted to know where the Baker boys were headed.

"Fred? Jordan is out cruising near the Head Light. Do you need him to do anything? Over," said the harbor pilot.

"Yes, give me a minute," said Fred.

Fred put down the handheld marine radio and picked up his cell phone. Some of the pilots knew the secondary frequency he used when he wanted a private conversation, and he wanted this request to be entirely private. He trusted Jordan, or else he would've gotten into a boat himself.

The cell phone rang once. "Fred?"

"Yes. Sorry for the secrecy."

"No problem. What is it?"

"I just saw the Baker brothers loading an excessive amount of fuel jugs onto Randy's lobster boat. Then they took off. I can't tell if they're leaving the harbor or just relocating."

"Is this in connection with the fuel spills?"

"It could be. Hell . . . it could be connected to the murdered tourists too. Those two are up to something," said Fred.

"I hear that. Who needs that much fuel? And why go out at night?"

"Exactly. The husband's body had been covered in fuel when they fished it out of the drink. Who knows? Maybe everything's related."

"Shit. You're right. Okay, I'll call Jordan and ask him to get eyes on the boat. ASAP. I'll get back to you in a few," said the pilot. "But the pilot boat isn't exactly inconspicuous."

"Do you trust Jordan?" said Fred.

"One hundred percent."

"He doesn't have to get too close," said Fred. "I just want to know where they're headed."

"Copy," said Steve.

Fred disconnected the call. He paced around the waterfront, the docks, and then back to the shed as he nervously waited for Steve's call. Nearly forty minutes later his phone buzzed.

"What's the news?"

"You were right. Those two are up to something."

"I knew it! What did Jordan see?" asked Fred.

"They cruised past the Portland Head Light and out toward the no-dumping zone. Something's going on. I think we should alert the Coast Guard."

"Yes, I'll call Detective Clark and the Coasties right now. Maybe they can nail those guys. I'd love to get them off the waterfront. They don't belong here."

Fred quickly called Clark. He answered on the first ring.

"Detective, it's Fred May. I think we finally have something on the Baker brothers."

Fred told Clark everything and the approximate position of the lobster boat. The location would change quickly once the men left the no-wake zone, allowing them to pick up speed. The powerful lobster boat engine had been designed to move fast through even the choppiest seas. On a calm night, the boat would quickly slice through the sea, putting a great distance between the men and their potential captors. Hopefully the Coast Guard had someone in the vicinity already. If not, they'd never know what the men had planned.

"Thanks, Fred. I'll call it in to the Coasties. I know they have extra people on patrol in the area. We might just get lucky," said Clark.

Before Fred could respond, the detective ended the call. Typical. He'd never liked the guy. That said, Fred hoped tonight would mark the end of the Baker brothers.

Chapter 54

Kari opened her eyes and scanned her small bedroom. The hospital had released her on the condition that she would rest over the weekend. If she lost consciousness, she would have to return to the hospital. Jimmy forced her to rest in bed, not the couch as she preferred.

Jimmy had shouldered the worry for her health as she'd bobbed in and out of lucidity during her two nights in the hospital. What a reckless idiot. She felt ashamed of her impetuousness. She could have easily died that night if Jimmy hadn't been there.

Her apartment smelled of fresh-cut flowers. Other lawyers and college friends had sent her well-wishes, food, and bouquets. Hani brought them fresh food. The warm spiced lentils, breads, and rice dishes soothed her as only a home-cooked meal could.

"Awake, sleepyhead?" said Jimmy cheerfully.

He walked into the bedroom, carrying a tray of food and a jug of water.

"Barely. I still feel groggy." Kari sat up slightly and pulled her hair into a high ponytail.

"It's normal. I felt like that after my concussion during high school football," he said as he placed the tray on her bedside. "Groggy is normal; not showering is just gross. Maybe today is the day you remove the layer of scum?"

"Geez. I was wondering what the funky smell was," she said. Turning to him, she took a moment and then said, "I've been such a jerk to you since I came back. A real asshole."

"Yeah . . . I'm used to it. You've always been an asshole." He smiled.

"Thank you for rescuing me. I don't know what could have happened if you weren't there. I just . . ." Her lip quivered as she inhaled a deep breath, trying not to cry.

"We rescue each other. You're here for me. I'm here for you. Remember?"

"I guess even a jerk like me can manage that," she said.

"Get some rest. Sleeping Kari isn't an asshole." He winked at her.

She squeezed his hand as he tucked her back under the covers. He stuffed the blanket and sheet under the sides of her legs, just as he had done when they were kids. She had insisted he do a full tuck so spiders had no way of getting inside the bed. Even to this day, this small gesture made her feel secure. Loved.

Chapter 55

Mack moved his mouse to awaken his computer. He cracked his knuckles and grabbed his favorite pen. Guilt had dealt him a big sucker punch. The follow-up jabs had reinforced his screwup. He should have been there when Kari took matters into her own hands. If he'd been up in Maine, not in Boston helping rich old ladies, her "accident" would never have happened. He'd protected her so many times over the years yet had failed her when she really needed him. What a dope.

"The guy drove a silver Tundra, Maine plate, with a NAVY bumper sticker" had been all Jimmy told him the night of the accident. Like somehow he could pull a magic trick and materialize the man.

"Here goes nothing," he said to the computer.

He had various investigatory platforms at his disposal. Maybe he would get a hit. And maybe he'd win the lottery. *Could happen.*

The search for all Toyota Tundras registered in the state of Maine resulted in close to thirty thousand vehicles. Not exactly a workable pool.

To narrow the results, he added a gender filter. He sought only men who had registered Toyota Tundras. The filter for gender had not decreased the list by much, probably because in Maine so many people drove a truck. Next, he added a filter for those registering as veterans. He knew some people chose not to register as veterans but figured why not see if the filter helped. The number of possibilities dropped to under two thousand. Now he had gotten somewhere.

He adjusted his wide girth on the sagging office chair. The bright light from the computer in the dark room burned his eyes, prompting him to flip on the desk lamp.

Finally, he added filters for geographic location and age of vehicle. Jimmy mentioned that the truck looked newish. He set the vehicle age to no more than five years. The list shrank to fewer than three hundred. The final filter for geographic location resulted in narrowing the list to eight individuals.

He entered each name into the unified investigatory database to obtain the criminal records of the men. Several had minor scuffles with law enforcement. Nothing that jumped out at him. Then he sought employment records. Only one name jumped out . . . Ron Baker. Employed at Bath Iron Works. Navy veteran and registered owner of a silver Toyota Tundra. Bingo.

Mack stared at the driver's license photo of the man who had forced Kari off the road and perhaps the man who had killed Irene Simmons. He needed to let Kari know right away.

He grabbed his phone to call her.

"Kari?"

"Hi, Mack," she replied.

She sounded so weak. Still. Even after staying a day in the hospital. "I finally found something."

"Really? You're kidding? The proverbial needle in a haystack?"

"Something like that, yes. It took a while, and I'll save you the drama and get right to the point. I think the guy who likely pushed you off the road was Ron Baker. He's a former navy guy, the registered owner of a silver Toyota Tundra."

"Damn. I knew it. He abused and stalked Irene Simmons. He must be the killer, not Ahmed."

He stood, ran his finger through his hair, and let out a long exhale. "Turn everything over to the police. Now. They need to investigate the murder again, and specifically Ron Baker."

"Okay, you're right. I'll call Clark right now. As much as I hate the idea of talking with that guy or helping him do his job."

Mack knew Clark from his days on the police force. They'd never worked a case together, but their paths had crossed here and there. The guy had always been a special sort of asshole.

"I know. Would you like me to accompany you or be on a three-way call? Maybe I can call the station, grease some wheels?"

"No, it's fine. I can handle it. Jimmy gave the police a description of the truck that ran me off the road. I'll bet they never bothered to follow it up."

Shaking his head, he said, "Probably not. I'll email you everything I found connected to Ron Baker. That'll help. And . . . yeah . . . you can handle them and so much more. I'm proud of you. You're nailing this one."

"Thanks. It's nice to hear. Oh, and send me your bill. I don't think we've paid you for your help in a while."

"Not a chance. This one's on me."

Mack sent everything to Kari via email, hoping she would turn the information they had acquired over to the police immediately. He worried about her safety. She might be smart as a whip and tough, but even tough people needed protection sometimes. Ron Baker knew she had investigated the fuel theft at BIW. He also probably knew Kari had survived the crash. Her involvement in the case became extremely dangerous the night she went to BIW. A guy like Baker would stop at nothing to get what he wanted. Kari's life depended on the Portland Police Department picking up Baker, or she'd never be safe.

Chapter 56

Ahmed's case had taken a radical turn the night Kari conducted her amateur stakeout at BIW. Mack had confirmed her suspicions that Ron Baker had been the man to run her off the road. She had to assume he was the man who'd stolen the fuel. She had a hunch that somehow the fuel made its way to the no-dumping zone outside of Casco Bay. But how?

Based on her conversation with Lorraine, Irene's Simmons's best friend, Kari suspected Ron Baker of Irene's murder as well. If Irene had confronted him about the fuel theft, he'd probably become violent, as he'd done in the past. Mack had been right when he asked her to turn everything over to the local police, even if that meant talking to Clark. However, before she did that, she needed to do one thing.

She opened a link to Facebook, which she rarely used. She searched for John King, a friend from the navy. He'd attended Naval Justice School with her and had then entered the fleet as a JAG. They'd lost contact after they had been assigned to different duty stations. Unlike her, John had never gone into private practice after his commitment to the navy ended. Instead, he'd cross-decked into the Coast Guard, where he continued to serve.

She found his Facebook page and sent him an instant message asking him to call her at his first opportunity. Within seconds he responded, *How's now?* She gave him a thumbs-up and then waited for her phone to ring.

"Hi, John, thanks so much for calling," she said.

"Not a problem. You caught me blowing off work to surf the internet. It happens."

"Oh boy, do I ever miss government practice. I still haven't figured out a way to bill my clients for online shopping time."

She missed talking with John and felt bad they hadn't kept in contact over the years. Like so many people she'd served with, time and geography had a way of fading connections.

"It's nice to hear your voice, Kari. But I get the feeling this isn't just personal. What's up?" asked John.

She gazed out her window toward the harbor. Rain came down in hard sheets, obscuring her view.

"Same, John. And you're right. It's not. I have some information that might help with an investigation the Coast Guard is handling off the coast of Maine, near Portland Harbor."

Despite the rain, Kari stood to open the window a crack to let in the fresh air. Briny air flowed into her small office, bringing the scent of rain and sea.

She heard the rustling of papers, and then he said, "I'm stationed in Florida, but I know someone up in that neck of the woods who's probably involved. I can pass you on to her. Does that work?"

"That would be fantastic."

"I'll do an email introduction. Her name's Elizabeth Strout."

Kari's impatience increased as she waited for Elizabeth Strout to respond to John's email. She'd hoped to bring the Coast Guard into the loop before speaking with Clark. Kari estimated that even if Clark chose to ignore the evidence, the Coast Guard would not. Finally, Elizabeth responded with her cell phone number. Kari picked up her desk phone and dialed.

"Elizabeth Strout."

"Hi, Ms. Strout. This is Kari Sharpe. Thanks for agreeing to speak with me."

"No problem. I'm intrigued. It's not often I get a call from a civilian attorney about an active case."

"I can imagine. And, yes, I am a civilian. I'm also a former navy JAG and reservist. I represent Youseff Ahmed in connection with the murder of Irene Simmons. As part of my case preparation, I've been looking into various matters involving the theft of fuel at Bath Iron Works."

"Interesting. So you must be calling me about either the fuel spillages or the murdered tourists? Am I correct?"

"Yes, exactly. I have a working theory I'd like to run past you."

"I'm all ears," said Strout.

Kari described her suspicions that Ron Baker stole fuel from BIW and then gave it to his cousins the Baker brothers.

"I don't have all the answers for you, only basic connections. I suspect the Baker men might be selling the stolen fuel out past the no-dumping zone. Perhaps they're transferring fuel and it spilled in the process? I'm not sure," she said.

"Interesting. We've also had reports of new trawlers trying to establish themselves off the coast. It's a competitive business. Inexpensive fuel could be a game changer for them."

"Exactly. The margins are so tight that even a small difference could be meaningful for their bottom line. Fuel appears to be taken from BIW approximately every other Wednesday. The next theft should occur on September seventeenth, according to the schedule they have used in the past."

"That's this week."

"Yes, but there's something else," said Kari.

"Go on. This is the first solid lead we've received on the case," said Elizabeth.

"Stupidly, I conducted my own stakeout, and the guy stealing fuel, Ron Baker, saw me. It nearly got me killed."

"Geez. You okay?"

"Yes. A bruised ego more than anything."

"I'm glad you're okay, but that could have a chilling effect on their operations," said Elizabeth.

"I know. I should've waited for the professionals to handle it."

"Don't beat yourself up. Maybe they've gotten a taste of the money they're making on the little enterprise and feel bold enough to continue. Criminals usually aren't that smart."

Kari laughed and said, "That's probably why they get caught."

"It's *always* why they get caught," said Strout. An announcement could be heard over the loudspeaker somewhere in Strout's office. She paused, then asked, "I'm wondering if this is the same crew responsible for the death of the two civilians on the sailboat? The husband's body had been covered in fuel when he was located. Any thoughts on a connection?"

"I've been wondering the same thing. Maybe the couple had been in the wrong place at the wrong time? I really don't know. All I know is that I think Ron Baker killed Irene Simmons, and now my client sits in lockup awaiting trial for a crime he never committed," said Kari.

"Have you alerted the local PD? We've been working with a . . . Detective Clark," said Elizabeth.

Kari bristled at the mention of Clark. "Yes, my next call is to local PD to keep them in the loop. I'm hoping they'll be able to help pull everything together."

Despite her words, Kari refused to believe Clark would do his job. She rubbed her tired head, willing herself to stay with the conversation. Something about the mere mention of Clark's name distracted her. She needed to focus.

"Okay, I'll get this right over to the lead investigators. Thanks very much for your assistance and hard work," said Elizabeth.

"I'm happy to pass this along. Let's hope I'm right. I'd hate to waste anyone's time."

Kari hung up the phone and jotted down a few notes in Ahmed's file. As she saw it, Ron Baker stole the fuel and gave it to his cousins on the waterfront to sell. If Irene Simmons had discovered his enterprise and somehow made it known, maybe Baker had permanently silenced her. An eyewitness saw a truck matching the type of truck he drove near the scene of the crime on the morning of the murder. Baker and Simmons shared a long and at times violent history. It was workable as a defense of Ahmed, if needed.

Now came the hard part—talking with Detective Clark.

Chapter 57

Kari arranged for a meeting with both Detective Clark and Attorney Parker, the assistant attorney general in charge of prosecuting Ahmed. To facilitate their meeting, she had prepared a summary of her investigative file. Ruth had made two extra copies for the men in preparation for the meeting.

"Kari, they're here," said Ruth.

"Okay. Get them settled into the conference room and I'll be right down."

Showtime, thought Kari as she collected the file and descended the steps to the lobby conference room.

"Good morning and thanks for coming in," she said to them.

She shook Parker's hand, but Clark never extended his to her. Instead, he sat quietly, looking at her with his hands folded across his chest. She felt the same way. No love lost between them.

"Your client must be pleading guilty, I assume?" sneered Parker.

Her fists clenched at the mention of Ahmed pleading guilty. *How dare he start this crap again?*

"Not even close, but nice try," she said. She rounded the conference table and took her seat. "I brought you both here to request that the PD formally reopen the investigation into Irene Simmons's death."

The men sat stone silent as she proceeded. "I have reason to believe I've found the real murderer."

"Do tell. I'd love to hear this one," said Parker.

Parker practically laughed in her face, but Clark said nothing. He sat stock still. His eyes bore into her with intensity.

"Before I provide you with my file, I want two things," said Kari.

"This'll be rich. Go on. Ask away," said Parker, spreading his hands wide.

Parker sat back in his chair like a king peacock who held all the cards. Kari felt a red-hot flash of anger at his arrogance. *Let it roll.*

"First, immunity for Ahmed for the statements I intend to provide, and second, I want to be involved in the takedown of the murderer," she said.

Parker laughed at her for a second time, pissing her off. He needed to agree to immunity; otherwise Ahmed's statements regarding his actions the day of the murder would be used against him.

"No way. We have an airtight case," Parker said.

Clark jumped in. "Do it. She's right. There's more to this case than we originally thought. I want to know what she learned."

Stunned, Kari couldn't believe her ears. Had Clark just supported her? He'd known something all along and chosen not to bring it to the attention of the prosecutor. The bastard. His silence would be the end of his career if he'd sat on exculpatory evidence.

"What do you mean? You told me there's nothing to worry about with this case!" whined Parker, who suddenly appeared flustered and unsure of himself.

Kari jumped in. "I prepared an immunity agreement for your signature. Once you sign it, I'll tell you everything I know."

Parker turned to Clark, who nodded.

After the immunity agreement had been executed, Kari proceeded to tell them everything. She started with Ahmed's omission that he had been at the scene of the crime. She told them about the witness seeing the silver Tundra the day of the murder and how Jimmy saw it the night she had been run off the road. Then she turned to the logs.

"Where did you find these?" asked Parker.

"They were buried in her seabag."

Clark picked up the picture Kari had taken of the unopened seabag and said, "Our guys never found the seabag."

"No, they wouldn't have. It was in Irene's sister's garage, not the back stand-alone garage used only by Irene. They would have had no reason to obtain a search warrant for the garage as part of the investigation. Unless of course probable cause existed to suspect Samantha Simmons of the murder," said Kari. She paused, took a sip of water, and continued: "Irene Simmons conducted her own investigation into the actions of her abusive ex-boyfriend, Ron Baker. I believe Baker murdered Irene to silence her because she discovered his fuel theft. I also believe he gave the fuel to his cousins down here on the waterfront. I think the cousins have been selling the fuel to trawlers in the no-dumping zone. This might even relate to the murder of the tourists."

The men sat quietly reading through the file she had provided. She gave them everything except the logs. Finally, Clark looked up from her file and said, "I need to meet with Baker. He called me a little over a week ago to ask about the investigation into the Simmons murder. I thought it seemed odd at the time. Now I have a reason. I also had investigated the Baker brothers. They have lengthy rap sheets. Their involvement in this little scheme wouldn't surprise me at all."

"I can do one better," she said.

Kari handed them the logs and continued: "These are copies of Irene's logs. They establish a four-month pattern of behavior. If I'm right, we can catch Ron Baker in the act of stealing fuel tomorrow night."

Kari was taking the chance that Ron Baker would be bold enough to steal again despite Jimmy seeing him at the scene of the accident. She counted on Baker not realizing the various connections they had made throughout her investigation. Hopefully the gamble would pay off. She feared a no-show by Baker would result in the entire investigation staying locked in place, leaving her to defend Ahmed in court.

"Who is this guy, Jesse Helms? His name's circled. I don't see Ron Baker's name anywhere on these logs," said Clark.

"No, his name isn't on the logs because he simply took the keys to the skiff from Jesse Helms on certain nights. He never signed out the skiff or put his name on the fuel logs. However, each circled entry contains a capital *C* in the margin. Ron Baker had been a navy chief and insisted everyone call him Chief even after he retired from military service. I believe the *C* in the margin was Irene's note that the entry involved Chief Ron Baker."

"Fine, but there's no 'we' in this investigation. I take it from here," said Clark with finality.

"Not a chance. Either I go with you, or I go by myself. Either way, I'll be there tomorrow night," said Kari.

Clark turned toward the bank of windows, considering his options, then said, "Fine. But you're staying away from any action. The last thing we need is for an untrained civilian mingling into the mix and ruining our investigation."

His comment landed hard. She felt her cheeks redden in embarrassment. The last time she'd been at BIW, she'd found herself at the bottom of a ravine. Clark probably knew. She wanted to be part of a sting, but this time from a safe distance.

"Well, I'd prefer not to sit around all night on a grubby stakeout. Let me know what happens. In the meantime, I'm still preparing my case against Ahmed. Nothing's changed. You've given me some interesting information, but I have enough on Ahmed to convict," said Parker.

Kari leaned forward, lurching across the table toward Parker, and hissed, "You either file a motion to stay the matter for two weeks, or I file a motion to have you removed and a Rule 11 Motion for Sanctions. Your call."

"Rule 11? What's that?" asked Clark.

"Go ahead, Parker. Tell him," she said. She leaned forward, placing her elbows on the table, steepling her hands.

Parker twisted in his chair and looked down at his feet. Kari spoke. "No? Feeling a little shy? Well, allow me. A Rule 11 Motion for

Sanctions is appropriate when a lawyer has done something unethical in a case."

"Unethical? Parker? What the hell's going on here?" asked Clark.

Parker glared at her and then at Clark. He looked like he was about to start crying.

"Our friend here chose to personally call Ahmed's family and pressure them to convince Ahmed to change his plea to guilty. Too afraid to face me in court."

Parker had started to say something when Clark cut him off. He turned to Parker, glaring at him, and said, "Come on, seriously? This case can't get worse." He absently pulled on his earlobe, lost in thought. Then he turned back to Parker. "File your motion today. This shit needs to get fixed. Now."

"Fine. But you'll see. I'll convict Ahmed. He did it. End of story," whined Parker. He hastily got up from the table, collected his things, and said, "I assume that's everything?"

"Yes, we're done here," she said with a dismissive flick of her wrist.

He had started to leave when Kari added, "And the motion to stay? Make it a consent motion to stay."

"Fine," said Parker.

Kari caught the slightest flash of a smirk on Clark's face before he composed himself. Parker was a prick. They saw eye to eye on that.

She and Clark arranged a time for her to be picked up by a uniformed officer on Wednesday evening. If they caught Ron Baker stealing fuel, they could conduct a full search of his vehicle and home in connection with the theft. Kari hoped a search would result in the police finding the ring she suspected had imprinted on Irene's bruised face.

Chapter 58

Clark strode quickly into the police conference room, taking his place behind the lectern. He tapped the microphone, cleared his throat, and said, "Okay, shitheads, quit flapping your jaws and take your seats!"

The task force he had assembled for tonight's sting consisted of roughly twenty-five officers. If they had a chance of pulling this off, every one of them needed to play their role. Most of the men and women continued to chat despite his call to order. *Idiots.* Kari had provided them with everything they needed to change the direction of the investigation. He had to give her credit. She had identified a massive criminal scheme that had taken place right under everyone's noses.

"Shut the hell up and sit down!" he yelled into the mic.

His shout caused the speakers to screech with so much force it finally caught their attention.

"Geez, Clark!" said one of the women.

The room came to order, finally. "Listen up. As you know, tonight's operation is joint with the Coast Guard and Bath's local PD. If tonight goes as planned, then we'll catch Irene Simmons's murderer as well as whoever killed the tourists."

Clark had his doubts that they could accomplish so much in one night, but you never knew in this line of work. At the very least, they would be able to catch Ron Baker in the act of stealing fuel. Not a total loss.

Clark clicked on the overhead, pulling up a detailed map of the area in Bath surrounding BIW. "Alpha Team meets here." He pointed to the location. "That is where we will load up into our undercover vehicles. Those have been provided by active duty personnel assigned to the ship. The tagged vehicles are our best hope of getting onto the BIW campus undetected. Remember we are borrowing civilian vehicles. That means keep your grubby fingers off the windows! I'm looking at you, Hensen."

The room erupted in laughter. Flipping quickly to the map of BIW, Clark continued: "Once Alpha Team swaps rides, we'll station ourselves here, here, and here." He jabbed his pen at the map as he spoke. "From these points, we will be able to watch the waterfront and the parking lots. Bravo Team is assigned to the #146 overpass in unmarked vehicles. Charlie Team is on the Portland waterfront. Best-case scenario: we nab all three of the Bakers in one night."

The women and men flipped through the pages on their tablets as he spoke. Each of them had been given the sting details on their field devices.

"Once I get the go from our civilian point of contact that Baker is on the move, I'll send an alert to everyone. Keep the chatter on the group line to a minimum. We will need to be in constant contact to cover the extensive sting area. Any questions?"

After the meeting Clark grabbed his go pack and headed to his unmarked vehicle. Thirty minutes later, he swapped his official car for the civilian one assigned to him. Kari Sharpe had used her military connections to arrange the transport for the Alpha Team's part of the sting. Clark hated to admit that Kari Sharpe impressed him. She was the right combination of tough and smart. He'd never thought she or any Sharpe could make anything other than a surrender date to jail. Even that had been questionable. The night of Doug's arrest he'd seen her trauma and, on many levels, had enjoyed it. He had enjoyed the power it gave him. Despite how he'd treated her, she'd handed him the evidence he needed to turn the case around. A real class act. He didn't deserve it.

Clark had worked with local PD and Sheila Rainey, supervisor at BIW, to arrange the sting. Rainey had confirmed Jesse Helms had signed out the skiff. If Helms had signed out the skiff, then Rainey would watch Baker, alerting Clark if he obtained the keys to the skiff. Clark hoped the woman would be able to manage the task. It only involved her observations. No interaction with Baker. Handling the matter any other way would likely risk tipping their hand, alerting the suspect.

The joint task force had determined it to be imperative that Baker remain oblivious to their investigation. For all he knew, today was no different from any other Wednesday.

Clark jammed his earpiece into his left ear and then adjusted the thing to get a snug fit. "Is everyone in place? Sound off." One by one the men and women of the task force identified themselves as being in place. All they had to do was wait. The shittiest part of any sting.

Clark settled back into the little shit car he had been assigned. He glanced around the messy vehicle and wondered how anyone would want to drive in a rolling garbage can. Fast-food wrappers littered the front footwell. The side of the black gearshift looked like coffee had been spilled on it and never cleaned. A thick layer of dust covered the dashboard, making Clark wonder if it was safe to breathe in the disgusting vehicle. His personal car had never been excessively neat, but at least he took out the trash occasionally. Whoever owned this vehicle had never bothered to do even a basic cleanup before turning the keys over to the task force for the night. Sitting in the mess made Clark so miserable that he hoped tonight ended fast, even if that meant no arrest.

Chapter 59

Sheila Rainey had never imagined herself involved in a police sting operation, yet here she sat, waiting to text Detective Clark. The Portland and Bath Police Departments had collaborated to catch Ron Baker in the act of stealing fuel from BIW. The joint task force sting operation seemed excessive, but she was no cop. What did she know?

Sheila's sweaty hands trembled as she pretended to work. Clark had told her not to raise any suspicions, to act normal. Easier said than done. It had to appear to Baker as though nothing had changed about the day, leaving him confident to proceed as intended. She peeked out her window toward the skiff docks for the hundredth time in the last five minutes. Letting out a shallow breath, she determined to let it go for a few minutes. If Baker made a move in the direction of the dock, she'd see it.

Finally, out the corner of her eye, she detected movement. Ron Baker confidently strode across the parking lot toward the skiff docks. Moments later, Jesse Helms drove up to the shed. Sheila watched as Baker slow jogged over to Helms's vehicle. He stood by the open driver's-side window, laughing, then walked away. She picked up her device and texted Clark: Baker and Helms just met. Baker is headed toward the docks. Moments later Clark responded, Thanks, we've got it from here. Go home and be safe.

Sheila quickly snatched up her bag and headed out of the office. If Irene had been murdered by Ron Baker, she had no intention of sticking around. It was bad enough that she'd had to "act normal" all day as she'd interacted with Baker. Fear followed her as she dashed out of the building toward her waiting car.

Chapter 60

After receiving the text, Clark drove his borrowed vehicle to the edge of the lot and got out. He jogged the distance toward the docks, where he met a few of the plainclothes officers involved in the sting.

"You guys have a good visual on the skiff dock?" he asked.

The man next to him nodded and said, "Yes, everyone's in place. We put cameras on the fuel dock as well. If he makes a move, we'll see it."

"Excellent. I'm going to reposition to meet the men on the 295. With any luck, we aren't wasting everyone's time tonight."

The officer listened to something in his earpiece and said, "Baker just pulled off from the pierside. He's headed toward the fuel dock. Tonight's a go." The man's voice cracked with a spark of excitement.

"Roger that. I'll make sure everyone's ready," said Clark as anticipation rippled through him.

Clark sped through the BIW campus. He needed to ditch the borrowed car and get back to his unmarked cruiser. The officer stationed along the I-295 corridor planned to tail Baker as he left BIW. They had hoped to snag the entire operation tonight, including the Baker brothers on the waterfront. The first step involved obtaining proof of Ron Baker's theft. Then they wanted to witness him turning the fuel over to his cousins, who would then transport it to sea for sale. As tempting as nailing Baker had to be to everyone, shutting down the entire scheme mattered more.

He parked the vehicle in a predesignated location, then left the keys in the visor as instructed. His unmarked cruiser sat a few spots away.

His radio chimed. "Clark? You there?"

He recognized the voice immediately as Beth Holloway's.

"Yes. I'm here. Do we have reservations for dinner this evening?" he asked.

"Yes. I just made them. Should be good!"

"Oh, great! I'll let my family know and see you there," he responded.

The simple message conveyed by the team on the waterfront indicated that Baker had stolen fuel from the dock. Tonight's sting had a chance of working. Clark's adrenaline pumped with anticipation. Nothing excited him more than a good takedown. Electrified chatter rippled through the assembled team as they conveyed updates.

Chapter 61

Kari sat in an unmarked police vehicle near the Portland waterfront. Her knees bounced with anxiety as she tried to remain still. She and Officer Bennett waited to hear if Baker had stolen the fuel. She flipped her wrist over for the hundredth time to check her watch as time failed to move. She made polite conversation with the officer who'd begrudgingly allowed her to ride along. Jimmy hadn't been so lucky. The police had no intention of allowing two civilians near a complex sting operation, much less one who'd recently been arrested. He sat at home, texting her for updates.

"Bennett? Are you there? Over."

Officer Bennett snatched his headset off its holder and spoke. "I'm here. Over."

"We're getting takeout at eight, if you want any."

"I'm starved and will be ready at eight. Thanks. Over," said Bennett.

Kari heard the entire exchange, waiting for it to end. Finally, she said, "Does that mean it's a go?"

"Sure does, ma'am. Baker is on the move, headed in this direction. Should arrive in under ten minutes," he said.

"And they confirmed he stole the fuel?" she asked. Kari could barely contain her excitement.

"I assume so, or the sting would be over," he said.

"Great. I'll just grab my things and . . ."

"Negative, ma'am. I need you to stay put. This could get dicey, and we don't need to worry about a civilian casualty."

Kari had known this would happen. She and Clark had compromised about her involvement in the sting. She knew staying out of the way had been his only stipulation.

"Okay, I'll stay up here and far out of the way, but I need to get out of this car. The hours of anxiously sitting have balled me up. I desperately need to stand," she said.

"Okay. But stay close by. I need to move into place on the waterfront," said Bennett.

The young officer got out of the vehicle and moved quickly into his preassigned position.

Moments later, the bright headlights of a large vehicle shone into the dark marine parking lot. The oversize pickup truck barely slowed as it screeched into a slot. The doors flashed open, and two men jumped out, oblivious to the presence of numerous law enforcement officers.

Chapter 62

Ron Baker heaved the last of the heavy fuel jugs into his vehicle near the BIW fuel-skiff docks. He hated transporting the jugs to his car, but it couldn't be avoided. Greg and Jeff had decided that moving the fuel over land had been the quickest way of delivering it to them. The location of the BIW fuel dock had been so far from the Portland Harbor that meeting him near the area would use more of the precious, expensive commodity than they would be able to sell. Over land had been the best choice, even if it meant dragging the heavy, dirty containers. Luckily, they'd sprung for the wheeled jugs.

He slammed the back of his truck closed. Finally finished. The engine of his Tundra roared to life. Within seconds he had every window down, allowing the crisp night air to mingle with the fumes from the fuel jugs.

He rumbled up to the night drop box and tossed the key to the skiff into the locked box. The key jangled and thudded into the wooden bin. Then he pressed hard on the accelerator, lurching the truck forward.

Baker hated that a JAG had come to BIW, asking questions. Even though Detective Clark had assured him they had arrested Irene Simmons's murderer, he had a sinking feeling he'd missed something important.

Baker's mind returned to the night he'd run that nosy-bitch attorney off the road. Served her right. He searched his memory for the events of the night. She'd seen him near the skiff. No way would he risk going to jail. No way. Not for some self-righteous attorney. Not for Irene Simmons. His actions had stopped the attorney in her tracks. Nothing had changed since that night, as far as he could tell. No police surveillance that he could detect. Nobody asking questions on the waterfront. Perfect.

Maybe the accident had shaken sense into her?

He sped down the I-295 to the Portland Harbor, dreaming about how he would spend the spoils from their latest fuel sales. The money had been fantastic. Nothing unimaginable, but an unexpected windfall. Fuel prices had soared over the past few months, making their enterprise a welcome relief for the men who had purchased the fuel and nearly tripling his slice of the pie.

The minor risk associated with refueling in the no-dumping zone hadn't deterred their customer base. The eager men showed up in their trawlers for the fuel at every opportunity. Then his cousins had started stealing lobsters. Pure genius. The money had rolled in, significantly padding Baker's retirement account. Between his navy pension, his Bath Iron Works 401(k), and the fuel scam—he had nothing to worry about. The two bitches who had gotten too close were out of the way. One scared stiff. The other dead. He just needed a little more time to collect some more money and get clear of the mess his cousins had created with those tourists. If all went well, he'd be in Belize within a few months, impressing the ladies with his success. Maybe keeping an eye out for a few opportunities.

When he arrived at the main Portland Harbor pier, his cousins stood in front of their truck, casually raising their hands to greet him. Both Greg and Jeff were fifteen years his junior, so he planned to make them haul the load of heavy fuel jugs to the water. Rank had its privileges. Not that those two had ever served.

Chapter 63

Clark watched the waterfront from his predetermined location. Prior to the sting, plainclothes police officers had met with Fred May to do a walk-through of the area. Fred had helped the police designate several vantage points where the team would remain concealed. Clark's aging knees wished he had chosen a standing spot for the sting.

The silver Tundra thundered into the still lot, disgorging its felonious occupant. Greg and Jeff Baker met the truck with a wave, then set to unloading its contents. Clark adjusted his binoculars as he watched the men haul the fuel jugs to their waiting lobster boat.

He whispered into his headset: "You guys getting all of this? Have enough yet?" His voice was just a wisp of sound.

"Yes. We've gotten still and video shots. I'd say it's a wrap," said a fellow officer.

Clark started to stand. "Go time!" he yelled into his microphone and the air. Most of the officers sat close enough to hear him.

In unison the officers descended on the Baker trio in a loud, chaotic swarm. The women and men ran toward the men with a thunderous clatter, appearing from their concealed locations as though materializing out of thin air.

"Get down! Get down!" yelled an officer.

"Hands on your head where I can see them!" shouted another.

The officers immediately grabbed both Ron and Greg Baker, dropping them to the ground.

Chapter 64

Jeff Baker heard the shouts of the cops. *Shit! We're surrounded!* Panic propelled him forward. He bolted toward the waterfront in a mad dash for his freedom. His feet pounded the gravel as he closed the distance to the waiting lobster boat. *If I can just get to the boat . . .*

Rounding the length of the dock, he sprang onto the boat, causing it to dip violently before righting itself. He yanked the line free from its cleat and gunned the engines. The black sea and freedom awaited him. All he had to do was make it through the harbor and the cops would never find him. Maybe he would disappear in Portsmouth or Boston. Anywhere but here.

Suddenly bright lights turned on from every direction, changing night into day in an instant. The intense beams shone into his eyes, blinding him.

"Stop! This is the United States Coast Guard! You are under arrest!" shouted a voice over and over.

Numerous Coast Guard cutters swarmed the harbor, thwarting his efforts to run for the open water. They quickly circled his boat, spraying water in every direction. A violent wake rocked his lobster boat, nearly toppling him. He closed his fist tight on the console, steadying himself.

Jeff rammed the side of one of the boats, then ripped the helm in the opposite direction, hoping to outmaneuver the cutter. Every direction he turned, another one of the swift boats prevented him from passing. Cold seawater pelted him in streams as he maneuvered.

"Stop! You are under arrest! Surrender or you will be shot!" shouted a female voice.

He bashed into another one of the cutters, determined to push it out of the way. Then, over the deafening clamor of the engine, he heard the distinct whizzing sound of a bullet as it sped past his head. *Are they shooting?* Plunk, plunk . . . the side of the lobster boat took hit after hit. A hissing sound blared from the outboard engine as one of the bullets punched a hole into it. The next few shots thumped holes near him in the cockpit.

"Those are your last warning shots! You are under arrest!" shouted the woman. "Shut off your engine and put your hands up!"

"Okay! I'm stopping!" he shouted breathlessly.

Once he cut the engine, the boat slowed, and several lights hit his face, blinding him. He lowered a hand to cover his eyes. "Keep your hands in the air!" Either shock or disbelief caused him to ignore the command. In response, a few substantial thunks drilled into the hull of the lobster boat. He froze. Several uniformed Coast Guard officers effortlessly leaped on board and threw him down. Smashing his face onto the hard deck of the lobster boat.

"Search it!" one of the men yelled.

Chapter 65

Clark could barely make out what had transpired in the harbor but assumed the Coast Guard had the situation in hand. The Coasties took down far worse individuals along the shores of the United States. The likes of Jeff Baker would be no match for them. Clark returned his attention to Ron and Greg Baker.

"Anything you say will be used in a court of law. You have the right to . . ."

One of the officers read them their Miranda rights as they shoved the handcuffed men toward the waiting police vehicles.

Kari Sharpe slipped out of the shadows toward them.

"Remember me?" she sneered at Ron Baker.

Baker looked at her, stunned, then looked away. The officer shoved him in the back of an unmarked cruiser.

"Nice work, Attorney Sharpe," said Clark as he extended his hand to shake.

Kari glanced at his outstretched hand, hesitated, and then shook it quickly without making eye contact.

"Thanks," she said with a quick glance at him. "You didn't do a bad job yourself."

"Did you catch the ring he had on? Looks to me like I need to send it up to Augusta for forensics," said Clark.

"No, I couldn't see it. His hands were behind his back. Does it look like something that could leave an impression on a cheek? Specifically, Irene Simmons's cheek?" asked Kari.

"Sure does. I plan to spend some time with our friend after he's been booked," said Clark. He flashed a grin at her and walked away. Clark had every intention of obtaining a full confession from the Bakers. The case would not be the end of his career, nor would it haunt him for years to come. He needed to do the right thing by the victims and Ahmed. His years on the force had not been stellar. Choosing power, brute force, and bullying over honesty. Over the years, his shittiness had taken a toll on him. Guilt dogged him many nights, chasing the possibility of sleep. Tonight he'd make up for the crap he had done.

Before Kari could walk away, he slow jogged toward her. "Attorney Sharpe! Hold up." He closed the gap between them quickly. The other officers lingered a distance away from them. Giving him the privacy he wanted. He needed to get this off his chest. Tonight.

"Look . . . I wanted to say. Well . . . I'm sorry. I . . ." He looked down and then back to her. Shifting his weight side to side. He waited for her to say something.

"Sorry? What are you talking about?" Kari looked at him like he'd sprouted an extra head.

"You know what I'm talking about. I'm sorry for that night. You were just a kid, and I was a total asshole. You didn't deserve it. Your family had been through enough already. That's all."

He felt naked, exposed as he admitted fault, especially to a Sharpe. To Kari.

Without skipping a beat, she launched at him. "No—I didn't deserve it and neither did Doug. You took it way too far. Then you had the nerve to ask me about him like it's funny? Take your apology and shove it," she said loudly. She turned to walk away.

He needed to say something. "Hey. Listen . . . I know. I know. I was out of control that day and on the ship. I asked about him before I could stop myself. I knew better. I'm sorry. You did a hell of a job breaking this case. I couldn't have done it without you. We both know it. You really made something of yourself, despite the odds. I'm still working on it."

She looked away from him toward the harbor. Even in the darkness he could tell her eyes shone with tears.

"We good?" he asked. What else could he say? Their history locked them together. This moment determined their future and his peace of mind.

She simply turned and walked away.

Chapter 66

The next morning, exhausted, Kari collapsed into her office chair. The sting had gone smoother than she'd anticipated. She waited impatiently for Detective Clark to contact her regarding forensics on the ring and any statements made by the men. The Portland Police housed all three men, but the Coast Guard planned to question them in tandem with the Portland PD. She knew better than to hope she would hear anything today, but still she sat distracted, waiting for his call.

Kari picked up various files, trying to focus, only to close them and stare out the window. Her mind returned to the events of the previous night. Nerves had a way of blotting out her ability to work effectively. She stood for the fifth time in thirty minutes and grabbed her mug for another cup of coffee or tea. Anything to distract her.

She hated Clark. As a young woman, she'd dreamed about the man who had taken away her brother. The man who had violently and needlessly hurt Doug and then laughed about his tragic death. She'd vowed to extract pain from him. Yet last night he'd apologized for his actions. He'd taken responsibility for her pain. No one had ever acknowledged hurting her, except Clark. It gave her an unexpected lightness, as though a large object in her body had moved. Last night she'd slept with a soundness she'd never known. Maybe people changed. Maybe not. She had no idea. All she knew right now was that Clark had been on her side for this one. And he'd apologized. It meant something.

Kari chose not to bring Ahmed or his family into the loop on the ongoing investigation into Ron Baker's activities. She feared she might give them false hope. Until she knew more, she told them only that she was working on an alternate theory to explain Irene Simmons's murder.

Her device buzzed, indicating a text had been received. You free to come to the station? I have something to show you. The message had been sent by Detective Clark. *Something to show me? What had happened overnight?* she thought. Then she typed out a quick reply: Yes—on my way to you now.

The Portland Police station sat just a few blocks from her waterfront office. She grabbed her bag, a fresh legal pad, and Ahmed's file before heading out for the short walk. The gloomy gray day heightened the colors of the redbrick buildings in the Old Port. Tourists walked in and out of the small stores along the cobblestone streets, oblivious to the stress she felt for Ahmed and many of her other clients. Fresh flowers had been placed along the waterfront for the slain tourists.

At times the magnitude of responsibility for the lives of clients weighed heavily on her. Today she hoped the weight would lift, even just a little.

Once at the station, she shivered as she waited in an overly air-conditioned conference room. After a few minutes, Clark barreled in.

"Thanks for coming in, Attorney Sharpe. I thought you might want to see what we have on our friend Ron Baker, rather than just telling you on the phone," said Clark.

"This should be good. I'm hoping you found something connecting him to the Simmons murder."

Clark smiled and picked up a remote. The large flat screen on the wall in front of Kari came to life. Clark quickly navigated through a projected desktop interface to open the "Baker, Ron" file. Then he opened the "Photos" file.

"After I met with you regarding this matter, I pulled all the camera footage I could obtain in the area surrounding where the Simmons body had been found. This is what I discovered," he said.

The images he projected onto the screen had been grainy, but the existence of Ron Baker's Toyota Tundra had been clear.

"The time stamp on these photos corroborates what Meg Shore saw on the morning of the murder? Ron Baker had been in the area when Irene Simmons died," said Kari. She half asked and half stated her response to the pictures as she watched the pictures flip from one camera angle to another.

"Yes. We can pin him to the location on the date and time of the murder," he said.

Clark opened his file again and retrieved a large photograph of a navy chief's gold insignia ring. The ring contained the letters *USN* and the gold anchor associated with the rank of chief. Many chiefs wore the large, expensive ring well into their civilian life.

"This is a picture of the ring Ron Baker had been wearing last night when we arrested him. I've sent it to Augusta for forensics. I'm not expecting much by way of DNA to be found on the ring, but if we compare the injury on Ms. Simmons's face with the curve of the ring, in this area, I believe it will match," said Clark as he traced an area of the ring with his pen.

"Sounds to me like we finally have the real murderer," she said.

Kari let out a long exhale and sat back into her chair.

"We absolutely do."

Kari believed in her bones that Ron Baker had murdered Irene Simmons after learning of his abuse. However, she had been surprised by how quickly Detective Clark had made the leap. In her experience, the police took their time when moving from one suspect to another. The jump seemed almost too easy, too good to be true. Clark must have sensed her astonishment.

"I haven't shown you the best part," he said.

"There's more? So far you have him at the scene and potentially a partial imprint of his ring on the victim's face. Not sure you need more to drop the charges against Ahmed."

"There's more. Just watch."

As Clark navigated to another file on the screen, the door flung open. Bob Parker, the prosecutor, walked into the conference room. He took a chair a few seats down from Kari and said, "You started without me? Thanks."

"Some things just can't wait. We're getting to the main event. You haven't missed too much," said Clark.

The detective returned his attention to the screen in front of him. The screen went blank, and then the date and time displayed prominently in the center. The room looked like a typical interrogation room. A small desk, two chairs, and bright lights. After a few seconds, Ron Baker entered the room. He sat, waiting until Detective Clark entered and sat across from him.

"I'll spare you the boring parts and get right to the action," said Clark.

He fast-forwarded the video. As the footage advanced, Kari watched Ron Baker talking, shaking his head, getting up to stretch, and then putting his head on the table.

"How long did you question Baker?" asked Bob Parker.

"A few hours," answered Clark.

"I assume he had been properly Mirandized and frequently asked if he wanted counsel?" asked Parker.

"Sure was. We did it several times throughout our questioning of him. We even gave him breaks," said Clark.

He stopped and backed up a little to get to the right time-stamped location on the video.

"Here it is," said Clark.

Kari leaned in and listened intently to the statement provided by Ron Baker to Detective Clark.

"Irene told me she figured out that I had been stealing fuel from the dock. She said either I came clean, or she planned to go to Sheila Rainey with the evidence. I went to her house early that morning to talk some sense into her. I thought maybe if I offered her a cut, she'd just let it go. She had my whole life in her hands. If I went down for this, we both knew I faced

financial ruin and possible jail time, all because of her. I had to talk with her, convince her to give me a break."

Baker sat back in his chair, then rubbed his eyes.

"Did you manage to convince her?" asked Clark.

"No, she refused to listen and told me to get away from her. She needed to go for a walk before work. She moved quickly to the forest to take the path she liked. I followed her. I just wanted to talk to her. She wouldn't listen. Why wouldn't she listen? I didn't want to hurt her; I just needed her to listen. She had a way of frustrating me so much."

He balled his hands into fists and pounded the table.

"Did you murder Irene Simmons?" asked Clark.

Baker paused for so long, Kari had to check the time stamp to be sure the video feed had not frozen. Finally, he placed his head in his hands and began to speak softly.

"I didn't mean to hurt her. I loved Irene more than I have ever loved anyone or anything. She meant everything to me. I just needed to make her listen to me. But she just kept walking away."

"What happened when she walked away?" asked Clark.

"I followed her into the forest. When she wouldn't stop, I grabbed her arm and spun her around to face me," Baker said.

"Is that when you murdered her?" asked Clark.

"I just wanted to knock some sense into her . . ."

"You get the idea," said Clark as he stopped the video and turned to Parker. "I think you've seen enough. He signed a full confession and a waiver of his rights to counsel. It's as airtight as I've ever seen. We've booked him for murder."

Kari spoke next. "I expect all charges against my client will be dropped. Today."

"Well, not so fast. I'll need to review everything again. There is no doubt that your boy Ahmed had been at the scene of the crime. Maybe I'll charge him with fleeing or interfering in a police investigation. There are so many options and little reason for me to simply let him go," scoffed Parker.

Kari stood so quickly she nearly toppled her chair over. She turned to Parker with an intense glare and said, "This ends today. Either you file a motion dropping all charges and directing the immediate release of Ahmed, or I make your life uncomfortable, starting with Rule 11 sanctions. Then everyone in Portland, including your country club chums, will know you used the word 'boy' when referring to a Black man. Not sure people will want to be friendly with a known racist. This ends today or I'll finish you personally and professionally. There is absolutely no reason for you to continue to hold my client."

Parker sat quietly, staring intently at Kari. He seemed to be calculating his next move, somehow unwilling to admit he was wrong. Clark had started to say something when the door opened.

"Detective Clark, you have a call from Officer Pazzulo on line one."

"Perfect. Thanks. I'll take it in here," said Clark. He snatched the massive telephone console on the large conference table and slid it in front of himself. "That's my Coast Guard contact. I asked that they call me with any updates."

Picking up the receiver, he said, "This is Detective Clark."

He nodded his head frequently and then said, "Perfect. That buttons it up. I appreciate the call." Without saying goodbye, he hung up the phone.

"The Coasties found a large hunting knife on the Bakers' lobster boat. They also found traces of blood in the area where the knife had been thrown. During questioning, Greg Baker turned on Jeff and said he witnessed Jeff killing the tourists."

"Nice family," said Kari.

"Those guys are real losers. It only took a minute for Jeff to turn on Greg, blaming him for killing the wife. They are being charged with the murder of the Kadys along with various other marine-related shit I could not care less about."

Parker let out a long whistle and said, "Looks like you cops had a good night. Well, my work here is done." He had started to get up when Clark's head snapped in Parker's direction.

"Not so fast, honcho. She's right. We have no reason to continue to hold Ahmed. This ends today. I'm going to send this up the chain of command. Either you get ahead of it or you'll look like the asshole you are when my report comes out. Trust me. If you wait, it'll get worse for you. And for the record . . . Attorney Sharpe had a good night. She brought us the evidence we needed, and you know it," shouted Clark.

As Clark spoke, he stretched his large torso across the conference table toward Parker, pointing at him in an intimidating manner. Parker shrunk into his seat, averting eye contact.

Then he cleared his throat, stood, and said, "I want to see the written confession before I do anything."

"I already made a copy for you. I'm going to alert lockup that Ahmed is to be out-processed today. You better start typing, counselor," said Clark as he slid a sheet of paper toward Parker.

Parker snatched up the document, glanced at Kari, and then stormed out of the room.

"Well, that's not exactly what I expected for today, but I'll take it," said Kari.

"The guy is a fool. It's about time his fancy, privileged, shit-ass self did something right."

"I couldn't agree more. How long will it take to out-process Ahmed? Assuming Parker files the motion?"

"I'd say by four he should be walking out of the station a free man. And don't worry. He'll file it. He and I have a long history together. I've seen this behavior before."

Chapter 67

Kari sprinted to the lockup area immediately following her conversation with Clark and Parker. She wanted to be the first to tell Ahmed the good news. She sat in the counsel room, impatiently waiting for Ahmed to be brought into the cramped space. The beat-up room, with its heavily scuffed floors and cheap furnishings, had been the same one where she'd first discussed the case with Ahmed following his arrest.

A soft knock on the door preceded its opening. "Ma'am? You ready for him?"

"Yes—thanks."

Kari stood to greet her client, something she did only for the clients she liked.

Once they finished their greeting, Kari launched right in. "I have good news for you," she said.

"Good. I could use some," he said.

The heavy dark circles underscored Ahmed's dark eyes. He looked exhausted. Lacerations on his right knuckles and fresh facial bruising indicated a recent fight.

"Ron Baker, a former navy chief who works as a civilian at BIW, has confessed to the murder of Irene Simmons. You're a free man."

Ahmed appeared not to hear her. He merely sat with a blank expression on his face; then he looked down.

"Ahmed? Did you hear me? You are a free man. They'll begin processing and have you out of here in a couple of hours, maximum," she said.

Her words seemed to land after she repeated herself. Stunned recognition and understanding of the weight of her message crossed his gentle face. Then the tears started.

"Are you messing with me, ma'am?" he croaked. He shook his head, rubbed his face vigorously with his hands, and looked at her.

"No, Ahmed, I would never do such a thing to you or any of my clients. You are walking out of here today. A free man. After we are done talking, I'll ask that they bring you to a different area, away from the other detainees. There's no reason for you to spend even a second longer near the men who have abused you in here."

After a moment Ahmed's tears slowed and he said, "Does my mom know?"

"Not yet. I came here immediately when I heard the news that Ron Baker had confessed. Would you like to call her?"

"Can you?" he whispered as he shook his head.

He'd barely managed to softly utter the words when the tears of relief returned. The salty liquid dripped unabated down his smooth skin onto his prison uniform.

"Let's do it together."

Chapter 68

Kari had needed time to decompress after Ahmed's case was resolved. She'd chosen to take off the rest of the week after the sting and the release of her client. She'd needed a break. The unexpected time off had worked wonders on her stress, leaving her feeling rested and whole again. Returning to work on Monday morning had not felt nearly as daunting as she'd imagined. She reviewed her agenda and to-do list for the day and marveled at the influx of new client meetings Ruth had set up for the week.

The local newspapers had interviewed her regarding Ahmed's case. She and Ahmed had sat in her conference room, patiently answering the questions posed by the reporters. After the articles and broadcasts aired, her office received so many calls for criminal defense work that she considered hiring an associate to help her with routine hearings and motions. She also increased Ruth's responsibilities. Ruth managed to handle the added duties with ease. Kari often overheard her bragging to other paralegals about the things "her JAG" asked her to draft.

"Kari? I have Captain Pearson on line one. Do you want it?" asked Ruth.

Captain Pearson had asked her to meet with Ahmed on the day of his arrest. His phone call had set the wheels in motion for Kari to represent Ahmed.

"Of course I'll take it. Please put the call through."

Seconds later Kari's internal line buzzed again. "Here he is, Kari!"

"Lieutenant Commander Sharpe," she said.

"Hello, Lieutenant Commander. I'm calling to congratulate you on your success with Petty Officer Ahmed's case. You did an amazing job. I know I speak for the command and everyone in the JAG when I say your efforts in representing Petty Officer Ahmed were nothing short of exemplary, as always."

"Thank you, sir. I appreciate the call. I'm thrilled that an innocent man did not end up being wrongfully convicted."

"Me too. I'm sure you know by now that everyone here is abuzz with this case. Sailors all over the fleet will be requesting your assignment on their matters."

"That's very flattering, sir," she said as she attempted to stifle her emotions. A lot had happened since their first phone call. The weight of it hit her all at once.

Kari had already experienced the case's impact on her local practice. She had never considered how the fleet's accused may handle the news.

"Congratulations again. I'm sure it won't take me too long to be calling you back."

"I look forward to hearing from you again, sir."

"Famous last words, Lieutenant Commander. Famous last words. Careful what you ask for."

He disconnected their call before Kari had a chance to respond.

The clomping of Jimmy's quick footsteps up the staircase outside of her office brought her back into the room.

"You ready, sis?" said Jimmy.

"More than ready. I'm starving."

"In that case, I'm glad it's your turn to pay," joked Jimmy.

The siblings walked out of her waterfront office and onto the floating docks. A stiff chill moved into Portland, Maine, heralding the beginning of fall. Kari embraced the brisk air, easing her mind.

The End

Acknowledgments

Adrift could not have come to life without the support and wisdom of several remarkable individuals.

To Grace Doyle, thank you for believing in me enough to pass me along to the awesome editorial director Jessica Tribble Wells. To Jessica Tribble Wells, I am in awe of the work you do. Your vision, creativity, and foresight brought my work to life. You helped me be less "clinical," shaping *Adrift* into the novel it became. I'm so happy and feel so lucky that I have had the joy of working with you and getting to know you.

I extend my deepest gratitude to my developmental editor, Clarence Haynes, for helping me to see the emotional side of life. Through our copious chats and your extensive editorial letters, you taught me how to feel each character's emotions, whether I wanted to or not. Your insights and guidance have been invaluable throughout this journey.

To my entire editing and marketing team at Thomas & Mercer, I greatly appreciate the hard work each of you poured into my novel. It would not be the same story without your attention to detail, kind corrections, and positivity.

With heartfelt appreciation,
K. T. Konkoly

About the Author

K. T. Konkoly is a practicing attorney who started right out of law school as an officer in the US Navy Judge Advocate General's Corps, where she served as a criminal defense attorney at the naval base in San Diego, California. Upon leaving the navy, she moved with her family to Portland, Maine, where she rose to partner in one of the city's biggest and most respected law firms. Konkoly has always been a litigator, staying close to the courtroom action as both a JAG and private attorney. Outside of work, Konkoly enjoys spending time with her family and her dog, Tony—not necessarily in that order. She also enjoys sailing, traveling, gardening, reading, cooking, and spending time with friends. *Adrift* is her first novel.